Her own sensuality began to reawaken. She could feel a nagging ache beginning deep within her abdomen. Her hands clutched him a bit tighter as if to strain him to her.

Abruptly, he stepped back, holding her at arms' length. "This goes too fast," he said a little breathlessly. "We must go slower."

"But why?" she objected.

"Because we have the chance to," he replied. "We can turn the duke's vicious tormenting into pure pleasure. Are you willing?"

Her eyes lighted at the thought. Without hesitation she nodded.

He lifted her into his arms, holding her high against his chest. "Put your arms around my neck, and kiss me."

She smiled hesitantly as she complied. Her lips touched his cheek, kissed it, then traced a path across his cheekbone to his ear. Her breath warmed it before she kissed it too.

"Is that what you want?" she whispered, her lips moving against the curve, fanning the tiny almost invisible hair there.

He gasped as his arms tightened painfully around her. "Beware, Joanna. . . ."

In a few swift strides he carried her to the bed and stretched her on it. Half covering her with his body, he began to caress her slowly.

Consumed by passion's fiery need, she shivered and pulled him closer. . . .

Lovefire

Deana James

ZEBRA BOOKS
KENSINGTON PUBLISHING CORP.

ZEBRA BOOKS

are published by

Kensington Publishing Corp.
475 Park Avenue South
New York, NY 10016

First printing: October 1985

Printed in the United States of America

For Clif Warren

Teacher, Mentor, and Friend

Prologue

"Bring forth the children!"

As heavy boots thudded in the hallway outside the suite, the guttural command rang out. Joanna sat bolt upright in her bed, staring into the cold darkness. The warmth of the down comforter was no help against the fear that chilled her blood. Both hands flew to her throat where she felt the skin prickling. Even as she heard her little brother's terrified squeal, the door to her own small chamber flew open, allowing the pitiless light to blind her.

A tall man in a dark uniform pushed aside the cowering *femme de chambre* and peered in. "Is this the daughter?"

Terrified into speechlessness, the woman nodded.

"Well, hasten, woman. Drag her out of that bed."

Dropping a hasty curtsey, the shivering creature slid around the door facing, twitching the skirts of her night robe aside to avoid even the touch of the officer's boots. "My lady . . ." She reached trembling hands toward the pale little figure.

"Bring my robe." Her lips felt so stiff that Joanna doubted her command could be understood.

The woman hesitated, casting a quick look over her shoulder at the implacable figure silhouetted in the brightly lighted rectangle. "My lady Joanna, please . . ."

"Bring my robe." Obdurate pride flashing to her aid, Joanna raised her chin defiantly as she enunciated each word clearly.

The officer's eyes widened in anger. His hand fell to the hilt of his sword. His body swayed toward her. Then his attention was distracted by the scuffling and wailing in the outer room. With a curse, he strode from Joanna's line of vision.

"Do as I command," she hissed.

"Yes, my lady." The woman dropped another curtsey and stumbled to the chest at the end of the bed. As she caught up the velvet folds, her hands fumbled nervously, causing the garment to slip from them and fall to the floor. A small sob of fear and weakness escaped her as she darted a glance first at the small figure sitting upright in the bed and then at the doorway to the other room.

From the main chamber of the suite, Joanna heard a sharp slap followed by a high-pitched shriek that trailed away into sobs. "Holy Mary, Mother of God," she breathed. As the maid crouched, trembling, beside the bed, too terror-stricken to rise, the little girl thrust her bare feet out from under the covers and pattered down the three steps to the floor. Stooping, she rescued her robe from the maid's nerveless grasp and slipped it on over her nightdress. Buttoning it at the throat with fingers that felt more than ever like dead sticks, she knotted the belt tightly around her waist.

In the other chamber, her brother Charles began to curse. His words were cut off by another slap. She shivered. The floor was like ice beneath her bare feet.

She dared not glance about her. To do so would have broken her determination. From the very depths of her spirit she summoned the courage to walk proudly into the lighted room. Four steps . . . five. On the sill she paused, blinking in the light.

The scene almost drove her back into the darkness. Her

8

brother Charles, her senior by some eighteen months, writhed, whimpering, in the grip of two burly men in the uniform of the Valois guards. Her younger brother Luis, just eight, dangled like a puppet, the collar of his nightgown clutched in the fist of another guard. His eyes were glazed with shock, his cheek glowed bright red.

Only one of the frightened servants, Charles's manservant and valet, dared to protest. "His Royal Highness King Charles of Navarre will hear—"

The officer whose back was to Joanna threw back his head in an impudent bark of laughter. "Oh, indeed he will—and see too." At his last words, all trace of humor vanished from his face and his voice dropped to a menacing hiss.

The valet stumbled back a step at the ominous threat.

Smiling in grim satisfaction, the officer surveyed the scene. Suddenly, he remembered the princess. Mouth open to bawl a command, he threw a quick look over his shoulder. The sight of the small girl surprised him into silence. No cowering, whimpering child this. Instead a silent presence with its own particular dignity.

In stark contrast to the pale magnolia of her skin, her ebony hair curled in masses of ringlets about her face and shoulders. Her eyes, dark as her hair yet with crystal fire in their depths, dared the king's man to do his worst.

For a moment he stood speechless; then lifetime habits asserted themselves and his hand flew to his head to drag off his hat and sweep it gallantly before him. Even as the gesture was completed, he recovered himself and remembered his mission. His expression changed to one of angry mockery. "Ah, the princess," he sneered.

Proudly, she inclined her head. "What is the meaning of this intrusion?" Her light young voice carried a hint of a tremor as she struggled for control.

"The meaning is justice, young daughter of treachery." Replacing his hat, he loomed over her, engulfing her in his shadow as one hand found the hilt of his sword. "Your

9

father, the dog of Navarre, has turned traitor. As to be expected, he cared nothing for his word, so he forgot his children. We merely seek to remind him of what we hold."

"My father is not a traitor!" This from Charles, who had ceased to struggle and stood scowling resentfully at the scene. The fact that this man had not struck his sister but had treated her with every respect had not gone unnoticed on his part. Suddenly, he was aware of his lack of dignity as he stood in his nightgown held tightly in the grips of two common soldiers.

"Ah, but he is," the officer turned back to face the thirteen-year-old lad who stood a head taller than the little girl but whose bony feet, thin legs, and tear-stained face gave the lie to any pretensions of maturity. "He is a treaty breaker, but we shall persuade him to mend that which he has broken." With these words he nodded shortly to the man who held Charles's right arm.

Without releasing his grip, the guard drew a knife from his belt, not a dagger of the type usually carried but a heavy blade such as a cook might use to cut meat.

Charles's eyes widened in terror. "No," he gasped. *"Oh, no! Swine!"*

Joanna felt her stomach heave. Swallowing convulsively, she managed to control herself. On leaden feet she took two steps into the room. "You cannot," she croaked. "Think what you do. You have not the right—"

"Oh, I have the right." The officer extracted a rolled parchment from his doublet. "I have more. I have my orders."

"You cannot shed the blood royal!"

The officer ignored her. "Do it!"

Charles's voice rose to a shriek as the man efficiently grasped the boy's hand. Holding it tightly with his own left hand, he used the knife in his right to pare off the little finger. The prince's screams were deafening, and they continued until the other guard flung his body into the arms of the stupefied valet.

The commander withdrew a small leather pouch from the breast of his doublet and opened it to receive the bloody object. "Now the younger."

Luis's terrified shriek ended abruptly when he fainted from the pain and fear.

The torturer turned toward Joanna, who stood frozen to the spot, her black eyes dilated in her bloodless face. Terrified almost beyond thought, she blinked rapidly, then drew a deep breath. Pride, her mind whispered. Be brave. You are a king's daughter. You must not show fear. Stiffening her spine, she fastened her eyes steadfastly on the officer's face. Like anthracite they blazed, as she took a single step toward him. A faint ringing sounded in her ears; dizziness threatened to overwhelm her.

But when the torturer would have moved, his approach was stayed by the upraised hand of the officer. "We have enough," he said, suddenly nervous before her proud stare.

The man muttered an unintelligible protest which was instantly quelled by a commanding gesture.

"A girl is of little importance." The man drew the leather pouch closed with a decisive tug. "We have what we came for."

As swiftly as they had come, the soldiers withdrew. The terrified servants crept out from the corners in which they had cowered. The valet speedily clapped a heavy towel to his charge's wound and bade the younger boy's nurse do the same for Luis.

Finally, when his hysterical sobbing had died away, Charles began to curse. Uttered in his hoarse exhausted voice, the words took on a demonic character. His glittering black eyes slid feverishly around the room until at last they alighted on his sister standing numbly only a few feet from the door to her bedchamber.

"It should have been you," he snarled. "But you're worthless. They could have chopped off your head and no

11

one would have cared."

The valet glanced in her direction and tried to smile feebly in reassurance. "Hush, young Prince," he soothed, interposing his body between the boy and girl. "The officer said he had enough. He was being chivalrous, for which thank God and all the saints."

"If she hadn't been so worthless, he would have taken her finger," Charles insisted deliriously. "She's worthless. The man said so."

"Drink this." The valet raised a cup to Charles's moving lips. "It will relieve the pain and give you rest."

"Worthless," Charles sobbed.

"Come, my lady." Joanna's maid touched her arm. "He will be better in the morning. Think not on his words tonight."

Joanna shook her head dazedly. Turning stiffly, she allowed herself to be led back to bed.

Part I

The Duchess Of Brittany

Chapter 1

The wind from the land caressed Joanna's cheek as she stared into the darkness toward the north. To the east lay the coast of France, to the west, the calm waters of the Golfe de Gascogne. For several days the royal barge had hugged the coastline, as was the custom, rather than risk sailing out of sight of land. Tomorrow she would begin to swing to the west as they passed La Rochelle and Les Sables d'Olonne.

Standing at the rail, Joanna rested her hands lightly on its smoothly polished surface and set her feet slightly apart to maintain balance against the gentle roll of the waves. Fog swirled around the sides of the ship, blanketing the water in grayish white. Undimmed by the moon, stars blazed crystal fire from above.

Alone except for the helmsman who stood above and behind her, Joanna opened her black velvet cloak and draped its edges over her shoulders. The gentle wind caressed her body through her white linen nightdress.

Somewhere out there in the darkness was Jean, Duke of Brittany, her husband. She had never seen him and knew surprisingly little about him, yet she was sailing to meet him and to take her place beside him in his château at Rennes . . . and in his bed. She shivered. Although the wind had not changed one jot, the chill of dread spread through her body. He was old, older than her father.

Charles of Navarre had informed her of her marriage on the day before it had been performed. With a wave of his hand toward his secretary, he had indicated the parchment which he, as her father, had just signed. Its seals and ribands dangled impressively from its corners. Her approval, indeed her consent, had not been necessary.

Charles would have punished her severely had she objected. "You are fourteen, almost fifteen. . . ." His black eyes had looked to her for confirmation which she had hastily provided with a nod of her head. "You will marry tomorrow. The Breton ambassador will take part in the ceremony. I shall send someone to fetch you directly after noon." He chewed his lip thoughtfully.

Joanna clenched her fists in the folds of her skirt and waited.

The King of Navarre returned to the documents he was studying. The secretary cleared his throat. Annoyed, the king looked up. "Was there something else?"

His daughter raised her eyes. "Whom am I to marry?" Her normally husky voice trembled and rasped due to nervousness.

Charles stared, surprised, into black eyes like his own yet different. Where his were opaque, without light of any kind, hers held peculiar shadings. Sometimes they glittered strangely, as if lit from within. "You will find out in good time," he replied cruelly. "You are not to question my choice."

"No, Father."

"You are *not* questioning my commands, are you, Joanna?" He rose from behind the desk and came to stand before her. His short frame had put on flesh in his middle years so that he cut an imposing figure. Even though father and daughter were of the same height, she took a step backward.

"No, Father. I merely wondered whom you had selected

16

for me."

He snorted dryly. "I have selected an alliance that will benefit Navarre, as well as my plans. The Valois will find himself ringed by enemies."

Joanna waited. If he chose to tell her, he would do so. If not, she would be dismissed. To beg would only rouse his ire. Charles of Navarre was a bad man to anger. His temper often exploded due to some slight provocation and woe betide the hapless person who stood closest to him.

But the king was in an expansive mood. "Your husband is rich." He smiled thinly. "Richer than I. His land is rich too. Brittany is a fertile country, suited to farming and surrounded by rich fishing waters." He studied his daughter's fragile face.

"Then my husband is" —she paused, swallowing to relieve a constricted feeling in her throat—"a lord of Brittany?"

Charles nodded proudly. "The Duke of Brittany himself."

Not by a flicker of a muscle did Joanna betray her feelings. Her fists, within the folds of her skirt, remained perfectly still. Her lips did not move, either to smile or frown.

Her father grinned maliciously, slapping her cheek lightly with his square hand. "So controlled. But I know you. Yes, madam, I know you. I have watched you as I have all my children. You hide behind that iron control. Are your feelings, too, encased in ice? I wonder." His hand dropped menacingly onto her shoulder and slid down her arm.

Too late she relaxed her fist into a limp open hand, for her father had seen. "A fist!" he snarled. "You dare to make a fist in my presence." Then he grinned. "You do not care for the Duke of Brittany. Perhaps you have heard rumors about him. Perhaps you think him unsuitable." He stared intently into her eyes.

"I think nothing, Father."

Brutally, he squeezed her wrist, feeling her blood pound in the abused veins. "See that you do not. Your life will be much easier if you think nothing. Women who think too much come to a bad end."

He released her wrist, allowing her hand to fall limply back into the folds of her dress. She did not move. "May I retire?"

"Jean de Montfort is an elderly man, but powerful." Charles turned away ignoring her request as if it had not been made. "He has no heirs. His previous marriage was not blessed. Your duty will be to produce heirs for him. You are young. You have been capable of performing the woman's function for almost a year now. Your sons will create a strong alliance. I need not tell you how politically strong I would be with my grandson as Duke of Brittany."

"No, Father," she whispered.

"No, Father," he mocked. "A man can never tell what you think. I shall be glad to have you out of the court. A man cannot have too many sons, but daughters are a different matter." He seated himself on the edge of his desk, regarding her keenly. "You are not ill featured. Perhaps Jean de Montfort will look on you with favor. School yourself to please him," he advised. "Put aside this secretive behavior. Flatter him and study his moods. If you produce healthy children, your life may be pleasant."

Joanna inclined her head. "Thank you, Father, for this good advice."

"And look you," he warned, "surround yourself with loyal subjects of Navarre. They will enable you to contact me rapidly." He caught her chin and lifted her face to study it.

She smiled thinly, for his fingers pinched. "I will, Father."

He grunted, suddenly remembering the presence of his secretary who was studying the parchment in front of him as if he sought to memorize it. "Remove yourself from my presence. Dress yourself in your best tomorrow. The ceremony will take place in the chapel and will be followed by a feast of sorts. Is that not correct, Diego?"

The secretary snapped to attention. "All is being prepared, Your Highness."

18

"Not too much expense. Since this is merely a proxy ceremony, there is no need for . . ."

Joanna did not wait to hear what economies her father intended to practice. Dropping a low curtsey, she left the chamber. Only when the door closed behind her in her own room did she give in to the emotional turmoil that raged within her slender body. Tears slipped down her face as she lowered herself carefully into the carved high-backed chair at her writing desk.

Stiffly she clutched its arms, hoping that feeling their rigidity would still her whirling world. She should not have been surprised. Jean de Montfort was a powerful man. Her father had supported him in his successful quest for the suzerainty of Brittany at the battle of Aurai. When the other claimant, Charles of Blois, had been killed, the ducal seat had gone to Jean by default.

She shuddered again. So many, many years ago . . . The man was older than her father. The battle had taken place five years before she was born. Her stomach clenched. How could she endure?

Six months later, standing on the deck of the *San Juan el Ibérico,* Joanna realized her fingernails were scarring the smoothly polished wood of the rail, so tightly was she clutching it. Fog shrouded the sea around her, yet the wind blew gently against her cheek. As the sails billowed above her, the rigging creaked softly. Best not to think of the past. The peace of the sea seeped into her spirit. Her hands relaxed.

As they did so, she became aware of the strange quality of all around her. The scents and sounds of the sea faded. The white fog crept upward, ever upward, from the waves. Inexorably, it rose around the hem of her nightdress. The gentle rolling of the deck beneath her feet intensified the feeling that she was floating. The stars began to dim as the crescent moon slipped from behind the cloudbank to the west.

Navarre lay in the darkness behind her. Forever . . . With a lightness of spirit she realized that she would never see it again. Navarre and her father, whom the world called Charles the Bad, no longer existed for her. She clasped her hands together on the rail as if it were the altar of a church. As her confessor had assured her, nothing was so bad that some good did not come from it.

Closing her eyes, she composed her mind to give thanks as she had been taught, but pleasing words of comfort, those of saints and priests, did not come. Instead came the words of romances, visions of knights who vied and died for the love of their ladies. She had been a princess. Now she was a duchess, yet no man had ever touched her. Releasing her hold on the rail, she raised slender fingers to her lips. If a knight were to love her, what would he be like? She could almost picture him, broad shouldered with a narrow waist and hips. He would have the strong, muscular thighs of a horseman. His head would be raised proudly on the strong column of his neck. His hair and eyes would be dark as ebony like her own.

She would stand proudly at the top of a grand marble staircase and watch the fight below. In the romances the hero always fought in the field or a hall while the heroine looked over the rail of her balcony or stood at the top of a staircase. Such a knight would slay the cruel warlock or monstrous devil that held her enthralled or bedeviled.

When the evil creature lay dead, her love would fling aside his bloody sword and rush to the top of the stairs or climb the rail of the balcony and kneel at her feet. She would extend her hand for his kiss. She would feel a thrill of ecstasy—whatever that was—before he rose to his towering height.

Their eyes would meet. His would glow with love and desire. He would tenderly place one arm around her shoulders, and would enfold her hands in one of his. *Every beat of my heart will tell you of my love. . . .*

"My lady . . ."

The grating, whining voice of Isabella de la Alcudia shattered her reverie. "My lady, you will catch lung fever standing here on the deck with your cloak thrown open. For shame! For shame! Suppose someone should appear. You must remember the dignity of your position at all times. Your father remanded you to my care until your husband can assume his authority over you. How dare you expose your person to the poisonous night vapors?"

The woman's hands, like claws, plucked the black velvet cloak from her charge's shoulders and dragged it together across Joanna's young breasts. Anger flamed in Joanna's mind. Her peace, so carefully engendered, was lost, as was her pleasant dream. The *hechicera* had followed and found her; for such she had called the old woman in her mind. *Witch!*

Unwilling to trust his daughter to surround herself with people loyal to Navarre, Charles had sent a hand-picked group to accompany her. Through them and others, he maintained a network of spies throughout France and Spain. Isabella de la Alcudia had stood at the shoulder of the royal princess since the King of France had released the children two years ago.

Ignoring the woman's rantings, Joanna spun on her heel and strode back to her cabin. When she would have slammed the door shut behind her, Isabella caught it with her palm and pushed it open, continuing her tirade as she catalogued the princess' shortcomings and failings.

"Fetch me a beaker of mulled wine," Joanna commanded when the woman paused for breath.

"You need nothing." The woman denied her angrily. "Climb into bed and pull the covers up. You will be asleep in—"

21

"Fetch me a beaker of wine," Joanna repeated. "I am not sleepy in the slightest. Your scolding has irritated and upset me."

"You deserve to be scolded," her companion replied. "The king would do more than scold if he knew of this escapade. He would—"

"My father is not here." As Joanna's voice rose, her fingers clenched and unclenched. "Nor is it likely that I shall ever be in his presence again. Indeed, I shall take great pains to avoid him, if at all possible." She drew herself up angrily. "May I remind you that you are supposed to be my servant. If you wish to remain so until the end of the voyage, then I suggest you assume a more submissive demeanor. Otherwise, I shall summon the captain and have you locked away."

The older woman's nostrils quivered. A muscle flickered in one sallow cheek. "You," she snarled, "would be well advised to watch your tongue. You think to run free, but you do not know the way of the world. Your ignorance may lead you into trouble far more serious than you can imagine. Then you will see how well your father has protected you."

Turning away quickly from Isabella's mocking gaze, Joanna bit her lip to repress the reply she longed to make. Her best judgment confirmed that the woman spoke the truth. Rumors, unsettling in the extreme, had reached her ears about the court to which she traveled. Always at the heart of these rumors was the duke himself.

Behind her, Isabella's voice whined on and on. "His Royal Highness King Charles knows well how to protect his own. He pays his servants well, and in exchange, we who serve him know well how to protect his interests. You would do well to remember that his arm is long and his people are everywhere. This presence may stand you in good stead." The bony fingers rested on her charge's shoulder in a proprietary way. "Now go to bed like a good girl, and we'll say no more about this untoward behavior."

22

Anger, fear, frustration swept over Joanna in waves. She could not bear the idea of subservience to this woman. Only the Duke of Brittany, when she reached his side, had the right to command her. She was the duchess.

Nevertheless, a hard school of experience gave her the self-control to hide her feelings. Resolving to dismiss Isabella at the first opportunity, she slid her body between the damp sheets and huddled there shivering.

Looking more than ever like a witch as the lantern distorted her features and figure, Joanna's companion bustled officiously around the cabin, opening and closing the lids of trunks and refolding articles of clothing. Her black eyes glinted from beneath her lashes as she kept shifting them sideways to study her charge.

Determined not to be treated as though she were a child bidden to go to sleep, Joanna followed the woman's movements with her eyes. Her lips curled in mockery as she watched Isabella's increasing irritation, revealed in her movements which became jerky and clumsy.

At last Isabella closed the last trunk with a disgusted thump. Twitching her heavy skirts aside, she dropped the barest suggestion of a curtsey. "Have I your permission to retire, my lady?" Her voice was a sarcastic whine.

"No," Joanna replied silkily. "I requested a beaker of mulled wine. Your thumping and thudding have been most disturbing. I insist that you fetch it to help me sleep."

The clash of wills charged the atmosphere of the small cabin with electricity. Like duelists who stare at each other across their rapier points, the women measured each other, circling, mentally watching for an opening or weakness.

Stubbornly, Joanna refused to yield. Her stare never wavered. The light from the gently swaying lantern picked out gold flecks deep within her eyes. Determined that Isabella should bring the wine, she drew a deep breath and clenched her small fists beneath the sheet.

23

With a shrug of her stooped shoulders, the woman consented. Pressing her lips together, she bowed her head. "At once, my lady."

Later, with the pewter beaker warming her hands, Joanna stared into the shadows in the corner of the cabin. She did not fool herself. She had not won a total victory, only a minor skirmish. The *hechicera* would continue to seek to dominate her, and no doubt all these tiny rebellions would be carefully recorded to report to her father.

But what could he do? His arm was long, but even he could not dissolve her marriage and return her to his control.

On the other hand, her husband was old. If he died before she produced the required heir or when the heir were still an infant, Charles of Navarre would most certainly seek to have himself named guardian of his daughter. Since the loss of his Norman lands some dozen years ago to the Black Prince of England, their return had become an obsession.

Joanna's head whirled. Feelings of desperation made her stomach ache. How could she hope to win? How could the pawn defeat the king? Somehow she must find her own way. She . . .

She determined to think no more on it. To do so would drive her deeper and deeper into depression. She took another small sip of the warm wine. It was sweet and soothing. Although she had not really wanted it when she'd directed Isabella to bring it, now it comforted her.

She was a long way from home, bound for an alien land. The language spoken there was strange to her. The members of the court, she knew, spoke French, but the people spoke Breton, a language with which she was totally unfamiliar. She doubted if one person at the court spoke Spanish. At least there was Latin. She comforted herself with that thought. She could always find an understanding ear in the church.

Grimacing, she took another sip of wine. She had found

24

little comfort in religion. Her father was not religious, except for form's sake. She had a confessor who traveled with her, but she had precious little to confess. So closely guarded was she that she had never had an opportunity to commit even the smallest sin.

When her confessor had suggested that she might have sinful thoughts, she had closed her lips firmly and shaken her head. Her thoughts were her own. Since she suspected that he might carry any significant revelation to her father, she would not expose her feelings.

She shook her head ruefully. Isolated in the court, kept from the society of young girls her own age, she felt stifled. Her companions had always been women of Isabella's age or older. Her older brother Charles had never cared for her. Her younger brother Luis had taken Charles's attitude as his cue. Both had treated her with rude disdain whenever their paths had chanced to cross in the royal palace. Consequently, she had been left alone with her duennas and tutors.

Her tutors . . . She had almost cried when she had been forced to say good-bye to good Brother Francisco, who had taught her mathematics, history, and geography, as well as Latin and French, for seven years. He had gone with her to France when she had been held hostage. She had begged to have him to accompany her to Brittany, but her pleas had been ignored. She was a duchess, no longer a schoolgirl. Besides, in her father's opinion, she obviously knew too much already, much more than she would ever need to know. So Brother Francisco had remained in Navarre along with her dancing and music master.

No, she had no feelings of nostalgia, experienced no emotional wrench at being parted from well-loved family or friends—only from a host of enemies who sought to use her for their own profit. Her father's reputation, which had spread far and wide from serf's hovel to royal palace, had placed her and her brothers in constant jeopardy. Guile had become a way of life to the princes and the princess. The lessons of a lifetime would stand her in good stead.

She made a wry face as she realized her last sip of wine had drained the beaker to the dregs. With a sigh, she leaned over to set the vessel on the floor beside the bed. Her head spun dizzily as she hoisted herself back up. Slumping down against the bolster, she stared at the canopy above her.

The barge swayed gently on, carrying her farther and farther away from Navarre. With a wisdom unusual in one of her years, she determined to concentrate on what lay ahead. Surely Jean de Montfort could not be worse than Charles the Bad.

She smiled sleepily as the motion of the water and its rhythmical slap against the side of the barge lulled her, the barge rocking her as would a giant cradle. Her past had consisted of dreary monotony interspersed with moments of nauseating terror. No future, she assured herself, could be worse than that past. She must look to the future.

Watchfires guided the barge into the mouth of the Vilaine. A river pilot came aboard to steer it northward to Rennes. With him came a welcoming committee of one, the Chevalier de la Roche-Bernard, whose château stood gracefully on a pleasant hill overlooking the river.

The chevalier, a rotund man, glared first at the captain, second at Don Rodrigo, third at Doña Isabella, and last at herself. His darkly red complexion betrayed his irritation.

Joanna watched him from behind a façade of cool self-containment. "My lord." She acknowledged his bow with the barest of nods. Don Rodrigo de Bustamonte interceded with formal introductions all around. By the time they were completed, the Breton was shifting his weight restlessly.

"His Excellency Duke Jean desired that I accompany you to his side." The chevalier explained his presence with barely concealed irritation. His voice shook slightly. Nervously, clutching his tall sugar-loaf hat of dark brown velvet, he glared at the new Duchess as if she represented a particularly unpleasant task that he approached with grim distaste.

Even as she acknowledged his speech, his red-veined eyes flickered over the deck; the captain, whose lips were tightly compressed; and the crew drawn up rigidly to attention. "I will bring aboard my men," he informed the captain in a speech that too hastily followed Joanna's expression of appreciation.

The officer shot a glance at Don Rodrigo, whose brows drew together in suspicion. The don cleared his throat officiously. "Is there some problem in Brittany?"

The chevalier gaped, hesitating to answer. "There is always some problem somewhere, Don Rodrigo. One cannot be too careful. Treacherous forces are at work."

"We are on a bridal journey," Don Rodrigo informed him smoothly. "If there is the slightest reason to doubt the safety of Her Excellency, we shall return immediately to Navarre." He nodded in Joanna's direction. "This gentle maid—"

"Oh, no. Indeed not." Sire de la Roche-Bernard clutched his hat even more frantically until Joanna was sure it would never recover its shape. "I merely meant that my retinue will escort the duchess more safely . . . that is . . ."

"My men are the finest of Navarre," Don Rodrigo insisted haughtily. "They were especially chosen. Every one would give his life for her."

"No doubt. No doubt. I meant no disrespect. My men's familiarity with the land—"

"Then they will ride along the banks on either side," Don Rodrigo decided. "That way their familiarity will be to advantage."

"An excellent idea, Don Rodrigo," Joanna seconded. The Breton's whole demeanor had been insulting. Obviously, he did not welcome her with open arms. Why he should have

27

been sent to escort her, she did not know, but the presence of many armed men of uncertain sympathies would only create problems for Don Rodrigo. "While your men are being informed of their role, my lord, may I invite you to partake of some refreshment?" she offered smoothly.

He glared at her again. She had the distinct impression that his rotund body was somehow poised for flight. Then he shrugged. A fatal calm seemed to settle over him. "Thank you, my lady," he murmured, bowing.

In the salon, they sipped sherry and nibbled small honey cakes brought from Navarre. The wine of Jerez de la Frontera was rich and golden. The chevalier regarded it lovingly. "Delicious," he pronounced, patting his heavy belly. "Reminiscent of the English mead."

Joanna smiled sweetly. "I understand that my husband is a great friend of the English."

His affable expression cooled. He set the glass down heavily. "Yes," he admitted. With those words he rose, signaling the end of the interlude. "I must beg your leave to instruct my men."

"You will take supper with us, Sire de la Roche-Bernard?" Isabella inquired.

"No, madam. I thank you. We will make landfall north of Redon. I will have much to do to see to my men. Messengers will be sent ahead to inform His Excellency of the approximate time of your arrival. The last-minute preparations will have to be effected."

"I thank you then," Joanna extended her hand.

"My pleasure, madam." He bowed low over it, his lips never quite touching her cool skin. With a nod to the other occupants of the salon he was gone.

"All is not well," Isabella de la Alcudia began, but Don Rodrigo hushed her with a look.

"We will deliver the princess to her husband as ordered."

Joanna shuddered. To be delivered . . . like a parcel. Briefly, she reflected that less than fifty miles remained of her journey to her husband's side. Slowly, inexorably, she was being brought together with him across time and space. More than ever she felt herself a pawn in a gigantic game of chess, being moved ever forward until at last she was moved into the path of a powerful opposing piece who would mercilessly knock her from the board.

Chapter 2

The *San Juan de Ibérico* bumped gently against the hastily constructed dock jutting out into the Vilaine River. The rough boards had been covered, first with straw matting and then with a succession of carpets of every color and design stretched end to end to the bank. A black closed carriage waited, the crest of the suzerainty of Brittany prominent on the door.

Isabella and the two other ladies chosen to accompany Joanna from Spain had spent all morning bathing and dressing their charge in the garments Charles had provided for his daughter.

Now she sat on a stool amid the confusion of the cabin. A deep rose red velvet gown covered her from chin to toe, its color a stunning foil for her magnolia skin and blue-black hair. The sleeves, their scalloped edges lined in paler rose taffeta, trailed on the ground, and a girdle of wrought silver set with pearls gathered the garment in just below Joanna's high breasts. The underdress, likewise of rose taffeta laced tight to cover her arms to the wrists, rustled at her every movement.

With growing frustration, Isabella brushed the curly black hair until it shone. At last in despair, she gave up trying to make it lie smooth and finally contented herself with deep waves that ended in curls which she coaxed into submission with her fingers. Finally, sighing disgustedly, she met Joanna's eyes in the mirror.

"I cannot help my hair, Doña Isabella," the girl apologized humbly.

"'Tis no matter. After tonight it will be tucked away in a snood or braided into a coronet as befits a young matron," Isabella snapped peevishly.

Her words caused Joanna to pale. To meet her new husband, she wore her hair down in token of the gift of virginity she would bring to him. But after tonight, she would no longer be a maid.

Her mouth was dry. She longed to ask someone, even Isabella, what would happen to her tonight. Not one iota of information had ever reached her ears, so closely had she been guarded. Her husband would have dominion over her body. But what did that mean? A wife must be submissive to her husband. She had been submissive to her father, but there would be more to her submission with her husband. Yet what?

She bit her lip in an effort to stop its trembling.

"Her Excellency is a beautiful bride." Old Doña Catalina's voice trembled as badly as her hands as she lifted the chaplet from its box. It was of the same design of filigree silver as the girdle. She held it aloft while Doña Maria Dolores tossed a veil of exquisite, palest pink sendal over Joanna's head. The sheer material covered her to her fingertips.

Isabella then took the chaplet from the old woman's quivering fingers and set it firmly, but gently, around the new duchess' brow.

Joanna could barely suppress a moan. As the cold of the silver seeped through the thin silk, she began to shiver. Nervous tremors shook her from head to toe.

Isabella caught her arm in a punishing grip. "Here! Stop that! Catalina, a bit of mulled wine. She needs some refreshment."

The wine steadied her just before a knock sounded on the cabin door.

"We are ready," Isabella answered. "Now."

Jerkily, Joanna rose to her feet, swaying slightly although the barge had stopped all but the most imperceptible rocking. Maria Dolores knelt to arrange her sleeve and skirt on one side while Catalina bent stiffly to do the same on the other. Isabella adjusted the veil slightly.

"You are lovely, my lady. Your father shall have no cause for displeasure tonight." The words were spoken more as a warning than an encouragement.

"No." The word was only a breath of sound.

Doña Catalina straightened and hurried to swing open the door. From outside the cabin, men's voices reached Joanna. They were awaiting her. Placing each foot carefully as if a sudden movement might shatter her, she covered the distance to the cabin door.

Dimly, she was aware of Don Rodrigo de Bustamonte bowing low to kiss her fingertips, his breath warm through the sendal. At her left she recognized the Sire de la Roche-Bernard, his brow knitted in its usual angry frown. Beyond him stood the captain of the barge. The rest were strangers.

Between two lines, she passed, followed by her ladies in waiting. Her demeanor was cool, her vision focused distantly on the edge of the ship where steps had been constructed for her to descend onto the dock. The steps too were covered with matting and carpet.

Later she would not be able to remember whether the sun shone brightly or whether the heavens opened themselves and wept for her in fear and sorrow. She supposed, since she could not remember being wet, the day must have been fair.

The ground was suddenly firm beneath her feet. She stumbled slightly and a gloved hand caught hers. Grateful for the warmth and firmness, she raised her eyes to the face of the man who steadied her passage.

He was young, very young, only a few years older than

she, and his eyes were blue as lapis lazuli. His beard and hair, uncovered as he held his hat beneath his arm, were so pale a yellow that they appeared almost silvery on their tips.

"Careful, my lady," he murmured in peculiarly accented French. "You have not lost your sea legs yet."

At the mention of her legs, she blushed slightly. No man should mention the word in a lady's presence. Quickly, she withdrew her hand from his and murmured something indistinguishable. Thereafter, she covered the distance to the coach rapidly. Another gentleman handed her into the interior, where she sank gratefully onto the velvet cushions.

The carriage swayed again as others entered it, but she did not notice. Her attention was directed back to the man who remained standing on the dock. He had replaced his hat, flung the liripipe across one broad shoulder, and looped it around his arm. He stood at ease, staring at her, a smile curving the corners of his mouth.

As he caught her eyes on him, he inclined his head at the same time he shot her a half-teasing, half-reassuring smile. Hastily, she drew back into the interior of the coach as, with a jolt, it pulled away.

A few people stared from the doors of small shops as she was drawn through the streets of Rennes, but they made no gestures of greeting. Clearly, she was unheralded. The carriage rolled out into the open countryside and began to climb. A troop of mounted men preceded it, another followed.

"We are well guarded," Don Rodrigo remarked with satisfaction.

"That we need to be does not speak well," Joanna dared to comment.

The envoy drew himself up haughtily. "It is the prestige that is due your rank, my lady. You would be shamed if only a couple of men comprised your escort. No. Your lord has done everything that is right and proper."

"Except meet me himself," she whispered.

"He has many responsibilities," Isabella chided.

"Everyone always has."

Don Rodrigo held up his hand for silence. "You will do well to accept with good grace all that is done for you and ignore that which is not," he told her firmly. "I speak boldly because I must, my lady. You . . ."

At that moment the carriage passed through an ancient stone gateway so narrow that the driver scraped the side of the carriage on the gray stones. The occupants were thrown sideways. Don Rodrigo recovered himself, cursing under his breath.

Beneath her veil, Joanna could not restrain a smile. Despite his sanctimonious lecture, the envoy was tired and upset. His control was slipping. He probably was counting the hours until he could accompany the royal barge back to Navarre.

Clattering over the flagstones, the carriage turned in a wide circle in the courtyard and then drew up before a canopied entrance.

"At last," Isabella murmured.

Joanna stared as huge double doors creaked open and liveried servants lined up at attention on the steps. Nervously, she gathered her gown in her fists. The door to the carriage swung open, and the same young man held out his hand. His smile was sympathetic as if his eyes saw beneath the sendal and read the expression in her frightened young face.

Trying to smile, her mouth trembling slightly, she placed her hand in his. With a start he felt her coldness through the thin leather of his glove. He longed to say something comforting, but to do so would draw censure onto himself and perhaps onto her. "Take care, my lady," he muttered.

She caught up her skirt with the other hand. "I will, my lord."

Then another took her away from him to lead her forward to mount the stone steps that were covered with more carpet.

On the threshold, Joanna paused while the other occupants of the carriage climbed out and arranged themselves behind her. Horsemen were dismounting as well, some handing the reins of their mounts to others while they, too, arranged themselves behind her.

A procession, she thought. For the first time, I get to lead the procession. Suddenly she could not suppress a tiny hysterical giggle. Her hand flew to her mouth. Doña Isabella would box her ears. Quickly, she coughed to disguise the sound.

At her left shoulder Don Rodrigo leaned forward. "Are you all right, my lady?"

Compressing her lips firmly, she nodded. His question restored her sense of decorum.

"Then we are ready."

Joanna folded her hands together at her waist. Bowing her head ever so slightly and lowering her lashes until they screened her eyes, she led the way into the hall.

The rows of servants gave way to rows of ladies and gentlemen of the court. Their elegant and colorful garments were obviously donned for the wedding celebration. Every face was alive with curiosity as they stared avidly at the girl beneath the veil. In front of her was silence; behind, a buzz of comment.

"The Spanish princess . . ."

". . . such a beautiful gown . . ."

Through her lashes she could see a group of men waiting at the end of the hall where a dais had been erected. In the center of the group, seated in a heavily carved chair, was her husband. His whole body appeared twisted to the side; his right shoulder dropped several inches lower than his left as he leaned on his right arm. His right leg was extended toward her, the foot propped upon a stool.

Despite the rigorous discipline drilled into her by years of terror and enforced submission, she could not quell the sick feeling that settled in her stomach and spread outward to all parts of her body. Her limbs began to tremble and her foot turned, causing her to stumble slightly.

Biting her lower lip, she recovered her balance but not before she felt Don Rodrigo's hand touch her elbow briefly. This time, however, his touch did nothing to comfort her. Quite the contrary, it seemed to be forcing her forward against her will.

Jean de Montfort had not escaped the battle of Aurai unscathed. His horse had fallen with him, breaking his right leg in two places and smashing his knee. In the process of healing, the leg had been drawn up several inches. Later, lacking movement in his knee, his right hip had become involved in the injury to the extent that his balance was permanently disturbed. With the passing of years rheumatism had inflamed and swollen his joints until he could barely walk.

After one swift glance Joanna kept her eyes suitably downcast, until she halted before the duke's chair.

Don Rodrigo stepped forward. "Her Royal Highness, Princess Joanna of Navarre," he announced grandly.

At his words Joanna raised her eyes to meet the "most quarrelsome prince in Europe." Brittany's face was dead white and lines of pain heavily etched his forehead and the sides of his mouth. His green velvet hat had at least two yards of liripiping which were draped round his cadaverous face. The color proved an unfortunate choice since it accented the green cast to his skin. The effect was frightening. Behind her left shoulder, she heard a slight hiss as Don Rodrigo released a long breath.

Brittany's eyes were a unique shade of pale gray that made the blackness of their pupils stand out starkly. Now those eyes collided with hers. Languidly, he gestured with his right hand.

With a rustle of taffeta skirts, Doña Isabella stepped forward to lift the veil. Shorter than her charge, she fumbled with its folds as she slipped it back over Joanna's head.

"Bend down," she whispered. But Joanna was too horrified to register the command.

One half of the veil was back, but the other drooped down across the left side of her face. No one moved to help the mortified duenna. Then, from somewhere off to the side, aid presented itself.

Interposing his tall lean body between Joanna and the duke, the young man who had helped her twice before gently turned the veil back from her face. He smiled briefly at her. She acknowledged his help with a tiny nod. Then he, too, stepped aside.

"Your Grace." He bowed low, sweeping his hat off in an elegant gesture. "Behold your bride."

The duke smiled slightly then—a very wintry smile to be sure. There was only a hint of pleasure in it as if he had not smiled in a long time and as if he were a stranger to pleasure of any kind.

Joanna clasped her hands so tightly together that the knuckles showed white. She could not, for her very life, return his smile. All her strength of will was bent on suppressing the shudders that coursed through her body and down the length of her spine.

"My lady." The old man drew a deep breath and released the words in a sigh. His voice was a raspy whine reminiscent of a tired old hound's.

Stiff as a statue, she felt Isabella's hand at her waist. As she pretended to arrange the veil, the duenna delivered a sharp pinch to the soft flesh above Joanna's hip.

The pain was sufficient to break Joanna's trance. Bowing her head, she sank into a deep curtsey. "Your Grace," she murmured.

"Approach us so that we may see you properly," Brittany commanded. "Bring a chair." He directed this command to the young man who had thrown back her veil.

When it was done, Joanna was conducted to the chair at

her husband's right. "Did you have a comfortable journey, my lady?" the old man inquired politely.

She nodded shyly. "The voyage was peaceful, my lord."

"And were you pleased with your welcome?" The pupils of the strange pale eyes slid along the lines of assembled nobility, studying them as they listened for her answer.

Joanna hesitated. She did not know how to answer him. Was he referring to the carpets laid end to end across the straw matting leading to her carriage? Her gaze followed his. "I am pleased to have arrived safely at your side," she murmured at last.

Raising his right eyebrow, he turned his face to stare directly into hers. "Did la Roche-Bernard provide you with a suitable escort?"

Puzzled, she nodded. "He did, my lord. He came aboard the barge while his men rode along the banks. Most conscientious and dutiful."

Brittany smirked. "He has played into my hands." Even as he spoke, he gestured to a man who stood at attention apart from the clusters of people engaged in conversation. The man turned on his heel, his right hand going to the hilt of his sword, and slipped as unobtrusively as possible from the room. Few had noticed his leaving.

Joanna stiffened. She had dwelt too long in the court of Charles the Bad to be surprised by treachery. Coldly, she realized that her husband had used her as an instrument by which to draw an enemy into a net. Though her intervention would do little good, she nevertheless forced her stiff lips to move. "He did everything that was right and proper for me, my lord," she whispered.

The duke's eyes narrowed. "He could do no less," he rasped.

"He could have taken me prisoner perhaps and held me for hostage."

"He would not have dared," Jean de Montfort replied

haughtily. "Furthermore, Bustamonte had his orders."

Joanna's eyes flew to Don Rodrigo. He had withdrawn and was unable to hear them. However, his attention had never wavered from their faces as he studied their reactions to each other's conversation. "From whom did he receive them?" she inquired huskily, striving to conceal the anger in her voice. Treachery among her own retinue. "I understood he was my officer at my command."

Her husband frowned, heavy lines deepening in his face. "He is your father's man. Charles and I do favors for each other. La Roche-Bernard . . . ah!" He broke off as the officer returned with a guard of armed men. At a harsh command, the portly Breton found himself surrounded. His bright red face turned purple with anger.

"Montfort!" he shouted. "Treacherous dog!"

The officer smashed a studded gauntlet across the man's face. A woman screamed. Men arranged themselves in front of their womenfolk as several dress swords slithered from their sheaths. Prudently, the guests quit the area around the struggling man. Helpless in the hands of the soldiers and deserted by his friends, he hung panting and groaning while the officer spoke in a clear ringing voice. "Raoul de la Roche-Bernard, I arrest you for the crimes of treason and calumny against his grace, the Duke of Brittany."

"Treachery," the chevalier moaned. "To me, friends. I—"

"Take him away." The duke gestured peremptorily. "The marriage feast will begin presently. He spoils the pleasure of the day. My bride is upset." His sidewise smile at Joanna resembled nothing so much as a sneer. "But look you, Captain d'Angers, see he reveals the names of all those in the conspiracy with him before he hangs."

At the word conspiracy the hum of comment increased in volume. The pale eyes of the duke shifted to the huddled groups of members of his court. The atmosphere in the room thickened perceptibly. A rather pretty lady in blue gave a noisy sob and buried her face in the shoulder of her escort.

"I beg you, Your Grace . . ." Joanna touched her husband's arm.

"What, my lady?" His pale eyes fell to her fingertips, then rose to her face.

"The chevalier treated me with every courtesy and he took great care to insure my protection. Surely, there must be some mistake."

The man's jaw clenched in anger. "Your concern becomes your womanly heart, my lady, still he is a traitor."

"But might not clemency be granted on the celebration of our wedding? We would not want so unpleasant—"

Brittany drew in his breath sharply. *"You will not question me."* Each word was stressed and enunciated with the venomous intention of committing Joanna to her place once and for all.

She bit her lip. Terrified, she nodded, dropping her eyes and jerking her hand away from his sleeve to bury it in the folds of her dress. "No, Your Grace."

He stared silently at her as the guards hustled the chevalier's wretched, stumbling figure from the room.

As if on cue, a liveried servant entered through the same double doors which had just closed behind the guards and the prisoner. Advancing to the center of the room, seemingly oblivious to the tragic drama just ended, he spoke in sonorous tones. "The wedding feast, so please your graces."

"Geoffrey!" the duke snapped.

The silver-haired young man hastened forward. Mounting the dais as one long familiar with this procedure, he eased the duke's foot down from its stool. Then placing one hand firmly under the duke's arm, he steadied the bent man to his feet.

"Joanna!"

Resentment stained her cheeks at this rude bawling of her given name. Yet she rose, out of long habit responding to the tone of command.

"You take my other side." He gestured irritably, capturing her small hand in his. "Your hand is like ice," he commented. "The wine will warm you tonight. Right, Geoffrey. I have caused to be brought from the valley of the Marne the wine of Épernay. You will like it, Joanna. It is delicate and difficult to obtain since it does not travel well, but this is a celebration for my bride." He laughed amiably enough as he hobbled down the steps between the two young people.

With some shuffling and fumbling the young man called Geoffrey managed to get Brittany seated at the head of a long table. His main task accomplished, he pulled Joanna's chair out from the table for her. This time when she caught his èye, he did not smile. His eyes focused deliberately on a spot a few inches to the right of her ear.

Puzzled and faintly hurt, she seated herself while he stationed himself at attention behind the ducal chair. She did not have time to muse on his attitude, nor on the fact that he did not seat himself farther down the table with a group that obviously consisted of squires of the knights. Lackeys immediately began to serve the banquet while a group of musicians in the gallery began to play.

A long silver plate and a silver loving cup were placed between the duke and his new duchess. With a knotty white finger Jean de Montfort pointed out the initials B and N—Brittany and Navarre—entwined in an elaborate design of fanciful leaves. Both plate and cup were marked alike. "In your honor," he informed her expansively.

Geoffrey leaned between them to fill the cup with the bubbling wine of Épernay called champagne after the district where its grapes grow. Servants then brought basins of warm water scented with rose petals so the guests might wash their hands. With a leer Jean plucked the linen towel from the servant's arm and dried Joanna's hands between his own. Then tossing the towel in the man's face, he pressed his thin pale lips to the throbbing pulses in each of her wrists in turn.

At this gesture, Joanna could scarcely resist the desire to twist her hands from his. Jean de Montfort became even more frightening with each passing minute. The realization that this man had dominion over her body nauseated her. Sweat dotted her brow.

As the basins of water were removed, another group of servants carried in great platters of venison and boar as well as piles of small fowl and fish. When each was presented to the duke, he placed a generous portion on the silver plate. A platter piled high with loaves of fine white bread was set in front of them, flanked by a plate of mounded butter and a cellar of salt.

"My lady, you must taste this first. This deer came from the forest to the north. Geoffrey shot it himself and brought it home for the wedding."

Joanna blinked. Nausea and fear combined had sent her into another world; now his rasping voice called her back. Extended to her mouth on the tip of her husband's dagger was a sliver of tenderloin. As she stared at it, uncomprehending, a drop of red liquid collected on its tip and dripped onto the white cloth spread over the board. The sight was too much.

Helplessly, she swayed in her chair then slumped over the arm.

While the duke, bemused and irritated, stared at his unconscious bride, Geoffrey sprang forward and knelt beside the chair. Cradling her pale face against his shoulder, he dipped his long fingers into the chilled wine and moistened her lips.

Meanwhile, Brittany turned irritably to Don Rodrigo on his left. "She is not sickly, is she?" he bawled. "I was assured that she was healthy and strong, capable of bearing sons."

"Madre de Dios!" Rodrigo exclaimed, also rising to his

43

feet. Others had noticed the bride's sudden swoon and the hum of comment rose again. The royal houses of Europe had their troubles with weak bloodlines. Sickly heirs and barren women were not uncommon and were grounds for divorce or at least annulment. "I swear before . . ." He hastened to hover anxiously over her.

But Geoffrey's champagne had already restored her.

With her head tipped back against his arm and his fingers on her lips, Joanna regained consciousness. When she first opened her eyes, she could not imagine what had happened to her. Her head spun; she remembered nothing. Geoffrey's fair handsome face hung above her, its expression anxious.

"My lord," she whispered.

"My lady, you fainted."

She sighed. "I never faint. You must be mistaken."

With a rueful smile, he shook his head. Reaching for the cup, he held the champagne to her lips.

"Your Grace?" Don Rodrigo's excited voice queried.

Remembering who and where she was, Joanna straightened in her chair. "I am all right," she insisted shakily. Quickly she looked at her husband. "I pray you pardon me, my lord. I was doubtless weak . . . from hunger. I have had nothing to eat all day." With a sick feeling in her stomach, she remembered the proffered meat. Her eyes flew to the spatter on the white tablecloth and then away again.

Jean de Montfort shrugged. "Then eat," he commanded, his voice gruff. "Sit down." He motioned to the envoy. Thereupon, he turned his back on Joanna and grabbed Bustamonte's arm. "You had better be right. If she is sickly, I will send her back by the same barge that brought her."

The man's face turned deep scarlet. "I swear, she is healthy. Never a day of sickness in her life. Look at that skin. The blood comes to the surface like fine wine. Such color could not be achieved if she were ill. I beg you. Remember she has had a long journey. Those women kept her standing all morning in the cabin. Stupid old crones! They are to blame for this." Don Rodrigo fell to cursing Doña Isabella and the others.

Jean de Montfort looked over his shoulder at her. "Well, we will give her a few more minutes to eat; then I will have the bedding ceremony immediately. If I find her blemished or weak in any way, back she goes."

Chapter 3

The duke spoke loudly making no attempt to prevent her overhearing. Indeed, the other men seated beyond Don Rodrigo heard also and grinned. One leaned far out over the board and stared at her in amused speculation.

Her cheeks, pearly white from her swoon, now blushed a fiery red. With a coarse laugh the man drew back, gesturing in her direction with the point of his knife.

Brittany broke off his conversation with Don Rodrigo to turn and stare at her with renewed interest. "So." He chuckled. "A little color back in those cheeks. Good! Good!" He waved a hand at the silver plate. "Eat! You will need your strength. I want no fainting in my bed tonight."

From hurt and embarrassment, her emotions changed to fury. She was a princess. How dare he insult and denigrate her before her face in the sight and hearing of this whole assembly! Forgetting her father's words of advice, forgetting that she was in a position of extreme vulnerability, she clenched her jaw. Staring haughtily into his pale gray eyes, she straightened her spine. "I shall do all that is required of me this night," she replied icily.

His entire face contorted in a snarl of anger at her show of displeasure. "You may be sure of that, madam," he informed her drily; then he leaned toward her so that none might hear his next words. "You may also be sure that emotional displays of that type will be dealt with harshly and immediately should they occur again. You have dared to show your temper twice in the short space of time since our meeting. I shall not tolerate a third time. Be warned."

He turned again to Don Rodrigo. "She is not biddable," he commented angrily.

Bustamonte shot her an angry look over the duke's drooping shoulder. With studied diplomacy the don attempted to soothe him. "She is very young, Your Grace."

"Nonsense. That is no excuse. Because she is very young, she should be infinitely tractable. I can only surmise that her father has not disciplined her as he should. Girls in France are taught their place from earliest babyhood."

"She is still young," the don insisted. "You have time to train her as you wish. A few months of your direction, and she should know your every want and need before you even speak. She is not simple but infinitely teachable."

The suggestion appealed to the duke. The corner of his mouth quirked upward in an unpleasant smile. He turned back to her. "It is true," he mused. "I do have the pleasure of training you."

Not only his words, but the darkly evil secrets of his eyes made Joanna shudder. Her breath caught in her throat as she clenched her hands in the folds of her skirts. The horror and vulnerability of her position terrified her. She had leaped from the devil she knew to the devil she did not. Charles the Bad had never beaten her severely. Her body had been a marketable commodity. Now it had been sold to the highest bidder. This man could use it as he chose. He would cast it aside when he had done so. Unless she became pregnant immediately, she did not doubt that he would arrange to cast her aside in the most humiliating and painful way possible. And when he finished with her body, it would be no longer marketable.

With trembling hands she reached for the silver loving

cup. Her husband was there before her. His hand closed round the opposite handle. When she drew back, he shook his head. "Drink with me, wife," he commanded.

"I . . ."

"Come, Joanna." His voice was a threat.

She had no choice. Taking the other handle, she bent toward him. As was the custom, they raised the cup to their lips. In order to drink together without spilling the fine champagne, she had to join her mouth with his at the rim. With his thin lips touching hers, he dropped his hand onto her thigh, his knobby fingers squeezing her painfully.

She could hear the applause and raucous laughter and cheers. She tried to tilt the cup away, but her husband's grasp held it firmly against their mouths. At the same time his fingers thrust themselves roughly against the mount at the jointure of her thighs.

His rough handling terrified her, but she knew instinctively she dared not pull back. If she caused a drop of wine to be spilled, he would strike her here and now in the presence of the company. Silently praying for strength, she endured while the lewd comments went on and on.

At last when the noise seemed to peak, he tilted the cup back down. At that time, however, he did not let her sink back in her chair. Instead, he glued his mouth to hers and thrust his tongue against her locked teeth. Her resistance must have increased his ire, for his knuckles moved up her belly, prodding her roughly.

When she gasped in pain, he thrust deeply filling her mouth with his plundering tongue. Having achieved his purpose, he pulled away to face the table with a sneer of triumph. Struggling to his feet with the aid of the ever-present Geoffrey, he raised the loving cup that he had wrenched from her nerveless grip. His face was flushed with lust. "My friends, I beg you drink to my health and to the future succession of my line."

Hearty cheers greeted his command, for while the guests

49

had not been drinking long enough to be really drunk, the frightening episode preceding the wedding had created tension in them. Now their anxiety dissolved in a frantic storm of gaiety. Lackeys ran among the guests refilling the emptied goblets.

Out of the corner of her eye, Joanna caught Doña Isabella's movement as she pushed herself out of her chair. Events were moving too fast. She felt swept along as by a great tidal wave. This was to be her wedding supper. Yet she had had no pleasure from it. Not one toast had been drunk to her health and happiness. Instead she had been insulted, abused, and terrorized. She had eaten hardly a bite of food, drunk no more than a few sips of wine.

Tears were very close to surfacing as she grasped the edge of the table to steady herself. The day had gone from bad to worse. Now the worst seemed to be ahead.

The duenna's heavy hand rested on her shoulder. Geoffrey dragged back her chair, pulling her hands loose from the edge of the table.

"Go!" the duke commanded grandly. "Prepare my bride." He leered into her face which paled white as chalk in startling contrast to her midnight hair. He caught her chin in his hand as she rose swaying. "Give me another kiss."

Terrified, she stood frozen while he tilted forward unsteadily on his arthritic legs, to plant hard lips on her soft trembling ones. Abruptly, he pulled away, staring with satisfaction into her ebony eyes, reading in them her fear. "Go," he commanded again, his own lust stirred by the fresh sensuality of her young body. He felt eager and excited.

As the duenna led Joanna away to be joined by several other ladies, the men cheered and drank again. Brittany felt himself a good fellow. This night was going to be a memorable one. Brushing aside the silver loving cup, he called for a goblet more convenient to his grip.

Geoffrey thrust him one filled to the brim with more champagne. At one end of the table, a man sprang to his feet to propose a toast to marital bliss. The musicians struck up a lively tune and a troop of dancers and acrobats ran into the room.

Joanna and her ladies were hurried to the bedchamber by a woman in a huge heart-shaped headdress supported by metal cauls of filigreed silver. As they crossed the threshold, the princess groaned aloud. Not at the sight of the huge canopied bed with green velvet hangings and coverlet that dominated one side of what was clearly the ducal bedchamber. There she would perform her duties for the first time as a wife. She had been reared to accept those duties and regarded them as her lot in life.

Her dismay was caused by the sight of the chairs and the heavily laden buffet table that filled the other side of the room. Clearly, the bedding ceremony was to be more than a mere formality. At least a dozen people would be able to sit and eat and drink through the night while her husband consummated his marriage.

She had little time to think. Isabella's hands were already lifting the chaplet and veil from her head while Catalina and María Dolores began to unlace the tight taffeta undersleeves. The Frenchwoman in the huge headdress hastened to the buffet and poured a goblet of wine which she carried with both hands to the trembling girl. "Drink, Your Grace," she commanded not unkindly. "It is the fine golden wine from Jerez de la Frontera."

Obediently, Joanna lifted the goblet to her stiff lips.

The rose velvet dress was lifted over her head, then the taffeta underdress. She stood shivering in her undergarments, even though the room was almost hot from the blazing fire in the huge fireplace and the tall trees of candles placed in each of the four corners.

Old Doña Catalina's joints creaked noisily as she knelt to unfasten Joanna's garters, roll down the silk stockings, and unbuckle the straps of her rose leather shoes. Isabella slipped the strap of her chemise off one shoulder while María

51

Dolores did the same on the other side. The loose undergarment fell to her feet leaving her naked from the waist, for her slender figure had been too delicate to warrant a *cotte*. Her *braies* were swiftly untied and slipped down also.

Raucous laughter and the shuffling of many feet echoed down the hall.

Joanna turned in desperation, her hands seeking a robe of some sort, but Isabella smirked nastily and shook her head. Taking her charge firmly in hand, she held her by the shoulders as the men threw open the door.

A sigh of pleasure was the only sound as the first comers stopped short, at the sight of her slender pale nudity. Behind them others crowded in, bearing on their shoulders the duke himself still clutching a goblet.

"My bride," he wheezed. His pale gray eyes surveyed her figure minutely as his friends lowered him. He hobbled forward unsteadily, his tongue licking across his lower lip. "Well, now."

At the expression in his eyes Joanna felt a huge cold hollow space open beneath her ribs. Her stomach seemed to drop away, leaving her with no strength and only cold terror and weakness in its stead. All eyes in the room, all eyes in the world, seemed to be turned on her at this moment. She swallowed convulsively.

A man in the duke's retinue laughed uproariously. Clapping his nearest companion on the back, he made a lewd remark. The others laughed too, hesitantly at first until the duke himself joined in, nodding delightedly and finishing the wine in his goblet.

This he thrust at Geoffrey, who set it aside on a table near the door and hastened to undo the buttons at the neck of his master's surcoat. From the moment he had entered the room, his eyes had steadily avoided Joanna's form. Now he turned his back to her completely.

With many a chuckle and leer the others fell to divesting

the duke of his garments. As his body emerged, Joanna's [...] increased until she swayed where she stood, only held upright by the hands of her ladies.

"She is not sickly, is she?" Jean de Montfort asked again of Bustamonte. "I can see no blemish on her body, but this fainting . . ."

"I assure you . . ." Don Rodrigo began.

"Let her await you in the bed," Doña Isabella suggested, daring greatly to interrupt the envoy. "She did not eat much perforce. But she will be able to do all that you require of her tonight. She is strong and healthy. I have been with her since babyhood. She has never had a sick day."

Without waiting for permission, she guided the trembling, fainting girl to the bed and helped her in, leaving the covers turned down to expose her from the waist up.

The men had meanwhile succeeded in getting the duke's *chausses* off, so he stood naked at last except for an undershirt of thin linen.

"Geoffrey!" he barked.

The young man put his arm under his master's shoulder to help him to the bed.

Before he climbed in, the old duke bent his mouth close to Geoffrey's ear. "Draw the curtains tightly around the bed," he commanded in a harsh whisper. "And look you, encourage these fools to leave swiftly, then return alone."

"I will, my lord."

As the green velvet walls closed round them, shutting the newly-married couple from the eyes of the witnesses, Joanna closed her eyes. At least in the green darkness, she did not have to see the withered white limbs with their swollen arthritic knobs at the joints.

Then his hands found her. "Move close to me." His voice trembled even as it commanded. His breath rasped harshly as if he had been running hard.

Joanna tried to speak, but her mouth and throat were dry. She could not have moved had he prodded her with a spear.

nds fumbled, slid off her shoulders, to grip her
ns. "I said, 'Come.'" His actions suiting his words,
ed their bodies together until they lay with his ribs
g in and out against her.

Fumbling at her chin, he lifted up her face and kissed her.
With their mouths locked together, he began to fondle one of
her small breasts, pinching the nipple as he would have done
had she been an experienced woman. At his touch to that
part of her body which had known no man's hand before, she
began to struggle.

In silent terror, she fought him, but his hands and tongue
were everywhere. No sooner had her hand pushed him away
from her breast than he shifted his grip to her buttock. With
an angry whimper she swung her arm wide, flailing his
shoulder until he caught her wrist and brought it down
behind her back to lock both wrists together in his long
knobby fingers.

"Stop that!" he whispered angrily. Groaning at the
unaccustomed effort he threw one leg across the tops of her
thighs. "You must not strike your lord and master. A good
wife submits." Held fast by the weight of his body and his
grip on her wrists, Joanna could only writhe helplessly.

His other hand then roamed familiarly over her breasts,
squeezing them roughly before he pinched and tugged at her
nipples. "You are not doing your duty," he panted. "You are
my wife. You ought to be doing this for me. I am the one who
needs skillful hands. But that will come later." He chuckled
softly. His fingers crawled down across her belly to insinuate
themselves roughly into the cleft at the joining of her thighs.

Ignorant as to his purpose and ashamed that a man would
touch her there, she cried out. Her cry was hailed on the
other side of the curtain as men smiled at each other and
drank a toast to the new heir.

"My lords and gentlemen." Geoffrey's voice rose above
the general merrymaking. "His Grace has instructed me to

conduct you again to the hall where you will be pleased to continue the banquet and to enjoy the entertainments he has provided."

While some of the company would have preferred to stay and drink the excellent wines, they were forced to follow the example of the others. A few of the men rose immediately, their eyes fiery, their own desires aroused by the muted sounds issuing from behind the green velvet hangings.

"*Par dieu,*" one remarked to his fellow as he led the exodus with a will, "I never could sit out a joust."

"Nor I," his companion agreed. "Always preferred to take a turn with the lances myself." Their coarse voices carried clearly through the curtain as did the laughing ribaldry that followed them.

The uncaring remarks struck chords in Joanna's mind, penetrating the horror being inflicted on her, driving out her terror on a wave of fierce proud anger. They had left the room. The monsters had left her to her cruel fate in the arms of this horrible old man. She would receive no help from any of the witnesses and certainly no mercy from her husband.

The fierce temper that her upbringing had tried unsuccessfully to suppress rose to the surface in a scream of rage accompanied by an unexpected attack upon the duke's body. Knotting herself into a ball, she kicked out violently. Her bare feet came into contact with his thighs, pushing him away from her at the same time she flung herself backward through the velvet curtains.

She landed on her naked shoulders, her head striking the chilled stone floor with a shock. The force of her fall was the last straw to her overcharged senses. Her naked hips and legs slid nervelessly over the edge; her body crumpled bonelessly in a pathetic heap.

Fortunately, her unconscious state spared her the sight of her husband's livid face bathed in perspiration. Gasping with pain, Jean raised himself on one elbow to glare over the edge of the high bed. One of her feet had delivered a hard blow to

55

his manhood, destroying his desire abruptly. Boiling with fury and frustration, he swung his legs over the side of the bed and dropped down painfully onto his knees.

The contact of his arthritic joints with the cold floor wrung a shriek of agony from his lips. Collapsing against the side of the bed, he cupped his trembling hands around them as tears spouted from his eyes and trickled down his sunken cheeks.

Gradually, his pain lessened from white hot pulsations to a dull throbbing exacerbated by contact with the icy floor. Moaning faintly with each breath, the duke looked around him warily. Fortunately, Geoffrey had led the wedding guests from the chamber. No one had witnessed his humiliation.

But what was he to do? The agony in his limbs receded to be replaced by a more severe agony of mind. From the depths of his being, it arose, bitter as gall. He could not consummate this marriage. Indeed, he doubted that he could have done so had the girl been willing and eager. His body was too old, too used up, too much a prisoner of its own deformities.

Pulling his hands from their task of soothing his knees, he clasped them round his head. Blood pounding in his temples, he faced the end of his dynastic hopes, the falling away of his followers when his failure became generally known, and the eventual loss of the suzerainty for which he had schemed and fought for so long. His entire life, its purpose, would amount to nothing without the heir. He must think.

His mind, honed to razor sharpness by decades of statecraft, spun in intricate circles, darting like a spider back and forth across its web. His eyes rested on the white form before him. Running his gaze over her dispassionately, he noted that she breathed. That single fact was sufficient. Beyond that he had no curiosity about her condition. He dare not let her leave this room unless a solution could be found to his dilemma. Yet he dared not kill her, the daughter of his most powerful ally.

Geoffrey found him thus. "Your Grace!" He sprang forward, throwing his arm around the duke's thinly-clad shoulder. "My God! Your Grace, what happened?"

The duke raised his head tiredly to stare up into blue eyes. Geoffrey's young face held no condemnation, only pity and concern. For a full minute the old man stared, his mind whirling and turning. Then a gem of an idea was born—an idea so outrageous that at first he rejected it with a shake of his head. However, it would not go away.

"What happened?" the younger man repeated anxiously. "Are you all right? Are you in great pain?"

Slowly, Montfort shook his head, his eyes never leaving Geoffrey's face. Gradually, they assumed a hooded expression.

Satisfied that the duke was safe for the present, Geoffrey scrambled around the flaccid body of his master and knelt beside Joanna. Straightening out her crumpled limbs, he arranged her body in a more normal position. As he lifted her head, he felt a huge lump on the back of her skull. Alarmed, he placed his hand on her breast. With a relieved sigh, he felt her heart's irregular thumping. At least she was still alive, although she probably had a concussion.

Sinking back on his heels, he returned his attention to the duke whose breath rasped in his throat. The man's strange pale eyes were reduced to white rings around the enlarged pupils that stared, unblinking, at Geoffrey as he worked over the unconscious girl. "Your Grace?" he queried uncertainly.

Brittany did not answer. His falcon's gaze slid over the youth's body, taking in the breadth of shoulder, the strength of thigh.

Geoffrey stirred nervously beneath this unblinking scrutiny. "Your Grace, let me help you to rise. The cold floor will sink into your joints."

Brittany nodded slowly. His body was cold as ice, but its chill came from within, generated by the enormity of the gamble he was about to take.

Geoffrey slipped both hands under the man's shoulders and hoisted him to his feet, propping him up against the bedpost. Brittany looked ghastly, his body shrunken in appearance. Never had his age been more apparent.

Whipping the coverlet off the bed, the young man draped it toga fashion around his master's body.

"Thank you," came the shivering croak. The words were the first the duke had spoken since his lackey had entered the chamber.

Geoffrey smiled to himself, shaking his head slightly at the unaccustomed words. "Let me help you back to bed," he suggested.

Furtively, the duke glanced across the room checking to see that no one lurked in the shadows to carry this tale beyond the chamber. Satisfied of privacy, he scanned the crumpled body at his feet. Suspiciously, he nudged it with his foot.

Geoffrey flinched. Hurriedly, he knelt to gather up the doll-like figure. She was surprisingly light, her body fine boned for its length. Lifting her onto the bed, he straightened her limbs and gently eased the long fall of black hair that had caught under her body. She lay as one lifeless. Had it not been for the slight rise and fall of her chest, Geoffrey would have believed her dead.

Dark smudges had begun to appear on her breasts and wrists. As their import dawned upon him, he swallowed convulsively. He could no longer maintain his detachment. Against his will his hands began to tremble, his head to spin. He had witnessed men put to the torture; he had served as a second in a duel in which one man had been killed. What had happened in this room tonight? The duke was capable of anything. What maltreatment had he visited on this young and tender form?

Leaning his forehead against the bedpost, he drew in a long deep breath.

Behind him, he felt rather than heard Brittany move.

"You must do it." The words were spoken in a raspy whisper.

Geoffrey did not understand. If the duke were ordering him to kill the girl, he could not do it. He was no paid assassin. His body straightened. Wheeling, he shook his head. Standing face to face with his master, he snapped, "Never."

"You dare to say me 'never'?"

"I am no murderer."

The duke sighed with relief. "I did not mean for you to commit murder, my boy."

Geoffrey stared at the old face, its lines bespeaking the crafty unscrupulous mind behind it. His brows drew together in a frown.

"You must do it," the duke repeated.

"What?"

The older man hobbled across the room, his shortened right leg more noticeable than ever. The blue knotty veins about his right ankle and calf distended with each step he took. Slumping down in a chair beside the laden table, he pulled the wine to him and slopped some into a goblet. "Lock the door."

With a feeling of mounting dread, Geoffrey did so. The room seemed unnaturally quiet. The flames had died on the hearth leaving only silent glowing coals. Many of the candles, especially those nearest the door where the draught had been stronger, had guttered down in their sockets. Soon the room would be in darkness.

Brittany quaffed the wine in the goblet and poured more, filling a second goblet for his man and indicating with a sweep of his hand that Geoffrey should sit in a chair opposite. "I am cold," he whispered.

"I'll stoke up the fire."

"Leave it."

Geoffrey clutched the stem of the goblet.

"Leave it. These things are best said and done in the dark."

"I shall not—"

"Silence," the duke's voice never varied. "I do not ask you to do murder." He stared at the pale young man. His hair was like silver in the waning light, his eyes like silver too, gray, yet lighter at the edges of the irises so no clear line delineated the color from the white. His body was still slender, somewhat lanky, its musculature immature.

Geoffrey shifted under the duke's stare, turning his head slightly to one side and focusing on a spot about a foot beyond the older man's drooping right shoulder.

Jean de Montfort sighed. "You do remember that I brought you with me out of England?"

The muscles around Geoffrey's finely sculpted jaw tightened. "I remember everything. You took me from the abbey. The prior had beaten me so often my back was never healed from one time to the next. I swore to follow you forever."

"Did you never think why you were in the abbey in the first place?"

"They told me. My father placed me there because I was a bastard. My mother was dead. They told me that too. I was to be trained for the Church."

"Just so," Brittany nodded. "You were a bastard. And you have been . . . pleased to be with me?"

Gray eyes met the older man's. "I have been pleased."

"You have been given the education of a knight," the duke reminded him. "You have had every comfort."

Except acceptance, Geoffrey thought. I drew the bastard's lot because blood ties legalized by contracts and religious vows are everything.

"Sometimes I have been harsh," Brittany admitted. He studied the wine in the goblet. One by one the candles in the tree behind him guttered out. Only the red glow from the hearth remained. "I am not an easy man. My life has not

60

been easy. But I have reared you to be hard."

Geoffrey said nothing. What could he say? The beatings administered by the prior had been no different from the beatings administered by the lackeys at the duke's command. Only afterward the care of his body had been different. His stripes had been anointed with soothing salve and he had been put to bed between cool linen sheets to think on his multitude of sins and the ways to avoid the same punishment.

"Now I need your obedience," the duke sighed and shrugged. "I cannot do it myself. Perhaps had she been willing, not so frightened, not so angry, I might have been able." He stared at the green velvet hangings. "She is beautiful."

An idea was forming in Geoffrey's mind, so outrageous, so unbelievable that he at first rejected it outright.

"You have seen her nude body, lifted it in your arms," the duke smiled at his retainer. "You are a young man, lusty. You have had your turns with women."

Geoffrey swallowed. He nodded his head. Not for the world would he admit that he had had no turns with the women. His bastardy had put him beneath the notice of the ladies of the court. Barely seventeen and constantly in attendance on the crippled duke, he had had no opportunities to tumble the serving wenches.

The duke leaned forward, placing his hand on the young man's knee. "Then you will do it," he whispered. "Do it tonight. Do it now."

He rose and clapped Geoffrey on the back. "Now! To the good work. The girl awaits you. She is guaranteed to be a virgin. With your young strength you should be able to break open her body and ride her well."

The crude description of the part he was expected to play made Geoffrey's stomach churn. "She will know I am not you."

Brittany snorted. "That hysterical baby. She is unconscious now. If you get to it, it will be done before she awakes."

"Make love to an unconscious woman?"

"The best time. No fuss. No crying and complaining. Just take your pleasure and be off. The best of them are really no better than the worst." Exerting pressure with the arm he laid around Geoffrey's shoulders, he forced the young man toward the bed.

The room was almost totally in darkness now; only a faint red glow emanated from the hearth.

Before the curtains the duke began unbuttoning Geoffrey's tunic. The air of the room was warm, but the youth's body was sweating profusely. "Your Grace, I beg you—"

"Hush." The duke's voice lowered to an insidious whisper.

Geoffrey shivered at the cold rush of air on his shoulders as the duke drew the tunic off. The touch of the duke's hands against his skin caused something to snap in his brain. A servant he might be—and a bastard—but he would be driven no farther if he died for it. The duke's fingers fumbled at the lacings holding the codpiece to the hose.

"I can take care of that." Geoffrey's voice sounded steady. The breath he drew swelled his chest and flexed his broad shoulders.

The duke's hands dropped away instantly. Turning his back, he limped away into the darkness.

With stiff fingers Geoffrey stripped off the rest of his garments. The performance of these natural acts calmed him somewhat. Naked, he faced the curtains. The turmoil in his mind had given way to a perverse excitement. He would think no longer of the reasons for the act. Instead he trained his mind intently on monitoring the sensations of his body.

His muscles shuddered and jumped as he drew aside the bed curtain and lifted one knee onto the sheets. There he paused to listen intently. Only the sound of labored breathing reached his ears.

Hoisting his body inside the canopy, he drew the curtains closed, welcoming the impenetrable darkness. Crouching on his knees he found her nude body with his hands.

She lay just as he had left her although now her skin was chill. Pity touched him briefly; he had not thought to cover her when he had laid her down. He ran his hands across the bed until he encountered the covers, pushed aside in the struggle. Straightening them somewhat, he stretched out beside her, then pulled the covers over them both enclosing them in a cocoon.

As he gathered her against him, she moaned. The sound froze his muscles. Suppose she awoke and began to fight him. He could not bring himself to hurt her. He recalled the delicate face he had seen through the veil of palest pink silk. She had been so brutalized. He visualized the bruises empurpling her slender neck and breasts.

But she remained still, her breathing even, although strained. Even before their nest began to warm, he became aware of her body leaning limply against his. With one hand he encircled her shoulder while the other trailed delicately over her hip. Unlike his skin, hers had a smooth, satiny feel. His trembling fingers explored further, discovering the delectable curve from her waist to the top of her thigh.

Gently, reverently, he touched her cheek with his lips as he pulled her lower body against his. Her hair smelled of exotic flowers. A soft moan slid between his parted lips at the feel of warm smooth flesh against his manhood. Dear God! This was almost worth dying for! He had never imagined such delight. His muscle began to throb painfully as the slight movements of their breathing stimulated him unbearably. He must have her. He must.

Conversations with older boys, discussions overheard at the table after the ladies had left, his own observations of animals had given him a rudimentary knowledge of the act.

Tipping her onto her back, he found her knees in the dark and parted her legs with trembling hands. Her very lack of

63

tance sent a wave of shame sweeping over him, lessening desire. She was unconscious, and he was molesting her. Momentarily, he sank back onto his heels glancing hastily at the closed bed curtains.

He really had no choice. Brittany waited. A wave of anger made him tremble. Honor, like a bright flame in his mind, made him tremble. He bolted upright in bed, flinging the covers aside. Cool air struck his chest sobering him. He reached out a hand to throw the curtains aside and refuse this shameful task.

He clenched his fists and drew back. The duke would have him killed before he got to his room.

And what of the girl? Another would most surely take his place. That man, whoever he might be, might use her cruelly, might take his pleasure without thought for the delicacy of her body.

Her slim warm body drew Geoffrey's hand like a magnet. Like a man in a dream, he reached out to trail a hand along the inside of her thigh. His fingers found their way into the soft nest of curls at the joining of her body. His throbbing need, which had eased slightly, began again in earnest.

He had to have relief. He had never felt so male.

Hastily, he fumbled for the opening he knew to be there. It seemed unbelievably small. With his other hand he grasped himself, not surprised to find himself swollen and wet. Consciously, he measured his own size against hers. No wonder it hurt a woman. His tender heart felt deep sympathy for her plight. Perhaps Brittany was right; perhaps unconscious was best.

Positioning himself carefully, he slipped his hands under her hips, cupping her buttocks, and lifting her toward him.

As the sheath of muscle began to stretch to accommodate him, he found the virginal tissue so lauded by the men in their discussions at table. Again he paused, shuddering with unsatisfied lust. A tiny corner of his mind rebelled at the intrusion. She had fought the good fight. Now unconscious

64

and in the hands of her enemies, she had only this last frail barrier.

He must have leaned forward slightly, for she moaned as if in pain. She would wake before the task was done. With a quick intake of breath, he lunged forward.

She shrieked, that is, in her mind she shrieked. The actual sound was more like a dry rasp. Her shocked body would not obey the commands of her brain. Torn from her semiconscious state to agonized awareness, Joanna lay shocked, not recognizing what had happened to her in the smothering darkness.

Memories and nightmares flooded her mind; reality mixed indistinguishably with fantasy. Impenetrable smothering blackness was before her eyes, and her body was being split apart.

The torture chamber! Her last conscious act had been a violent one against the Duke of Brittany, her husband. He had condemned her to torture.

The pain eased for a minute as the instrument of her torturer was withdrawn from her body, then it slid back in again deeper than before. Terrified, she tried to scream again. But this time the sound was cut short as a hard-muscled form settled atop her. A hand cupped her shoulder, as her breasts were flattened beneath a warm chest. A man! It had to be. His lips touched her cheek. His breath panted in her ear. The other hand brushed through the tangled curls at her temple.

Again came the impaling movement. But the pain was bearable this time. He trailed his lips to the corner of her mouth, then captured it with his own. Whimpering soundlessly in fear, she wrenched her head to the side. Not to be denied, his lips trailed down her neck, bestowing a caress that was much like a benison on the place where her blood pounded hot and terrified.

The hard instrument within her drove deeper than ever; then, suddenly, she felt her tormentor's body stiffen. A guttural sound grated from his throat as if he had sought to remain silent but could not. When he collapsed on her, nearly crushing the breath from her body, his head fell onto the pillow. His harsh breathing sounded loud in her ear.

Immobile, pinned by the weight of his body, she waited fearfully for the next act. When he had rested a moment, would another take his place? Would he begin again? She tried to speak. Her throat was dry with fear; her lips, dry and cracked. Oddly, the lack of the capacity to speak drove her into a panic. She could not even beg for mercy.

Unbelievably, his hand moved from her shoulder to her throat, caressing her gently. Still she was terrified. The gentleness might be a trick. The hand could close and strangle her in an instant; it might break her neck if he felt her helpless straining. Frozen, she waited.

But the strong warm fingers caused no pain. Instead they massaged her rigid muscles gently. As they soothed her, she became aware of other parts of her body. The hard object within her softened and slid from her, followed by a flood of hot liquid.

Instantly, she stiffened again in panic. Suddenly, she knew. The thing that men did to women had been done to her. She was bleeding. The realization increased her fear. A few tears of helplessness trickled from the corners of her eyes, but they were soon shed. She was exhausted. Pain, fear, more pain, stark terror—all combined with excitement, the lateness of the hour, and the lack of food to drain her limbs. Suddenly, she no longer had the desire to struggle. So this was what was meant by submitting to one's husband. Now she knew the worst and had endured the worst.

Ineffectually, feebly, she pushed at the hard-muscled shoulder pressing down her breasts. Her strength was as nothing.

Somewhat to her surprise, her tormentor moved. He reared himself over her, supporting his weight on his arms, and then lowered his face again to hers. His lips touched her cheek, found the salt trails of her tears. He breathed a sigh. Then the tip of his tongue gently licked away the moisture.

Confused by this unaccustomed caress, she shivered. Her clenched fists gradually relaxed. Trembling, she lifted one small hand to touch the body that pressed her down. She found warm skin, slightly damp with perspiration, stretched over muscle and bones. Ribs. She was touching a man's naked ribs. Instantly, her hand pulled back.

The caresses on her face continued. Gentle lips replaced the soothing tongue. Suddenly, he shifted his weight, rolling from her body, leaving only his leg thrown across her, the inner side of his thigh resting on the part which he had so lately abused.

As he drew the covers securely around her, she could picture him lying beside her in the darkness, his upper body supported by the arm which pressed against her side. Still he continued to kiss her. Her lips, her cheeks, her chin, the tip of her nose, her forehead, all received his silent apology. Finally, he bestowed a kiss on each of her eyelids in turn.

She tried again to speak, this time managing a low hoarse croak.

"Shh-shh," he hissed warningly and laid a finger across her lips.

She obeyed him instantly, nodding her head in the darkness. Too exhausted after the ordeal to resist, she lay perfectly still beside him, not daring to breathe.

And then he began to caress her with his hand.

Geoffrey traced her smooth shoulder with his fingers, finding the division where the underarm joined her body at the swell of her breast. Sliding his fingers into the warm crevice, he allowed his palm to cover the sensitive point. She would like that, he thought as he rotated it evenly.

Her breathing quickened slightly as the tip hardened. He would take it between his thumb and finger the next time he touched it, but to do so now might frighten her. And she had been frightened enough.

He smiled briefly. What optimism! Probably he would never touch her again. He might well be dead tomorrow. He did not believe the duke's promise.

That sobering thought stilled his hand for only a moment. Then he continued its path. If this were his last night on earth, what better way to spend it. His fingers slid down from her breast and into the exciting curve of her waist. She was perfectly formed. He explored her navel, again eliciting quickened breathing accompanied this time by a fluttering of stomach muscles.

Shifting his thigh lower, he touched the curls at the bottom of her belly. They were still moist and slightly stiff. Her hands grasped his arm as her thighs tensed beneath his leg.

Reluctantly, he drew back. He had thought to soothe the abused edges of her body, but he recognized the fear that his painful entry through her virgin tissue had generated. She had been hurt too much that night. Instead, he placed his hand firmly at her waist and drew her warmly against him. Again he kissed her cheek before laying his own head on the pillow beside hers. Deliberately, he relaxed his body, seeking to draw deep even breaths.

He could feel her body lying tense beside his for several minutes. Finally, reassured as he had intended, her limbs relaxed. She was asleep and the time had come when he must face the duke.

His own fears had kept him awake. Now the moment of reckoning made him sick. A prey of conflicting emotions, almost weeping now that he had to part the curtains, he drew a deep breath. Even as he gently separated himself from her side, he heard a faint noise from the room beyond.

"Hsst!" Jean de Montfort had returned and was growing impatient.

With no hope for the morrow, Geoffrey slipped from beneath the covers. For a moment he paused, kneeling above the figure on the bed. With gentle hands he tucked the blankets around her body to protect it from the night's chill. He longed to bestow one more tiny kiss on her face but feared to awaken her. If she did not know that he was not Brittany, she just might survive.

Sighing, he slipped, naked, from between the curtains and straightened in the chill room.

A tiny fire flickered on the hearth. From it, the duke extracted a slender brand to light a candle. Holding it aloft, he stared at Geoffrey's body. Following his stare, Geoffrey flinched, then paled at the dark smears on his thighs.

The duke's face was impassive. After one glance he turned slightly aside to set the candle on the table and lower himself tiredly into a chair.

Thankfully Geoffrey reached for his hose which lay in a heap on the floor. Hastily, he drew them on and pinned up the codpiece. His linen shirt and tunic followed.

When he was decently covered, the duke handed him a goblet of Spanish sherry. "To my good and faithful servant," he mocked softly.

Geoffrey would have liked to decline to drink with the man, but his need was too great. His mouth was dry as a desert, and his fear of his impending fate made his whole body tremble. Thankfully, he accepted what was thrust into his hands and took a huge gulp. Its rare flavor was lost on him but not its restoring strength. As its warmth entered his blood, he closed his eyes in relief.

"Tell me exactly what happened." The duke refilled the goblet and motioned the younger man toward the chair beside the fire.

Geoffrey's pale eyes flashed upward in angry defiance. This question was the last straw. Ignoring the chair, he strode toward the door.

"Oh, spare me," Brittany snarled, waving his hand tiredly. The night had been long, cold, and exhausting for him. He was sick with disappointment at his failure to consummate his marriage. The knowledge that he might never impregnate his bride weighed heavily on his proud spirit.

"My lord?" The valet paused at the door.

"I care not for a recital of your adolescent gropings. But if I am going to carry this deception off to my credit and your safety, I must know what *I* did to the lady, so that my story will corroborate hers."

For the first time Geoffrey felt a faint stirring of hope for his life. Never moving from the door, he nevertheless turned back to face the duke. "The marriage was consummated as you commanded." He replied in the formal voice of one delivering a message. "Beyond that I cannot tell you."

"And she was not suspicious?" Brittany sighed wearily. "You did leave her asleep, I assume."

"Yes, my lord. Exhausted." Geoffrey's own head felt light and filled with feathers. Perhaps he should not have imbibed, but in truth, he realized that he wanted to get very, very drunk.

"Good. Good." Brittany nodded with satisfaction. "You took her without a struggle."

"I did all that may become a man."

"Very like. Very like." The duke accepted the proud tone without demur. "And she . . . ?"

"She did as she should." In truth, Geoffrey had no idea what Joanna should or should not have done. But his sense of dignity rebelled at the idea of discussing this very private act more. Tears of weariness and frustration were very close to the surface as he regarded this horrible old man who seemed to think it was his due to know what had occurred. Lest he betray himself, Geoffrey dropped his eyes.

The duke stared at the bent head. Rumpled waves of fair hair fell forward over the young man's forehead, concealing his expression. He sensed that his vassal would be pushed no farther. Only one more question would suffice.

"And did I speak to her?"

"No, my lord. You only hissed at her to keep her quiet." The duke was silent a moment, staring intently at his servant's stiff figure. In the glow of the single candle, the youth's pale hair gleamed like a cap of silver. "Why then, I thank you," he said at last, his voice only slightly tinged with mockery. "No man could have a better vassal than you."

Geoffrey raised his head, lines of strain deeply etched on either side of his straight mouth. Both he and the duke knew he was no vassal. He was a servant of the lowliest sort, little better than a slave. He was neither fish nor fowl, isolated from the others by his nationality, his birth, his language, and his ambivalent position in the duke's retinue.

The duke sighed regretfully. "Have you told me the truth?"

"Yes, sire," Geoffrey said simply.

"Then go to your bedchamber. I will take my place beside my bride." The duke grimaced as he rose on his arthritic limbs. "Help me," he commanded in the tone he always used.

Out of habit, Geoffrey sprang to his feet and offered his strong young shoulder. As one man they moved slowly toward the bed. "Wash the witness off your body," the duke instructed him, *sotto voce*. "Change into fresh garments and come to wake me early, accompanied by several lords and ladies to break the fast. Be sure that Don Rodrigo and Doña Isabella are among them. That Spanish duenna will have the sheets paraded before the others almost before I can get out of them. Fools about that thing!" He was rambling tiredly, and he knew it. "God! 'Tis terrible to be old, but worse to be old and crippled."

"Yes, my lord."

He turned to face Geoffrey; both hands went to the young man's shoulders. "I suffered the agonies of the damned to get this Brittany," he whispered. "Now the injuries I received prevent me from keeping it."

Geoffrey thought his master had never looked older, nor more feeble. In a sort of wonderment he realized that the duke spoke by way of explanation for the shameful act he had asked the young man to perform. "You should try to get

71

some rest, my lord."

"Thank you, Geoffrey. Thank you, my good and loyal vassal. Yes." He parted the curtains of the bed and slumped onto the mattress with a groan. "Yes. I shall sleep tonight beside my bride . . . my bride," he whispered.

Geoffrey raised the old man's naked feet and legs and swung them onto the bed, then drew the curtain closed. Returning to the table, he reached to snuff out the candle. His eye caught the half-filled decanter of sherry. "Why not?" he murmured. Defiantly, he hooked it in his fist as he blew the candle out.

When the laughing, chattering guests entered the ducal bedchamber at midmorning, both occupants of the bed stirred painfully to wakefulness. Joanna groaned, suddenly aware that pain wracked every muscle in her body. One hand flew to cover her naked breasts, the other dropped protectively to screen her mount from eyes that would subject it to lascivious interest.

Beside her the duke raised himself with a moan, but he managed to throw an arm and leg across her as the curtains were parted by Doña Isabella.

"Your Grace." The lady swept a low curtsey.

"Why it is morning, Joanna," the duke announced for all to hear.

"'Tis time to break the fast." One of the duke's friends flung aside the curtains at the foot of the bed and stared avidly at the two who lay within, limbs entwined. The nobleman's hand snaked out and dragged the covers from their bodies.

Joanna lay on her back, her limbs still relaxed as they had been in sleep. The stains of her ravaged maidenhead showed clearly on her thighs and on the sheets beneath her.

Several ladies and gentlemen broke into light applause, while the man who had torn away the covers cheered lustily.

"Long live Montfort!"

Geoffrey stepped forward, clad in a fresh tunic of dark burgundy wool and black hose. Bowing low, he rose to assist the duke to rise, flinging a robe over his body.

Servants entered, efficiently cleared away the remains of last night's buffet, and replaced them with fresh steaming dishes. More champagne was poured into fresh goblets.

"Long live Montfort!" The guests all raised their voices.

"My friends." He smiled benignly, acknowledging their congratulations. Turning to Bustamonte, the duke raised his goblet. "Last night I was in Navarre," he laughed.

Everyone responded merrily to the small pun.

"I see the climate agreed with you," the don replied with a smile.

"Indeed, a most fair and welcoming country." Brittany drank, inviting all the guests to follow suit.

Geoffrey retired stiffly to stand by the door. With a painful ache in his middle, he watched the duchess' ladies help her from the bed and into the steaming bath the servants had brought for her. He watched her stumble and clutch at old Doña Catalina's arm as her feet touched the cold floor. As she sank into the warm water, he saw her grimace as it rose around her loins.

Suddenly, he realized he was sweating; his fists were clenched; his teeth, locked. Her pain was his. God knew her body was his. Desperately, he turned his eyes toward the ceiling.

As the duke had predicted, Doña Isabella swept the sheet from the bed as if it were a banner of victory. "See!" she exclaimed proudly. With a look of almost religious fervor, she draped it across her arms and carried it among the guests for all to inspect.

Geoffrey swallowed convulsively. He had never been sickened by the sight of blood. Now he felt his own blood draining from his face. Sternly, he drew himself up and sank his teeth into his lower lip. The pain staved off the dizziness.

73

He watched impassively as the guests clapped the duke on the shoulders and drank and ate. The noise grew.

Across the room, old Doña Catalina bent over Joanna and rubbed the sponge gently between her legs. The girl sat as one stunned, but high color stained her cheeks. Humiliation and resentment combined to created a writhing seething inferno within her body.

No one cared about her at all, not one of them. She was a thing of no value . . . worthless as a person. While Geoffrey watched, her fists clenched on the edges of the tub.

Then Doña Isabella returned with the sheet, throwing it back across the foot of the bed so that all might see it again should they care to. "Rise, Your Grace," she instructed Joanna. "María Dolores. The towels." The woman came forward with a length of linen as Doña Isabella took Joanna's hands and tugged the reluctant girl to her feet.

At the sound of the water splashing, Brittany turned to regard the pale nude body with possessive satisfaction. "She has served me well, Don Rodrigo," he remarked expansively. "Be sure to convey my pleasure to your sovereign."

"I shall, Your Grace." Don Rodrigo bowed low.

Doña Isabella nodded pleasantly, ignoring the chalk white face of her charge as she slid her arms into a high-necked robe of dark green silk.

Chapter 4

In agony Joanna awaited the second night of her marriage, but the horror of her wedding night was not repeated. Indeed, her husband did not come to her. The duke merely gave his bride a chaste kiss on the forehead and limped away on the arm of the ubiquitous Geoffrey.

The third day and the fourth nights he did the same. She could not eat her meals; the food stuck in her throat. She could not sleep at night but spent the hours between dusk and dawn pacing the floor, alarmed at every sound.

When Don Rodrigo prepared to return to Navarre, he presented himself before the duchess in the solar of the château. "Your Grace." The velvet liripipe of his hat swept the floor at his elegant gesture.

Dark circles rimmed her ebony eyes. The healthy magnolia bloom of her skin had been replaced by a translucent pallor. She merely nodded at his gallantry, fixing her eyes on the golden medallion suspended on a thick chain about his neck. She cared naught what lies Don Rodrigo might spin as he bade her farewell. She had planned to order him to take Doña Isabella with him on his return to Navarre, but now she did not believe that he cared about her well-being, much less that he would help her. He had been among the other men who had filed out laughing and joking, leaving her to be brutalized and raped.

"I sail for Navarre on the morrow."

When she did not answer, he stirred uncomfortably. "Your Grace, have you any message for your father or brothers?" He spoke gently, referring to them as her family rather than as the king and the princes.

Her eyes flickered to his face. For a minute he did not think she would answer him. Then she let a small ironic smile play about her pale lips. "You may tell my father that my marriage is everything he hoped it would be. He will fully appreciate the message."

Don Rodrigo nodded slowly. He was not by nature a cruel man, merely an envoy who did the bidding of Charles of Navarre. He hoped he was mistaken in his assessment of the duchess' condition. "And may I tell him you are . . . happy?" He could have bitten his tongue as soon as the words were spoken.

Her pallor increased although he would not have believed that was possible. She sat like a plaster statue. "Tell him what you will." Her eyes returned to the spot on the wall.

He withdrew in some confusion, to be detained in the outer chamber by Doña Isabella. "You must find some means to enliven her," he ordered sternly. "Otherwise, your position here will not last six months."

But Doña Isabella shook her head, her voice tinged with satisfaction. "She will recover. She is but cowed. He used her badly on their wedding night, but it is just as well that he begins as he means to go on. It is also well that she is young and strong. Once she conceives, he will leave her alone, and her interest in the baby will revive her."

"But she is lifeless," Don Rodrigo objected. "I have not seen her eat a bite of food since the wedding."

Doña Isabella lifted her shoulders in a slight shrug. "She is very proud, being the daughter of a powerful monarch. The duke has taught her humility."

The man stared at the woman, aghast at finding her so

devoid of any sign of human compassion. He was not surprised to hear, even obliquely, of the violence of the duke. Men had total control over the bodies of their wives, and a knight trained from boyhood to be hard frequently forgot his own strength. Nevertheless, he was surprised to find that a woman chosen to be the companion of a young and tender princess had no feeling for her charge. If the Duchess Joanna had requested it of him, he would have forced the duenna to return with him to Navarre. Since she had not, he shook his head. "Serve her faithfully," he admonished.

"I am a loyal subject of Navarre," she replied cryptically, showing him the door to the apartments.

That night the duke appeared, accompanied by the ever-present Geoffrey, to take supper in the duchess' apartments. A table was set for two. Doña Isabella was dismissed as were the two young bretonnes, the attendants Lady Lisette and Lady Thérèse. Servants set covered dishes on the table across the room from the great bed and departed.

"Come, my lady." The duke held out his hand to her.

Clenching her jaw to still the chattering of her teeth, Joanna laid the tips of her fingers across the edge of his hand, wondering how she could endure the ordeal awaiting her. At that very moment a sudden movement could bring a twinge of pain between her legs. Smiling suavely, the duke led her to the table. When she was seated, Geoffrey helped the duke to a seat opposite her.

His body slouching to the right as always, Brittany regarded her white face with an annoyed frown. "Busta-monte conveyed some very unpleasant news to me before he departed," he began without preamble.

Her hands doubled into fists within the folds of her skirt. Frantically, she recalled her conversation with Don Rodrigo. Nothing she had said could have aroused his displeasure. She would deny everything else. A slight flush rose to her cheeks as she prepared to defend herself.

"He told me you have eaten nothing since our wedding." Brittany eyed her critically. "You do seem somewhat gaunt. Geoffrey, do you notice a difference?"

Joanna's eyes flew to the servant's impassive face. His constant presence was becoming annoying. Resentful that he should even be consulted, she glared at him, daring him to criticize her.

To Geoffrey, the change from the exquisite vital girl she had been on her arrival to the haunted fragile creature she had become was obvious. He longed to express his concern, yet he hesitated. Which answer would be in her best interest? He could not bear to cause her more pain. He tilted his head to one side as though studying her. "Perhaps a trifle," he replied noncommittally.

Fearfully, Joanna returned her gaze to her husband. Her hand rose to her throat. Full well she knew the power her husband had over her. His will was every bit as strong as her father's. She was merely a vessel to hold his heir until it should be born. She should expect no consideration. With the future stretching bleak and loveless before her, she had lost her appetite. Yet she dared not tell her husband of her feelings. A man who had taken advantage of her unconscious state on her wedding night would not hesitate to use her cruelly; perhaps he would even beat her if he were displeased.

She made an effort to smile as if in gratitude for his concern. Then she dropped her eyes to her lap. "I am perhaps a little homesick, my lord."

"What? Speak up?" Brittany barked. "What did she say, Geoffrey?"

Geoffrey bent to his master. "She pleads homesickness, Your Grace."

"Oh." Brittany appeared to study this idea while he laughed to himself. He had not forgotten his anger in the nuptial bed. To his way of thinking his punishment for her resistance had been lenient. He could have had her hauled out of bed and beaten till the blood ran. On the other hand, Jean was not by nature a vicious man. Like all the powerful princes of Europe, he merely punished swiftly and mercilessly those who offended him. One pale eyebrow rose quizically.

"Pour us some wine, Geoffrey."

The room was silent except for the faint splash of the dark red liquid into the goblets.

"Madam, I would see you drink with me."

Steeling herself, Joanna raised the vessel to her lips and took the tiniest of sips. The wine was much stronger than that to which she was accustomed and it had a distinctly resinous taste. Lowering the goblet, she swallowed cautiously. The taste made her ill, but sensing he was testing her, she managed a wan smile.

The duke laughed. "Geoffrey, the duchess has a lovely smile, does she not? Joanna, we would see it more often. Indeed, we would see it whenever we come near, or we shall know the reason why. Furthermore, any Navarrese ambassador or messenger will see it in a face blooming with healthy color." The command was implicit in his voice.

"My lord." Joanna bowed her head. "I am happy to do as you request."

"Geoffrey!" Brittany waved his hand languidly. "The duchess has chosen an unfortunate gown. Black is most unsuitable for a newly wedded woman. Undoubtedly 'twas that which caused Rodrigo's concern. Furthermore, the neck is entirely too high." He stared meaningfully at the silver-piped scallops that brushed her chin and jaw. "Unfasten that gown."

With a gasp of horror, Joanna's hand flew to her throat. "My lord . . ."

"You are my wife," he reminded her. "You must prove your submission. Geoffrey," he repeated sternly.

His face sympathetic, the youth moved to the back of

Joanna's chair.

"No, please."

With fingers that trembled, Geoffrey's hands touched her beneath the fall of heavy black hair that had been enclosed in a snood of silver mesh at Doña Isabella's smug direction.

She winced away, her skin prickling. "Damned lackey," she whispered out of the side of her mouth.

He smiled ironically. At least her spirit was not quite broken. "Your Grace, permit me."

Suddenly her shoulders slumped. "Do as you were commanded," she hissed.

In perfect silence he undid the buttons that began at her hairline. Where his fingers inadvertently touched her, her skin seemed to burn. She experienced an involuntary tightening of the muscles of her thighs and belly. In another instant she felt she would scream. One button, then two, then half a dozen. When he was halfway down her back, she threw a furious glance across the table. "Is it your wish that he undress me, Your Grace?"

Brittany grinned. "Enough, Geoffrey. Now push the gown forward and away from her neck. A little farther, Geoffrey. Let the tops of those creamy breasts show. Ah, yes."

Humiliated to tears, her face and throat white as alabaster, Joanna endured the amused stare of her husband. "Your Grace, I am not a courtesan."

"But I am your lord and master," he replied. "You will grant me total dominion over your body?"

She drew in a deep shuddering breath.

"Answer me."

"Yes, my lord." Her voice was so low, he could only guess at her answer. A treacherous tear spilled from one of Joanna's shimmering eyes.

He smiled expansively. "Then you will join me at meals henceforth and present a beautiful and smiling face."

Joanna stared straight ahead, tears on her cheeks which had reddened with embarrassment. "I shall do as you command, my lord."

"'I shall do as you command, my lord,'" he mocked her. His voice rose in a terrifying roar that caused her to jump. "But it shall not seem a command, my lady. You shall present to the world and to me an amiable and a docile nature so that Don Rodrigo or anyone who comes or goes to Navarre will carry only the most glowing accounts of your happiness."

Frozen in a tableau the three remained silent until suddenly Jean relaxed again. Like a parent who tells his child to smile after a punishment, he laughed, amused at the idea of fooling the world.

For Joanna, although tears continued to slide silently down her face to drop like crystals into the hollows of her shoulders, had managed a wan smile at his command.

He raised his goblet in a toast. "To our happiness, my dear. Geoffrey, is your mistress' cup filled? See that she drinks deep. Drink and be merry is the adjuration of the ancients, Joanna."

His hand shaking slightly, Geoffrey took the goblet from her slack fingers and refilled it. "I pray you pardon me, my lady," he murmured.

Panic almost overpowered her. Would he never stop? He would drown her. She had never drunk so much strong wine at a time. The smell filled her nostrils and her head began to swim.

At last he stopped pouring. Under her husband's merciless scrutiny she lifted the cup to her lips and drank deeply, pretending appreciation although the wine's resinous quality rasped against the soft tissues of the inside of her mouth.

The duke watched her, a satisfied smile twisting his face, until she set down an empty vessel. "Good." He chuckled. "Now, Geoffrey, you may serve me."

Throughout the meal the duke ate in high good humor. Soup, fish, meat, vegetable, sweets, and a cheese were served him, and ever the wine. With each sip the duke took, he gestured to the servant to serve the duchess.

In the end Joanna found her head spinning dizzily. Her brain was numb but, ever at his behest, she smiled. Silently she sat, nodding slightly, her modesty overcome. Across the table the duke stared his fill at the tops of her pale breasts and found himself pleasurably titillated by her dishabille.

Hovering about the table, refilling her goblet, and serving the plates, Geoffrey struggled for self-control. His view was much more revealing than the duke's and he found himself sweating.

At last the duke pronounced himself finished. He pushed back his chair and hobbled to her side. "Do you think you will ever resist me again, Joanna?" he asked equably.

She did not look at him. Her ebony eyes were slightly glazed.

Laughing, he patted her bare shoulder, allowing his fingers to slide far down over her fair white skin. "Send for her women. They will undress her and put her to bed. I shall visit her tonight. She will not resist." He shook her gently by her bare shoulder. "Do you hear me, Joanna? I shall visit you tonight. You will do your duty."

Still she did not look at him.

"Answer me!"

"Yes, my lord."

"'Tis well." He laughed as he transferred his grip to the shoulder of his servant whose face was almost as white as his lady's. "Help me to my chambers."

Doña Isabella found her as they had left her. With the aid of Lady Lisette and Lady Thérèse, who sighed and simpered romantically over her, Joanna was undressed and slipped into the great bed to await her lord. Again the curtains were drawn and the room darkened.

Joanna's head spun. She could not keep her eyes open. Although her fear was extreme, the deadening influence of so much wine with so little food left her almost paralyzed. At least there will be little pain, she thought.

Experimentally, she raised a wavering finger to touch her lips. Numb! The only response was a strange tingling feeling. She smiled slightly at her secret. She would not be able to feel much of what was done to her. The curtains were drawn so no light entered. She could not see anything. That was not such a bad thing after all. No sight of her husband's ugly knotted hands and twisted frame. No pain when he thrust into her and she did her duty.

She felt faintly nauseated. "Did her duty." She wanted to rage and scream. The lowliest peasant woman in the filthiest hovel was no worse off than the Duchess of Brittany.

But she would not weep again. She had wept over those things before. She would never weep over them again, she vowed.

She thought she heard the chamber door open and close. Did she hear the shuffling of the duke's footsteps accompanied by the lighter, catlike tread of Geoffrey? Her mind was whirling. She could not think. Better to close her eyes in the velvety blackness.

Then she felt the bed give as he climbed in. His hands touched her, caressed her cheek, her shoulder. At least he was not hurting her—not yet. She kept her eyes firmly closed. Someone, an old groom, had told her to close her eyes when he had pulled a splinter from her hand. What he could not see, a man felt less, he had said.

Warm breath brushed her cheek. A tender kiss. Hands drew her limp body against hard muscles. Now a hand commenced to stroke and cup her breast.

In her wine-dark state she stirred involuntarily as her skin began to tingle. Her movement brought her more firmly against the lower part of the male body with its upthrusting muscle. Fearfully, she moaned, but her partner kissed her lips gently in a manner that was oddly reassuring.

Perhaps he had punished her as much as he wished to?

83

Perhaps he would not want to hurt her any more? Hesitantly, she returned his kiss, her untrained lips moving softly.

She felt him tremble. His body actually trembled. Disbelieving, she kissed him again, and the reaction was the stronger. One of his hands moved to her breast and titillated the peak into a hard point. Unconsciously, she arched her body, trying to increase the delightful sensation.

And then his mouth was on her nipple. Suddenly shy, she gasped and pushed against his shoulders with her hands, but he was kissing the sensitive nub of flesh so pleasantly, taking it between his lips and drawing on it. An entirely different kind of moan broke from her.

Turning her over onto her back, he began to kiss the other breast, his hand touching her hipbone. While she waited breathlessly, his fingers tiptoed down the edge of her hipbone to the fullness of her thigh.

Stiffening against the pain she was sure would come next, she squeezed her thighs together, but his fingers did not seek to part them. Rather they teased and played along the crease, before they fell to twisting and ruffling the tight soft curls at the base of her belly.

The sensations were electric. The tingling sensation increased until she could not lie still beneath his ministrations. She drew up one knee and pressed upward, vaguely intending to throw off his hand; but, of course, the tantalizing fingers followed her movements with ease.

"Umm-m-m . . . my lord," she whispered, straightening out one leg at the same time she drew up the other.

He did not answer, but slid his leg in between hers, pressing his thigh up firmly against the opening of her body.

She should be afraid. It was coming. He was going to stick that huge thing she had thought to be an instrument of torture in between her legs again. Her brain whirled, befogged at first by the wine and then by physical sensations that confused her.

As if he sensed her confusion, he continued to kiss and caress her. Now his teeth were nipping at the tips of her breasts, the sweet pain somewhat pleasurable as it caused her to rub and press herself against his thigh.

His thigh rubbed between her legs, titillating her mount. Like an itch that once scratched requires more scratching, each rasp of his flesh against hers required another and then another.

She did not realize she was moaning. She did not know that the hands on his shoulders, which had first sought to push him away, now clutched him to her. At last he drew back for breath. By that time her breasts were aching. She clasped her hands in his hair and pulled him back against her.

She needed something. Her body was aching, almost as if it itched inside. But it was more than an itch. It was a burning . . . a pain. The pain was within herself, not outside. His touch did not cause it, but he could end it. She was sure of that.

"Please," she sighed. "Please."

Again his finger fell on her lips.

"But . . ." Her objection ended in a sob. She must not object, but oh, her need was great.

Again the admonishing finger stopped her words. He withdrew from her entirely. His hands pressed outward against the inside of her thighs. This time she did not resist. Trembling with excitement and a little fear, she felt his hardness at her welcoming opening. So moist and hot was she that he was halfway in before she realized. Then her muscles responded, closing round him and ushering him into her.

He gasped, a short expulsion of agonized sound. When he would have drawn back, she wrapped her legs around his waist and held him. With an agonized groan he clasped her waist, then slipped his hands up to squeeze her breasts.

She thought she would die from the sensation. Her softest

parts both within and without were throbbing with the agonizing pleasure his body created. Helplessly, she writhed, squeezing his waist with her thighs and arching her chest under his hands.

Like a wild thing never before caressed, she could not get enough of the sensation once she accepted it. Mindless, her brain afire, her breath coming swift and hot, she twisted as he rolled the aroused points of her nipples between his fingers and held himself hard and deep inside her.

Too soon the pleasure mounted to an unbearable peak. Wildly, she strove, bucking her body upward until only her shoulders supported her on the sheet. All the fear and frustration, all the anger and resentment dammed inside her for her whole life exploded within her.

With a wild keening cry, she stiffened. The muscles sheathing him contracted fiercely, then relaxed as tremor after tremor gave her body release. Her eyes flew wide open, but the darkness was impenetrable. At the same moment her overcharged senses, unable to absorb more, refused to respond at all. Then she slipped back onto the bed unconscious.

Happily, Geoffrey felt her relax. His own pleasure had peaked with hers, but she had been unaware of it. Now he slid off her, stretching out beside her, gathering her limp perspiring body against his own, and pulling the covers around them.

With reverent lips he kissed her hot face, brushing the fine hair back from her temples.

His subtle questions among older knights had not gone for naught. The lady had been aroused as they had said she would be, but nothing in their bragging reminiscences had prepared him for her response. The crude admonition of the duke's, to ride her well, had been amazingly correct. Once aroused, she had been like a wild animal.

Regretfully, he suspected that his own lovemaking had not been so much responsible as the fear and hatred she harbored within her. Each time he had served the wine tonight, her eyes had blazed eloquently, damning him and the duke to the fires of hell.

As well they should be.... His whole soul revolted against the use the duke had put him to, yet his whole body had eagerly responded to the duke's command this evening. The desire for her was a taste he had acquired with the first sip. What would become of him when he could no longer drink from her sweet well?

With a little sigh, she turned her face into his shoulder and drew her hands up under her chin like a child. What a bliss it would be to lie here with her in his arms all the night—a dream he could not hope to have. He tortured himself by picturing them waking together in the big bed, by thinking of the joy they would find in each other's bodies, both young, both strong and eager.

But he must not allow the duke to grow impatient. How much longer would His Grace be satisfied to wait while his servant enjoyed the pleasures of the duchess' body?

Bestowing a lingering gentle kiss on Joanna's smooth forehead, he slipped away from her warm side into the chill room.

Tonight the duke had dozed off in his chair, thus allowing Geoffrey time to dress. Once aroused, the older man looked blearily around him. He did not even speak but merely nodded as he allowed the valet to help him to his feet. Wearily, Montfort realized that the knowledge of what had gone on in the room should have aroused him. He should feel his own body tighten, but nothing happened. Bitterly, he faced the fact that his excesses in food and drink had combined with the general deterioration of his body to render him impotent.

Looking into his master's face in that moment, Geoffrey felt the hair rise on the back of his neck. Hatred and jealousy burned fiercely in Montfort's sunken eyes, and they spelled danger and death for his servant. Numbly, Geoffrey guided the older man to the door. Had the executioner's axe struck off his head at that moment, he would have died unsurprised.

When the pair finally gained the duke's apartments and Montfort was abed, the old man spoke. "Did it go well tonight?"

Geoffrey stiffened. To be forced to recite even one word of that earth-shaking experience would make him vomit. Still as a stone he stood, his mouth set in a grim line. He was, after all, a man.

"Damned idiot!" the duke snarled.

"Yes, Your Grace."

"Must I take you to the dungeon and have the information beaten out of you?"

Geoffrey's impassive expression never wavered, though his fair skin paled. As if the duke had not spoken, the valet turned to his own pallet.

Propped on pillows, Brittany stared at the youth who stretched himself on the pallet he now occupied as a matter of course. There was no hint of insolence in his manner, merely an exhausted resignation.

Of course, Brittany realized he would not take his servant to the dungeon, unless he did so to have his tongue torn out. But what good would that do?

As the young man drew the covers up to his chest and dropped an arm across his eyes, the duke shrugged. What did he care? Such things were never discussed between men and women anyway. At last he cleared his throat. "We must repeat this every night for a week or ten days." Brittany might have been discussing the most mundane of duties. "I trust you are willing and able. At the end of that time we will wait and see. If she has her monthly flux, then we must do it over. If not, then you need not trouble yourself again. I am sure you will be glad of that." This last remark dripped with sarcasm.

The candles were burning low. Brittany sank down beneath the covers and his arthritic hands drew them up to his chin. Closing his eyes, he tried to compose his mind for sleep. The girl and boy were two healthy young animals. He smiled sardonically. No doubt a week or ten days would suffice.

On the pallet across the room, Geoffrey rolled his head toward the bed. In the light given off by the guttering candles, he could see the duke's profile through a glaze of tears.

His emotions were tearing him apart. Uppermost in his mind was fear of torture and death. He was not a fool. The deeds he did on command were treasonous offenses. The duke would abandon him on a whim.

Standing behind Brittany's chair the day before, he had witnessed the torture of the Sire de la Roche-Bernard in the cellars of the château. The man had screamed and screamed as heavy leather boots had been placed on each foot and then boiling water had been poured into them. His feet had finally cooked, skin and flesh floating away from the bones and overflowing onto the floor.

Meanwhile the man had confessed his treason, naming associates. Names had flooded from his mouth, names of relatives, names of friends, names of enemies, names of people long dead. At last the duke had pronounced himself satisfied and the torturer had garroted the suffering man.

In some measure Joanna had been responsible for that man's death. Doubtless, she had participated in the plot to bring him into the duke's trap. With the heedlessness the very powerful showed to those who served them, she would bring the same fate on his head.

He bit his knuckle until the blood came. Christ! He was doomed, trapped between them. His body was theirs to use as it pleased them.

Her thighs had wrapped around him, holding him tightly

89

while she took her pleasure. She would do it again. If she knew his identity, she would have him killed immediately. But, of course, the duke would probably have him killed at the end of the month.

The candle guttered out, leaving the room in haunted darkness while Geoffrey tossed wretchedly on his pallet.

Chapter 5

The following day Joanna ventured from her apartments.
The small formal gardens of the château were her goal.
Accompanied by her three ladies, she made her way
determinedly through a maze of corridors and down several
flights of steps onto the middle terrace.

The day was fair, a balm to her wounded spirit. Between
carefully trimmed parterres of boxwood, she followed the
path of crushed red stone to a central fountain. There in the
pleasant shade of clipped yew trees, she sank down on a
small white marble bench and drew in a deep breath of warm
summer air.

Doña Isabella pressed her lips into a tight disapproving
line. "Your Grace should not be sitting on the cold marble. I
suggest you continue your walk and return to the solar. It
would not do to take a chill from the vapors rising off the
river."

Lady Lisette laughed nervously as she sat on another
small bench placed at a right angle to the stone fountain
from which the waters of the Vilaine trickled cheerfully. "I
hardly think vapors are rising at this time of day, madam,"
she ventured. "The air is so sweet and warm."

Doña Isabella flashed the younger woman a look of pure
malice. "The duchess has not yet recovered from her

journey," she snapped. "She must take especial care."

"I am taking care, Doña Isabella," Joanna insisted firmly. Although speaking still caused her pain, she nevertheless intervened in defense of the young woman who sought only to please her. "Please seat yourself and let us enjoy the garden. Thérèse, will you play for us?"

Obediently, the quiet one of the group swung her hurdy-gurdy from under her arm and began to turn its handle slowly. At the same time her skillful fingers held down the strings strung to the handle. A soft rondo tinkled and plunked in accompaniment to the splash of the fountain.

Joanna sat with head bowed over her hands. Her face was largely concealed beneath the edges of the veil that swung between the horns of her headdress. In this peaceful setting the music induced in her a wave of self-pity. She had pictured for herself the life of a beloved lady in a romance, that of a woman who lived happily ever after when her lover was revealed to be a prince or duke. Here she was in a warm summer garden amidst green hedges and bright fragrant blossoms, her ladies gathered around her to entertain her with sweet music and pleasant talk, but the picture was distorted.

While the outward appearance suited her romantic ideal, the actuality was horrifying in the extreme. Just so did her rich and elegant clothes conceal the terrible bruises on her body. She was the picture of a beautiful lady in a romance, but her duke, instead of being handsome and gentle, was old and cruel. Furthermore, she doubted strongly that anyone would come to rescue her.

Long years of discipline as well as long years of hiding her feelings would stand her in good stead, she reasoned. She would keep her face immobile, her eyes blank, and trust no one.

Lady Thérèse's hurdy-gurdy stopped abruptly.

Joanna raised her head to see Geoffrey striding down the red stone path toward them. Instantly, she stiffened as a wave of resentment and dislike rose in her throat. This lackey, this servant, this nameless creature had witnessed— had been party to—her humiliation. Now he dared to approach her alone.

"Your Grace." He swept his hat from his head in a graceful bow.

She acknowledged his courtesy with an icy nod.

"The duke offers you compliments of the day. He hopes you find the gardens to your liking."

She gazed round her as if coldly appraising the scene. "Very pleasant."

He studied her impassive face. "My lord will be pleased. He bade me come to you and guide you through them. Since he can walk only with difficulty himself, he sends me in his stead."

"He puts himself to too much trouble for me, sirrah." Her tone was cool, but he noticed she hid her hands in the folds of her skirt.

Geoffrey bowed before her, offering her his arm. "It is his wish, my lady." His own feelings were mixed. She was his first woman. He knew her body in the dark, but her mind and heart were strangers to him.

Her hands moved beneath the folds of her skirt, unclenching and rearranging her fingers into a smooth languid pattern. Without further comment, she placed the very tips of her fingers on the gray wool sleeve crooked toward her. With a nod to her ladies, she rose to walk beside him.

Lady Lisette and Lady Thérèse strolled along several yards behind the couple. Only Doña Isabella had the temerity to follow close enough to overhear their words.

"These gardens are laid out much like English gardens," Geoffrey began as they passed under an arch of carefully clipped yew.

"Indeed?" Joanna replied sarcastically. "How do you know of English gardens?"

"I am an Englishman," he told her.

She looked at him directly for the first time since their walk. "An Englishman? How does it happen that you are attendant in a French court? An exile?" She hazarded a guess.

"The duke needed a servant while he was in England several years ago. He took me out of an abbey where I had been since birth. I have served him faithfully ever since."

"Then your name is? . . ."

"Geoffrey." He shrugged.

"No surname?" she inquired cruelly, knowing the answer before he spoke.

"No, Your Grace."

She walked on between the perfect parterres. Ahead beyond another arch a fountain spilled clear water into its stone basin. The day was summer still, only an occasional breath of air stirring. His quiet acceptance of her condemnation made her ashamed of herself, yet she would not apologize. "You are very fortunate," she said at last.

"I am persuaded that I am," he agreed gravely.

"Even though you participate in scenes such as you did last night?" she whispered angrily.

"Even though I witness scenes such as the torture and murder of the Sire de la Roche-Bernard," he replied coldly.

"The torture and murder? . . ."

"Aye, lady. Those were my words." His eyes never wavered as the color drained from her face leaving her white to the lips. "But, of course, you doubtless approve of the punishment of traitors to your husband. You must have been gratified to be the instrument of his entrapment."

She looked away hastily, concentrating on the rivulets of sparkling water that overflowed from the petals of a stone flower into the basin beneath. Her stomach roiled with the knowledge that she had not left torture and murder behind in Navarre. Despite herself, her fingernails clutched at the sleeve of Geoffrey's tunic, only for an instant. Then her iron control reasserted itself.

She leveled a cold stare at her husband's servant. "Indeed," she replied, "I am ever loyal to my husband." Let the spy take that back to his master, she thought.

Beside her, Geoffrey drew in a deep breath. He had been right in his assumption. She was as pitiless as her notorious father. Doubtless cruelty was a family trait bred in the bone. His own position grew even more precarious. An icy frisson scudded down his spine as her cold black eyes scanned his face.

"I think I have seen enough of the gardens for today . . . er . . . Geoffrey. I plead weariness. Last evening was an ordeal, as you well remember." It was her turn to shudder, recalling the feel of this spy's hands on her. Would he someday be ordered to close his hands around her neck and break it as easily as he had undone the buttons of her dress?

She stared at the long white fingers curled in a loose fist only a few inches from her own hand. Were they the instruments of her eventual death? She swallowed painfully.

Geoffrey smiled slightly. "It will be my pleasure to escort you wherever you wish to go at this hour in the afternoon," he informed her. "The duke takes his rest at this time and bids me see to your needs."

"Oh, but—"

"It is his command." The young man hesitated. His pale gray eyes drifted to the water splashing into the basin. "I obey his commands faithfully—even those in which I take no pleasure."

Was he offering her a sympathetic word? She dared not trust him. "He taught me a stern lesson." Her voice faded to a shamed whisper and she raised one hand to her throat.

"*Mea culpa,* my lady," he bowed over her other hand, raising the slender fingers to his lips. "I have aroused memories when I know how very painful they must be."

"I accept your apology," she whispered. "You have been

most pleasant to me. I shall inform my husband of your attention."

"I thank you." He turned with her. "I believe this way leads most directly back to the gallery. The maze is confusing to anyone walking in it for the first time."

That night, after she had drunk wine with her husband, she retired dizzily to the bed behind the curtains. In a few minutes, she was joined within the cavernous blackness by the same familiar body she had known twice before.

He caressed her briefly, his hands moving over her body perfunctorily as if assuring himself that she was prepared to accept him. His fingers merely brushed across her breasts before seeking the juncture of her thighs. The warmth and moisture there signaled her readiness as did her tremulous gasp of anticipation. Without delay, he pulled her legs apart and pressed himself home in the core of her body.

Then, while shudders of ecstasy were still rippling through her, he drew away from her, parted the curtains of the bed, and left her alone. Bereft, she could not restrain the hand that reached out timidly for him even as he slipped away. She longed to call out, beseeching him to return and hold her for just a few minutes, but stubborn pride restrained her as did the certainty that her request would be denied. He cared nothing for her once his own pleasure was satisfied. Remembering the humiliation of their first night together, she considered herself lucky that he had touched her before the act so that she might be prepared to accept him.

Weary and not a little heartsick, she curled herself into a ball under the covers in the big bed and closed her eyes.

But sleep would not come. Instead she thought of Geoffrey. She could picture the valet's tall form, his broad shoulders and narrow waist. His arresting eyes haunted her. Did she imagine they had regarded accusingly? Surely he had no reason to look upon her with anything but favor.

He was an enigma to her. Raised with utmost strictness, she had never been allowed to carry on conversations with young men and her curiosity about members of the opposite sex had been discouraged by the aged women in her entourage. Now an incredibly handsome young man was presenting himself to be her companion. His presence was somehow exciting.

She recalled an illustration, in one of her books, of a knight so handsome she had dreamed about him for many nights. He had been called the Knight of the Sun. He had knelt at the feet of his ladylove, his head thrown back, his arms extended. His fair face was lifted toward her in a look of such adoration that Joanna had felt herself grow warm with delight. Like Geoffrey he had bright golden hair.

If only a handsome knight would look at her like that . . . If only Geoffrey were a knight instead of a baseborn bastard servant . . . That thought filled her with regret. She had enjoyed his conversation today. He was so strong, so handsome, so grave, so sincere. She was certain he would be as loyal and faithful as the knights of the *chansons*.

Life was unfair. She was not vain, but she knew herself to be young and comely. The face her mirror revealed to her was regularly featured with fair skin. Of course, her hair was not straight, but since she was married, it was out of sight most of the time. Why could she not have married a handsome young man—a prince or a duke?

Why was Geoffrey not the duke? The thought struck her forcibly. She could be happy with Geoffrey. She knew it instinctively. If she allowed herself to think about him, he would set her pulses throbbing. His body was lean and tall and straight, not crippled and crooked as her husband's. His eyes were kind and his voice gentle. Montfort had coldly calculating eyes and a mocking sneering mouth.

She remembered Geoffrey's hands; the fingers were long and tapering. Now that she knew what went on in the marriage bed, she could imagine what those long hands would feel like on her body. There would be no need to make love in pitch darkness; it would be a pleasure in the light. She would like to see his face as he kissed her. Would he smile like the Knight of the Sun?

She shivered deliciously at the thought. What would he say to her? Would he pay her extravagant compliments and bring her rich gifts and . . .

Angrily, she flopped over on the bed. Such thoughts were a waste of time. She was a princess of the blood royal. Despite the fact that her husband was ugly and old, he was also of noble blood. Even to contemplate tainting it was an affront to the ideals by which she had been so carefully reared. God ordained the births of all His people. Some special few He chose to be rulers and mothers of rulers. She was one of those. Despite Geoffrey's handsome face and figure, he was unsuitable for her to associate with except as a servant. God had ordained his role as that of a servant. She must always keep herself aloof and him in his place. She heaved a soft regretful sigh.

For almost a month the pattern of Joanna's days remained the same as the lazy warm summer spun away. Geoffrey walked with her in the afternoon. At night the duke plied her with drink, either in her own apartments or in the hall. Then with her mind clouded, she lay enshrouded in impenetrable darkness and awaited her lover's caress. Sometimes he was swift and left her side almost as soon as he had come. Sometimes he took his time, caressing her to madness, kissing her in places shocking to her mind but wildly exciting to her body.

She tried to hold herself aloof. All her self-protective instincts told her that these feelings were dangerous. This faceless lover was her lord and master. If she revealed too strongly the resentment or the pleasure his treatment of her aroused, she would be punished.

She could not forget his cruel hands on her body when she had fought him the first time. The second time, she vented her anger in another way. That too was dangerous. A woman should not be aggressive. Passive was best. She struggled to remain still, repressing her natural inclinations until she thought she would die from negating the wild sensations his hands evoked.

After he left her, she would throw aside the curtains and stoke up the fire. Alone, she would sit in a high-backed chair drawn close to the hearth. Sometimes she would stare into the fire; sometimes she would pace like a lioness measuring the confines of her cage.

Sometimes she would read. Unobtrusively, she had collected the few books in the château and had hidden them in the bottom of one of her chests, and in the small hours when the nightmares and shadows preyed most fiercely on her mind, she would drag them out and huddle beside the fire, bitterly reading the sweet lies of the *chansons de geste*.

Meanwhile Isabella de la Alcudia observed the duchess with growing satisfaction. The girl bore no love for her husband. Her emotions were steadfastly locked away behind a barrier of ice. Her already slender body had lost flesh. But that was natural, the duenna reasoned.

"Your flux has not appeared, Your Grace," she observed serenely one morning as she helped Joanna to bathe.

The snide words echoed like thunder in Joanna's ears. The washcloth she was lifting toward her breasts froze in midair, and warm water dripped onto her knees unheeded. She swallowed painfully before dropping her eyes to the slightly concave surface of her belly.

As if she had been stabbed to the heart, Joanna stared at the part of herself that was not herself. In her imagination she felt again the invasion of her body by the thick muscle of her husband, recalled the violent shudders that racked him when he expelled the seed that now had taken root in fertile ground. She carried it now within her body.

Fierce burning hatred threatened to consume her. All color drained from her face. Fortunately for the peace of mind of the duenna, Joanna's black ringlets fell forward around her face to mask her expression.

With stiff motions Joanna lifted the washcloth, not to her breasts but to her face, covering the emotions she might reveal. When she removed it, the warm streams of water had washed away every trace of a frown and had brought a becoming blush to her smooth white cheeks.

"I am sure you presume too soon, Doña Isabella," was all she said. Her voice had almost resumed its normal tone, except for an underlying thread of huskiness which would not seem to disappear. The sound was oddly old to issue from such a young face.

"I feel sure that we should make the announcement to His Grace immediately." Isabella held the huge linen towel for Joanna to step into. "He will be most gratified to know that in all probability his heir is on the way."

Joanna's black eyes narrowed. "And suppose you are mistaken? Suppose you have miscounted? Suppose I am merely late? The . . . changes in my life in the last month might cause me to be so."

Isabella pressed her lips together angrily, but her stubborn expression bespoke her certainty.

Throughout her toilette, Joanna felt the woman's eyes surveying her, measuring her. Were the tips of her breasts swollen and darker? Was her belly already distended? Once clothed, she pressed the palms of her hands experimentally against her stomach. She could feel no difference. Absolutely none. But she was late. She tried to remember when last she had had the illness. They had been at sea, so she had claimed to be seasick for the only time during the entire voyage.

Doña Isabella adjusted the silken veil so that it fell smoothly from the silver filigree basket into which she had tucked Joanna's heavy hair. "You must eat well from now on," she admonished. "The babe needs your special care, so he will grow strong."

At the mention of food, Joanna winced. She considered it the ultimate in depersonalization to no longer eat to please herself or as her appetite demanded. Instead she must eat for the "babe."

In the garden she stared unseeingly at the hint of yellow in the leaves of the blooming shrubs. The boxwood and yew remained as green as ever, but the flowers were beginning to fade. The petals of some had withered slightly at the edges and the ground was littered with the fallen stalks of others.

Autumn comes early this year, she thought. She was much farther north, no longer in sunny Navarre, but in cold harsh Brittany where the chill wind blew incessantly outside the walls of the middle garden.

Lisette and Thérèse were chattering happily to themselves. Lisette had been contracted in marriage to a minor baron whose home was far to the west. To Joanna's surprise, the girl was quite happy, eagerly planning her wardrobe and discussing what linens and plate she would take to her husband. The fact that he was considerably older than she did not bother her.

"He will be kind to me," Lisette assured her mistress. "His first wife died in childbirth, but she was my aunt, my father's younger sister. My father said that he was most kind to her and wept most grievously at her death." She sighed mistily. "Do you not think it romantic that he has come to marry one near in blood to her so that he may know her again if only for a little bit?"

Personally, Joanna thought the idea sounded ghoulish.

Furthermore, she strongly suspected that the marcher baron did not want to give up the sizable dowry that Lisette's aunt must have brought him. She wondered if Lisette's father had had to give a dowry with Lisette, was curious about the provisions of the marriage contract. But she said nothing. Lisette was happy. She would leave her to her innocent ignorance. Lisette could do nothing about her plight anyway. Better to leave her to happy fancies.

Thérèse unslung her hurdy-gurdy and began to play a lilting festive tune frequently heard at weddings in the north of France. As she recognized the first notes, Lisette giggled happily and began to sing in the Breton language Joanna could not yet understand. Nevertheless, she smiled, infected by their obvious happiness and the gay melody.

Through the arch at the end of the aisle of parterres, Geoffrey strode toward them, his step faster than usual. His fine brow was wrinkled in a frown that marred his usual cold impassivity.

To her surprise he dropped to one knee before her and bowed low. The melody of the hurdy-gurdy faltered. Automatically, she extended her hand. Something extraordinary had occurred. Was it her imagination, or did his fingers press hers a bit tighter than usual? There was a question in her eyes as he raised his head. "Your Grace, will you walk with me?" His voice was a little huskier than usual.

Since she never refused him, the question was irrelevant. Despite her resentment of his continual presence, not to speak of her angry embarrassment at his constant presence in her bedchamber, she never allowed her true feelings for him to show. No doubt the sounds she could not suppress as well as the sounds her husband took no trouble to suppress filled the servant's ears every night. Much as she hated to reveal herself to her husband, she hated the thought of Geoffrey's hearing her expressions of passion more.

Yet all these feelings, she concealed behind a façade of

bland indifference. With a nod of acquiescence she allowed him to draw her up from the white marble bench and lead her away through the arch toward the central fountain in the maze.

Despite himself, he stared at her, unable to admit that he was deeply concerned. The white veil fluttering behind her revealed her fair profile from brow to wimple. He had not noticed before the dark smudges beneath her eyes nor the sharpness of her cheekbones. She did not look well.

"Doña Isabella is with the duke," he said at last.

Her reaction was instantaneous. She stumbled slightly, a muttered exclamation escaping her before she clamped her lips tightly together. When they reached the fountain, he stopped to face her.

His eyes were darker than usual she noted; their usual pale gray was almost stormy. What was he concerned about? Why did his eyes bore into her?

"She tells him . . . good news." Geoffrey was picking his words carefully. He glanced away from her to stare at the clouds scudding across the sky. He was a fool for coming to her. This dash into the garden like an eager expectant father was ill conceived. He had no right to hear her confirmation, and yet he wanted to. With thudding heart, he realized that he wanted desperately to hear it from her own lips.

Coldly, her anger tight-leashed, Joanna shrugged. "I had ordered her to wait until such a time as I was sure. 'Tis early days yet."

He swallowed, trying desperately to control his eyes. They would not behave but dropped of their own accord to the waistline of her dress.

Her affronted gasp dragged his eyes back to her face. The ebony gaze was hard. "You forget yourself, Geoffrey," she sneered.

"*Mea culpa,* my lady," he whispered softly, dropping to his knee again. His face flushed with embarrassment.

103

The sight of his discomfiture pleased her. "I should not like to report your rude behavior to my lord." Her voice carried an implicit threat.

Instantly, he was terrified. Now it begins, he thought. I have served my purpose. The hair on the back of his neck prickled and he expected to hear the thud of boots on the red stone paths at the duke's guards came to arrest him for treason. His eyes flew to her face, in supplication.

Their glances held. Neither could understand the other's emotions. He struggled for control of his private fears. She read his fear, although she could not understand it. Her threat had been idle. In the first place, her husband would not punish or dismiss a favorite servant on the whim of the wife whom he regarded as little more than a broodmare. In the second, she could not bring herself to cause hurt and unhappiness to one who, although his presence infuriated her, could not be held responsible for his situation. Even as she, he was subject to the whims of the duke. A faint flush of her cheeks bespoke her shame.

"Rise, Geoffrey," Joanna bade him coldly. "You are in no danger from me."

Hastily, he straightened, throwing back his shoulders. His bright head caught the rays of the sun. In his usual dark gray wool, he looked suddenly weary and colorless but for the glinting sunlight on his hair.

She drew a deep breath. "I appreciate your interest . . . and concern," she acknowledged at last. "Do you come to bring me to my lord?"

He started at the question. How could he have forgotten his mission? In his own desire to know the truth, he had completely forgotten that he had been sent posthaste to the garden to bring her to Brittany. "Yes, Your Grace," he admitted miserably. "Will it please you to come with me?"

She looked around her sadly. Suddenly, she felt very tired. The garden was the same, yet not the same. The clouds had begun to gather. A breeze scrabbled through the blossoms in the center of the boxwood parterres. "Yes, Geoffrey," she said at last. "Bring me to my lord." She placed her hand on his crooked arm.

He smiled reassuringly. Then daring greatly, he placed his hand over hers covering it with his warmth.

Not by any sign did she acknowledge his act, but she did not draw her hand away.

Chapter 6

Early on Christmas Eve the heavens threw down an avalanche of snow on the château. Huge flakes whirled round the gray walls and drifted into deep banks around the boxwood in the middle garden, totally obscuring it in a solid blanket of white.

The Duke of Brittany suffered greatly during the cold dampness. His rheumatism settled alarmingly in all the joints of his limbs. Grotesque feverish swellings rose on his elbows, wrists, knees, and ankles; and his temper was taut as a bowstring. More often than not his targets were the duchess, whom he kept within his sight for hours at a time, and Geoffrey, who never left him.

His form distorted as a demon's in a religious painting, he now hobbled forth from his bedchamber in the middle of the day. Leaning heavily on the arm of his servant, he dragged himself painfully to a private room off his audience chamber. Since early October, he had ordered it kept uncomfortably hot for any normal occupants. A trestle table had been erected before a heavily padded chair. Seated in the chair, both legs stretched out on a leather embroidered hassock that had come his way from Outremer, he dispatched Geoffrey to fetch Joanna.

"Surely, my lady will join you shortly," the youth dared to

object. "'Tis Christmas Eve. She will be engaged in the solar."

"I want her to spend the day with me," Jean de Montfort snapped irritably. "She carries my heir. I do not want her busying herself with servants' doings. Let *la garce* Alcudia prepare the Christmas livery. Summon her!"

Bowing, Geoffrey made a wry face as he hurried from the chamber. A wave of frustration made him hunch his shoulders and knot his fists. His own feelings for the duchess grew deeper with each passing day. Yet he could not reveal himself to her, nor could he ease her way. In the door of the solar he halted. His eyes found her amongst her ladies and caressed her unawares.

Joanna stood at the side of Lady Thérèse, advising her as to last-minute details on the finishing of a garment. All servants of the château received a new livery of forest green wool on the sixth day of the new year. Less than two weeks remained for Joanna and her ladies to sew these garments. The measurements had been taken weeks ago and the material cut, but the real work was the sewing, for each stitch was done by hand.

Since Geoffrey did not enter the solar except by invitation, his presence at the door was not immediately noted. Quietly he waited, enjoying this opportunity to observe her. As she stood, she placed her hand absently on the small of her back in the age-old gesture of gravid women whose burdens pulled heavily on their slender spines.

Her pregnancy had not been easy for her. She did not sleep at night, nor had her appetite been good. As she pointed to a spot on the work in Thérèse's lap, he was struck by the extreme slenderness of her arm. Her distended belly and enlarged breasts proclaimed her pregnancy, but the rest of her body resembled a lanky child's.

As he looked, his heart leaped within him. He wanted her. Since Doña Isabella had announced her pregnancy in August, he had not been to her bed. Indeed he had not been to bed with any woman. Now his loins ached at the sight of her.

When at last she saw him, she heaved a sigh of irritation. The past four months had been stressful times. The duke watched her every moment, studying her belly as if she were made of glass through which he could see the babe grow. Excusing herself to Thérèse, she came to the door of the solar. "I cannot get the Christmas livery done if I have no time to work on it," she informed the waiting servant without preamble.

He looked reproachful. "Do you send me back to tell him that?"

The corners of her mouth twitched upward ever so slightly as she shook her head. His presence irritated her still, but she could not doubt his sincerity in seeing to her welfare. Indeed, Geoffrey clucked after her much more than his master did. Shrugging in acquiescence, she laid her hand on his arm. "Lead me to my chamber. I must throw a surcoat over this gown. The way he stares at my belly I fear the babe will be born with a hole in its backside."

The truth of her remark made Geoffrey chuckle softly as he escorted her down the hall. Her lack of respect for him allowed her to indulge in casual comments she dared make to no one else. Lady Thérèse was too delicate and ladylike to hear such things while Doña Isabella would have disapproved vociferously. Only with Geoffrey could Joanna relieve the tension that permeated every aspect of her life.

Furthermore, she trusted him insofar as she trusted anyone. Due to his nameless bastardy, she held him in low esteem so she said exactly what she thought to him, believing rightly that he had no one with whom to gossip. Their relationship had taken on an easy naturalness that soothed them both although neither acknowledged friendship with the other. Indeed, if questioned, either would have denied any friendship existed.

As she walked beside him, she fretted about the tasks she

was being pulled away from. She no longer thought of Geoffrey as a spy. Her common sense had told her that she had made too many slips in front of him. If he were collecting evidence, he already had more than enough. Moreover, Brittany knew that she bore him no love. He did not expect her to.

In her tiring room she smoothed the surcoat over her gently rounded belly. The garment was a beautiful thing. Made sideless to reveal the gown beneath, it consisted of broad bands of white velvet that encircled her shoulders and hips. Connecting the two bands were equally wide plastrons of the same material at her front and back. Below the band at her hips hung a full skirt of emerald velvet, and only the long sleeves and the upper sides of her dark gray wool undergown were visible. In this garment her burgeoning figure was effectively concealed. The style was new-fashioned for Brittany, although it was part of her trousseau from Spain.

As she stared at herself in the small silver mirror, she smiled grimly. Obviously, the surcoat had been chosen for her with her eventual pregnancy in mind. Odd that the idea had not occurred to her when the gown had been chosen. Now the scales had been lifted from her eyes, and she saw the method in many inconsequential acts. Suddenly she felt very old. Mentally bracing herself, she joined Geoffrey where he leaned against the wall across the hall from her doorway.

His eyes inspected her, smiling approval at the bright emerald green. The color relieved the severe gray. He did not like to see her wear gray. If she were his wife . . . He cut short the thought. "The surcoat was a wise choice, my lady," he said by way of a compliment.

"Thank you," she murmured as she laid her hand in its accustomed place on his arm. She felt infinitely tired and depressed. Her sleep was still troubled. The babe kicked and pummeled her all night long. Indeed, whenever she lay down, he invariably decided to wake up and play. Worse than that, she had had nightmares. Unconsciously, she shuddered.

"My lady?"

Her hand resting on Geoffrey's arm had communicated her distress to him. Instantly, she drew away.

"Are you cold?" His voice was so kind, so genuinely solicitous that she felt closer to tears than ever.

Biting her lip, she shook her head.

"If you truly feel unwell, I will return you to your chamber and placate His Grace somehow." His gray eyes searched her face. Before she could rebuild her façade, he had caught one of her hands in both of his. The thinness and coldness of it alarmed him. "My lady," he pleaded anxiously, chafing her flesh briskly, "you must eat more and rest longer. You are too thin."

She shook her head, swallowing a dry sob. "I eat enough."

He caught her chin and forced her to look into his accusing eyes. "You eat almost nothing at table. You will starve yourself and the babe."

Furiously, she struck at his wrist. "You forget yourself, Geoffrey. I am not your concern nor is the welfare of this babe."

He dropped his hand, clenching it into a fist at his side. His eyes, however, never left her face. "We are all concerned with the welfare of you and the babe," he insisted.

Her hands went to her swollen belly. "You are concerned for the welfare of the heir," she spat. "I am just a broodmare, a vessel to carry it in. It will eat off my body whether I eat or not. It is likely that I will die during labor, but the babe will live. Pray God it is a boy so some poor hapless fool is not forced again into marriage with—" Her voice which had risen to a hysterical peak broke off abruptly. She dared not go on. To continue would have been treason. While she trusted Geoffrey with minor complaints, she did not trust him enough to say what she really thought of Brittany.

Picking up her skirts, she began to run down the hall. A flush burned in her cheeks and her eyes prickled with tears.

Beside her in a couple of strides, Geoffrey caught her arm above the elbow and turned her toward him. His other arm went around her, dragging her into the circle of his arms. "Please, Your Grace," he begged. "Please, don't . . . I never meant to upset you. Believe me. I truly care about you. Truly. I care about you and the babe. Whether it be boy or girl, it is still a babe and precious." The words tumbled from his mouth. His whole soul was rent by the need to comfort her without giving away his true reasons. The agony of his secret was like hot knives piercing his lungs.

She stood stiffly in his arms uncertain what to do. She was shocked by his touch, shocked by the intimacy of his body so close to hers. Not a single person had so much as put an arm around her since the conception of the babe had been made known. Except for Geoffrey, she touched no one. Except for the impersonal dressing of her body and hair by Thérèse and Isabella, no one touched her.

Her initial impression was of warmth enfolding her. She was aware of the texture of his clothing, the rough wool of his tunic, the smooth knobs of buttons down one side of it. Secondly, she was aware of his scent, a clean smell, not like that of some of the lords who sat close to her at her husband's table. His hands were strong, yet gentle. He put no bruises on her body where he touched her. Instead one hand cupped the back of her head and guided it to his shoulder while the other soothed the strained muscles at the small of her back. It was at that very spot that she ached most persistently. How had he known? With a low sob she leaned her body against him. The swell of the babe was warm and firm between them.

Then reason reasserted itself. She was the Duchess of Brittany. He was a lackey who had laid hands on her body. "Release me," she hissed in a low, angry voice. Stiffening her spine, she pushed away.

He obeyed with alacrity. The color drained from his face, leaving it almost as white as the snow that swirled around the château. He stepped back, awaiting her will.

Her black eyes blazed golden fire from their depths. Her sense of dignity was deeply offended by this nameless lackey's presumption. Her first impulse was to report him immediately to her husband. He would be punished. She told him as much. "I shall have you whipped," she threatened him coldly.

While she watched him closely, he merely nodded.

"You would doubtless be banished from my husband's service."

Again he nodded. His face had assumed the blank impassivity she had grown accustomed to when she had first known him.

"Perhaps doing manual labor in the fields or stables would teach you proper respect for your betters?"

He did not plead. Instead he stood at attention, his back straight as a lance, the skin around his mouth compressed into a white ring.

His silence made her uneasy. As her anger cooled, she realized that she really did not want to harm him. After all, the incident had been of little import. He had not touched her to do her harm but merely to keep her from running and perhaps falling and injuring herself. Now that she thought of it, it all seemed perfectly natural.

Her color returned to normal. The babe kicked strongly, reminding her that she was standing in the hall and that standing tired her. "I do not want you to touch me again, Geoffrey," she said at last.

He nodded, his gray eyes staring straight ahead.

She thought he breathed a little easier. "Brittany is doubtless growing more and more impatient. I think we should join him before *you* get into more trouble," she added.

Bowing with studied politeness, he held his arm for her. "Your Grace."

"I meant what I said, Geoffrey," she reiterated. "I do not want you to touch me ever again."

113

"Never, Your Grace."

Brittany scowled furiously at the two who presented themselves in his study. The duchess looked drawn but composed. A frown line creased her white brow between the black wings of her eyebrows.

"Your Grace." She dropped only the suggestion of a curtsey, her hand still on Geoffrey's arm.

The duke's scowl darkened. "Stop that damned formality when we are alone, Joanna," he commanded. "You are my wife. You carry my child. I would not have you expend any energy that is not necessary."

She did not express her gratitude for his magnanimity but merely nodded as Geoffrey escorted her to a chair close to the blazing fire and retired to his accustomed station behind the duke's chair.

Brittany shrugged. He cared little what she thought. Women had almost no education because their intelligence was so mean they could understand almost nothing. Even an animal would lick a man's hand in gratitude, he thought. Undoubtedly, his wife had less sense than Brutus, his favorite hound. Staring pensively at the table in front of him, he rubbed his hands absently in an effort to ease their everlasting throbbing.

The fire crackled in the hearth as Geoffrey lowered himself noiselessly onto the stool he had long ago moved beside it. The duke frequently forgot him entirely. When he had first come from England, he had stood for hours. Many nights when he had been dismissed, his legs and feet had been swollen so badly from the knees down that he could not sleep for the pain. Soaking them in salt water had relieved them somewhat, but finally he had carried a folding stool into the duke's study. At first he had hidden it behind a tapestry, but when its presence was not commented on, he had simply left it against the wall.

114

If the duke noticed his lackey's defection from discipline, he did not comment. His own condition occupied his mind when he was not concentrating on keeping the suzerainty for himself against Bretons such as the late unfortunate Roche-Bernard.

His wife regarded the fire for a few moments before turning in his direction. "Did you wish my presence for some specific reason, Your Grace?" Her eyes were fathomless pools of mystery in her small pale face.

"Eh . . . what?"

Joanna's mouth curled ever so slightly. Her fingers tightened on the arm of her chair. "I asked if you wished me to be here for some specific reason. I have all the ladies working in the solar on the Christmas livery for the servants. We have less than two weeks to complete it," she reminded him patiently.

He continued to stare at the parchment in front of him. "What are you doing directing work?" he barked suddenly. His pale eyes darted from the document to appraise her with some surprise.

She blinked in amazement. "Your lady directs your household, Your Grace. I accepted the keys to all the locks in the château soon after I arrived. I have been trained well, and Doña Isabella and Lady Thérèse advise me if there is anything I do not understand."

Brittany stared at his fifteen-year-old bride. Already the babe was dragging heavily at her slight frame. Only her toes touched the floor where she sat. Her stomach already made an obtrusive mound in her lap. "When will you be sixteen?" he asked in an apparent *non sequitur*.

"In April," she flashed defiantly. Her Spanish temper rose swiftly as high color stained her cheeks. "But I am well trained, Your Grace. The liveries were all measured and cut weeks ago and —"

He waved her into silence. "I did not bring you here to discuss the servants, madam."

115

She subsided, returning her gaze to the fire. "No, Your Grace."

"Geoffrey!"

He rose swiftly. "Your Grace."

The duke drew a key from his purse and passed it back over his shoulder. "Fetch the coffer from the chest. There are several keys to the household that you do not possess," he told his wife smugly.

She did not answer but continued to stare into the fire.

When Geoffrey set the iron-banded box on the table, the duke extracted still another key from his purse. Chuckling softly as if at a good joke on his wife, he fumbled with the stubborn lock. "Not been opened in a long time," he confided to Geoffrey in a companionable manner.

The lackey watched curiously. As the seconds passed, the snow turned to sleet which slashed against the oiled hide at the window. The room seemed to grow colder with each passing minute.

The duke groaned as the key defied his stiff, painful fingers.

"Allow me," Geoffrey reached over the hunched shoulders.

Brittany sighed. His crooked members rested useless on the edge of the table as he watched Geoffrey's long supple hands easily turn the key. When the lid was lifted, he pushed his young servant aside irritably and scrabbled through the velvet and suede pouches that gave off muted clinks as they were moved.

At last he found what he sought. With an unfamiliar grin on his face, he withdrew a small pouch of dark crimson. Pulling it open, he emptied its contents into his hand.

"Duchess," he called.

Obediently, she rose, resisting the urge to put her hand to the small of her back. She wanted no sympathy from him. Instinctively, she knew that any such movement would be greeted with a knowing smirk since it confirmed his opinion that women were weak, ineffectual creatures.

"I have a gift for you for the Christmas tide," he announced grandly, including Geoffrey in his smile. He dangled the bright object from his hand. "See," he invited. "'Tis not a ruby although it is almost as red. The setting is real gold. It should become you beautifully. I wish you joy of the season, my dear Joanna."

She stared at the necklace as it caught the light and glittered in his palsied hand. The dark red cabochon stone looked like a drop of dried blood. She swallowed as her stomach protested the thought.

"Geoffrey will fasten it for you. I would do so myself, but I do not want to make you kneel down." He smiled at her. "You see. I *am* most concerned about your welfare."

As he spoke, Geoffrey took the necklace and came around behind her. She felt his hand at the back of her neck. Her black hair had been bundled into a long net that hung down to the middle of her back. With one hand he brushed it gently aside. Where his fingers touched her, they seemed to burn through the material of her gown.

Then his arms came over her shoulders, bringing the necklace down in front of her eyes to rest on the gray material of her gown. She lifted the hair to help him encircle her neck.

Then he was fastening the clasp. In the dimness of the room he bent toward her to see better. Where the back of her neck was most vulnerable, she felt his breath. Her skin prickled at the subtle stimulation. The sensation was devastating to her senses. Another second and she was sure she would have to twist away.

At the crucial moment his hands fell away and he stepped back. She drew a deep shuddering breath, one hand fingering the stone.

"Well, Joanna." The duke's voice shocked her overcharged senses.

She raised her eyes. Geoffrey's closeness had brought a

117

becoming flush to her cheeks. Despite her drawn thinness, she looked almost as she had the day she had disembarked from the *San Juan el Ibérico*. "I am most grateful, Your Grace," she whispered. "I . . . It is too much. I did not think . . . that is, I have no gift for you."

Well pleased with her color, which he attributed to pleasure at his gift, Brittany leaned back expansively in his chair. "You carry within you the greatest gift a man can receive from a woman, my dear. Pray God, it is a boy. You will never want for anything so long as you live."

"I do so," she replied, her smile a frozen mask.

Behind her she was aware of Geoffrey's breathing; he still stood at her back.

"I would like you to wear the jewel to the Christmas mass this midnight," her husband continued. His attention returned to the table in front of him. "Lock this up and clear it away." He gestured to the treasure coffer.

While Geoffrey obeyed, he stared at his wife. "So you are working on the Christmas livery?" he queried.

"Yes, Your Grace."

"I would not have believed it. I am surprised to find you so efficient. I would not think, given your young age . . ." He shrugged his crippled right shoulder. "Perhaps your industry bodes well. You must be stronger than you look." He studied her. "Madam, come here."

She caught her breath. Rooted to the spot, she clutched nervously at the stone in the necklace.

"Come here," he commanded impatiently.

When she stood before him, he put out his hands to touch the mound of her belly. "Your Grace," she protested fearfully.

"Stupid." He sneered. "I merely want to feel my son kick." He brushed aside the protective hands she had curved around her.

As his hands fumbled beneath the white velvet plastron,

118

her eyes found Geoffrey's face. He was not watching her. Instead, his pale gray eyes were focused on the duke. To Joanna's surprise they were furious, and his mouth was curled back from his even white teeth in a wolf's snarl.

Then her attention was diverted as the duke slid one hand around her waist to press against her spine and arch her forward. The other hand was splayed over her belly. As impersonally as a physician, he handled her. Then the babe moved within her. She could feel the tiny body turn and thrust. In embarrassed agony she looked down at the head of the old man who chuckled gleefully and squeezed her even harder.

"My son. My heir," he cackled.

"Your Grace," she protested.

"Only a minute more, woman."

His hand stayed only a bit longer, feeling the tumbling body, but his next move frightened her even more. Black spots flickered across her vision as she felt his hard gnarled fingers move upward to close over her swollen breast. As if she were a cow, he squeezed. More sensitive than ever with her pregnancy far along, his rough handling wrung a cry from her as she threw back her head and pushed against his shoulders.

"Your Grace," she gasped.

"Good," he laughed, squeezing it harder than ever. "Good. You should be able to nurse my heir with ease." He flung this information over his shoulder at Geoffrey, whose white furious face he could not see.

The duke released her so abruptly that she staggered back against the wall, her hands clutching at the tapestry that masked its rough surface. As she struggled to regain her balance, Geoffrey sprang from behind the duke's chair. His strong hands grasped her shoulders, righting her and shielding her with his body from the duke's sight as if by so doing he could protect her.

119

Their eyes met: hers, shocked and frightened like those of a child who has been punished for it knows not what; his furiously angry and wild with helpless frustration. Not knowing what she had done, but responding to a need to soothe his savagery, she impulsively laid her hand on his chest. The world faded into shadows for a moment.

"Is the stupid creature unhurt?" The duke's querulous voice catapulted them back into the cold room outside which the wind howled like a frightened ghost.

As a shudder racked his lean frame, Geoffrey stepped away from her. "She is well, Your Grace. She did not fall."

"Stupid creature." The duke addressed Joanna directly. "I was not going to hurt you. You were never in danger. Nervous. This violent shying away does not become a mother-to-be, Joanna." He gestured for her to come to him again.

Angrily, she shook her head.

"Come back here," he insisted irritably.

"No."

"I promise not to touch you again. Just let me take a good look at you and at that pretty thing you wear around your lovely neck." His voice took on a wheedling, whining tone as he reminded her of his Christmas gift.

But she stubbornly shook her head. Her fear and embarrassment had given way to anger. In this instance she knew he would not hurt her. He was too concerned with the welfare of his heir to do much more than issue a few weak commands.

"Geoffrey," he commanded, "you bring her here."

A moment's silence preceded his answer. "Perhaps I had better take the duchess back to her chamber, Your Grace," he proposed tactfully. "She will need time to check the progress of the work in the solar before she dresses for mass."

The duke scowled angrily, but Geoffrey hurried on. Crooking his arm for Joanna, he bowed slightly. Bemused by his daring, she placed her hand on his sleeve. "She must

120

have some food," he explained. "We have fasted since midnight to receive the Host, but the babe must not." He smiled winningly at his master.

The duke's scowl lightened. He chuckled drily. "Right. The babe must not fast. Take her away. I will see you at midnight." He turned back to his papers. As he sought his place, his hands resumed their compulsive rubbing.

Chapter 7

Outside the chamber, Joanna gave a low protesting moan and staggered away from Geoffrey's supporting arm. Sinking to her knees by the wall, she retched violently. Because she had preserved the obligatory twenty-four-hour fast before midnight on Christmas Eve, she had eaten nothing all day. Her stomach heaved, but she had nothing to bring up.

"Your Grace! My lady! Joanna!" Geoffrey dropped to his knees beside her, frantic with fear as he felt the spasms shake her body. "I beg you, Joanna. Please . . . lean back against me. Try to relax." He gathered her shivering body into his arms.

Tears flowed down her cheeks. Her humiliation, coupled with the touch of Brittany's hands on her belly and breast, had reawakened the submerged memories of her wedding night.

"Joanna," Geoffrey crooned. "Joanna. Please. Such terrible weeping will injure the babe. Do not. I beg you. Breathe deeply. You must not give in to such . . ." As he talked, he tilted her head back against his shoulder, and his hand stroked fine tendrils of hair from her hot, damp forehead and cheeks.

The audience chamber was dark at that time in the late

afternoon, but soon servants would be coming to light it. Mass would be said here tonight rather than in the chapel, since all the residents of the château would gather together at midnight on Christmas Eve.

"I must get you out of here," he murmured. "Joanna, I am going to carry you to your chambers. If you will allow me?" Without waiting for permission, Geoffrey swept her into his arms.

With her hot, flushed face buried in his neck, he hurried along the hall, praying as he went that he would meet no one. The thudding of his boots on the floor alarmed him, but he sacrificed stealth for speed.

Her sobbing slackened. Her hands crept round his neck. "Geoffrey," she whispered, her voice hoarse and raspy. "Please. Do not take me back to my chambers. Doña Isabella will be there. She will . . . she will . . . Geoffrey!" Her voice broke again. "I cannot bear more. Please. I beg you."

He stopped at her words. "But, Your Grace—"

"Please hide me, Geoffrey," she begged. "Please. Just for a little while. I can bear no more. Truly." She began to sob again with renewed violence.

Nonplused, he halted with his burden. Where could he take her? His own small chamber was but a dusty hole. Since he now spent all his time with the duke, he had not used it in months except to dress. Furthermore, to take the Duchess of Brittany to a servant's cubby would mean her disgrace and his death if she were discovered there.

The chapel. No one would be there tonight since both priest and acolytes would be elsewhere preparing for the midnight mass in the audience hall. He retraced his steps and entered the small room, now dark except for a pair of candles lighting the altar. Though the room was cold, it welcomed them.

Still holding her in his arms, he lowered himself to a bench and began to rock her gently. She kept her face in the hollow of his throat and her arms tight around his neck.

Her body, its temperature higher than normal from the presence of the baby, was wet with perspiration. Its gentle curves pressed against his own as her subtle perfume rose around him. Closing his eyes, he shuddered inwardly as he sought to quell the pain her body caused him. Her swollen breasts pressed against his chest. The curve of her hips fitted between his thighs.

Holding her in silence, he waited until her sobbing gradually subsided. Her breathing became regular as her body relaxed. Carefully he loosened his arms; she did not move. She had fallen into a deep sleep. The drains on her body had demanded their toll.

Feeling like a thief, Geoffrey touched his lips to her hair. She did not respond. Emboldened, his mouth brushed her forehead, then her cheek. His heart pounded as he felt himself grow hard and throb against her soft flesh. She would never know. Surely Almighty God would allow him to sit in His sanctuary a moment before this humble altar and endure the sweet torture of her shape.

The babe moved. The flesh of his flesh she carried within her moved against its father's body. Geoffrey held his breath.

The candles on the altar flickered out; the intruding wind, whipping wildly from all directions outside, must have found a chink in the walls of the château. The man sitting alone welcomed the ensuing darkness as a friend. The body of the woman he worshiped was clasped in his arms. They were alone for the first time in their strange relationship. No one lurked in the shadows and listened to what they did.

He kissed her again, this time with gentle light feathery brushes across her face. If he died for them, they would be worth the pain. His free hand strayed possessively over the sweet curve of her thigh up to the hard-stretched mound of her stomach. He drew in his breath sharply. The desire to see her nude, to caress her tightly-drawn white skin, to worship her with kisses was a knife to his vitals. Continuing his blind adventure, he cupped his hand around her breast beneath the white velvet plastron. To his delight and agony it was full and ripe. She had changed from the girl whose small budding bosom he had caressed. The nipple was swollen as was the aureole around it. Again he longed to see her body.

Her breast heaved under his hand as she drew an uneasy breath. Burning with pain and passion, he waited as she stirred, then quieted.

Cradling her body in one arm, he wiped his hand across his sweating face. She carried his child. And this child, if it were a boy, would someday be a duke. The thought was a bitter one.

All the pain of his bastardy—his nameless state, his total dependence on Jean de Montfort for the bread in his mouth and the clothes on his back—swept over him in an agony of humiliation so intense he had to set his teeth against it. Even his sexual initiation had been at the sufferance of the duke.

Sliding one hand under Joanna's hip, he turned her to him. Her breasts pressed against his chest, their child was cradled between them. His hands cupped her shoulder and supported her hip. She was all in all to him, yet she could never know.

He realized he was weeping. Tears trickled down his cheeks as pain mounted in his swollen throat. From his earliest memories he had never wept. His orphaned state had earned him no sympathy from the monks at the abbey. He had quickly learned that a stolid impassive face concealed all emotion and drew the least criticism. A smile was looked upon as a lack of reverence. To weep showed a lack of strength.

Now, in the lonely darkness, his overwrought emotions betrayed him. Fight them though he might, he could not suppress them. With a shudder, he bowed his head over her and gave himself up to them.

The room grew frigid. Geoffrey felt the cold spreading to his feet despite his leather boots. He clenched his teeth to keep them from chattering. Joanna stirred in his arms. With a soft groan, she opened her eyes. Where was she? Her first thought was that she was in her own bedchamber with the duke's arms around her. Against her will, he would penetrate her body with his own while his hands slid over and over her and created the strangest sensations.

Then she remembered: Geoffrey held her. It must be he. She could feel strong arms around her, hear the thudding of a heart beneath her ear. She could see nothing. "Where are we?" she moaned.

His chest heaved. "The chapel," he muttered, his voice hoarse.

"Are you catching cold?" she asked.

"Probably." He coughed self-consciously. "The floor is a sheet of ice. A draft blew out the candles long ago."

She put her hands down to push herself up, then slumped back against him. "I feel so weak," she muttered apologetically.

"I was taking you to get some food," he reminded her. "You should never have observed the fast." As his voice regained its normal timbre, he felt himself regaining control.

"I suppose not," she agreed. Simultaneously, her stomach growled, and the babe kicked vigorously. She groaned. "I am receiving the same scolding from everyone here. You, my stomach, and now the babe." She patted her belly reprovingly. Clumsily she worked her way around on Geoffrey's lap until she could swing her legs off onto the floor.

He had to set his teeth as her buttocks and thighs rubbed across his arousal. "If you will wait, I will set you down," he told her, speaking as mildly as he could manage.

Surprised at his aggravation, she sighed. "I am sorry to be so unwieldy. 'Tis not my fault."

He helped her to stand, then rose himself, ignoring the thousands of needles that shot from ankle to knee. "You are not at fault," he murmured. "Can you walk now?"

She took an experimental step. "Oh, yes. Actually, I feel quite rested. I must have fallen asleep."

He took her arm in the darkness. "Go slow," he cautioned. "Let me guide you. You must not fall." Ironically, his own plight was more precarious than he realized. His feet felt like lumps of ice at the ends of his legs. At his first step he stumbled and fell to his knees with a muffled curse.

"Geoffrey!" She bent over tugging at him. Her voice was shrill with concern. "Geoffrey. What?"

"Nothing," he growled. "My feet went to sleep."

Pressing her hands against his cold cheeks, she felt his face. "You are half-frozen," she accused. "You kept me warm while you froze."

He pushed himself up, abruptly afraid that her fingers would find the paths of his tears. "You exaggerate. I had my feet on the floor while yours were on the bench."

His aloof manner drove her back. Stiffly, she backed away from him until her legs encountered another bench in the dark. He stamped his feet until he could feel them below his ankles. "I can walk now," he gritted out. "Let me take you to find some food."

Their hands fumbled in the dark, met, and clasped. This time she did not put her hand in its accustomed place on his arm. Instead their fingers entwined as he locked her arm inside his own against his body. "Ready?"

"Yes."

The door of the audience chamber burst open. A chaos of noise and cold erupted into the room previously quiet except for the intoning of the priest and warm because of the great fires in the hearth and the myriads of candles. The howling wind immediately extinguished all light except the leaping flames in the huge fireplace along one side of the room.

A half-dozen crossbowmen sprang through the door, their

weapons cocked. Instantly, their arrows flew toward their marks, the duke and his personal guards.

Seated on a high-backed chair, his leg propped on the footstool, his body covered in furs, Brittany was at a disadvantage. Nevertheless, his early years of campaigning had fine-tuned his reflexes. Old and crippled he might be, but not so old that he could not push his foot against its rest and send the chair toppling to the side.

The arrow thudded into the shoulder of the man kneeling behind him. The man screamed, clutched at the shaft, and toppled over backward. As he sprawled awkwardly among the others, unbalancing them and sending them into confusion, Geoffrey leaped over the flailing body and flung himself in front of Joanna.

As he grasped her arms to pull her to her feet, his hands spasmed painfully and his back arched in agony.

"Geoffrey!" Her wide frightened eyes searched his contorted face.

"Come, Your Grace," he hissed through clenched teeth. "I must get you out of here.'

All around them, women screamed and men cursed. The raiders had caught the men out of armor and for the most part unarmed except for a few ornamental dress swords. Pandemonium disrupted the quiet service.

"Kill the impostor! Remember Roche-Bernard. *À Blois! À Du Guesclin!*" These cries identified the force as supporters of the men whom Jean de Montfort had killed and imprisoned to become Duke of Brittany.

Shielding Joanna with his body, Geoffrey staggered toward the entrance to the hall.

"You are hurt!" Her frightened eyes fastened on the shaft sticking out of the back of his left thigh.

"Run!" He growled, hopping as swiftly as he could, his arms around her shoulders as he pushed her in front of him.

Behind them the duke's forces began to rally. Montfort

climbed to his feet, shielding himself behind his chair. His own voice, harsh and fierce, rang out. "Defend me, friends. These are treacherous dogs who break the peace of God. Their leader is dead. Roche-Bernard is dead. *À Brittany! À Montfort!* Roche-Bernard is dead!"

Thrusting Joanna before him, Geoffrey stumbled into the hall. His efforts to slam the door were thwarted by a terrified girl who lunged after them. "Wait! Help me!" she cried. Her voice ended in a shriek as an arrow plowed into her back just below the shoulder blade. Her hands clawed at Geoffrey's belt.

"Thérèse!"

Ignoring Joanna's horrified cry, Geoffrey pushed her through the door.

"I will take care of her," he urged. "Go on. Go!"

With Joanna safely in the hall beyond, he turned to catch the injured girl. Even as his arms received her, her eyes began to glaze. Blood trickled from the side of her mouth. Gently, he supported her limp body to the floor.

As he straightened, a mailed figure leaped at him, shouting unintelligibly. The point of a heavy sword lunged straight for his belly. Despite the wound in his thigh, he side-stepped, slashing down with his own blade. He was able only to partially deflect the thrust. The point sliced through the flesh at his waist before it tore through his half-cloak and pulled him off balance. Through the whole length of the gash, blood welled in a bright red sheet.

"For Roche-Bernard!" The man yelled triumphantly, drawing back to lunge again.

Silently, Geoffrey parried the next wild slash. The fire was beginning in his thigh, and his blood trickled in a hot stream into his boot. Now his other side was also wounded although he felt nothing there but hot wetness. He must end this quickly before he became faint. Surprisingly, he never doubted the outcome. He would win because he did not fight for himself. He fought for his lady whom he must get to safety.

Again Geoffrey heard Brittany's deep cry. "Roche-Bernard is dead! *À Montfort!*" A grim smile of admiration writhed across his set lips. The duke was at his best as the old campaigner rallying the troops around him. With great courage and coolness he proved his claim to his seat.

Beyond the fellow's back he saw the men of Brittany, those left standing after the surprise attack, form a protective square around the duke, who himself had drawn his dress sword and was waving it in exhortation. Fighting furiously with their inadequate weapons and the swords they had caught up from the enemy dead, they moved in a rough formation in the direction of the chapel. A good place to defend, Geoffrey thought. Most of the enemy concentrated on them. Only his adversary was still battling independently.

The man swung at him again. This time he was clumsy or perhaps overeager. His blade went wide. Geoffrey deflected the poorly placed slash and straightened his own sword, extending to the length of his arm.

Too late the man realized the danger in his own overextension. His frantic attempt to draw back was thwarted by the pool of blood from Thérèse's body. His foot slipped, and Geoffrey thrust home.

Ripping his sword from the man's body even as it fell, Geoffrey whirled on his good leg to lunge clumsily for the door. His hand caught for the facing but to his surprise, he missed. Instead his bloody hand fastened in the tapestry hanging beside it. As it swayed, he swayed. Dear God! He was faint already.

Bracing himself, he made another grab for the door, found it, and staggered through. "Joanna . . ."

"Geoffrey." She darted out of the darkness, catching his arm.

"Hurry," he whispered. "Lead the way."

"Where?"

He shook his head dazedly.

If the defenders lost the château, his own room at the back would be among the last searched. Vaguely, he realized that he must get her someplace temporarily so he could bind up his wounds. He was losing too much blood.

"Through the solar to the servants' quarters . . ."

"Yes." Picking up her skirts, she hurried down the long hall. Fortunately, the battle had turned away from them entirely. No one cared to pursue a lone woman and a wounded man.

Geoffrey leaned against the wall, trembling, his vision swimming as streaks of red flashed through the dimness of the `hall. He must summon the strength to follow her. Pushing himself onto his feet, he staggered a couple of steps. Desperate, he swore, using foul words he had heard only from the most vicious of men. The arrow in his leg tore his flesh and grated against the bone. The pain nauseated him. Swallowing gamely, he tried to hop, supporting himself with one hand on the wall.

In his other hand, he held his sword, the point dripping blood.

Ahead of him, down the dark hall, a lighted rectangle appeared. Joanna turned to wait, silhouetted in the glow of the candles in the solar. Hands on either side of the door, her figure slightly thickened at the waist, she stood. "Geoffrey," she called.

"Go on," he croaked as each step required a bit more of his failing energy. She was wavering before his eyes.

He took his hand from the wall to wipe it across his face in an effort to restore his fading vision. The move caused him to totter sideways. As his weight shifted to his injured leg, a cry ripped from his throat. The excruciating agony steadied him, propelling him down the hall rapidly. But he was so cold and his throat felt dry.

In the doorway of the solar Joanna lifted one hand to her throat. Geoffrey staggered toward her. He was hurt. Geoffrey was hurt! The light spill glistened off the red liquid that dyed his hip on one side and his legs from both knees down. The same red dripped from the tip of his sword. She shook her head, struggling to control a feeling of faintness.

He reached her side, leaning his temple against the side of the door. "We must hide," he whispered.

"In my room?"

"*No!*" His voice betrayed his fear for her. "No, 'tis the first place you would be sought."

"They would not dare to harm a princess of Navarre."

He smiled mistily, his eyes slightly glazed. "A princess of Navarre, no. But a duchess of Brittany, one who carries the heir within her body, yes." When he reached for her, she drew back. His hand was bright with blood. "Your pardon, Your Grace," he shivered grimly. "If you will follow me . . ."

"Where?" she asked fearfully, following him across the solar.

"To my room in the servants' quarters. 'Tis the last place they would look."

Bloody footprints now marked his trail across the solar. Hurrying along behind him, she swallowed valiantly at the sight of the shaft of the arrow protruding from the back of his thigh. He was limping badly. Suddenly ashamed of herself, she caught up with him and thrust her shoulder under his armpit. "Lean on me," she ordered. "We can make better time."

He did not answer. As she glanced upward, she saw his throat work as he swallowed against pain or nausea or the threat of unconsciousness. She could not imagine which, but she knew he could not keep going much longer.

This part of the château was eerily silent, its occupants had been attending the midnight mass. Hopefully, they had scattered before the attack. She shivered as she thought of those who lay dead. Thérèse! Was her dear gentle musician badly wounded? Joanna would not allow herself to think that Thérèse was dead.

Geoffrey sighed between his tightly clamped teeth. "Loose me, Joanna," he gasped. "I . . . I . . ." He rallied. "Keep going straight till you come to the stairs at the very end of this hall. Go up. And up."

"Save your breath," she gritted out. He was heavier than she had expected. Although he was slender, he was all bone and muscle.

"You will hurt yourself," he protested hazily. "The babe—"

"I am sure he is asleep," she grunted as they came to the foot of the stairs. But realistically, her heart sank. She could not hope to mount those stairs supporting Geoffrey's weight.

"Leave me," he moaned again. She could feel his legs begin to buckle.

"No!" She fell to her knees as he collapsed on the first step. Backward he sprawled, his eyes only half open. He was barely conscious.

"Geoffrey," she cried, tugging at his arm. He moaned faintly through tight-clenched lips. Frustrated and frightened, she struck him. Her hand flashed out and delivered a ringing slap to the side of his face. "No, Geoffrey! You will not lose yourself here at the stairs. You have dragged me this far. You must take me the rest of the way. I demand it of you."

He rolled his head weakly, the slap had cleared his head a little. "The head of the stairs . . . back down the hall . . . up a small flight to . . . garret." He wearily waved his hand in that direction.

"Then you must take me there," she insisted. "I cannot go alone. I will not go without you. You must escort me. It is your duty." She was surprised that she directed such cruel words to the suffering youth. Perhaps she was more

Navarre's daughter than she knew.

"Your Grace . . ." He groaned.

She tugged at his arm. "Up, Sir Geoffrey," she ordered.

His wounds shrieked messages of protest to his disordered brain, but her command became paramount.

Blinded with pain, faint from loss of blood, he nevertheless stayed on his feet as she tottered up the stairs with him. Although barely conscious, he realized the terrific effort she was exerting. Her small face was pressed against his chest. Her slender arm encircled his waist and one hand clutched his belt. Each breath she drew sounded like a moan of pain.

At the top of the first flight, she gasped for breath. With one hand she cupped her belly, feeling it cautiously. It felt still but normal. The babe no doubt is sleeping peacefully, she thought with a tired smirk. Her own panic and excitement had given way to near exhaustion as she called on the last reserves of her strength. "Are you sure there is a room up here?" she panted.

He swung his head dizzily. "The very coldest . . . in . . . château . . ."

As they hesitated, faint shouts reached their ears. Footsteps thudded in the hallway below. "We must hide."

He nodded. "Only small . . . steps . . ."

In the end they mounted them together, literally crawling the last few on their hands and knees. Panting, gasping, straining, she dragged him upward when his weakened legs could no longer bear his own weight.

Her questing fingers found the latch, lifted it. The door creaked open. A musty smell filled her nostrils. *"Santa María,* Geoffrey! How long has it been since you have been here?"

He did not answer. He lay on his face on the landing, his feet hanging over the stairs.

The room was pitch-black and only different from the outdoors because the wind did not blow through it and the snow did not drift about its floor. Its tiny hide window was sealed, but the temperature must have been well below freezing.

Geoffrey must be gotten warm, or he would die. She was not sure she would not die herself once the heat of her exertions faded from her body. Sweeping her arms in great circles before her, she encountered a chest. Her fumbling fingers identified the stub of a candle with flint and tinder beside it. She was not good at this operation, but fortunately her skills were equal to the task.

The light revealed a cell no bigger than her private tiring room. Behind the chest were a narrow unmade bed with rumpled covers and a tiny table. Nothing else. The whole room was no more than seven feet by five feet. She sighed angrily at this evidence of how badly Geoffrey was treated. He did everything for the duke, yet he received no more recompense than this.

Regretfully, she cast her eyes toward his still form lying just outside the door. He had interposed his body to protect her. No doubt he had taken the arrow meant for her, and now he was bleeding badly.

She vowed he would not die. The babe hung heavy on her tired frame, but she put both hands under it and pulled it upward, easing herself of its weight for a moment. Drawing a deep breath, she straightened and then threw back the covers on the bed. At least the linens seemed to be fairly clean although in the dim light, she could not be certain.

Hurrying back to his still form, she caught him under the arms and started dragging him through the door. Her heart pounded as black spots whirled before her eyes. She gulped in air, then heaved and rested, heaved and rested.

Finally, he was beside the bed, the door closed behind him. Just before she had closed it, she had heard muffled screams and shouts from the lower floors. These sounds had sent her flying to shut them in and throw the bar. Not that the door would offer much protection, she realized, but it made her feel safer.

Dropping to her knees beside his body, she bent to examine his wounds, but a black tide rolled across her vision Forced to give in to the demands of her overtaxed body, she leaned her cheek against his shoulder. Then, without knowing she did so and without a struggle, she closed her eyes and lost consciousness.

Chapter 8

She was freezing, particularly her legs and buttocks. Grumbling to herself, she rubbed her hip and discovered in doing so that she was uncovered. With one hand, she searched for blankets. She must have kicked them off in the night. But her upper body was lying on a warm surface that moved rhythmically.

With a start Joanna opened her eyes. Suddenly, she remembered everything. Kneeling to see to Geoffrey's wounds, she must have lost consciousness. Every fiber of her being rebelled at the thought of moving, but she sat up with agonizing slowness. She buried her face in her hands. Oh, for a chance to go back to sleep and awaken to a different world. How she dreaded getting her feet under her and rising.

A glance at the candle told her that she had been unconscious only a few minutes, but the temperature of the room had been unrelenting. Forced by the biting cold to act, she crawled on her knees to the chest and brought the candle back to Geoffrey's side.

The sight of his bloodied body made her head spin dizzily, but she steeled herself. If he were to survive, she must bandage his wounds and get him into a warm bed.

Looking first at the long slice in his side, she was relieved to see that it had stopped bleeding almost completely. In that regard, the cold of the room had helped him.

Ripped by the sword that had torn his side, his half-cloak lay partially covered by his body. She tugged it free and tore it into long strips. Panting and grunting, she managed to pass one length under his body. Making a pad out of another, she bound it across the wound.

Gritting her teeth, she touched the bloodstained shaft. A feeling of helplessness settled over her. Her shoulders slumped in despair. She knew nothing of nursing, nothing of wounds or the procedures for treating them. Should she attempt to remove the arrow? Arrows had terrible barbed heads that tore the flesh around them. But how could she bandage him and make him comfortable without pulling it out? Bowing her head, she prayed for strength.

The arrow must come out. He was unconscious now, seemingly insensible to pain. At least she could not hurt him more than anyone else who would pull it free—and it must be freed.

Raising her head, she cleared her mind of all thought except the exhortation to herself to be strong and quick. Her hand closed over the shaft, moving it slightly to test its depth. At first it did not move. She knew a moment of panic. Suppose it were embedded in the bone.

Gently, she pressed it toward the outside of his leg. As she did, it moved easily. It might be lying beside the bone, so it would not move easily in the other direction, she reasoned shakily.

"Holy Mary, Mother of God," she whispered with closed eyes. Taking a deep breath and biting her lips between her teeth, she took a firmer grip on the shaft.

Embedded in the heavy muscle at the back of Geoffrey's thigh, the arrow resisted her first gentle efforts to pull it free. Blood, which had almost ceased to flow, welled out from the wound.

A self-pitying sob burst from her clenched lips. She was not fitted for this. Her birth, her upbringing, her education

140

had all been focused on an existence free from the realities of life. She was supposed to sit sedately in the solar and direct her ladies in their various pursuits. Her children were supposed to cluster round her knees, their adoring faces turned up for her to kiss.

Bitterly, she pushed the picture away. Here was another flash of the reality that had become more and more familiar since she had come to Rennes.

"Oh, Geoffrey," she whispered. "I *am* sorry." Placing her other hand on his buttock, she exerted the strongest, steadiest pull of which she was capable, groaning at the intensity of her effort.

His body contorted as he gave forth a terrible groan that ended in a scream.

Abruptly, the arrow came free, spattering blood across the front of the white velvet plastron. Blinking in horror, open-mouthed, she stared at it. Her first fear was that the head was still in the wound. She could not know that the arrow had been a barrel-point, a type made specifically for slipping between the links in chain mail and consequently having no barbs on the point. Flinging the arrow aside, she turned her attention to the moaning pain-wracked man.

Geoffrey rolled onto his back, away from her, his face contorted. "Christ, have mercy!" he exclaimed.

"Please," Joanna held out her bloodstained hands toward him. "Please, Geoffrey. I did not mean to hurt you. But the arrow . . ." Tears streamed down her cheeks. "I did not mean . . ."

His vision cleared. "Yes . . . you . . . only . . . help . . ." Each word was a painful gasp, and his chest heaved in a tremendous effort to achieve control.

Sick with pain and fatigue, they stared at each other, their anguished eyes sunk in their chalk white faces. Both looked decades older than their years as they struggled for the courage to go on.

Wiping the tears away from her cheeks with the back of

her hand, she offered him a travesty of a smile. "Will you let me help you onto the bed?" she whispered. "Now that you are conscious, you should not lie on the cold floor any longer. Once on the bed I can bandage your wound and cover you."

He nodded. Drawing a shaky breath, he tried to push himself up, but his arm quavered, threatening to drop him onto his injured side. Hastily, Joanna climbed to her feet, suppressing a groan as her numb flesh responded stiffly to this demand. Bending over him, she placed her hands under his arms and heaved.

"Joanna, think of the babe." But even as he protested, he exerted his strength so her effort would not be in vain. As she released a muffled cry, his body sprawled backward half on, half off the bed. Unbalanced by his considerable weight, she fell across him and lay panting, her face against his neck.

At last when her breathing had steadied somewhat, she gathered herself for one more effort. "Now," she whispered against his neck. "One more try. Then you can rest."

"My lady," he murmured. "My love." One hand trembled against the back of her head in a sweet caress.

She dismissed the act along with the words. He was doubtless delirious with pain and exhaustion. He probably did not know to whom he was talking. Pushing herself off him, she stood erect and pressed her hands hard into the small of her back. To her the wonder of all this was that her babe lay still within her body. How oblivious he was to the terrors that besieged his mother!

Stooping she lifted Geoffrey's legs onto the bed. Her act drew another smothered groan from him. Ignoring it and working like an automaton, she tore the required strips from the cloak and bound his thigh tightly. After the struggle to get his side attended to, this procedure seemed anticlimactic.

Pulling the covers up over his chin, she crossed to the door and opened it, listening for searchers. Hearing nothing, she returned to the bed. Geoffrey's eyes were pale gray wells that stared at her out of sunken sockets. Now and then a shiver racked him.

Suddenly, she too was very cold. Her efforts over, she sank down on the chest at the foot of the bed. Hugging her arms across her breasts, she set her teeth to stave off their chattering.

"Joanna," came the hoarse whisper. "Climb into bed with me."

She shook her head. "No. I shall just sit here for a few minutes until I get my breath back. Perhaps the duke and his men won. I think I should slip down and see."

"No!" His voice was surprisingly strong. He raised himself up in bed. "Climb into bed with me and warm yourself. When we have both rested, then I will investigate."

"You can barely sit," she scoffed, "let alone walk."

He set his teeth. "Either you get warm, or I climb outside the covers and pass out on the floor again."

"You are acting like a child," she accused.

"Will you get into bed with me?" He raised the covers. As she still hesitated, he snorted in exasperation. "Good God, Your Grace, what can I do to you? I cannot stand as you said. I certainly cannot harm your body. The most I can do is bleed on you."

She shuddered, then shivered. Shrugging angrily, she crawled into the bed beside him.

Their commingled warmth was like heaven to their sorely strained bodies. His arm arranged the covers over her, then settled proprietarily across her waist.

"Geoffrey," she whispered wearily. "You forget yourself."

"I am freezing," he insisted. "You keep me warm. 'Twould be a shame to work so hard to save me, then lose me to lung fever."

She did not answer his pitiful attempt at humor, but her weary body relaxed instantly and she fell into a deep sleep.

This time he followed her into a deep well of unconsciousness.

Frost formed on the inside of the hide-covered window. The light was dim, at best a pitiful glow filling the room with shadows. Outside the wind continued its bleak howling although the whirling blizzard had slackened.

Joanna stirred first. Turning on her back, she pressed a cold cheek against Geoffrey's chest. Her eyes still closed, she thought to drift back into sleep, but it was not to be. The babe gave a great wiggle and began to kick vigorously against her diaphragm. Instantly, her eyes flew open. Her stomach growled, and she had to swallow as her mouth began to water.

Sweet Mary, but she was hungry! She placed a placating hand on her stomach only to feel the insistent kicking. Seeking relief, she turned over on her side to face Geoffrey, but the babe, not to be daunted, somersaulted within her and butted his head against Geoffrey's ribs.

Gray eyes flew open and stared into hers in a dazed fashion.

"He kicks hard." Her voice was a husky rasp.

"Aye, he does." Geoffrey had no voice at all, only breath coming from his dry throat. A flush stained his cheeks. The fever was already rising in him.

"I am so hungry," she whispered. "I must eat or die."

His face looked like an old man's in the gray half-light, but he rallied with a tired smile. "Then I shall fetch you something."

Shrugging her shoulders mentally, she waited. He could no more rise than a sick babe, but he would find that out by himself more quickly if she did not argue with him.

He raised his disordered silver blond head from the pillow. He could go no farther. As pale as death except for the hectic flush on his cheeks, he caught his lower lip between his teeth and made a game try. He could not lift his shoulders from the bed. From the depths of his body came a low moan eloquent of despair.

"Satisfied?" she asked politely.

"I . . ." He had to clear his throat. "I will be stronger in a minute."

"I will wait," she agreed. "But only for a minute. Then I shall rise and try to discover what has happened in my own château overnight."

"No . . ."

"Yes."

He caught hold of her arm. "If the duke was taken—"

"We will be found in a matter of hours. To hide here in this cell is the height of foolishness."

"I will regain a measure of strength; then I can get you to safety."

"Not without food and drink, you will not." She pushed her feet from under the covers. "Sweet Mary, I hate this cold. Does it do nothing in this cursed Brittany but snow?"

He struggled to rise again, but weakness and fever defeated him. He had lost a great deal of blood the night before. His thirst raged so fiercely that his tongue felt swollen.

She flung back the lid of the chest and bent over it. "Do you have another cloak in here?" Her voice sounded hollow coming from the depths of the chest.

"Yes, but—"

"Good. I will take off this surcoat—'tis ruined anyway—and throw a cloak over me. That way if an enemy sees me, he may let me pass as a woman of no importance." She smiled hopefully as she drew his heavy gray garment from the chest.

"Joanna—"

"Be quiet, Geoffrey." She drew the surcoat over her head and tossed it over the end of the bed. With a wide swing, she

145

settled his cloak around her shoulders. Its extra length pooled on the floor around her feet.

"You cannot go. You . . . the babe . . ."

"The babe is kicking me to pieces." She groaned. "If I do not feed him soon, he will break a rib from the inside. Then there will I be." She came to the side of the bed to bend over him and laid a hand across his forehead. Casting levity aside, she searched his gaunt suffering face.

He caught her wrist. "You must not go," he whispered. "I will protect you. Just give me a few minutes to regain my strength and . . ."

She twisted her wrist from his grasp in a salutary demonstration of his strength. A superior smile curled her mouth at one corner. "Geoffrey. Rest easy. I shall return with food or help or both."

He fell back onto the pillow, his face stark as a martyr's on a cross.

Pity for his plight moved her as well as for his pride, which was strangely at odds with his baseborn position. He had brought her to safety but now found himself too weak to protect her further. She touched his cheek with gentle fingers. "Geoffrey, you have saved me. Do not chastise yourself when you have no strength left. No queen could have a more valiant and faithful servant than you."

He did not answer, nor did he remove his arm from across his eyes.

She turned away, kicking the overlong cloak aside, and hurried out, closing the door behind her.

The hall was much darker than the room. Cautiously, she felt for the top of the little flight of steps leading down from the garret. She had no desire to risk an accident and her body was unwieldy.

The upper hall was deserted. There was no sign of a servant. She tried to find hope in the thought that the staff might be going about their tasks as usual. She had no idea of the time. It could be morning, noon, or late afternoon. She had no way of knowing how long she had slept.

At the head of the stairs leading to the main hallway, she paused to listen. Again there was the same deathly quiet. Had the château been overrun? Had its conquerors taken the duke and his followers captive and borne them away? Or were they besieged? Were the defenders manning the outer walls? A hundred possibilities raced through her mind as she crept cautiously down the steep flight.

Finally, she came to the door of the solar. Surely it would not be empty. All the women of the house traditionally gathered there to work, to chat, to entertain themselves with stories and songs. At the thought of music, her heart went out to Thérèse. Where was her sweet lady?

Cautiously, she lifted the latch, pushing open the door a fraction of an inch at a time. The room was cold and empty. Its candles had been allowed to gutter out in their sockets, but natural light streamed down from the skylights that had been fitted with blown-glass panes, an innovation that added immeasurably to the comfort of women trying to sew by hand to create the steady stream of garments required to outfit the large number of servants who worked in the château.

She paused, her hand on the door latch, uncertain what to do. Should she try to find the duke and his retainers, or should she try to find something to eat? Her stomach growled alarmingly at that moment, and she swayed where she stood as hunger pangs reasserted themselves, gripping her stomach.

Food! She must find something for herself and Geoffrey. A table was always kept set in the main hall. It had been laid the night before with every possible delicacy to be consumed after the Christmas mass. That would be the most likely place to try. Surely, all that food would not have been eaten.

Determined to feed herself before she did anything else,

she started across the room. The sight of the floor brought her to a quick stop. Dark brown stains, drops of blood and bloody footprints, made a trail across the floor. If anyone had come to find her, he would certainly have had an easy trail to follow. Unless, of course, no one cared about her anymore.

Such speculations were making her desperate. Shaking her head to throw those thoughts away, she circled the solar, carefully avoiding the stains.

In the hall beyond, she heard sounds of voices. Feeling a mixture of wild relief and dread, she hurried toward them. So hungry was she that she could not think what would happen if the room were occupied by the men of Roche-Bernard. If the duke were dead, surely they would give her a meal. She would pretend to be a serving maid. Hastily she checked her throat, hands, and arms for jewelry. During the peculiar chain of events of yesterday, she had never gotten around to donning any, except for the duke's gift which she thrust out of sight beneath her gown. Her unadorned condition along with her disheveled appearance must be her protection.

Trembling, she opened the door a tiny crack. A wave of relief so palpable that she felt like crying swept her. The room was alive with the duke's people while Brittany himself sat in his righted chair, his foot propped on his ottoman, directing the proceedings.

Among the people bustling about, Doña Isabella sat rigidly upright in a straight-backed chair. Her face was gray and set; her hands fingered her prayer beads. At the sight of Joanna standing in the door, the duenna's rigid face contorted. To Joanna's surprise, the woman so forgot her stern dignity as to run to the door to greet her charge. "My lady!" she exclaimed, lapsing into Spanish in her excitement. Her face almost cracked in its effort to smile. "You are safe." The older woman took Joanna's hand and looked deeply into her eyes. Then her sharp gaze inspected the ugly brown stains under Joanna's nails and in the crevices of her fingers and palm. "You *are* safe?" she questioned.

"Yes, Doña Isabella." Joanna patted the woman's clawlike hands and was further amazed to find that they were cold and shaking.

From his chair, Brittany had seen her. He straightened eagerly, directed a relieved smile at her and motioned her forward. "Joanna!"

Before she approached his chair, she smiled again at her duenna. "Will you please bring me something to eat, Isabella? I faint from hunger."

"At once," Isabella turned away abruptly, seemingly glad of the task since it gave her the chance to recover after her uncharacteristic display of emotion.

Jean de Montfort regarded his duchess' approach with a combination of relief and guilt. She had not been harmed; the heir for which he had sacrificed and schemed was still safe within her belly. Yet he had not given her a thought until he had seen her walk into the room. His eyes narrowed as he studied her face. Would she accuse him of neglect and make a scene as women were wont to do?

"Your Grace." She dropped a perfunctory curtsey before him.

"I am pleased you are well, Joanna."

She smiled sarcastically. "I was well attended throughout the battle."

He flushed. So she did realize that no effort had been made on her behalf. He had expected that she would. She was too perceptive by half.

Before he could comment, Doña Isabella approached with a pair of servants: one bearing a basin, a towel, and a ewer of hot water; the other bearing a platter of carefully chosen delicacies.

Joanna bestowed a warm smile on her duenna. With

149

intense relief, she dipped her hands into the water and laved away the traces of the ordeal she and Geoffrey had shared.

Brittany took a startled look around him, as if suddenly recalling that his most faithful attendant was also absent. Then his eyes dropped to the stained water.

"'Tis Geoffrey's blood," Joanna informed him coldly. "He took an arrow meant for me, and his side was slashed in a fight covering our flight. Your men defended you most admirably, my lord, but you should give instructions to them regarding your heir."

Ignoring her sarcastic thrust, he leaned forward anxiously. "Then he is dead?"

She shook her head, drying her hands on the towel and returning it to the attendant who bore it away. "Only gravely wounded. He hid me safely before he collapsed. I bandaged his wounds. He, even now, lies waiting anxiously in his bed. I beg you to send servants to see to him."

The duke nodded. Summoning his butler, he sent the man scurrying for the surgeon who had only just collapsed in the corner with a tankard of beer and a hunk of bread. "He shall have our thanks. He has protected that which is most precious in Brittany."

"The heir," Joanna remarked *sotto voce* as she took a bite out of a boiled egg that had been pickled in spiced wine vinegar.

The duke scowled. "You too, my dear," he admonished. "You are also precious to me."

Turning to face him full on, she stared into his pale gray eyes. His face looked much the same; no deeper lines marred it. The shadows beneath his eyes might have been incurred from a night spent carousing heavily with his cronies. Contrasting it in her mind with Geoffrey's pain-wracked countenance, she felt a surge of helpless anger.

"I believe that my father's alliance would still hold firm were I to disappear forever," she informed him bitterly.

His face did not change. "Doubtless," he agreed suavely. "Since he wants to go through Brittany to regain his lands in Normandy. Nevertheless, your presence is important to us both. I can depend on his unswerving loyalty if he knows I hold that which is dear to him within my grasp. Be assured, I hold it gently and carefully, but I hold it nevertheless."

She nodded, her appetite suddenly gone. She should have known better than to try to score off a fierce wolf like Brittany. He could gobble her in one bite if he took a fancy to the taste of her flesh. Handing the plate to the waiting attendant, she placed her hands carefully on the arms of her chair in what she hoped was a cold regal pose. "I should like Geoffrey moved from that horrid cell to the solar." While her words asked permission, her voice brooked no argument. "There my ladies and I may nurse him to insure his return to health. I will not have him neglected by servants who would attend him only when they thought about him or not at all. His room is the remotest in the château." She looked at her husband accusingly.

The duke shrugged. "It shall be as you wish, my dear. Although in defense of myself for what you obviously consider my ingratitude toward a good man, Geoffrey selected his own room. More often than not, he goes there only to dress since he attends me constantly these days." He shifted slightly in a vain attempt to ease his throbbing joints.

"That must be changed," she insisted; then she stammered because of the look that Montfort threw her. "That is, his room must be changed. He has served you most nobly this night. I beg you to reward him richly."

Had her hatred for Geoffrey cooled somewhat? Montfort wondered. Did she look on him with especial favor? He hoped not for her sake as well as Geoffrey's. He would not have his wife cuckolding him with his lackey. Only he had the right to cuckold himself. The irony of the situation struck him, bringing a grimace to his mouth. He had more than

151

once noticed Geoffrey's attention trained on the duchess when he thought no one was looking.

Suddenly, the duke felt a fierce burning anger at the very depths of his soul. The coils around the three of them tightened inexorably, hurting first one and then the other.

Joanna, who had been watching his face, shivered at the expression she saw there. Had she done Geoffrey a disservice in demanding that his situation be bettered? She had never asked anything of her husband before. Perhaps the duke was vindictive. Some men were. Her father, for example, liked to listen to the requests of people against whom he had some baseless grudge and then do the opposite of what they had sought.

She attempted to change the subject. "Did the attackers prove a serious threat, my lord?"

He regarded her for some minutes, during which his face took on the aspect of steel. "They are all dead, except for a few who wish they were. I intend to root out every sign of resistance to my right to rule as well as to the right of my heir," he nodded significantly toward her belly. "Those who opposed me and lived are even now bound, naked, their feet frozen in buckets of ice. They will soon speak with most eloquent tongues. Be assured, Joanna. I am every bit as merciless as Charles the Bad."

Nodding resignedly, she placed a hand to her temple where a headache began to throb. She was too tired to fence anymore. She had revealed too much, but the nervous strain of the past twenty-four hours had rendered her incautious. The duke's description of the fate of those poor tortured souls was the last straw. Signaling to Doña Isabella, who had retired just out of hearing, she placed her palms together in a formal attitude of reverence. "I beg your leave to retire and bathe, Your Grace. The past twenty-four hours have been most unsettling. Even though I did manage to sleep a bit last night, I still feel unusually exhausted."

Brittany smiled, the soul of generosity. He had not missed

the pinched look around her mouth as he had told her of the battle and its aftermath, nor the greenish tint to her skin. That would keep her in her place. She would not come before him soon again with accusations of neglect and demands for better treatment of his servants.

With a feeling of contentment, he watched Joanna's companion take her charge's arm as the two left the hall.

Chapter 9

Men may accept a bastard into their rough world if he be willing to fight like a tiger to prove himself to them. However, he is an embarrassment to all women, for he symbolizes a sister's fall from grace. As Geoffrey lay in the solar of the château at Rennes, his body soaked up the healing sunlight shining warmly through the leaden glass panes above him and his thoughts drifted idly backward. He tried to remember a time in his life when a woman had made a stir over him. Having no memory of his mother, only of the stern-faced monks of the priory, he had known no women at all until he had come to Brittany with the duke. Now he decided that he liked the experience above all things.

The surgeon had sewn his flesh together and had swathed him in bandages so tight he could hardly move. For twenty-four hours he had endured considerable discomfort as he'd drifted in and out of consciousness, during which time his fever crept ever higher. Joanna had cast about frantically until an old woman among the lower servants of the château had suggested that his gashes be kept clean and exposed to the light and air for a period of time each day. Such treatment she vowed was the best cure for wounds. Since all the servants swore by her, Joanna had eagerly followed her advice.

So now Geoffrey lay in the solar, a room reserved exclusively for the use of women, a place where a man set foot only on the most extraordinary occasions. His body lay on a wide comfortable bed fitted with lavender-scented white sheets, so clean they dazzled his eyes. Fires burned brightly on the hearth, and charcoal braziers radiated heat in every work area as well as beside his bed.

A screen had been brought to shield his bed from maidenly eyes when he lay unclothed, except for a loincloth, in the direct rays of the sun.

At first his embarrassment had been acute as he suffered his body to be stripped and bathed by gentle hands. To lie virtually nude made him nervous. Furthermore, he had tensed and frantically clutched at the covers every time someone had come close to the other side of the screen. But the warm rays streaming in through the skylight had gradually worked their particular magic on him. Nerves knotted since he was old enough to remember gradually stretched themselves. His body relaxed, and the healing of his gashes proceeded with relative freedom from pain.

Smiling foolishly, he lay at peace, feeling the soothing warmth on his skin and listening to the hum of conversation from behind the screen. Frequently, someone played a musical instrument in accompaniment to soft singing. The women had soft voices and laughed often. He could distinguish Joanna's tones from all others. To hear her all day long made him happy despite the nagging pain of the surgeon's stitches.

"Geoffrey," she called softly. "Are you asleep?"

"No."

"Cover yourself, so I can bring you a posset."

Obediently he drew the sheet and blanket over his limbs. "Come ahead," he called.

She seated herself beside him on the stool drawn close to the bed. "I have mixed the sweet wine of La Rochelle with an egg," she smiled encouragingly. "Lady Marguerite suggested this particular wine which she assured me is the most delicious in France."

Geoffrey returned her smile with a wry grin. Lady Marguerite, a middle-aged harridan with rotten teeth, had once made a great push to have Brittany send him away because she'd considered him a bad moral example to the servants. Now with Joanna championing him among the ladies as Brittany had among the men, he was approached with special friendliness and concern by women who had previously cut him directly when he'd happened to pass near them.

He grinned at Joanna after the first sip. "'Tis nectar," he agreed. "My gratitude to Lady Marguerite."

Joanna smiled gently. "You look better today." She felt his forehead. "I believe your fever has gone almost entirely."

He nodded. Her very nearness excited him. The gold bracelet on her slender white wrist flashed in the bright sunlight as she took her hand away. If she were his wife, she would kiss his forehead rather than just lay her hand on it. The futility of his thoughts made him uncomfortable. His eyes left her face to concentrate on the figures painted on the screen at the end of his bed. He swallowed and plucked at the edge of the covers. "I must be up and about my lord's business else I lose my position. I grow soft lying here being tended by those I should tend."

"Shall I step around the corner of the screen and let you rise?" she asked sweetly.

He looked at her quickly, catching her amused tolerant smile. "Oh, aye. I remember your face not so long ago when you waited for me to prove to myself that I could not rise, but you are wrong this time. I am gaining strength by the hour. A few more of these drinks, and I shall be ready to return to my work."

"Are you then so unhappy being cosseted a little?"

He drew a deep breath. "I have never been treated so well," he told her softly. "Never in my life have I been more content

157

despite everything."

"Then linger with us. Take a well-deserved rest."

He shook his head, his voice stern. "'Twill make it all harder to return to my room and my life."

She smiled. "You are not returning to that room, Geoffrey. I have had your things moved to a room down the hall from my lord's. You will live in a room with heat and light." His mouth opened to protest, but she raised her hand. "I have asked this of Brittany, and he has agreed. 'Tis already accomplished. Your old things are folded carefully in a chest at the end of a new long bed, more appropriate for your height. Furthermore, you have several new garments. We ladies felt that you had too few clothes and those not of such good quality as befits a loyal vassal."

"I am not a vassal," he protested grimly. "I am a bastard."

She shook her head. Rising, she laid a hand upon her forehead as she bent to take the posset from his hand. "Rest," she soothed. "All that is past. You have tired and excited yourself. I did not mean to make you argue."

When he would have protested further, she placed her fingers over his lips. Their tips were cool and soft. He had to steel himself to keep from kissing them. "When I leave, pull your sheets aside again," she instructed him. "You have not yet had your full two hours in the sun as Brigitte bade."

"You will have me so dark I will be taken for an Egyptian," he protested faintly.

"With your hair?" she scoffed. "I assume that you are practicing for the position of court jester."

He chuckled. As her bright skirts disappeared around the side of the screen, he threw back the covers. It was true that his skin had acquired a light tannish cast. He wondered idly if she would prefer his body pale or dark. That is, if she ever saw it. Would she be as attracted to him as he was to her? Would she want to kiss him and touch him in intimate places as he . . . He broke off this train of thought when he realized that he was sweating and aroused, and glanced hastily at the screen.

He really must control his thoughts. Someone was going to come across him in this condition and suspect his secret, but the pain of wanting her grew more intense every day. Mingled with that pain was the knowledge that in all probability he would never touch her again. He set his face in stern lines and closed his eyes. The sun warmed a visage of cold determination.

Therefore, before he could walk easily, he resumed his duties with the duke. If Brittany noticed the paleness under Geoffrey's newly acquired tan, the pinched look about his lips and nose, he made no demur. The valet who had been lifting and dressing him while Geoffrey recuperated had seemed more ham-handed with each passing day, whereas Geoffrey knew his master's body as well as his own. Brittany's swollen joints were not jerked or twisted by Geoffrey. Though the duke welcomed the youth back with only a formal acknowledgment, he sighed with relief when familiar skilled hands helped him to his chair and made his leg comfortable on the ottoman.

The term of Joanna's pregnancy was nearly up. The best midwives in Brittany had been summoned. The ducal bedchamber had been prepared for the lying-in. Members of the court had been ordered to be ready at a moment's notice to attend the birth. All was in readiness.

Joanna looked forward to the event also, but for quite different reasons. Her body was unwieldy; her stomach, enormous. Three inches below her navel extending to the top of her thighs, her skin was a tortured mass of flame red lines. All the nostrums of Doña Isabella, all the massaging by Brigitte had been to no avail. Her taut young skin had split rather than stretched.

She tried not to think about those marks, but she could not forebear the occasional tear as she sat in a chair beside a tub of warm water and sponged herself with a cloth. Doña Isabella would no longer allow her to sit in the bath water. She was short of breath, her swollen breasts ached, and the babe kicked and plunged so that she could get no rest.

The duke watched her like a hawk, insisting that she spend several hours a day in his room off the audience chamber. At table he selected the food that she ate and even had Geoffrey cut her meat. From the Isle of Jersey in the English Channel, he had imported a special cow whose milk was reputed to be the richest in cream. After its arrival, he insisted that she eat a small dish of the clotted stuff each night. Every bite brought on shudders of revulsion, but Montfort was adamant. She was too small and thin. The babe would not be strong.

So she ate, while within her hatred grew and festered. What she desired was of no consequence. Everything was for the babe—the heir. She was a vessel, of about the same importance as a wine keg. No one cared about the keg, only what was inside it.

Sometimes to spite Montfort, she would feign illness, so she could not come to the table. When he would have a meal brought to her room, she would dispose of it in the chamber pot. At such times, she giggled triumphantly while she scraped her plate. Later, when hunger pangs bothered her in the middle of the night, she hid her face, ashamed of her childishness.

Late in February her pregnancy became so advanced that she could hardly find comfort in any position. Her ankles were swollen; her breasts ached. Then the babe dropped noticeably.

Doña Isabella greeted the change in Joanna with great excitement. "We must hasten to His Grace with the news," she crowed. "He will not have long to wait."

"Doña Isabella!" Joanna exclaimed. "Do not say anything to him until I am showing more positive signs."

"Nonsense, this babe will come whether you will it or no. The father-to-be is already excited. Keep him interested. He will feel more charitable toward you if you share these things with him."

"I do not care for his charity."

"Then you should." Doña Isabella's face hardened. "He holds the power of life and death over you. Your fate hangs here on this child. If you produce a male heir, then all will be well for a time. If the boy is healthy, you will be rewarded as his mother. You will be consulted in his education. You will be able to exert a powerful influence on him." Raising her voice dramatically on the word *powerful,* she looked expectantly at Joanna.

Tired of the endless harangue and more than a little uncomfortable because of the strange griping sensation that she had just experienced, Joanna pressed her forehead against the heel of her hand.

"I will bring him the news immediately," the duenna insisted triumphantly as if her cogent arguments had changed Joanna's mind. Without a backward glance, she stalked out.

Angrily, Joanna swept her hand across the dressing table, knocking the combs and brushes, the pots and jars across the room. Her word counted for nothing now. Nothing! Isabella did not deceive her. If her word counted for nothing while she carried the heir, it would be worth less than nothing when her duty was executed.

Furious with rage, she stared at the looking glass shattered into bits that lay amid powder, blobs of rouge, and the clear liquids spattered across the floor. The combined scents of rose, jasmine, hyacinth, and of the heavier ambergris-based musk, which she did not use, were overpowering. A sob rose in her throat and was stubbornly swallowed. She would not cry. Not a tear.

Pushing herself out of her chair with incautious speed, she swayed dizzily as black spots swirled before her eyes. Another tightening of the muscles across her belly startled her with its strength. She gripped the edge of the table with

161

one hand and her belly with the other.

With a shudder she realized what was happening. Brigitte had told her in a private moment. This was the first sign that her babe would soon be born. Within a few hours, a few days, or perhaps a week the old woman had said. Joanna's muscles were at work without her behest, turning the babe and positioning him head down to be born.

Panic struck her, then hot rage. Even her body, her very own body was not her own. She had not the power to bid her muscles relax and wait. Her body would act of its own volition. She would be rent asunder as if she were a mindless, emotionless blob.

She had never felt so angry, nor so helpless in her life. Her black eyes were sparks of ebony fire in her white face. As she stared wildly about, the power of her emotions set her trembling from head to foot. Sharp pain lanced her between the eyes. At the same time her stomach roiled ominously.

As suddenly as they had come over her, the violent emotions faded. She must at all costs preserve control of her mind. Her mind was her last refuge. When all around her were forcing their will upon her, in her mind she was still free. She would never surrender that last bastion.

Drawing a deep calming breath, she made her way a little unsteadily to the outer chamber to ring for a maid. She would have the mess cleaned up and be about her business. Let Doña Isabella and the duke chuckle and plan. She would not join them.

With icy calm she faced the duke an hour later. Excitement crackling in his voice, he barked peremptorily, "*La garce* Isabella reports you are near your time."

Joanna did not flinch at the epithet bestowed on her duenna. Privately she thought the woman a bitch and more, but her mask firmly in place, she shrugged. "So she tells me, my lord."

He regarded her steadily. "Come here."

Steeling herself, she maintained her position.

162

"Come here," he repeated coldly. "I intend to feel for myself this tightening of which she speaks." When she did not move, he shook his head disgustedly, muttering a foul oath between his teeth. "Before God, woman, I am your husband. That babe got there because I touched your body. Come here."

Her hands clenched behind the folds of her dress. "What is it you wish to know, my lord? I will be happy to confirm or deny."

He crooked his knobby finger at her. "Come, Joanna," he wheedled. "Geoffrey! Bring the jewel coffer." He tossed the key over his shoulder with an irritated gesture.

His face pale, his eyes blank, Geoffrey rose from his stool in the shadows. Bending, he retrieved the key without a glance at the duchess.

Joanna raised her hand. "I do not want a jewel, my lord." Her voice trembled slightly.

"Well then, what do you want?" he barked in exasperation.

"I want to be left alone. I do not want to be felt of like a fruit in the market."

Dark red stained Brittany's high cheekbones. "What you want with regard to my son is of little consequence, madam!" he roared furiously. He struggled to rise from his chair, his anger making him incautious. Geoffrey straightened from getting the coffer from the chest to see the duke tottering on unsteady legs. Too far away to reach his side, the young man could only watch helplessly as the weak arthritic limbs gave way.

Like a tree Brittany fell forward, his hips too stiff in the joints to move properly. He put out his hands to catch himself, but his fall was hard nevertheless. Horror-stricken, his valet saw him measure his length on the floor in front of his defiant wife.

His scream of pain and rage was awful to hear. Joanna clutched her belly protectively. As she did, she felt a viselike

163

contraction push downward. Her small cry of distress was, however, drowned by her husband's curse. "Bitch! Black Navarrese bitch!" Instead of using the French, he yelled at her in his accented Spanish, making clear his anger at her.

In an instant Geoffrey knelt by his side, grasping the bony shoulders and pulling the duke to a sitting position. "Your Grace. Do not excite yourself so."

Recovering himself, the duke's rage turned to ice. "Get me up, Geoffrey," he commanded. The operation took at least a minute, during which time his eyes never left his wife's white face. "Bring me wine," was his next command.

When that was done, he stared at his wife as he would a rabbit wriggling in a snare. "You are foolish, Joanna. Most foolish. A wise wife would have gladly accepted the jewel I was about to offer and would have granted her husband his small pleasure. But *you!*..." The pronoun thundered throughout the quiet room. Despite herself, she jumped as did Geoffrey. "I have been uncommonly lenient ..." he began.

His words dropped off as she experienced another contraction. It drove her to her knees, her small cry of mingled fear and pain clear in the room.

What Jean de Montfort might have threatened was forgotten by both men as she clutched her belly and lifted frightened eyes to Geoffrey. "Please," she whispered. "Will you help me to?..."

"To the ducal bedchamber," Montfort commanded peremptorily. His face broke into a smile as his anger was forgotten. "Carry her there forthwith. Then summon her women, the midwives, the physician. As soon as they are with her, give instructions to the butler to see that all is set in motion." He laughed triumphantly. "My son is about to be born. I want witnesses—many witnesses to the event."

"Can you put your arms around my neck?" Geoffrey whispered as he bent over her.

She shook her head, her teeth biting down hard on her

bottom lip. "Help me to stand, Geoffrey," she commanded.

"But, Your Grace . . ." he protested, looking anxiously over his shoulder at Brittany. Within the pit of his stomach was a cold, sick fear for her.

"Help me to stand," she repeated, clutching at his arms. "Brigitte says I should walk for as long as I can. 'Twill make the babe come faster and more easily."

Doubtfully, his hands cold and trembling, he helped her to her feet.

Brittany studied them anxiously. "Damn what that old woman says. What about the midwives I have engaged for you? What do they say?"

Joanna threw him a withering glance. "I have not heard, my lord. They have spent their time in the kitchen and servants' common room drinking and swilling food. Both are excellent trencherwomen I have heard it said." Straightening herself carefully, she turned and walked toward the door with slow but steady steps.

Behind them Brittany called angrily. "Mind what I said, Geoffrey. Have the butler summon the witnesses and prepare the feast."

At first as Joanna labored, she clenched her teeth to hold back the cries of pain, determined not to entertain the many lords and ladies assembled on the other side of the room. The gathering became larger as the evening grew later. While many reckoned that their convocation was premature given the eagerness of the duke and the youth of the duchess, they dared not risk missing the event. Furthermore, the Lucullan quality of the feast with its gourmet dishes and excellent wines was an added inducement.

A great fire had been built in the fireplace, and the entire room was ablaze with light. To Joanna's perspiring body it was uncomfortably warm. Servants entered bearing trays of food and wine, and left carrying away the platters already emptied by the laughing, joking guests.

Since the wine and ale flowed madly in celebration, people became more and more noisy. A lutenist was summoned to play cheerful music and several couples found time to dance a few measures before their drinking drove them to sprawl ungracefully in the many chairs brought in for their rest.

The midwives hired by the duke made a great show of caring for their charge, running to and fro with commands for the lesser servants. At first they took turns informing the duke and the assembled company as to what they perceived to be the progress of the birth. Unfortunately, as the evening wore on, the company grew more drunken; so the announcements ceased to create any interest. At that time, the midwives themselves began to tipple at the wines so that both were in a daze by midnight.

Brigitte calmly slipped up to the one who lolled back in her chair dozing beside her charge. "I will take a turn," the old woman whispered. "From the look of her, 'twill be a long watch. Generally with first babes, the young body takes its own time. And she *is* very young. You must be well rested when the young count arrives."

The midwife stirred sleepily. "You are right," she agreed. She cast a glance at Joanna, who lay perfectly still, resting between contractions which had slowed to a remarkable degree. Recognizing the lack of activity, she shrugged. "'Tis just as likely to be a false alarm, but if the babe does not come by afternoon tomorrow, I will purge her." She glanced at the laughing duke. "He will grow angry if his heir does not put in an appearance within a reasonable length of time."

With that pronouncement, the woman took herself off to her bed, leaving Brigitte to wring water from a cloth and begin to sponge Joanna with its cooling wetness. "Now, my pretty," the old woman crooned. "Close your sweet eyes and rest. Sleep if you can." Just then one of the servants dropped a tray at the door and the loud crash made Joanna jump. "Men!" the old woman sneered over her shoulder. "What do

166

they know?"

"Might I have a drink, Brigitte?" Joanna's lips were cracked and swollen where she had clamped down on them.

"Aye, my pretty." Brigitte patted her hand reassuringly. She signaled to Geoffrey, who had stationed himself purposefully in the corner where he could see the bed and its occupant. He lunged across the room, his forehead wrinkled in alarm, but Brigitte intercepted him. "Bring snow," she instructed him. "A nice bucket of fresh snow—and look you, be sure to get it from a spot that is fresh and windswept. Do not dip it up from near the side of the building where it may be contaminated with soot from the chimneys. She needs a cooling drink. Poor little one. This room is much too warm for such hard work as she must do."

Geoffrey was off like an arrow and back in a surprisingly short time. "How is she?" he inquired of Brigitte.

"Resting," the old woman replied. She cast a dark look in the direction of the drunken witnesses. To a man they were either sprawled unconscious or reeling where they sat. "'Tis an old man's foolishness to set up a celebration in the birthing room. Babes have their own times and 'tis bad to try to hurry them." Her eyes narrowed angrily as she stared at the other midwife now sleeping upon a pillow across the room.

"But the duchess is all right?" Geoffrey insisted.

"Her, bless her. Yes. She be thinner than she should be, but that may be for the best. In my experience the woman who eats like a sow has trouble getting an overfat baby born safely."

Geoffrey blushed and shifted uncomfortably at the old woman's blunt speech. "Will it be a long time yet?"

"Probably," Brigitte nodded. "See. The sweet one has fallen asleep."

Geoffrey would have turned away to resume his post when her hand on his arm stopped him. "Look you. That toad's cousin that I replaced here talked of giving a purge to hasten the birth. Think you, you can prevent her coming back with such?" She eyed Geoffrey narrowly.

At his look of worry, she gave him a disgusted look. "She helped you," she reminded him. "She came for me when the surgeon had sewn you together and covered your wounds over with God knows what fearful stuff. You must help her now."

He nodded glancing in the direction of Brittany. The duke had fallen asleep in his chair. "I will see that she is the one who wakes up to a glass of wine with a purge in it," he grinned. "'Twill keep her too concerned about herself to worry about my lady." He started for the door, then turned back. "Shall I fix enough for the other?"

Brigitte chuckled. "'Twould do no harm. Doubtless all this wine and food has made them choleric. A purge is very soothing to such, I understand."

So both midwives spent the better part of the next day squatting over the jointed stools in the chamber assigned to them.

And the good dame Brigitte held Joanna's hand as the pains began to come the next day. "Draw the curtain across the front of the bed," she instructed Geoffrey with an angry look in the direction of the duke, who had rested most of the night in his chair and had now begun to break his fast. "She must pull her legs up and bear down. She needs no distractions. 'Tis a sin against her womanhood to put her on public display."

Geoffrey closed the curtain and then returned to the other side of the bed. At about eleven o'clock servants had brought a meal for all to break the fast. Now the valets and maids of the various gentlemen and ladies were bringing refreshing draughts. One man even called for a basin and bowl for his man to shave him.

"Bear down, my pretty," Brigitte counseled on the other side of the curtain. "Take a deep breath and yell." She clasped the young woman's thin hand, as the duchess arched

168

her back. On the other side of the bed, Geoffrey caught Joanna's other hand.

"You should not be here," Brigitte scolded.

"Yes," he replied simply. "I should." His gray eyes were bright with tears as Joanna threw her head back on the pillow and yelled at the top of her lungs.

Chapter 10

Jean Charles Godefroy Louis Philippe de Rennes, Marquis of Brest and lord of the newly acquired fief of Roche-Bernard was born in the midafternoon. The exhausted lords and ladies hailed his coming with joyous cheers. A lavish round of toasts to his health was drunk before the company retired quickly to their various bedrooms to sleep away the effects of the thirty-hour vigil.

Dame Brigitte presented his nude squalling form to his father, who counted the arms and legs, the eyes and ears, the mouth and nose, and happily observed the tiny pink worm at the botton of the small stomach. Almost beside himself with elation, he ordered the old woman to take the newborn count to his nursery.

"Geoffrey!" he called loudly. "Accompany this . . ." He paused scowling. "You are not one of those I hired."

Brigitte became very busy wrapping the blankets about the tiny limbs in such a manner that he would not kick them off and take a chill.

Geoffrey stepped forward. "Doubtless there is an explanation, Your Grace, but let us not delay this woman. She has proved herself a competent nurse."

The duke shrugged. "Oh, yes. Instruct Lady Marguerite to

171

oversee the servants in the nursery. Accompany this woman thither and return to help me to my bed." He gazed around him, suddenly remembering that his usual bed was occupied. "Select a bedchamber for me. Sweet Jesu, but I am tired. 'Twas a long vigil."

"Shall I have Thierry see you to your chamber?" Geoffrey waved his hand in the direction of the man who had been his substitute.

"Who?" Now that the excitement and suspense had ended, the duke looked exhausted. "Oh . . . perhaps so. That way I could get right to bed." He stared down at his right leg. "Swollen to twice its size," he commented. "Yes. Come here, you clod. Careful with that leg."

As Geoffrey hurried Brigitte out, he heard the duke cursing the unfortunate Thierry.

The halls of the château were icy cold, impossible to heat in winter. Putting his hand under the nurse's arm, Geoffrey trotted her to the nursery. There all was in readiness. A rush basket with clean sheets, blankets, soft pillows, and warm bricks welcomed the young lord into the cold world.

When he was safely deposited, Brigitte turned to Geoffrey. "I must return to her," she insisted sternly. "Not one person gave a thought to my lady. She may be lying there in her own sweat and blood. The afterbirth will have come and no one to receive it. The poor sweet child."

"But surely—"

"Did you see anyone give a care for her?" The old woman snorted in disgust. "They all went off to take their sweet rest—after she did all the work."

Geoffrey looked around the nursery with its full complement of servants cooing over the sleeping babe. "You are right. But do you dare to leave him?"

Brigitte stopped. A worried frown added to her wrinkles. "Perhaps not. The first hours after birth are the most dangerous. Once in a great while the little ones forget to breathe. Someone must watch them constantly."

"You stay with him," Geoffrey decided. "I will fetch help for her."

"Get someone other than those stupid toads. Where is the dark one?"

"She retired to sleep long ago." He patted Brigitte's thin shoulder. "Never fear. I will get someone to take care of her."

His search for competent servants to make Joanna comfortable proved more difficult than he had at first imagined. Since all of her attendants as well as Doña Isabella had been present at the birthing, they were one and all now sound asleep, most too drunken to be roused.

Likewise, the servants in the kitchen had joined in the celebration, reasoning rightly that their duties would be foregone that night. Searching the château with increasing concern, Geoffrey found no one to help him. Every single person was incapable of practical action except the women in the nursery in charge of the babe.

At last he returned to the ducal bedchamber. The huge fire had died to glowing embers; the temperature in the room was much colder. Ignoring the mess on the tables and the crazed arrangement of chairs, he went straight to the bedside. The condition of the bed and of its occupant made him swallow quickly to suppress his rising gorge.

The duchess had been neglected by all. Every servant in the room at the birthing must have done as he and Brigitte had been forced by the duke's command to do. They had left her lying, as if she were of no consequence, in the bloodstained welter of towels and sheets that remained after her labor.

Such neglect was nothing short of treason, yet the pattern for it had been set by the duke himself, who had apparently forgotten his young wife in the excitement of his celebration. Softly Geoffrey began to curse.

Joanna had had the strength to pull herself to the other side of the bed after she had expelled the afterbirth. She had drawn the thin covers over her and was now huddled in a tight ball in one corner.

Coming around to her side, he dropped down on his knees. His eyes, on a level with the bed, took in the paths that tears had traced on her cheeks. Her face was flushed. Timorously, he touched the back of his hand to her forehead. Her fever was already beginning.

She needed to be bathed and changed and put into a clean bed with warm bricks around her feet. She needed services performed for her that he could not guess at.

In anguish he rubbed his hand across the back of his neck. Heir or no, she must have Brigitte. That woman was the only one who could help her.

The thought was mother to the act. In record time he had brought Brigitte to the bedside, where the old woman moaned and wrung her hands in pity. Together they found sheets and cleared the mess away. The first mattress beneath her body was likewise soaked, but the second was clean.

While Geoffrey cradled the feverish girl in his arms, Brigitte made the bed. "Now, let me sponge the poor sweet while you find a nightshirt from among His Grace's things," she instructed. When he brought it, she bade him turn his back while she worked it down over Joanna's body.

"You are being silly, Brigitte," he chided. "I sat beside her the whole time. Her body is no secret from me."

She snorted. "'Tis one thing to look on a suffering, laboring body, young man. The look is one of pity. 'Tis quite another to look at a slim sleeping lady. That look . . . well . . . you could die for that look."

While he acknowledged the truth of her statement, he had to bite his lip to still his own eagerness for the sight of Joanna. The few minutes he had held her in his arms had revived all the old longings. She was the woman he loved. He wanted to see her as she was now that she had borne the fruits of that love. Was she much changed? Was she as slender as before? He greatly feared that she might be even thinner, for she had been perilously thin all through her pregnancy.

Moreover, he wanted to assure himself that she was well. The sight of the spots of color riding her cheekbones worried him more than he cared to think. What if she died? Many women died, almost one half at their first lying-in. He had never quite understood how that could happen, but now with the babe born healthy and strong and the mother burning with fever, he understood it as never before. Grimly he set his teeth as he recalled the criminal neglect that had been her lot. Immediately after the birth all attention had centered on the heir with such suddenness that no one had even been assigned the duty of making the duchess comfortable and clean after her labor.

"What can we do for her?" he asked shakily.

"Her fever will go higher," Brigitte predicted in a calm voice. "Take the bucket and get more snow. When you have brought it, I must return to the nursery. I do not really fear that the babe will be neglected but that he will be disturbed by overmuch handling by those trying to curry favor with the duke. You must wrap snow in cloths and put them on her wrists and forehead, to keep her fever down. Put them on her neck too if the fever seems to go too high. Get her to eat it every time she asks for water. Spoon it down her. 'Twill keep her cool until the fever burns itself out." Her instructions given, Brigitte drew a deep tired breath.

Observing her, Geoffrey remembered that she was a frail old woman who had not been to bed herself in more than twenty-four hours. "You need rest yourself," he told her softly.

She gave him a weary smile. "I napped between pangs, just as she did. As you get older, you will learn to husband your strength." She turned back to the bed and straightened the clean sheets. "Off with you now. Bring back that snow, so I can get to the nursery. Some of those women are so anxious to impress the duke that they would drag the babe up and down the hall all day long presenting him to his father."

In the wee hours of the morning, Joanna awoke. Her body was so sore she could scarcely move. Her thighs felt as if they had been beaten with sticks while the burning ache between them made her want to cry.

Her tongue was dry and stuck to her lips when she tried to lick them. "Water," she croaked in a flat whisper with only a thread of resonance.

A movement beside her drew her eyes down her body. In the dim light that came from the fireplace, she could discern Geoffrey's disordered silver head as it shifted restlessly beside her hand. Managing to raise her own head off the pillow, she stared in wonderment at the ruffled but nevertheless distinctive hair.

Why was Geoffrey sleeping in her bed? That is, not exactly in her bed, but sleeping with his head on it? He should not be anywhere near her bed. Where were her ladies? Where had everyone gone?

Dropping her head back onto the pillow, she groaned. She could not remember the pain, but the discomfort of her body made her remember the hard work. She had never sweated or strained so hard in her life. Then they had taken the babe away. She raised her head to look around her.

A wry smile curled her lips. She did not even know whether she had borne a boy or a girl. No one had bothered to tell her. She would be angry if she were not so weak and thirsty. With a grimace she pulled her hand and arm from under the covers and touched the top of Geoffrey's head. His hair was soft and springy. Like a live thing, it curled over her fingers.

"Geoffrey," she whispered throatily. "Geoffrey."

He groaned. One hand lay on the coverlet beside him. He rubbed it over his face and batted it about his head.

"Geoffrey." This time she spoke a little louder.

"Your Grace?" he mumbled. "Coming, Your Grace."

Clearly, he thought himself answering Brittany.

"Geoffrey, please fetch me some drink."

176

He raised his head to stare into her face without recognition. His own eyes were slitted in the dimness. "Wha? . . ."

"Water, Geoffrey, or some cool wine?"

Abruptly, his eyes opened wide. "Your Grace, Lady Joanna!" He sat bolt upright. His sudden movement toppled him off the stool. With a virulent oath he sprawled sideways on the floor.

She rolled over and hung her head over the side of the bed. "Be careful." She chuckled.

He looked so comical in his rumpled clothing, and she needed a bit of a laugh. He grinned at her when he saw her smiling. "How may I serve you?" He tugged at his forelock in mockery of a lower servant.

"Is there some water?" she asked for the third or fourth time.

He climbed stiffly to his feet. His limbs had been doubled under him on the small uncomfortable stool. Now they refused to obey his commands. "I have snow for you," he told her.

She had not known how thirsty and hot she was until she let him feed her the snow. She felt a little like a baby, eating snow, but she could not argue with the way it melted in her mouth, cooling her body at the same time it slaked her thirst.

"Did the duke get his heir?" she asked at last.

A flush rose in Geoffrey's cheeks. "You do not know?" he asked.

She turned her face away. "I would not ask if I did," she muttered angrily.

"A fine boy. Beautiful." Geoffrey frowned. He could not remember a single distinguishing feature about the babe. Brigitte had caught it as it slid from Joanna's body and she had carried it to the fire where she had wiped it dry and swaddled it. "Very healthy," he finished lamely.

She turned back to him, her face grim. "How nice. I am sure my lord was pleased."

"Oh, yes. He had the babe taken to the nursery immediately."

She was so tired. "Thank you for the snow," she murmured. She could not hold her eyes open. She closed them and allowed herself to be welcomed into oblivion.

Geoffrey touched her cheek. She seemed much cooler now. He smiled wearily. She would be better tomorrow. She was young and strong. Better still, she was a fighter. She would recover completely. He set the bucket to one side and stretched his back and shoulders. The pallet arranged for the midwife invited him. Stumbling over his own feet, he stirred up the fire, added charcoal, and slumped down beside the bed. Almost instantly, he fell asleep.

The christening ceremony took place three days later. Though she was hobbling around her own apartment, Joanna informed the messenger from the duke that she was unable to rise from her bed as yet.

Therefore, she wore a small secretive smile when she was borne into the audience hall in a litter. Beside the duke's chair, a couch had been prepared with four feather cushions covered in forest green velvet and tasseled with gold. Doña Isabella and Geoffrey, substituting for the duke, helped her from the litter and supported her up the three steps to the dais.

Montfort sat beside her in his chair, his foot propped on the inevitable ottoman. Before them in his basket draped in green velvet and gold lay the new little marquis.

At the blare of trumpets, the babe screwed up his tiny face and began to wail. Immediately, Doña Isabella sank to her knees beside him and patted him ineffectually.

The duke's proud smile slipped slightly. Like all men, he knew little about babies and cared even less. He stared at the back of the waiting woman's head, willing her to perform her function and silence the noise that disturbed the christening.

178

After all was said and done, this was essentially *his* celebration of his manhood.

The bishop entered, preceding a procession of acolytes, priests, and monks, all chanting amidst swirls of incense and the tinkle of bells. The lords and ladies genuflected as he passed, adding to the confusion by the shuffling of their feet and the hum of their conversations.

A banquet had been set up on trestles across one end of the hall to serve the guests when the ceremony was over. Servants continued to carry in the food and drink while the bishop performed his offices.

The six gentlemen of the court who had been named to serve as godfathers came forward, each with a gift and an elaborate pledge of fealty.

Joanna was bored and caught herself wishing that she had pleaded weakness so she did not have to attend. The babe wailed almost without ceasing. Each time he would settle down to a quiet hiccupping, the trumpets would blare, disturbing him again.

Finally the last personage had performed his part and all were arranged in the assembly in order of their importance. The young marquis had at last cried himself to sleep. Doña Isabella had turned him over on his stomach and withdrawn, her face red with mortification. The duke signaled to Geoffrey, who assisted him to his feet and knelt beside him on one knee as was his duty. Steadying himself by placing his hand on his valet's shoulder, Brittany addressed the assembly.

"My friends and comrades in arms," the duke began. "Your presence here assures me of the peace and friendship we will continue to have here in Brittany. A man can count himself lucky if he has friends such as you to fight beside him." His eyes and his smile traveled over the faces of the men who had defended him the night of the insurrection.

"I also count my son lucky. For the same loyalty that defended me will defend him. Of this, he is too young yet to know, and some of you, like me, will be here only a short while to defend him." A general dissent swept the crowd as well-wishers objected to the duke's grim statement.

He held up his hand. "Therefore, it behooves us to reward young men also, men younger than ourselves who may guard and guide his steps."

The murmurs of dissent turned to puzzlement. Clearly the duke had some young man in mind, but who?

"On that night not long ago, when all of us here were banded together as brothers against a common enemy, one young man performed with extraordinary bravery and rare loyalty in defense of me and mine. I now reward him with that which is most precious to him."

He tightened his hand on Geoffrey's shoulder. "I name him who placed his own body in harm's way in defense of the duchess and the heir she carried." He gestured to the bishop who stepped forward again with his instruments for christening.

"I name him who has been nameless. Geoffrey Fitzjean d'Anglais."

Geoffrey's face went white. A concerted gasp arose from the assemblage, followed by murmurs of surprise and shock. The faces of many reflected anger and dismay.

"The bastard!" a woman's voice hissed.

Joanna sat up straight on her cushions, conflicting emotions mirroring themselves in her face. On the one hand, she applauded the reward that the duke had bestowed on Geoffrey. His loyalty was unquestioned. In all probability had he not rescued her she would be dead. The arrow that had caught him in the thigh had been aimed at her. Her sweet Lady Thérèse had died from another arrow. The rebels had made no efforts to spare women.

His face turned now in profile to her, his head bowed and eyes closed, Geoffrey pressed his palms together in an attitude of prayer as the bishop pronounced his name and poured blessed water over his silvery blond head. The drops trickled down his temples and spotted the coarse gray wool of his tunic.

After the bishop bestowed the blessing, Brittany motioned Geoffrey to his feet. Then, leaning heavily upon the young man's arm, he gestured to Joanna. "Come forward," he called to her.

Forgetting her role as invalid, she slipped her feet over the edge of the couch and rose. With sure steps, although slow, she took her place on the duke's left.

Brittany's strong voice rose over the attendants' hubbub. "Be it known that these are the nearest to me. Pay honor to Duchess Joanna, my wife, with whom I am well pleased and to my son, Jean Charles. Geoffrey, will you present him?"

Like a man in dream, or like one whose dream has come true, Geoffrey gently lifted the sleeping babe from the basket and cradled him in the crook of his arm. His solemn young face glistened where the christening water left its trails. Seeing him, Joanna felt unbearably moved as she realized that his cheeks also glistened suspiciously.

A fantastic desire formed in her mind. The sight of Geoffrey's handsome face and form suddenly stirred her unbearably. The infant in his arms seemed to fit as though he belonged there. Geoffrey's fair skin and pale silver hair shone like a halo in the light from the myriad torches. Standing straight and tall, his expression ascetic in its seriousness, he looked like the knight in every romance she had ever read. He was El Cid Campeador and Roland, Galahad, and Siegfried. Her breath caught in her throat as she felt a hot flush suffuse her cheeks. Such thoughts were dangerous, yet she could not contain them.

In a moment of blinding emotion, she longed for what she could never have. If only Geoffrey could be her husband standing here beside her, their child in his arms. Intuitively, she knew that Geoffrey loved her. He spent hours with her each day, walking, reading, talking. He had sat beside her, reassuring her during the fearful pangs when her son was

181

born. Likewise, she had awakened to find him lying beside her, his head on the bed, keeping watch over her in her darkest hours. Only cruel fate or accident made him a bastard and the duke of the blood royal. Her ebony eyes closed as pangs of desire curled in her belly. She dared not show her thoughts. It would have been better had she never thought them, for now she would have to live with them for the rest of her life.

At the sight of the duke, his duchess, and the heir together on the dais, the marshal gave the signal to the trumpeters, who blasted the air with their celebration. As the trumpets ceased, the voices of the assembly rose in a chorus of cheers. *"Vive Montfort! Vive le duc! Vive la duchesse! Vive l'enfant Jean Charles!"*

Immediately, Jean Charles awoke, starting fearfully in Geoffrey's arms. His face twisted and he was about to cry, but the valet touched the babe's cheek with his finger and spoke soothingly. As the cheers died away, the babe settled down, finding his tiny mouth with his thumb and sucking vigorously. With the formal part of the celebration at an end, a nurse came from the crowd of assembled servants and took the babe. Geoffrey smiled fondly into the tiny face before relinquishing Jean Charles into her arms.

Swiftly, Geoffrey moved to the duke's right side and assisted him to descend the dais. With his valet on his right and his wife on his left, Montfort managed a slow progress among his vassals, accepting felicitations from them as he passed. Some of the men offered cool congratulations to the newly named d'Anglais.

At the first mention of his new name, Geoffrey blinked. He had been merely Geoffrey for so long, he could not comprehend his new status. The lord who had spoken, a grizzled veteran from the Aurai campaign, clasped the young man's hand and clapped him on the shoulder. "Well fought, d'Anglais," he growled. "The duke knows well whom to honor."

Geoffrey was taken aback. No man had ever shaken his hand before. Certainly no man of such importance as the one now congratulating him. His humble gratitude pleased the assembly.

Thereafter, several men behaved in a like manner, until the small processional grew into a long one that finally arrived and arranged itself according to rank on the benches for the feast.

For the first time Geoffrey found himself actually seated at table. Though he sat among those of the lowest rank, nevertheless, he was served by others when he had always served. His status was exciting and frightening. He found he could eat nothing. All around him words buzzed in his ears, but he could make no sense of them. He had a name. He was Geoffrey Fitzjean d'Anglais.

The Fitzjean amazed him more than anything. He could not think what the duke meant by inserting it. The name was a corruption of the words *"fils de Jean"* or son of John. Did that mean the duke was adopting him? He shook his head slightly, smiling faintly at the fantastic idea. The duke now had a son. He needed to adopt no one.

No, the duke undoubtedly meant to accept him into the family as a sort of guardian uncle to the babe. Mentally, he vowed he would protect Jean Charles with his life. Otherwise, he would go on as before. He would sleep in the bedchamber beside the duke's. A bell system had been strung so that Brittany could ring to summon him at any time, night or day. He would continue to dress him, to bathe and shave him, to wait upon his needs.

But how different it would be. Now he had a name. He had been given the ultimate status. Both the duke and the duchess . . . The duchess! How did she feel about all this? A frisson of nerves prickled along his spine.

Joanna was a puzzle. Sometimes she acted as though she hated him; sometimes she behaved as though he were the best friend she had in the world. Covertly, he raised his eyes in her direction.

She sat at Montfort's left hand at the head of the table. A small page offered her a goblet of iced wine which she accepted eagerly. Her color was high. Was it his imagination or did she seem a little flushed? Should she be sitting here at the celebration, or should she be lying down resting from her ordeal? A worried frown creased his forehead.

At that instant she turned in his direction. Their eyes locked across the room full of people. He could not look away, even though he should not be looking at her at all.

She was too beautiful. Her skin, like warm cream, was a perfect setting for her exquisitely arched black eyebrows and her lustrous black eyes fringed by thick black lashes. The flush of color, he decided in that instant, was natural excitement, not a precursor of a fever. She had taken a sip of wine at the boy's behest. Now the tip of her tongue slipped from between her lips and licked away a shimmering drop of liquid.

Instantly, hot blood surged through his veins. He wanted her so badly that pain lanced along his thighs and his maleness began to throb. As hot color flooded his face, Joanna smiled at him. Lifting her goblet toward him, she offered a silent toast of congratulation to him before returning her attention to the duke who spoke impatiently at her side.

The gesture thrilled him immeasurably. Hot with unsatisfied lust, warm with love, he burned in delightful misery throughout the rest of the meal. When at last the feasting was over, he was able to slip away during the eternal rounds of speeches.

To his horror he realized that the extremity of his position had intensified. Now his loyalty to Jean de Montfort must be stronger than ever. Not only was the duke the man who had befriended him, he was also the man who had elevated him. He owed everything except his birth to him. His unknown father could have done no more for him than Brittany.

Further straining his emotions was his loyalty to the heir. The babe was his own son. A betrayal of Montfort would destroy the babe's position at the same time it would visit ignominy on his own flesh and blood. At all cost that must be prevented.

Finally, there was his love for Joanna. Sweat beads formed on his forehead as he thought of her. They had shared the most sublime experience that a man and a woman can know. Yet she was unaware that his were the hands that had caressed her and driven her to the ecstasies of which she was capable. Her first timid responses had progressed to erotic embraces under his tutelage, driving him wild and bringing him all the sensual pleasure he had known in his young life. How could he see her every day for the rest of their lives and never reveal his love and desire for her?

Like barbed hooks his thoughts sank into his flesh and into his mind. To leave them there would cause him constant pain, but to tear them away would tear great pieces from his body.

The room where he stood was dark and cold, as was the stone on which he leaned his forehead. He must return to the feasting. The duke would be needing him. Clenching his fists, he steadied himself with a dint of will. He would go on as before. He really had no other choice.

Chapter 11

The whole of October was an explosion of scarlet and gold. The grapes and hops were harvested. The very air was redolent of brews and fermentations. The forests around Rennes rang with the deep tones of hunting horns as foresters went out almost daily to bring in game to fill the larders of the château for the winter.

Joanna became an avid huntress. A deadly shot with a bow, she enjoyed moving cautiously among the trees or stationing herself in concealment along a deer path. To her delight she found she had the patience to wait for hours, scarcely moving, until her careless quarry came within range.

She did not like to ride. When she had mentioned that she had been on a horse but seldom, Geoffrey had offered immediately to teach her the art. But the height from the ground, the movement of the horse, the speed of a mount terrified her. Even riding to a part of the forest where the hunting was better was an ordeal.

She much preferred to tramp overland. For that purpose she had had the shoesewer make her heavy leggings that laced around the back of her legs and rose almost to midthigh. Then, when she and her escorts were out of sight of the château and Isabella's critical eye, she would pull the back of her gown through her belt in front and draw on the sides as she had seen peasant women do while working in the fields.

Joanna's long hikes caused little comment. The same two or three foresters, old and trusted men, accompanied her regularly, and Geoffrey went along when he was not needed by the duke. More than once he had objected to her going off alone with the foresters, but she had grown angry and had coldly reminded him in harsh terms that he had no right to gainsay her.

In the week before All Hallows, the weather had turned foul so Joanna dressed more warmly than usual as she prepared for the hunt. Accompanied by Clothere, the head forester, some days ago, she had caught sight of a particularly large stag with an exceptional rack of antlers. The majestic animal had stood poised in a misty vale a far distance across the river from her stand, and she had determined to hunt him. At last she would have a worthy addition to the huge racks that decorated the audience hall.

Her enthusiasm had not been dampened by the weather. Today, bubbling with excitement like the child she was, she rushed out of her rooms before any of her ladies could scold her.

In the back hall she met Geoffrey. Her bow and quiver gave away her plan, but she still tried to brush past him innocently.

He caught her arm. "You must not go today," he admonished her sternly. "The clouds are building, the wind is fierce. By noon we will have a storm that no doubt will bring freezing rain and sleet. The autumn is over. You will hunt no more this year."

Haughtily, she thrust her chin out. "If you will let me go, I will be back before noon. You are delaying me. Furthermore, you have no right to tell me what I will or will not do."

188

If he had been coaxing, he might have won. A quick glance at the weather might have convinced her of her folly, but his peremptory manner, coupled with her desire for the trophy, made her angry. "Clothere is waiting for me. We have sighted a magnificent stag."

"You will not go."

"No one tells me what to do except the duke, and he does not care whether I hunt or no." She twisted her arm free from his grasp. "Never touch me again in that manner."

"He would care if I went to him," Geoffrey threatened.

"Ah! The upstart lackey now admits to being a talebearer. I have known all along the reason why you were set to watch me so closely. At last I hear it from your own lips." Her eyes glittered angrily in the early morning dimness.

Her accusation angered him. He had never been a spy for Brittany, never once had he betrayed a single word that she had spoken to him. Following her down the hall, he caught her by the shoulder and spun her around. "You know that is not so. I have never . . ."

His hands had closed over her upper arms bringing her small lithe body tight against him. Now they stood breast to breast, their angry breathing creating friction between them. "I have never . . ." he repeated. He could not control himself. Her color was high, her lips red. Bending his head, he kissed her hard.

She had never had a kiss such as that. Instantly, she recognized it as a punishment for her angry words. He could not beat her, but his lips humiliated her more. Their hard pressure crushed her own before she gasped in pain. As her mouth flew open, he thrust his tongue into its velvet depths, drinking in the taste of her. He could not think. He could only feel, her breasts heaving against his chest and her mouth a sweet, warm cavity for his delectation.

Not a little mad, he let his hands slide from her arms to

189

her shoulder blades, then down her waist and over the smooth curve of her hips to cup her buttocks and press her hard against him. In that same motion he straightened his tall frame and thrust himself against her lifted body pressing himself into her so that they touched on all points.

"Geoffrey!" His rough handling frightened and offended her. Her husband, whose lovemaking was all she had ever known, had always been kind and considerate. His hands had moved gently, but knowingly, over her body arousing her slowly.

Geoffrey's hands and mouth were creating a firestorm that she could not control, but feared. Dropping her bow with a clatter, she wrenched one hand free and caught at his hair. With surprising strength she managed to tug his head back. His eyes were closed, his mouth agape.

"Geoffrey!" she hissed furiously. "Look at me!"

As if he were startled, his eyes blinked open to focus slowly on her face.

"Let me go!" Each word was spaced for emphasis.

Suddenly aware of what he had done, he set her body down as carefully as if it had been breakable. Then his hands dropped away as he stepped back silently. The tone of her voice and the expression in her angry eyes acted as a douche of ice water over his body. He had undoubtedly sealed his own death warrant. Inclining his head, he waited for the axe to fall.

"Pick up my bow!" she demanded imperiously.

Dropping to one knee, he caught it up and held it out to her with both hands.

"Look at me!" she snapped.

He raised his eyes.

Drawing her gauntlets from the broad belt at her waist, she slapped him hard across the face. "You will not touch me again. You will not gainsay me." She slapped him again. The gauntlets were made of heavy leather embroidered with

190

silver and gold threads across their backs. A gold French knot left a small scratch across his cheekbone.

Her eyes never left his face as she drew the gauntlets on one at a time and took the bow from his hands. Her eyes bored into him like black star sapphires. Then, swinging on her heel, she left him kneeling in the dark hall.

True to her word, she returned triumphant in the midafternoon. The wind was a hissing serpent, spattering its venom against the windows and doors, but her color was high. Oblivious to the cold, her heart pumping with excitement, she presented herself in the audience chamber accompanied by two of Clothere's assistants bearing the huge stag on a pole between them.

Banging on the door of her husband's study, she called him out. Scowling irritably at her disturbance, he hobbled to the door with Geoffrey's help.

"See, Your Grace," she caroled excitedly. "Meat for the tables for the Feast of All Saints and a trophy for the roof." She swept her hand toward the magnificent racks decorating the rafters above their heads. "Look! Sixteen points! I shot him with one arrow!"

Montfort regarded her display thoughtfully. "You go hunting frequently?" he questioned.

"Yes, Your Grace," she nodded happily. "But I have never gotten so majestic a stag as this before. Clothere and I saw him not too many days ago. I was determined to kill him."

His pale eyes measured her, guessing at the strong slender body the heavy mantle and fur lined boots concealed. "You appear to be in excellent spirits," he observed at last.

Something in his tone brought her up short. A little color drained from her face. Her voice faltered. "I . . . ah, yes, I am."

"And in excellent health."

She stopped stock-still. He was getting at something.

Instead of continuing with his observations, however, his eyes shifted to the patient men. "Take the duchess' kill and dispose of it appropriately." He dismissed them languidly. "The cooks will be most pleased with the additional meat, and . . . ah . . . Clothere can mount the rack as she requests."

As the men bowed and departed, he returned his attention to her.

"Thank you," Joanna began nervously. "Thank you, my lord. I will just excuse myself, if I may and wash away the —"

"Come into the private study," he said brusquely.

As he withdrew, her eyes flashed to Geoffrey. Her mouth hardened. Her lips formed an epithet that would have heated the air had it been uttered. Determined to betray him, if he had told tales on her, she followed her husband into the private study.

When the duke was seated comfortably behind his table, he motioned for Geoffrey to close the door. With that accomplished, the valet returned to his place behind the high-backed chair.

"You are completely recovered from your *accouchement,* my dear," Montfort observed. "If you can hunt every day and ride for hours—"

"I do not ride," she stated. "I walk."

"'Tis much the same." He dismissed the interruption with a wave of his hand. "You are capable of healthful exercise. Your body is strong once again."

She nodded shortly, knowing he was leading to something but not sensing the direction.

His eyes slitted momentarily as he watched her; then he raised one eyebrow. "It should be no problem to resume your duties as my wife."

Her eyes widened in surprise and horror. "But . . . but you already have your heir."

"I want more," he replied blandly. "Suppose, God forbid, something should happen to little Jean Charles. The death of infants is common. When he gets old enough to ride, what if he is thrown, his neck broken? What if he is injured while he is being trained to use weapons? Suppose he develops the sickness that binds the jaws together . . . the plague . . . inflammation of the lungs."

She retreated step by step before his grisly list. "I have done my duty," she begged piteously. "You have an heir."

"A wife's duty to her husband is to submit whenever he should desire her for the purpose that God created her for," Montfort intoned with mock piety.

She shuddered. Her eyes filled with tears, but she strove to hide them. Hanging her head, she pressed her body back against the door. "It is so painful," she murmured.

Montfort was silent a moment. "Ah, well. There is that, but think what pain the man endures for the sake of the woman. You do not have to fight, to suffer grievous wounds, to undergo the rigors and deprivations of war. A few short hours and your labors are ended."

Her head came up. "You have done none of those things for me," she accused angrily. "You do those things for yourself. Never wrap it in clean linen by saying that men make war for women."

His fist slammed down on the tabletop. "You will prepare yourself for my visit this very night," he thundered, "and for every night thereafter until you have proved you are quickening again."

"I will resist."

"Do so and expect to be beaten."

She clenched her fists at her sides. Her helplessness made her ill. The happiness she had felt only a few minutes before was totally forgotten in the face of this new horror. She clapped a hand over her mouth to avoid being sick before the eyes of these two men whom she now had cause to hate with equal virulence.

Feeling a bit uncomfortable before the real fear in her eyes, the duke sought to placate her. "'Tis not so bad the second time," he told her gruffly. "The way has been stretched by the first babe. You will not labor so long, nor suffer so much pain." Inwardly, he doubted the truth of his own words. She was a small slender girl still, and her labor had been protracted before.

His eyes shifting to the right and left gave him away. She saw that he was lying. "God forgive you," she moaned. "And God forgive me for whatever I have done to suffer so." Her hand found the latch behind her and pressed it down. Even as he looked at her again, she had fled.

Montfort's dry chuckle sounded odd in the room. "Ready, Geoffrey," he gritted softly.

The valet did not answer.

"Instruct Doña Isabella to give the duchess a sleeping draught tonight. She must not discover the substitution." A crook of his index finger brought Geoffrey to his shoulder. He twisted his face up to look into the silver gray eyes so close to his own. "If she should discover it," he mused silkily, "the results for you would be quite painful."

When Doña Isabella brought the mulled wine, Joanna stared into its depths angrily. "Is it drugged?"

"Merely a mild substance to relax you," the duenna replied stiffly.

"I will not drink it." Joanna handed it back.

The duenna pushed it forward under the girl's nose. "Do not be a fool. What did you expect? That he would be satisfied with one heir. That he would not want to play the man's part on you again, heir or no. You should have remembered that you are young, and men find you beautiful." This last comment was delivered in a derisive tone heavily laced with satisfaction. "We all have to pay for the gifts God gives us."

"Get out!"

"Not until you drink the wine, Your Grace. Your foolishness will cause you great pain someday. Woman is totally dependent on man. That is the way God made her to be. She is a part of His plan."

Joanna made a rude comment about God and His plan.

"Do not add blasphemy to your sins."

"Get out, I tell you!" Joanna rose from her stool in front of her dressing table. Brandishing her hairbrush, she stalked toward her tormentor.

"Put that down."

"No! The duke may have the right to tell me what to do, but you do not. Get out this instant!" The hairbrush hit the tankard of mulled wine, knocking it from Doña Isabella's hand and splattering its contents over the front of her gown.

The woman cried out in fear.

"Get out! Go on! *Hechicera! Vaya usted!*"

Doña Isabella hurried to the door. "You will regret this," she shouted.

"Go!" Joanna threw the hairbrush with all her might. It struck the wood an inch from Doña Isabella's head.

When the duke arrived with Geoffrey at the door of his wife's bedchamber, he found the door locked. Angrily Brittany ordered her to open to him.

"No," she begged. "Please, my lord. I will take the veil. I have given you the heir you wanted. Please."

"Did not that stupid witch give you the draught?" he growled.

"She tried, my lord, but I refused to take it. Please, let me take the veil. You can divorce me. My father will—"

"Charles will do nothing, but I will beat you to death."

195

Brittany's face was the color of dark wine. "Open this door."

Fearfully, she pressed her face against the paneling. "No!"

"Geoffrey," he demanded.

"Perhaps we should return tomorrow. I will see that she takes the potion tomorrow evening." His whole body ached with fear for her.

The duke's anger knew no bounds. With a wide swing, he struck the younger man across the face. "Do as I command you without question!"

"Yes, Your Grace." Geoffrey put his hand against the door. "My lady," he called gently. "Do not be foolish. You must submit. Open the door so we may have peace."

"No."

With a sigh, Geoffrey drew back and thrust his foot hard against the door just at the spot where the bolt was thrown. His force drove the old rusted screws from their holes. Another good kick pushed the barricade half across the room.

"My lord," he stepped back. "Do not . . ."

But Montfort was now in a towering rage. The very strength with which Geoffrey had knocked the door aside reminded him of his own puny condition. Once, he would have broken the door with the same ease and tamed the stubborn wench. Beneath him, she would have begged for mercy. His anger at his own inadequacy was transferred to the terrified but defiant Joanna.

Managing to stride steadily into the room without a sign of a limp, he advanced upon the cowering girl. "Your place, madam, is in that bed," he pointed angrily.

"No . . . please . . ."

"Geoffrey! Carry her to the bed!"

"No!" She drew her hunting knife from its scabbard. "If you have him touch me, I will cut him," she threatened.

The duke laughed mirthlessly. "Take that away from her, Geoffrey, and bind her hands behind her."

As she crouched, Geoffrey saw in her eyes hysterical terror too intense to be reasoned with. The knife was more dangerous to herself than anyone else. Untrained in combat, she held it with the point toward the floor. In the time she would need to draw it back, he would have her wrist pinioned and twisted behind her back. "My lady," he began softly. "Submit. You have no chance. We are two full-grown men against your frailty. Think, Lady Joanna."

Her eyes searched his face, seeking a friend. "Please," she quavered. "Oh, please."

Even as she spoke, he made his move. His hand snaked forward, closing over the back of her wrist and his thumb and third finger pressed hard against the nerves and tendons on the underside. Her fingers released their hold. The knife clattered to the floor.

Effortlessly, he jerked her into his arms, spinning her around to gather her other wrist into his grasp. The work was neatly done without struggle and without harming her. Over her head, his eyes met the duke's in silent communication.

Montfort grinned. "Bind her," he repeated.

With the sash from her nightrail, Geoffrey tied Joanna's slender wrists. All fight left her as she felt him jerk the knot tight. She stood trembling, head bowed, her shoulders touching his chest.

"Fetch a draught," Montfort commanded next.

When Geoffrey was gone, the duke limped closer to his wife. "You are foolish beyond belief." He lifted her chin forcing her to meet his eyes.

Through a fine film of tears, she defied him still. "You do not have to suffer as I will."

He dropped her chin and stood back. "You will have your children to care for," he reminded her. "Women love their children."

She shook her head. "Do you see my child near me? Have

197

you ever seen him beside me? He is nursed and cared for by a whole group of jealous women who hate the very sight of me for fear I might interfere in their routine and keep you from rewarding them for their good care of him. He will scarcely know my face by the time you are ready to send him away to some other noble house at the age of six or seven."

"That is your own choice," he replied. "You could assert your authority in the nursery. I would stand with you in whatever you decided for my son."

Again she shook her head. "I do not care. I just want to be left alone."

Even as the duke opened his mouth to speak, Geoffrey returned, bearing a small tray with a steaming tankard. His face was impassive, his silvery gray eyes opaque as pewter.

Brittany closed his mouth. With a nod to the valet, he turned his back on the proceeding and hobbled to a bench beside the fire.

Behind him, Geoffrey approached Joanna. "My lady," he crooned softly, as if he spoke to a fearful animal. "Drink this with good will. I promise, it has a pleasant taste."

Suddenly she welcomed the oblivion it promised. At least she would not have to feel the duke's hands on her body. When Geoffrey held it to her lips, she swallowed it without demur.

"Good," Montfort called out when Geoffrey took the tankard away from her lips. "Now bring her over here to sit beside me for a few minutes."

When Geoffrey escorted her to the bench, the duke put his arm around her. "Now, we will be like a pair of lovebirds." He chuckled, patting her shoulder and slipping his hand into the neck of her robe to feel her breast.

She tried to concentrate on the flickering flames and avoid all thoughts of his clammy hands.

However, Montfort was determined that she should not do so. Rather than order her beaten, he had decided to

198

punish her opposition himself. His fingers found her tender nipple and pinched it hard, and he dug his sharp fingernails into her flesh.

She cried out under his torment, but he used his other hand to turn her face up to him and silence her with his mouth. Helplessly, she writhed, held on the bench by the weight of his arm on her shoulder and his other hand on her neck. Her body excited him. But even as it did so, he felt himself trembling weakly. His arthritic hands pained him dreadfully as he expended more strength than he ordinarily did.

With a sigh, he released her.

Shocked and breathless, she swayed sideways and toppled off the bench onto the floor.

He touched her contemptuously with his foot. "Carry her to the bed, Geoffrey. She has learned her lesson for now."

Drawing herself into a ball, she tried unsuccessfully to hide her face. Then the younger man's strong arms closed round her and lifted her as in a cradle. When he gathered her against his chest, her head swam dizzily. Was it her imagination? Was she so drugged, or had his lips touched the top of her head? "Shall I untie her hands?" Geoffrey's voice seemed a long way off.

"Yes . . ."

She lay in the Stygian darkness created by the bedhangings as they closed round her. Geoffrey had freed her hands and covered her. Her head was buzzing; her lips felt dry and slightly numb.

"Best wait a few more minutes, Your Grace." That was Geoffrey's voice.

"Nonsense. She was practically unconscious when you lifted her."

She heard the rustle of clothing. Fear shot through her, briefly dispelling the clouds across her mind.

199

"Get on with it. Get it over. I am tired. My right leg hurts." The querulous voice kept complaining. What did it mean?

The curtains of the bed parted. A man's form was silhouetted for a brief instant. His weight pressed down on the bed. Then warm hands groped for her, found her.

She was pulled gently into his arms; a soft sigh escaped him as his breath warmed the skin of her face. Her muscles were overly relaxed from the effect of the drug, but she found the strength to raise her hand to his shoulder.

Gently, softly, with infinite care, he began to kiss her face. Where the tears had left their paths on her cheeks, his tongue licked them away. His magic fingertips massaged her temples even as he turned her face to his to kiss her lips.

Despite the drug or perhaps because of it, her body began to heat as his maleness came into contact with her femininity.

His mouth trailed lower down the slope of her breast to her abused nipple. With something like a groan, he touched it gently with his tongue, tasting the blood that besmeared its surface.

Her other hand found his shoulder and then the back of his head. His hair was just as she remembered it. But when? When? From the time before, when he had gotten her with child more than a year ago?

She rolled her head irritably on the pillow trying to drive back the shadows that swirled around her and threatened to overpower her. His head dipped lower to touch her navel with his tongue's tip. She shivered as the sensuality of her nature threatened to overcome her. The combination of that and the drug were too much to fight.

His tongue trailed down the center of her belly, following the line of tiny hairs, flicking them as it created excruciatingly pleasurable sensations. When his hands lifted her buttocks, her thighs fell apart bonelessly. As she moaned in her urgency, he raised her sex to meet his mouth.

As his tongue found the very core of her being, she cried from the depth of her throat, her hands burying themselves in his silken hair, the disordered silver hair that had curled around her fingers when she had lain deserted by all on the night her son had been born.

"Geoffrey!"

Chapter 12

Even as Joanna spoke his name, her ecstasy began. Tormented sublimely by his mouth and tongue, her inhibitions overcome by the drug, she shivered convulsively in his grip as wave after wave flooded her nerves. Unbearable sensations pulsated outward from her center of pleasure as Geoffrey caressed it masterfully.

Yet as she spoke his name, his own blood froze in his veins. Mechanically, he held her until she had finished, then lowered her to the bed. She had enjoyed the full scope of her womanhood before the drugs had overpowered her. He, on the other hand, was so overcome with fear that he could do nothing but tremble weakly.

The hangings of the bed were thrown back. "How did she recognize you?" The duke's voice was an angry growl.

"I . . . I do not know that she did. Perhaps? . . ."

"Enough!" The duke stood in silhouette, his face masked by darkness. "Come out of there."

"But . . . I have not . . ."

"Too bad," Montfort commented harshly, as he turned away.

A troop of guardsmen pulled Geoffrey from his room less

than half an hour after he had left the duke. Before he could protest, a sack was thrown over his head and a strap was fastened tightly about his neck. His hands were manacled behind him. Roughly he was dragged, stumbling, through halls and down steep flights of steps. As he felt the temperature drop, his terror increased. His escort was taking him to the dungeons below the château. When he tried to protest, a blow across the side of the neck silenced him.

At last he heard the grating of rusty metal on stone. The butt of a lance in the small of his back shoved him to his knees. Its point, pricking his hip painfully, prodded him forward. When he had crawled several feet on his hands and knees, he was halted by a tug on the strap around his neck. His manacles were attached to a ring in the floor. Footsteps shuffled away; the door grated closed.

He was alone in the icy darkness. Immediately he began to shiver. He had not had time to dress but had been taken away in only a thin lawn shirt, hose, and boots. The dungeon floor, located below the level of the Vilaine River, was brutally cold and damp. His thighs and buttocks began to ache almost immediately from the chill, yet he could do nothing but sit as he had been left.

The horror of his situation struck him full force. Would the duke leave him here to die with a sack over his head? Would the guards return at some future date and bury his body beneath the floor? He could not doubt the possibility of such a fate. Yet reason told him that he was being spared, at least for the time being, for something more horrible. A sob swelled in his throat and burst from his lips. He was most certainly going to die and for nothing of his own doing.

How long he lay in the darkness and cold, he could not imagine. Only the beating of his own heart and the expanding and contracting of his lungs provided any sense of rhythm or of the passage of time. It might have been hours or only minutes before the door grated open again. His jailers detached his manacles from the ring and dragged him roughly from the cell.

The room to which he was taken was much warmer. His hands were released from the manacles and instantly chained to a frame that stretched his arms over his head. At the same time cruelly efficient hands attached fetters to his ankles. His very soul quaked at the knowledge that he was about to be tortured. Someone unfastened the strap around his neck and lifted the edge of the sack. He felt a surge of gladness at the thought that he would be freed of its smothering effect, but the hiatus was short-lived. A thick gag was thrust into his mouth and tied tightly with another strap before the sack was dropped back into place and refastened tightly around his neck. Tears stung his eyes as he nearly strangled on the foul wad of cloth.

Gradually, he became aware that at least two other men were in the room besides himself. One breathed in a wheezy labored manner as if he had a congestion in his nose and throat. The other stoked the fire which blazed up in an orange glow discernible through the fabric.

The sound of a heavy door grating open caused the man beside Geoffrey to wheeze loudly. Then many feet were stamping and scuffling on the floor. A slap rang out followed by a grunt and a hissed curse.

"Tie her to the chair, lout." The duke's voice conveyed impatience and irritation. "Surely four strong men are sufficient to subdue one small girl."

Furiously angry, Joanna flailed her feet until her toe found the belly of one of the "four strong men." The fiery temper she had hitherto kept tightly in check lashed out in all directions. After an inordinate struggle for one so small, she was finally subdued.

The strap was unfastened from around her neck, and the bag pulled away. Blinking in the light, her eyes focused first on the duke's face which had a faintly amused expression.

"My father shall hear of this outrage," were her first words.

"Not unless he can hear what goes on in this dungeon at this moment," was the bland reply.

When she would have continued her tirade, he raised his hand. "Hold your tongue until I have dismissed the audience." He jerked his head in the direction of the two burly men who waited patiently for his commands.

At the sight of them, Joanna shuddered. Both were bare to the waist, and their bodies gleaming from the heat given off by the large firepit that blazed beneath a huge gridiron. A tripod bearing a brazier of charcoal stood close by. As they passed by her chair on their way out, the odor of their unwashed bodies made her gag. Their heavily muscled arms and chests were covered with greasy sweat.

The door clanged shut behind them and the duke lowered himself onto a chair facing Joanna. "Now, my dear wife," he said calmly. "Tell me what you intend to tell your father."

But Joanna had recovered her control. "I cannot think for what reason you have brought me here, my lord husband," she replied calmly. "But I assure you I do not find it humorous."

"I assure you I do not find your presence here humorous either." His pale eyes studied her face, so as not to miss even the flicker of an eyelid. "Last night—"

"It *was* Geoffrey!" she blurted.

The duke winced. Drawing a deep breath, he passed a hand across the lower half of his face.

She shook her head as if she could not believe what she knew to be true. "You sent Geoffrey to my bed. That is why you insisted that I be drugged. You—"

"How did you know, my dear?" he interrupted her gently.

She looked at him, puzzled. His voice was kinder than she had ever heard it. He had certainly never called her his "dear."

"His hair," she replied truthfully. "I touched his hair when he fell asleep on the side of my bed the night Jean Charles was born. Oo-o-oh!" Her eyes opened wide as the truth of

206

the heir's paternity dawned on her.

She sat in shocked silence for several moments. The fire sizzled and hissed. Gradually, her face changed as the import of her deduction dawned upon her. "There is no heir. I was put to bed with a bastard. A nameless English lackey." She shuddered. "Oh, God! The son you wanted so desperately is no son of yours at all. You tricked my father into supporting you. Damn you! Oh, damn you! You have degraded me and ruined me." She writhed helplessly in the straps. Her movements were totally ineffectual, for her wrists were tightly bound to the chair's arms. Another strap passing about her waist and around the back held her in her seat.

"Silence." He rose and hobbled toward her, bearing as little of his weight as possible on his right leg.

"You monster," she snarled. "When my father hears of this—"

Her words were cut off by a sharp slap across the cheek. Despite the pain, she did not cry out.

"You will listen!" the duke thundered. "You will listen to what I say as if your life depended on it, for believe me, my dear princess, it does. You have been bred to a strong, young stallion. Many a woman would envy you the pleasure he gives you. No, do not deny it. Do not shake your head at me. I have heard your moans and cries as he rides you."

"Beast! Monster!"

Without anger, he slapped her again. "Do not interrupt. The paternity of my child will never be questioned."

"When I tell—"

"But you will never tell, Duchess. If you do, you will disinherit your own son."

She fell silent as she considered that fact. "What is he to me?" she said at last. "I have no reason to love or cherish—"

The duke sighed impatiently. "Then you must be given a reason." Without further conversation, he hobbled to the door. Banging on it with his staff, he stood back as the two men entered. "Gag her and turn her chair," was his first command.

Moving with fearsome swiftness, one pulled a filthy wad of cloth from a pocket in his loose trousers. Even as Joanna opened her mouth to protest, she found herself roughly and unpleasantly gagged, her jaws distended and her tongue pressed flat against the bottom of her mouth. That action completed, the burly henchman lifted her chair by its arms and turned it around.

She stared in numbed horror at the sight before her. A man hung before her, chained and spread-eagled on a huge metal frame. She knew he was Geoffrey, although she could not see his face. But he was the duke's spy, his lackey—she stumbled over the distasteful thought—her lover. Why was he chained?

"Take off that sack," the duke commanded.

In an instant, Geoffrey hung, blinking, in the sudden light. His fair hair, wet with sweat, lay plastered in dark ringlets around his face.

"Now, lady," the duke hobbled to a seat beside the duchess. "You have his fate in your hands. He will never speak. He is utterly loyal to me, but your knowledge condemns you both."

Her eyes flashed obsidian fire at him as she defied him.

He smiled a bit sadly. "Begin!"

With the same hideous swiftness which she had observed before, one of the men stepped forward. His hammy fist stripped Geoffrey's shirt from his body with one violent ripping movement. Joanna closed her eyes at the sight of faintly tanned skin and of the long white scar where the sword had sliced it. Without warning, the duke pinched her sharply.

"Look, my dear. If a man is suffering for you, you should at least have the decency to look. When I led men into battle, I did not hesitate to look at their wounds."

Without a flicker of emotion the torturer tossed the rags of

208

the shirt to one side; then he seized the strings of Geoffrey's hose and ripped them apart, pushing the garments down over the young man's hips thereby exposing his torso completely.

Half fainting with shock, Joanna's eyes filled with tears at the shame and indignity of the whole proceeding. While she watched, Geoffrey's face flamed in embarrassment before paling to colorless gray as the first man stepped back and the second approached, a glowing iron in his hand.

"Bring it here," the duke called, his eyes never leaving her face.

When the iron was only a couple of feet from her, he continued his narration. "He is going to brand him," he explained with a sort of clinical detachment. "Once the brand is placed on his body, it marks him forever. Ordinarily, it is placed on the cheek or the forehead. Because I still have hopes that you will reconsider your decision, I shall order it placed on his belly. Look you!" He motioned the man closer, so that the cherry red iron was only inches from her own cheek. "It is in the shape of a B. It marks him as a prisoner of Brittany."

Her eyes grew wide with horror as she felt the heat radiating from it. He could not mean to use it. He was staging this entire drama to terrify her. It moved closer, even closer to her cheek. Straining to avoid it, she pressed her head back against the chair.

"Shall I use it?" the duke snapped, motioning the iron away.

Maintaining a stubborn silence, she glared at him.

"Just inside the hipbone . . . on the right," he instructed, his voice flat and cold.

Over the back of the advancing man, Geoffrey's eyes met Joanna's. His look said a thousand things, but none she could understand. A plea for mercy might have been there. But pride and horror and understanding might have been there too.

When the man pressed the iron into the flesh, Geoffrey's head snapped back and his whole body contorted against his bonds, seeking vainly to escape. From behind the gag came a high keening. The nauseating odor of burned flesh filled the air.

Joanna could not see the rest clearly, for tears overflowed her eyes and streamed down her cheeks. She felt as if she were strangling in their flood as Geoffrey's pain became her own.

Flinging her head from side to side, she dashed the tears from her eyes. Furiously angry and almost insane with frustration, she pulled at the straps on her wrists until she succeeded in tearing loose the entire arm of the chair. Bending to reach her mouth, she ripped away the gag. *"God damn you! What do you want?"*

The duke looked at her with renewed interest. "I want your promise that you will become the third person in our little game. My wants are as simple and as complicated as that."

She panted as if she had run for many miles. "And if I do not . . ."

"Then I will torture him until you do."

She shook her head. "You lie. You would not kill so loyal a man."

His pale eyes glittered in the flickering light. "You think he suffers this on my order to trick you?"

"Yes," she sneered. "He is well paid. He has a name now, who was once a nameless bastard."

Brittany stared at her for a long moment. Her strength pleased him at the same time that it irritated him. Inwardly, he condemned himself for creating this hideous situation, but he had no choice. The fates had damned him just as they had damned these two at his mercy. Drawing a deep breath, he jerked his head toward Joanna.

Silent and numb with horror, she felt the torturers' swift, efficient hands release the straps, then hold her in a hard, strong grip. Allowing her feet to merely skim the floor, they carried her to the empty frame which she had seen when she had first been unhooded. The speed of it, coupled with the flickering shadows and the hideous odors, created an atmosphere of unreality. She was in the midst of a nightmare. She would awaken from the drugged sleep to which the duke had subjected her to find this had not happened.

Chains! They clapped them tightly about her wrists, her ankles. She was spread-eagled just as Geoffrey was. His suffering face, his silver eyes slitted against the pain struggled to focus on her as his head leaned to the side resting on his updrawn arm.

It was not real. The sweat-streaked men stood aside, waiting for commands. Her eyes burned fever-bright as she stared at the duke. He sat in his chair, his head swinging from Geoffrey's half-fainting body to her own. "Strip her to the waist."

No. She must have spoken the words, but she could not make the sound come from her lips. One man advanced toward her, knife in hand. Was he going to cut her? But no. He merely sliced the knife through the material at her shoulders. Then, his heavy hands at her throat, his foul breath in her face, he tore her gown away.

She was bare to the waist. The air which had been so hot, now seemed so cold. Her nipples hardened with the chill? Fear? She was terrified. Her breath caught in her throat. God help her! That night so long ago in Paris came back to her.

She was seeing her brothers' pain, hearing their cries.

"The same place," the duke commanded softly.

His voice seemed to come from far away. Geoffrey strained at his bonds. A grunting sound of protest came from

211

his throat. The torturer's hands were on her body pushing her gown farther down. Her navel was exposed, her hips, the skin of her lower belly crisscrossed with stretch marks from her pregnancy. In the midst of her fear, she felt embarrassment because the imperfections of her body were exposed to the eyes of these men!

The torturer approached, the cherry red brand preceding him like the extension of his own arm. She would not cry out, she vowed. She would not let this dog of a Frenchman . . . The glowing iron touched her skin just to the right of her hipbone. In that instant she broke her vow.

She was consumed in flame. Every nerve in her body—every muscle—contorted in an effort to escape the searing agony. Never had she felt anything like it before. Her heart gave a fearful leap within her chest as her lungs swelled and expelled like a bellows. An agonized shriek ripped from her throat.

Why in the name of all merciful God could she not faint? Her head fell forward on her chest after the terrible moment of contortion. Although the pain continued practically unabated after the torturer pulled the brand away, she was no longer capable of such a fierce spasm. Helpless groaning was all she could manage.

"Joanna." The duke spoke, but to her, his voice was coming from far away. "Do you believe that Geoffrey would endure such to trick you?"

One of the torturers spoke. "She may not know what you say, my lord. Sometimes they cannot hear. The pain deadens all the other senses."

The duke cursed angrily. "Then fix her so she can hear. It is most important that she hear."

The man who had spoken came to her side. He dipped a rag into a bucket of cold water. Wringing it out, he clapped it roughly to her wound. The other man approached her then and wiped her face and gaping mouth with another rag

212

wrung out from the same bucket. "Now, my lord."

"Joanna," the duke repeated. "Do you believe that Geoffrey would endure such torture to trick you?"

From somewhere deep inside her, she found the strength to raise her head. Across the room, she knew, hung a figure in agony. She tried to focus on him, but his form kept rippling as waves of pain swept her body.

"Joanna!"

"No," she croaked.

"You must promise, Joanna. You must promise to obey me, your husband."

"I promise."

"You must do as I tell you, do as I command you, give me the heirs that I require."

"Yes."

"Take her down and return her to the chair."

Only vaguely was she aware of the pain in her wrists as the manacles were unlocked. Her arms dropped limply to her sides as she waited for the man who knelt at her ankles to complete his task. The man was clumsy, giving her time to find her balance. The smell of her own burned flesh rose in her nostrils along with the sour sweat from the filthy unwashed bodies of the men who pressed against her, back and front.

Her spirit returned. Though the pain had abated not one whit in its intensity, she could cope with it now. When her ankles were free, she angrily pushed the men's hands away. With a steadiness that secretly surprised even herself, she managed to walk across the small space to the chair.

Nude to the waist, she nevertheless seated herself bolt upright, her eyes staring straight ahead as she drew tremulous deep breaths.

The duke watched her for a moment, his gaze speculative.

At last she spoke. "Take him down too." Her voice was hoarse as if she had screamed for hours.

The duke gestured to the two men who hastily released Geoffrey's wrists and ankles. When they stepped aside, he stood, swaying weakly. Then, with an agonized grimace, he stooped to pull his hose up over his loins. The burn was too painful to bear the cloth upon it, so he fumbled to adjust the hose in a roll around his hips. "Come here, Geoffrey." Brittany commanded. "She wants to ascertain for herself that you are none the worse for a little touch here and there."

Geoffrey found that the act of holding himself erect was painful. His body had been held for hours in bondage: first, huddled in the icy cell, then painfully extended on the frame. With a hand that trembled he pulled the foul gag from his mouth and dropped it onto the floor. His anger had not yet kindled. Moving as a man three times his age might move, he blindly positioned himself before them.

With a quick nod, Brittany dismissed the men. The scene was oddly reminiscent of a scene in the great hall. The duke and duchess sat side by side, their chairs not more than a foot apart. Their most trusted vassal stood before them awaiting their commands. The room was lit by the fire of the open pit as well as several flambeaux that smoked dully from sconces in the wall.

The duke's face was deeply lined, and there was a pinched look about his mouth and nostrils. He stretched his right leg straight out in front of him. Exhausted, he raised his right hand to pass it over his mouth. One look at his swollen joints discouraged him so that he let it drop back uselessly across his thigh.

The duchess sat like some pagan goddess from ancient Minos. Her black eyes blazed with outrage from a face so devoid of color that it might have been carved from marble. Her nostrils flared as she sought to control her agonized breathing. Falling in a heavy tangle of curls over her alabaster shoulders, her black hair hung so long it covered the rose-tipped mounds of her breasts.

214

Although nearly depleted by the extended ordeal, both men were stirred by her beauty. The duke braced himself as he read the anger in her face.

Joanna swallowed hard as she took in the drooping figure before her. The cataclysmic events had left her feeling strangely light-headed, even somewhat detached from her choking rage. The burning pain beside her hipbone made her weak and sick. Thirsty, she longed for some snow such as Geoffrey had fed her when she had been so sick.

That memory threatened to bring tears, but she sternly repressed them. Geoffrey and she both needed snow, a whole tub of it to cool their terrible burns and soothe their raging thirsts. She licked her lips. Not surprisingly, they were dry and cracked.

"Let this agony come to an end," she rasped, turning to the duke. "Give me your commands. I will obey them even as your bastard lackey will."

Geoffrey winced at the contempt in her voice, but Brittany nodded coldly. He commended her. "Very wise of you, Joanna. Here is what we shall do." His eyes moved to Geoffrey's swaying figure. "Sit down, man, before you fall down."

Geoffrey straightened his body, a tinge of color spreading to his cheeks. "I pray you, my lord. Do not be concerned for me." His voice although dry and raspy was strong.

The duke looked from one to the other. Admiration mingled with anger. Tortured at his behest and helpless in his hands, they both retained a proud demeanor. Neither groveled nor wept. He drew a deep breath. "Very well. Suit yourself and be damned. You will both leave here by secret stairs which will take you to a chamber not far from our own apartments. I shall have clothing brought to you both, and whatever bandages and unguents are necessary to treat those wounds. When you have cared for yourselves, you, Geoffrey, will escort Joanna back to the solar as if she had

215

been in private conference with me." He looked from one to the other to gauge their reactions.

Geoffrey stared straight ahead at some spot on the far wall. Joanna, on the other hand, studied the duke's face with narrowed eyes that blazed her hatred.

"You, Joanna, will remain in the solar for some little time so that none are suspicious. Then you may excuse yourself and retire for a rest. Geoffrey, when you have escorted her to the solar, you may go to your room. I will not need you for the rest of the day."

"Yes, my lord," came his emotionless reply.

"Neither of you will relate by written or spoken word what you are now a party to. If another person knows, he cannot be trusted. Agreed?"

"Agreed," Joanna spoke quickly.

The duke's hand snaked out to close on her wrist with fierce strength. "If you betray me, my dear, I will see that you die horribly along with Geoffrey and your son. The charge will be adultery and witchcraft, and you will be burned at the stake for it with the babe bound to your breast."

Her face was still as stone. "I will never reveal it, my lord Duke," she replied at last.

"See that you do not." He flung her hand down. "Geoffrey!"

The young man nodded. "Yes, my lord."

"We are ready to leave now. God will that we never return. Give me your arm. Joanna, yours on the other side."

While Geoffrey steadied the duke, Joanna made shift to cover the upper part of her body with the mutilated garments that clung around her waist. When she had done all she could, shuddering, she placed herself on the duke's other side. Long practice enabled her to take his velvet-clad arm in both of hers in such a way that he was not hurt. Together the three made their way from the chamber.

Outside the door, the sweating burly men waited. If they were puzzled by the strangeness of the trio, they made no sign but merely tugged at their forelocks as it passed.

The hall was freezing. Joanna immediately began to shiver, her teeth chattering noisily. The duke threw his cloak around Geoffrey's shoulders and put his left arm around his wife. So, dependent on each other, they made their way onward and upward through the icy gloom.

Chapter 13

"I will not bathe tonight," Joanna instructed her tiring women with a dismissive wave of her hand. With an inward smile, she realized she had no need to pretend exhaustion. The time she had spent in the solar in obedience to the duke's command had been agonizing. The slightest movement pressed the material of her chemise against the horrible burn. Furthermore, she had had almost no food or sleep for well over twenty-four hours.

The duke's men had summoned her from her chamber only minutes after her tiring women had dressed her for the day. Later she and Geoffrey had taken only a few embarrassed minutes to smear on a greasy unguent before dressing hastily and quitting the chamber. Then he had escorted her to the solar, bowed stiffly, and left her.

Now as she dragged off her clothing, she could not suppress tears of weakness. There was not a scrap of food anywhere in her chambers. Too well-disciplined to be a nibbler, she had not a sweet, not a piece of dried fruit, not a nut. She did not even have a small decanter of wine or sherry.

Her stomach grumbled loudly as she stepped out of her gown. Her saffron chemise clung stickily to her midsection where a large greasy stain revealed the extent of the burn. Sliding the straps off her shoulders, she pushed the linen garment down until she could gingerly pluck the material away from her skin.

The sight of the burn made her grimace and swallow. Her body must have spasmed wildly; for the lines of the B were blurred, and the skin around it was bruised and swollen as if she had been struck. Staring at her abused flesh nauseated her. Supporting herself by holding on to the furniture, she made her way to the bed and sprawled across it, her hand across her eyes.

The pain of the burn had abated somewhat, but hunger gnawed at her like a living thing. God! Would she never feel well? Was she the same person who had hunted and killed the stag with such delight? Was she who now lay limp and hopeless, a brand on her flesh like a common felon, a king's daughter? Her father should hear of this.

A hoarse chuckle erupted from her throat, ending almost immediately in a hacking cough. Her father would be the first to act as her husband had, should he need an heir and not be able to get one of his own. He might use the information for his own advantage against Brittany, but he would never help her because she had been insulted or ill used. She was immaterial to both men. No more than a broodmare bred to a handsome young stallion.

Clearly, she recalled the duke's remark. As a terrible anger rose in her, she clenched her fist and bit down hard to suppress a scream of outrage. Eyes wide open she stared at the canopy overhead. Gradually her exhaustion and hunger overcame her and her violent feelings diminished leaving her limp and apathetic. She must face the fact that she could do nothing. With only the appearance of power, she had none to wield. Her clenched fists relaxed to lie palm up, her fingers curling only slightly.

As the fire began to die, she roused herself. She could not lie like a lump and take a chill. Already her feverish flesh was beginning to prickle as the temperature in the chamber dropped. She pushed herself up on one elbow, then fell back as her head swam dizzily. How stupid, she scolded herself. It was only a tiny burn. No more than a couple of square inches of skin had been touched.

At last she managed to get to her feet and step out of the soiled chemise. Her nightgown floated down over her head swathing her from head to foot in its cool folds. Numbly, she climbed between smooth, clean sheets.

She met the duke at breakfast the next morning. His pale eyes surveyed her haggard face. With a show of exceptional solicitude, he ordered Geoffrey to bring her two coddled eggs in defiance of the fast day which prohibited any in the château from eating the "forbidden" meat products.

"My lord," Joanna protested softly, but he waved her to silence.

Geoffrey returned with steaming eggs set upon a toasted slice of fine white bread. As he bent over her, her eyes scanned his face, studying him as if he were a new species she had just discovered.

"Eat, Joanna." The duke smiled pleasantly. "I want you hale and hearty." He paused significantly. "I think we will institute a new procedure tonight. I shall send Geoffrey to escort you to my chamber. After all, you are much younger. . . ."

Joanna did not hear the rest of his reasoning. The bite she was about to take wavered in midair. Carefully she set down her spoon before turning to stare at her grinning, preening husband. A flush rose in her cheeks as she observed that the men beyond Brittany's chair had paused in their eating to listen to her answer.

Her popularity had never been great. Since she had taken to hunting and had been so successful at the sport, she had encountered masculine resentment although hunting was open to both males and females. She was aware that if she had been a poor marksman or a stupid clumsy hunter, she would not have drawn disgruntled looks from huntsmen who observed her returning with choice game when they returned empty-handed. Now they listened avidly, grinning as they hoped for her rebellion and subsequent humiliation.

Hesitating only to draw a deep breath, she spoke firmly and clearly. "If that is what you wish, my lord, I am ever at your command."

The duke stared into her flickering eyes for a moment, reading there her hatred and her frustration. His eyes mocked her even as he nodded in a show of civility. Turning from her, he addressed the table in general. "My lady is ever ready to please me. Her duty is more than an old man has a right to expect." At their murmurs of denial, he raised a hand. "Hear me, friends, honor to her is honor to me."

"If you will excuse me . . ." Joanna sought to rise, but his arm detained her.

"Joanna, I insist you eat the rest of your breakfast. You will grow thin and pale. In fact, you look so this morning."

She stared at him in amazement, trying to read the motive for the mockery which seemed to bubble wildly from his lips. Clearly, Jean de Montfort was exhilarated beyond all reason. Stiffly, she reseated herself. His knobby hand closed over her wrist which rested on the edge of the table. "Eat, Joanna," he commanded sternly.

Inclining her head slightly, she again raised the spoon. A man beyond her husband guffawed over a crude remark made by a companion. Her ears burned, and her hand began to shake.

Now she knew what she could expect from the duke. She would be baited until he grew tired ot it. Her pride would be ground into the dust. She could say nothing, or she and Geoffrey would both die horrible deaths. The wild temper of Charles the Bad swept through her, making her blood boil and her hands tremble with anger. Yet she dared show nothing but a cool façade to the world. Raising her chin proudly, looking to neither right nor left, she reached for her tankard of ale.

How she managed to eat her breakfast, she never knew. In

the solar the glances in her direction and the whispered conversations drove her mad. By the end of the day, she was wild with frustration. She was the innocent, injured party in all this, yet she was the one who suffered.

Her husband, that arch plotter, enjoyed his power and lauded it over her, mocking her helplessness, while Geoffrey escorted her about the château as if his newly revealed status in her life were perfectly normal. His face remained utterly impassive, no matter what his master said.

"That bastard," she hissed softly.

"Did you speak, my lady?" One of her maids turned from arranging her clothing.

Shaking her head, she clenched her hands in anger. Later, while Isabella supervised the tiring woman's brushing of Joanna's hair, she realized that every muscle in her body was strung as tightly as a string on a lute. Her body was literally vibrating with hatred and dread.

"You do well to obey your husband's commands." Doña Isabella's smirk revealed her own pleasure in the fact that Joanna's pride was humbled. "Your father would be most pleased that you have become such a dutiful wife."

"Then you must inform him of it in your correspondences, Doña Isabella." Joanna's black eyes shot sparks of obsidian fire that reflected off the mirror before her.

At the mention of the correspondences, Isabella paled. She had gone to great lengths to keep her messages secret, pretending the letters she wrote were only family notes of greeting. She carefully concealed the information in the packets by writing it in a gibberish only a few could decipher. She scowled angrily at Joanna's references to the messages before the maids.

"I believe the information of your change of heart would be more appropriate coming from you, my lady," she replied smoothly.

"I have not written to my father since I arrived here. Nor do I intend to. He would not care to hear anything from me

223

except the news of the birth of his grandson. I left that announcement to your good offices, Doña Isabella."

A knock sounded at the door of the suite. "My robe!" Joanna snapped to the maid who hastened forward with it. Shivering from head to foot as if she had an ague, she slid her arms into the fur-lined wool and belted it more tightly than necessary around her thin middle.

Geoffrey's arm was steady under her fingers as she walked beside him, her head held high. Despite the coldness of the hall neither felt the inclination to hurry.

Joanna's stomach quivered and churned as she tried to present a brave front. Over and over in her mind she searched for some way to excuse the shame she felt at the thought of his coupling with her and getting her with child, a child whose royal blood was now tainted. The whole horrible circumstance of childbirth was magnified by the knowledge that the prince of the blood royal was, in fact, the son of a nameless bastard. If she had been raped by a common peasant, she would not have felt more unclean.

And now the entire degrading act was to be repeated over and over until the Duke of Brittany, whose suzerainty had been gained by usurpation and assassination, was satisfied with her production. They had arrived before the duke's door. She shuddered as a sob escaped her.

"My lady," Geoffrey whispered patting her hand. "Please do not fear."

She snatched her hand away from him. "I do not fear," she replied stiffly, her voice almost drowned in tears. "After all, have I not the duke's promise that so long as I keep silent and perform the woman's part for you, I will have my life. I will not be tortured or burned at the stake."

Geoffrey regarded her silently, helplessly. He could offer no words of comfort since her pride made her despise him. "I would help you if I could," he said at last.

She nodded shortly. "Knock at the door. We must not keep His Grace waiting."

She had never been in the duke's apartments before. To her taste, they were overplain and umcomfortably warm. Fires blazed in two fireplaces. The duke sat at his ease in a huge chair piled with pillows, his foot extended on a large stool draped in green velvet, the only condescension to softness in the room.

Noticing her surveyal of the surroundings, he made a sweeping gesture. "Welcome to a soldier's rest, my dear wife. Not to your taste I see. I fear I became a duke too late to affect the luxury one comes to expect if to the manor born. A monk's cell is more to my taste. Is that not so, Geoffrey?"

The valet nodded stiffly. His eyes fastened on the wide bed raised on the dais and made even higher with its triple mattresses. Because of the duke's aversion to chill, it had no hangings. Instead the fires in the twin fireplaces were tended all night long by the gentleman of the chamber.

Until his elevation to Geoffrey Fitzjean d'Anglais, he had risen from his pallet at intervals to stoke the fires and add more charcoal. His eyes shifted to the pallet. Sick apprehension swept him. The hangings about Joanna's bed had created an illusion of privacy. In the blazing firelight no movement would be hidden from the duke's eyes should he care to watch. Geoffrey passed a hand over his face, wiping away a thin film of perspiration.

Joanna, too, stared at the bed. She did not see the lack of hangings. Their absence had not yet dawned upon her. The mere knowledge of what would happen to her there made her shiver uncontrollably. Embarrassment, loathing, and fear all combined to stifle her breathing. Her fingertips felt cold as she raised them to her throat.

"Some wine for my lady," the duke suggested.

Her escort led her to a chair opposite the duke's.

"And pour some for me and for yourself."

Geoffrey noted with some surprise that his hands were perfectly steady as he lifted the stopper from the decanter and poured the pale amber liquid into the silver goblets.

Returning with the tray, he presented it first to the duke and then to the duchess.

"Now." Brittany took a hearty swallow and smiled expansively. "We present a pleasant family portrait, do we not?"

Joanna stared into the depths of her wine, noting how the liquid quivered as her hand trembled. Perhaps, by closing her mind to the whole situation, she could retain some measure of dignity. Geoffrey had stationed himself behind the duke's chair and out of the duke's range of vision.

When neither of the young people answered, Brittany sighed. He could expect no more. Obedience was enough. "Drink your wine," he grumbled. "Both of you."

Obediently, Joanna raised the goblet to her lips and did not lower it until she had swallowed its contents. When she again faced the duke, the room seemed to tilt slightly, but she welcomed the sensation of unreality. Perhaps if she were drunk enough, she would not notice what was done to her.

"Now that you know all, Joanna, it is not necessary for you to be drugged or drunk," Brittany warned her drily. "The pleasure that such a fine young man as Geoffrey can bring to your body should be reward enough for a little discomfort in childbearing."

Her eyes flashed open contemptuously. "His touch degrades me," she snarled. "I am the blood of kings. He is a bastard of unknown origin."

Behind the duke's chair, Geoffrey swallowed the small amount he had poured for himself. His bastardy again. Being so highborn, of course, she would resent his unknown origins. Still her attitude galled him. He was a man like any other and better than some. His attributes, thanks to the duke, were the equal of any young man of his age. Angrily, he straightened, keeping his eyes on the bleak gray stone above the fireplace.

To his surprise the duke came to his rescue. "I think it not to your advantage to insult a man who has your pleasure and

226

peace at his discretion," he chided meaningfully.

Her eyelashes swept upward as fear flashed across the space between her and Geoffrey. She swallowed uncomfortably.

"Not that Geoffrey would hurt you," the duke continued equably. "He is a perfect gentle man." He emphasized the word *gentle*. "Many a woman has been treated so cruelly on her wedding night that she has been brought to bed for several days thereafter. Indeed, I know of men who have boasted in their cups of the brutality of their conquests." He glanced over his shoulder at the valet standing tall and aloof behind him. "Have you not heard such, Geoffrey? Why some make sport of it, saying how the woman was nigh split in two by the superior size of their manhood."

The wine was making Joanna dizzy as its fumes touched her sensibilities. With every word her husband said, she was feeling more and more depressed. She pressed her lips together to still their trembling and stared miserably at her hands.

The fire crackled and leaped. A log burned through and fell with a shower of sparks. The duke finished his wine and set the cup down on the small table at his left. "Well, you must get on with it. Geoffrey, you must take Joanna into the second chamber."

At this information, Geoffrey glanced thankfully at him before looking inquiringly toward Joanna. "Shall I light the fire, my lady?"

"No." The duke hastily raised his hand. "No. The room must look as undisturbed as possible. Certainly, it must seem that you, Geoffrey, merely slept there to be at my beck and call."

"Yes, Your Grace."

Another uncomfortable silence ensued. As he studied first one and then the other, Brittany experienced a shameful perverse excitement in their discomfiture.

Joanna felt that she must scream. Her nerves were

stretched to the breaking point. The muscles in her stomach were knotted and quivering. Her fingers were icy. Merciful God. She could not endure much more.

"Bah!" The duke's exclamation made her jump. "Help me to bed, Geoffrey. We shall leave the duchess to her deliberations while you help me to undress and dispose of myself."

In only a few short minutes, the preparations were complete. Brittany was safely tucked away under the covers, grumbling and groaning fretfully. The fires were built even higher.

The atmosphere of the room made Joanna think of the priests' descriptions of hell. Surely, it would be very similar, with its intense heat, its leaping flames, its strange dark corners. Moreover, an evil demon ruled here and even now moaned terrifyingly.

At last the moment could be avoided no longer. With a branch of candles in one hand, Geoffrey came to her side. Inclining his head, he offered her his arm as familiarly as if they were taking a stroll through the garden.

Her eyes flew to his face and then down again. She moistened her lips. She could not think. Unreasoning dread and hatred filled her mind, concealed only by a thin veneer of pride that would not allow these emotions to be revealed. She placed her hand in its accustomed place on his arm. Her back stiff as a ramrod, she rose and allowed him to lead her from the room.

Behind her, she heard the duke's wheezy chuckle.

The inner chamber proved dark and chill. Its furnishings were of the same Spartan quality as the other. The bed was a single narrow cot with a covering of wolf pelts.

Geoffrey left her side to set the candelabra on the small table. "'Tis little enough, my lady." His voice was rough with apology.

She clenched her fists within the folds of her fur-lined robe. She had no choice. None. Her fingers were stiff, her lips tender where she had bitten them. Her thoughts twisted and turned feverishly, seeking some means of escape.

Then he came to her, placing his hands gently under her elbows and lifting her lightly toward him.

"No." He recognized the panic in her voice. "For mercy's sake . . ." Her black eyes were enormous in her stark white face. Her breath came rapidly and unevenly as if she had run a great distance.

He shook his head. "Your Grace, calm yourself. You have nothing to fear. Absolutely nothing."

"But . . ." After what Brittany had said, she dared not tell him of her humiliation, of her sick disgust at the thought that he would touch the most intimate places of her body. As one born to the blood royal she felt herself ruined forever. Yet he was much stronger than she. She remembered the blood he had shed in her behalf, his terrible strength when he had fought the rebel soldier. In agony she would have bowed her head, panting as she struggled to get herself under control.

"Look up, Joanna." He shook her slightly. His grave face hung above her, his usually light gray eyes stormy. Grimly he studied the flickering emotions she could not conceal. "We have to do this thing," he went on in a low, gentle voice. "You understand? If we do not, we die. You do not want to die?" He shook her again, only this time the motion was more like rocking.

"No." She realized that his eyes and his hands were soothing her at the same time they were compelling a response.

"My lady, I am one who has been forced throughout my whole life to obey the will of others whether I would or not. It is hard. Sometimes you think you would rather die than submit to one more indignity. But somehow you never do. Life is sweet after all." He smiled, a slow sweet smile tinged with sadness.

She studied his face. "Yes," she agreed grudgingly. "Life is sweet."

229

"I learned to do things that made the worst seem somehow better." His hands slid up her arms and cupped her shoulders, drawing her closer to him until she had to tilt her head far back on her slender neck. "Will you be guided by me in this, my lady?" he asked lightly, his voice taking on a whimsical tone.

Even as she shook her head, she knew she would. Suddenly, she longed to be guided by someone else. "Yes," she whispered. "Oh . . ."

As she consented, he cupped the back of her head in one of his long strong hands and drew her close to rest her cheek against his chest. "The first thing to remember when you have a bad, sad thing to do, is that you somehow contrive to make it better." One palm stroked her hair, while the other pressed against the curve of her waist.

They stood like that for a long while until her trembling stopped and her breathing evened. At long last, he cupped his hand under her chin and raised it so she must look at him. With their eyes locked, he brought his lips down to brush hers gently.

She caught her breath sharply but did not pull away. His lips were warm and soothing. As he continued to kiss her and stroke her back, she felt her dread and hatred drain away. Her lips warmed to the touch of his. One small hand closed round his arm just above his elbow. The other clasped his shoulder.

The kiss deepened. He wrapped both arms around her and held her tightly against his chest, so that he could feel the rise and fall of her breasts through the layers of fabric that separated them.

Her own sensuality began to reawaken after the long months since the conception of her child. She could feel a nagging ache beginning deep within her abdomen. Her hands clutched him a bit tighter as if to strain him to her.

Abruptly, he stepped back holding her at arms' length. "This goes too fast," he said a little breathlessly. "We must go slower."

"But why?" she objected.

"Because we have the chance to," he replied. "We can turn the duke's vicious tormenting into pure pleasure. Are you willing?"

Her eyes lighted at the thought. Without hesitation she nodded.

"Then let us enjoy the opportunities that we have been given." So saying, he lifted her into his arms, holding her high against his chest. "Put your arms around my neck, and kiss my cheek."

She smiled hesitantly as she complied. Her lips touched his cheek, kissed it, then traced a path across his cheekbone to his ear. Her breath warmed it before she kissed it too.

She felt his arms shake. "Oh, my lady. Be careful. You excite me. . . ."

At his words she drew back, then kissed him again in the same place. "Is that not what you want?" she whispered, her lips moving against the curve, fanning the tiny almost invisible hair there.

He gasped as his arms tightened painfully around her. "Beware, Joanna. . . ."

"Nonsense," she interrupted sternly. "You cannot experience 'pure pleasure' if I do not do my part. You told me to kiss your cheek, so . . ."

In a few swift strides he carried her to the bed and stretched her on it.

The wolf pelts welcomed her and him too as he arranged himself alongside her. Half covering her with his body, he began to kiss her slowly and lingeringly over her face and throat.

As she shivered beneath his mouth, she fastened her fingers in his hair and sighed softly.

"Do you enjoy my kisses?" he whispered as her sighs turned to moans.

"Oh, yes."

"Then will you open your robe and allow me to kiss your beautiful breasts. I have never seen them, but I have dreamed of what they would be like." He drew back expectantly, his eyes glinting like silver in the candlelight.

With fingers that trembled slightly, she undid the fastening of her belt and pulled her robe aside. His mouth felt dry at the sight. Two perfect creamy mounds each peaked with a dark rose seared his vision. If he had been stricken blind in the next instant, he would not have bewailed his fate. Gently, reverently, he bent to kiss first one and then the other. As his lips closed over the tip, his tongue flicked it provocatively.

Joanna gasped for breath. The sensation had been electric. A wave of passion curled within her belly, making her unconsciously draw up one knee and clench her fists as she struggled for control.

"Do you like that?" he asked.

Her fingers straightened with an effort. One hand caressed his silvery blond hair while the other pressed hard along his spine. "Yes."

"Then shall I do it again?"

"Please."

This time he took her nipple to hold between his teeth while his tongue circled it. She surged upward under him, pressing him tightly against her.

After a few minutes, when she was twisting and shivering in mindless abandon, he drew off. "I would have you touch me too," he whispered.

Her eyes flew open to study his smiling face. "Very well," she said at last. Rising, he stripped off his tunic. In the act of lifting the fine white shirt beneath it, he paused when she held up her hand. "Leave it. You will be too cold. Come to me, and I will do to you as you have to me." Her expression was serious, a small frown marring her perfect forehead as though she tried to remember.

When he again stretched out beside her, she pushed his

232

shirt aside and began to kiss his chest, enjoying the feel of the softly curling hair across her lips. She tongued his nipples as he had done to her and then held one between her teeth as he had.

"My God," he whispered. "You are incredible."

"Do I please you?"

He groaned in acquiescence.

"Shall I do it again?"

"As long as I can bear it. And then again. We have all night," he reminded her, cupping the back of her head and urging her against him.

Chapter 14

Geoffrey's fingers were cool to her fevered skin. Joanna moaned in anticipation as he opened her robe to frame the rest of her torso, thereby revealing the cup of her navel, her slightly concave belly, and the jet-black plumage at its base. Over the burn she had fashioned a small protective pad held in place by strings around her hips. Worshiping her with his eyes, he caressed her creamy skin and stroked her soft curly hair.

She squirmed in delight at the sensations his touch provoked, a small smile curving her lips, her eyes slitted and smoky with desire.

"Beautiful," he whispered, placing his mouth to her navel and touching its center with his tongue. "My God, my lady. Your body is perfection." His tongue continued its license as his hands caressed the tender flesh of her inner thighs.

"Geoffrey," she gasped at length, "I am losing control. I . . . can . . . not . . ."

He smiled. His hands slid under her buttocks and lifted her to him. "Lose control, my Joanna," he whispered so softly that she could not hear him dare to speak her name. "Enjoy your body. Live for the pure pleasure of the moment." With those words he thrust his tongue deeply in her to caress the very core of her being.

A shrill cry of ecstasy burst from her, startling the duke who lay in his bed in the next room. Tormented as he was by the nagging pain in his swollen joints, Brittany grinned, then sighed sadly. If old age was purgatory, then surely a sick old age was hell. At least his sins of this earth were being paid for on this earth, he reckoned piously as he massaged his throbbing hands over and over beneath the covers.

The chill of the single narrow bed was dispelled. Both Geoffrey and Joanna lay naked, their bodies sharing the same heat. When she had been able to think again, she had guided him into her, entwining their limbs so they lay facing each other yet still joined together. Her hands played over his body, tormenting him delightfully.

She smiled as she felt him throbbing within her. Her thumb and finger pinched a tiny erect masculine nipple. Instantly, he responded, his manhood thrusting deeper into her soft interior until she moaned at the sweet pain of his size.

"Holy Mother!" he breathed. With eyes closed and head thrown back, he inhaled great lungfuls of the cold air in an effort to cool his blood and delay the exquisite torture as long as possible.

She was inexorable. Edging closer to him, she fastened her tiny white teeth in his earlobe and nipped hard. At the same time her fingers tweaked the silvery blond hair that mingled with her own below.

"Please," he moaned. "Oh, please. I cannot bear—"

"Ssh," she whispered. Her warm breath in his ear sent delightful shivers down his spine. He writhed. "Be still," she cautioned. "Am I not the duchess? Do you disobey me?"

He shook his head. "Never," he groaned through clenched teeth. "Never."

"Then you will be quiet and wait." She trailed tiny nipping kisses down the side of his throat and across his chest.

His fingers stroked her hair, then fastened in it. Roughly, he pulled her back to stare into her face. "What do you do to me?" he groaned harshly.

The dark pools of her eyes reflected the candlelight. "I give you pleasure. I make the bad things good. 'Tis what you said we should do."

"Yes," he sighed. "Oh, yes."

A demon leaped in her eyes and a cold expression flitted across her face. "Besides, he in the other room can imagine what we do. I take great pleasure in the thought. I hope his imagination puts him into a frenzy."

Geoffrey stared at her. His own sense of the perverse shook him, making him tremble from head to toe. The rush of desire generated by his thoughts flooded his body and overwhelmed his control. Uncaring of her soft flesh, he grasped her shoulders as he twisted himself upon her. Wildly, he plunged into her body exploding immediately into her welcoming depths.

Later, when he had rested, he rolled away to find he had dislodged the bandages with which they had covered their burns. Somewhere dimly he remembered her small cry of pain. Instantly, he knelt beside the bed. "My lady, Your Grace . . ." Aghast, he examined the wound.

She lay still, silently accepting his concern. She was suddenly very tired. He had brought her pleasure, and she was sure she had given him the same. Now reaction overtook her. The room suddenly seemed very cold, very cold indeed. She wished fervently she were alone and snug in her own bed.

She felt his fingers resting on the skin of her belly without daring to touch the dreadful wound. The motion of his body that had dislodged the bandage had also abraded the seared flesh. Now the burn stung furiously.

"What can I do?" he groaned anxiously.

She shook her head. Her voice drooped with weariness. "Help me to dress. Let us quit this chamber. We both need rest and sleep."

He nodded, rising to his feet and adjusting the strip of

cloth he had swathed about his own hips. With no wasted motion, he dressed himself and then bent to her. "My lady?"

She had tucked her head into the crook of her arm. Only when his voice startled her did she realize that she had almost drifted off to sleep. Drowsily, like a child, she allowed herself to be stood on her feet. Her arms were guided into the fur-lined robe before it was belted loosely around her waist. He even smoothed her hair about her face, before he tucked her arm through his to lead her out.

The duke's stentorian snores came rhythmically from the huge bed, but his body was buried under the mounds of covers and soft mattresses he perforce adopted. The fire had burned lower in the fireplaces, but the room was still very hot.

"The devil sleeps," Joanna whispered, shivering.

Instantly, Geoffrey's arm went around her, drawing her into the warm strength of his body. "He is only a man." His lips pressed comfortingly against her temple.

"An evil one."

He pushed open the door and escorted her swiftly down the hall. Their breath fogged before them. The château was cold as a tomb.

Joanna's teeth chattered. "Holy M-mother! Will we have to go through this every night until I conceive?"

He nodded wryly. "When summer comes, it will be better."

"Summer is a long time away. 'Tis still only winter."

Almost at a run, they arrived at the door to her chambers where she paused uncertainly. "I would invite you in," she apologized stiffly, "but I am really so very tired."

"You can never invite me in," he reminded her. "I am a servant. An escort. You are the duchess."

She smiled an ironic sort of smile. "Of course. I am the duchess. What power I wield! Best beware of me. Bah!" She clenched her hands together and wrung them angrily. "What a lie life is for a woman!"

He paused before opening the door. How he wished he could wipe her bitterness away! He was happier than he had ever been. In utterly strange and unexpected ways the most disastrous events had reaped him great benefits. However, in the dark and silent hall he could think of no words of comfort.

"My lady," he said at last, "be at peace. You will never come to disgrace or pain through me. I will be forever loyal to you."

But she was too angry to count his worth. A sneer curled her lip. "Thank you, Geoffrey." She brushed him aside. Her hand found the handle and pushed the heavy door open. Illumined by the lightspill, her face was as bitter and cold as if it faced a thousand winters.

Isabella's eyes burned like anthracite in her parchment-white face. Clasping Joanna's hand, she drew the duchess from the solar.

"My God," Joanna gasped. "What has happened?"

"The king, my lady . . ." Isabella burst into noisy sobs as soon as they were in the duchess' apartments.

"My father?"

Isabella nodded, struggling for breath and holding her throat. "The king is dead."

Joanna stared aghast. Her father was only fifty-six years old. He could not be dead. He must be playing a trick, she thought, then wryly, only the good die young. "He was not ill?"

Isabella began to curse. Her witch's venom poured from her mouth. "I suspect a plot. That murderous monster Valois!"

Joanna nodded. Valois was indeed a murderous monster, but her father was a crafty spider too clever to be caught in a madman's trap. Placing her arms around the shoulders of the hysterical woman, she supported Isabella to a chair and

239

wrung out a wet cloth for her face. "Tell me," she commanded when the woman had calmed somewhat.

Drawing a letter from her pocket, Isabella extended it. Unfortunately, when Joanna opened it, its contents were too badly inkstained to be read. "Tell me," she repeated.

"He had a f-fever. Just a s-simple fever. Nothing. But he was chilled. The doctor . . . a curse on his soul!" She began to rant and rage again. Her voice rose to a scream.

Deliberately, Joanna struck her across the side of the face. "Calm yourself, Doña Isabella. Tell me what happened."

"He was wrapped in cloths soaked in brandy to warm his body and cause a sweat while he slept. They were sewn in place each night to warm him, you understand."

A horrible premonition swept over Joanna. "Oh, no . . ."

"The valet dropped a candle on them when he was cutting a thread. Cursed be the day of his birth and those of all his kin." Isabella began to sob again, weakly and hopelessly.

"He burned to death." Joanna's voice was devoid of all emotion.

"Yes. Oh, yes. He was horribly burned."

"Dear God!"

Joanna walked away, her hands clenched at her sides. Her father's hard black eyes rose before her measuring, calculating. She had thought to write to him, begging to be allowed to return for a visit. Once in Navarre she would have told him all. Together they would have worked the knowledge to some benefit for her. She had even begun the letter a couple of times but had put it aside, uncertain as to how to pursue her problem. Now it was too late.

"Oh, my lady, we are so alone." Isabella fumbled for her rosary and began frantically to count the beads.

"We were always alone," Joanna murmured. She pressed her hands against her belly. Even now inside her an heir of Brittany was most probably growing. She would bear him and others until Montfort was satisfied. Under pain of her life, she would never dare to reveal that he was a son

240

of d'Anglais.

Dry-eyed, she seated herself at her dressing table and opened a small pot of rouge. Lightly, she touched a bit of color to her cheeks and lips. "I shall go now and inform the duke. If he has not yet received such swift correspondence, doubtless he will wish to know the news."

At the allusion to the duenna's espionage, Isabella stiffened. Her hands clutched the rosary beads. Her black eyes followed the slim straight figure across the room. "M-my lady," she quavered, "you will keep me with you, will you not? I swear I will serve you as faithfully as ever I served your father."

At the door Joanna looked back over her shoulder. La Alcudia looked shrunken. Her eyes were reddened with her weeping, and her gnarled fingers were entangled in the rosary beads as if clinging to them for dear life. "If it is your wish to remain with me, Doña Isabella, you are welcome to stay," she said at last. "No one can ever have enough faithful servitors."

The years after that came and went for Joanna. With a deadening monotony she coupled with Geoffrey on demand and bore the duke's heirs. After the second pregnancy to which a second son was born, Brittany allowed her a respite of a year and after each one thereafter until she had borne him four living sons and two living daughters.

They were never far apart, the three of them, Jean, Joanna, and Geoffrey. So usual did their association seem to the court that it was no cause for comment.

As the duke aged, his limbs grew more gnarled and twisted. The overwhelming of Charles of Valois had ceased to be of importance as the young king's madness became generally known throughout the royal houses of Europe. The king's uncles—Burgundy, Anjou, Berri, and Bourbon—quarreled among themselves, so no attention was paid to the outlying suzerainties. The small uprising of Roche-Bernard and his sympathizers had been so thoroughly quelled that none sought to follow him. The people of Brittany seemed to have conveniently short memories, forgetting that Jean de Montfort had ever usurped the duchy.

As Geoffrey matured, his lanky body fulfilled its promises of above average height and breadth of shoulder. When he was not caring for the duke, he rode for miles alone through the Breton forests, hunted the boar and stag, and practiced with the weapons of knighthood. If his face was bleak and his eyes held an empty coldness, none cared enough to comment. He was, after all, only a servant.

Joanna wondered sometimes about her brother Charles, now King of Navarre, who was winning a name for himself throughout Europe as Charles the Noble. No correspondence had ever been exchanged between them. So far as he was concerned, he might never have had a sister. Meanwhile, she conducted the business of the château and oversaw the raising of her children with a dedication tempered by control. None among them was her favorite, as each had a personal complement of nurses, tutors, and servants to see to every need; yet she organized these staffs intelligently and efficiently. With Geoffrey she was pleasant in company and coldly impersonal in private. Only on the narrow bed in the duke's antichamber did her passionate nature override her rigid control. There she moaned and sighed, fought and scratched, as dark emotions found release through Geoffrey's skillful lovemaking.

Her pregnancies did not wreak undesirable changes on her body, not after the first which laced her belly with silvery stretchmarks, nor did they deplete her. She was young and active, much more active than the other women of her court. She hunted with her faithful Clothere or his assistants, still tramping miles through the forests. Frequently she ran. Neither her husband nor Geoffrey knew she followed Clothere in this strictly masculine pursuit. Beneath her

242

hunting gown she would wear leggings such as men wore, bound in place with straps of leather. When she was well away, she would tuck up the skirt and follow the men at a jogging trot.

At these times, with the clean dark green forest around her, game afoot, and her senses keen, she felt almost happy. Freedom was a heady thing, she decided . . . and very rare. As she came to appreciate it, she realized that few people had the least notion of what it tasted and smelled and felt like. Sometimes she laughed aloud as the cool scented breezes blew into her face, but always she was forced to return to the smoky gray walls of the château.

Henry Bolingbroke, Earl of Hereford, arrived with little fanfare from England to escort the Duke of Brittany to the wedding of King Richard II to Princess Isabelle, daughter of Charles of Valois, King of France. "The wedding will signal the beginning of twenty-eight years of peace between the two countries," he said as he enjoyed the fine French wine and foods at the celebratory banquet.

"You do not need me," Brittany wheezed. "I doubt that I could stand the trip to Calais in October. My condition"— he lifted his hands helplessly, before letting them fall back onto the arms of his chair—"deteriorates rapidly as you can see." The duke no longer walked except with great difficulty. More often he was pushed in a wheeled chair by either Geoffrey or Joanna.

"My father Gaunt persuades me that you are most necessary to our festivities," Bolingbroke replied, inclining his head toward the duke. "He has told me that I may speak frankly with you." He looked meaningfully at Joanna who sat at his left.

"You may speak before the duchess," the duke assured him drily. "She is my wife now of eleven years. Her good care and unswerving loyalty provide one of the few joys left to me in this world." His pale eyes shifted beyond the Englishman to drift lovingly over Joanna's neck and shoulders clad in rich crimson velvet with gold embroidery at the throat. She had changed little since he had married her. He had almost forgotten that he had forced her acquiescence.

"Briefly, then. Richard, my cousin, wishes this French alliance. Many in England believe he will give back all his father won at Crécy and more besides. You know that Charles is mad. He even ran amok among his own men a few years ago killing several. Were it not for his uncle Burgundy, he would not keep his throne at all."

"An alliance between England and France might not be to my advantage," Montfort admitted. "Although it is many years, some might remember that Blois was the prior claimant to Brittany."

"Exactly." Bolingbroke sat back a little in his chair, relaxing somewhat. He took a long drink of the exquisite wine and touched the napkin to his mouth before continuing.

"Navarre would not profit by a strong Valois," Joanna remarked suddenly.

Bolingbroke's blue English eyes widened. He knew very little of women who held political opinions. His own wife, Mary of Bohun, dead now two years, had had little knowledge beyond the care of a household. His father's mistress, Katherine Swynford, whom Gaunt had married secretly in his old age, knew more, but she kept most of her ideas to herself. Now here was a woman who must have actually listened intelligently to a conversation and drawn an original conclusion from it. "You are right about that," he agreed, raising his goblet in salute to her. "Navarre can never hope to regain its lost lands to the east if France is strong and at peace with England."

"None of the smaller countries would profit," Montfort agreed, well pleased at the impression his wife had created in the visitor. "A strong neighbor without a strong enemy to

244

threaten him grows greedy and begins to look around for food to satisfy his hunger."

Bolingbroke sat back in his chair, including the duchess for the first time in his conversation. "You must attend the wedding, my lord," he looked from one to the other. "Your presence among the English knights would show an alliance that would protect Brittany from encroachment."

"It might incite a reprisal." Montfort shook his head knowingly.

"Then England would come to your aid," Bolingbroke promised.

Montfort eyed his calculatingly. *"You* would, son of Lancaster, but what of your cousin? I think he is not like his father."

"My father also misses his brother," Bolingbroke acknowledged, thinking of his own hero worship of the Black Prince. "He would have been a great king."

Brittany sat silent for a moment. "I cannot go," he said at last. "My body is too weak. But I shall send Joanna in my stead. You will escort her. She will represent both Brittany and Navarre at Calais. Valois will know, if he is capable of knowing anything, that we both retain our independence. Would you like that, my dear?" he inquired solicitously. "I recall that you have not been outside of Brittany since you came here as a bride."

Joanna's eyes sparkled. Even a political pawn could enjoy the pageantry of a wedding between two of the most powerful princes in the world. "I should like it above all things, my lord." She turned a dazzling smile from her husband to the Earl of Hereford.

"I shall take great pleasure in escorting you, my lady," he replied suddenly, remembering that he had been a widower for two years.

"Then it is decided." Montfort nodded. "I shall provide an escort of two dozen knights, led by my most trusted man, to add to your numbers"—he gestured to his right some distance down the table—"Geoffrey Fitzjean d'Anglais."

Bolingbroke nodded in the direction indicated. "I shall be glad of his company. I have heard of him," he added significantly.

Montfort paused in reaching for a goblet. He stared at the Englishman. "Have you now?"

"Indeed. From my father whose memory is long."

Montfort shook his head as he lifted the wine to his lips. "Ah, well. Soon there will be none left to remember. Your father is well?"

The talk continued for a time, but Joanna did not listen. Excitement surged through her veins. She was going on a trip. Before the year was out she would be on her way to Calais to a magnificent royal wedding. There would be celebrations of all sorts, banquets, entertainments, perhaps a tournament. She would be among young people of her own age with whom she could talk and laugh. She would see all the newest and most beautiful clothes and jewels.

She must have a whole new wardrobe she decided. Sighing, she feared she would be sadly behind the fashions of the times, those current in Paris and London. She would look quaintly provincial. She had had few dresses since her arrival here over a decade ago. Since Montfort entertained less and less and since she cared nothing for sewing, she had made fewer and fewer gowns. She shivered in anticipation of the great task of preparing herself for the trip.

Surreptitiously, she glanced aside. She wanted to spring to her feet and dance around and send for Doña Isabella and the other ladies of her court to help her to prepare. With difficulty, she counseled herself that tomorrow would be soon enough.

"When shall we be leaving, Lord Bolingbroke?" she inquired.

"The wedding is to be in October," he replied. "We need to leave within a week.

"Oh, no. I need a suitable wardrobe. I cannot be ready so

246

soon." She clasped her hands together in an attitude of prayer. "Please say that I may have more time?"

Henry stared a moment into the gold-flecked eyes turned so beseechingly on him. So she was a woman after all—a very beautiful one with that black hair and those strange shining eyes, he thought appreciatively. She would outshine any woman in England. Hating to disappoint her, he shook his head sadly. "Alas, my lady, it cannot be. We must leave immediately if we are to arrive in time. We shall have to travel overland to St. Malo and take ship there for Cherbourg and thence to Calais. As our schedule stands now, we will have to depend on luck and favorable winds. If a storm should blow up, we might miss the wedding altogether."

"You shall have all the women in the castle working on nothing else but your new garments," the duke reassured her with an indulgent paternal smile.

That night in bed she lay awake planning the garments she would take with her when a knock sounded at the outer door to her apartments. Sitting bolt upright, she clasped the sheet to her breast.

She heard her maid rise and open the door, a muttered conversation; then the woman appeared timidly. "The duke, my lady, has sent Sir Geoffrey for you."

Vastly annoyed, she struggled with the desire to tell Geoffrey that she would not come. How dare Montfort? But suppose he was ill. He had not wanted to see her in some time now, not since the last child had been born over a year ago. This might not be an ordinary summons. Furthermore, he might forbid her to go to the wedding if she displeased him.

They had not gone more than half the length of the dark hall when Geoffrey caught her arm. "You find Bolingbroke to your liking," he accused.

Startled, she faced him in the chilly gloom. She could smell the wine on his breath. Geoffrey, who was usually so abstemious, was drunk. "Did the duke really send for me?"

she asked suspiciously.

He ignored her question. His hands tightened around her upper arms. "He is an Englishman."

"And so are you." She shrugged angrily. "The duke did not send for me."

"I could not let you make a fool of yourself. You must not look on other men with such . . . such favor." His voice shook slightly.

Furious, she twisted in his grasp. "I do not look on him with favor. I merely sat at table and discussed politics."

"You smiled at him. I saw you. Time and time again." He swayed, then staggered against her, forcing her to stumble back against the wall.

"Geoffrey, you are drunk. Go to bed. I shall return now to my chamber. In the morning you will have forgotten all about this, or you will be sorry you have behaved so."

"Not sorry, Joanna." He stepped closer to her. "Never sorry about you. You . . . you . . ." Suddenly, he dragged her against him and began to kiss her neck and throat. "You're mine," he slurred. "You . . . my . . . wife." Suddenly, a sound suspiciously like a sob escaped him.

Terrified that they might be seen together in these intimate circumstances, Joanna began to push and shove at him. "Geoffrey," she hissed. "For heaven's sake, get hold of yourself and let me go. You will destroy us both."

"I love you," he whispered. She could feel his impassioned breath hot on her neck. "I love you. I would never destroy you. But you must have a care for yourself." He straightened, his shadow looming over her. Then his mouth came down hard on hers.

It was a kiss unlike any he had ever given her before. So terrible in its intensity that she could not help but respond. His mouth was sweet with wine as his tongue plundered the inner depths of her own. Then he drew off. "My wife. Mine!" he repeated sorrowfully.

They stood together in the darkness. She was hypnotized

for long moments by the intensity of his emotion. She had never seen this side of Geoffrey's character before. He no longer resembled the self-contained, impersonal valet who made love on command as easily and skillfully as he wheeled the duke's chair or accompanied her on walks around the garden.

The danger of what he was doing fled and was replaced by cold anger. "Let me go!" she hissed, pushing her hands hard against his arms. At the same time she ducked her head and butted it against his chest. Unsteady as he was, he staggered back. His hands released her and reached out behind him to keep himself from falling.

In that instant, she darted away from him, back down the hall toward her own apartments. But he caught her before she had gone more than a few steps.

"You must listen. . . ."

"No." As she spun, her hand lashed out to connect with the side of his face in a resounding slap. "I do not have to listen. I obey Brittany. He has said that I will go to Calais with the Earl of Hereford, and so I shall. And I will smile at whomever I please whenever I please."

"But . . ."

All vestiges of control fled. The fiery temper and diabolical pride that had made her father infamous throughout Europe rose in a red wave. *"You forget yourself, d'Anglais."*

Her words should have been enough, but the potent combination of sorely tried patience and drink had made him overwrought. He caught her in his arms, dragging her against his chest so hard she lost her breath. *"I do not forget myself, d'Albret!"* he thundered calling her by her long-forgotten family name. His mouth ravaged hers again. His hands moved hurtfully over her body, as if by forcing her into him, they would become one.

Immediately, she recognized the difference in his love-making. It was as if she had never known love before. She was responding, her own fierce desire answering his. She was melting, acquiescing . . . then she remembered. Tearing her mouth away from his, she struck at him wildly with her fists, bit at his cheek with her sharp white teeth.

The physical pain was as nothing compared to the emotional pain he felt. Somehow he had not expected this violent rejection. Just when he thought he could bear no more, she spat out an epithet so terrible that it was like a brand upon his flesh.

"Bastard!"

No sword had ever cut him so deeply. Like a blade in his heart he took the vile word. It turned him to stone. His hands dropped limply from her body.

"Bastard!" she said it again. "Filthy peasant bastard! Nameless dog! If you ever dare to touch me again . . . Never forget. I am the Duchess of Brittany! I will have you killed."

Before her wrath, he seemed to shrivel. "Forgive me, Your Grace. I do forget myself." With these words, he sounded like the old Geoffrey. Coldly devoid of any kind of emotion. "It was the wine." He might have been apologizing for forgetting her book or her kerchief. The words were low and even.

Thrown off balance by his sudden change, panting with exertion and her own emotional outburst, she stared at him in the semidarkness, trying to read his expression and so gain some idea of his intent. She could not see his face.

Like a statue he stood, awaiting her command. If she had driven a blade through his heart, he would have accepted it without protest.

Drawing her robe together at the neck where his rough handling had disarranged it, she drew a deep breath. "You need not see me back to my apartments," she whispered at last.

He stepped farther away from her bowing stiffly. "As you wish, Your Grace."

As he did so, his face was illuminated by the light of the

lantern he had set on the floor. She gasped. His eyes met hers and he straightened instantly, but too late. She had seen the chalk white skin with the smear of blood at the corner of his mouth where her teeth had bitten him. More than that, she had seen the tears sparkling on his cheeks.

"Good night, my lady," he said hoarsely. Without another word he turned on his heel and left her. The darkness swallowed him immediately, but his footfalls echoed in the silent hall.

Chapter 15

The pageantry of the wedding at Calais was all that Joanna had dreamed it would be. Dressed in forest green and gold with the arms of Brittany emblazoned on the skirt of her surcoat and on the canopy above her head, she watched from a specially constructed stand along with other ladies of the nobility.

Four hundred French knights, their swords in hand, knelt before four hundred English knights likewise encumbered while the two kings, Richard and Charles, met and embraced. Then, while tears flowed down the cheeks of many, the tiny princess walked proudly to meet her husband-to-be.

Just seven years old, Isabelle was almost lost in her gown of scarlet velvet, and her fingers, her wrists, her throat, and even her brow were wreathed in heavy, intricately worked gold set with emeralds. Like a tiny star she blazed, and Joanna remembering her own marriage and subsequent disillusionment wept hardest of all.

During the feasting that followed, Joanna enjoyed the constant attention of Henry Bolingbroke, who shared a golden plate with her and cut her meat with his own knife. "I promised Brittany that I would care for you," was his bland explanation when she thanked him profusely for the time he gave her. Only three years older than she and with a position worthy of her own, he charmed her while she basked in his light. Of Geoffrey she had no thought.

For himself the Earl of Hereford was enchanted. He found her an incredibly lovely woman with great intelligence and agreeableness. The fact that she was the sister of the King of Navarre and would in all likelihood shortly be the Dowager Duchess of Brittany made her a pearl beyond price.

They danced and flirted throughout the entire celebration. His heavyset rather short figure could be seen everywhere in English blue and tawny side by side with the slender duchess in forest green.

When the time came for him to return her to Rennes, they spoke together frankly. "Someday soon I will be Duke of Lancaster as well as of Hereford." His blue English eyes surveyed her meaningfully.

"I wish your father long life and you a happy one," Joanna replied.

"As I do your husband, madam."

"That will be as God wills."

"Joanna. I wish to look to the future, perhaps months, perhaps years from now." He took her hands in his. "I find you in every way my vision of a wife who would please me very much."

"I do not know. . . ." She thought with a shudder of the eight children she had already borne. Yet Henry already had his sons. Here might be the answer to all her problems. She did not relish the thought of remaining in Brittany after her husband's death. Her son would be under the direction and guidance of Bretons who would brook no interference from a Navarrese. She did not know her brother, nor did she know one person in Navarre who would welcome her.

As she weighed these unsettling thoughts, Henry studied her impassive face. "What are you thinking?" he asked at last.

She smiled a little sadly, then more gaily. "I was thinking

254

that I would be a fool not to come to you when I am free of my present lord, but I have nothing to bring you. My father never paid my dowry. My husband did not renounce me because of Navarre's death soon after the wedding although he would have been well within his rights to do so."

Her honesty pleased Henry, who smiled in answer as he told her so. "As to your wealth and dowry, your birth and your manner are all that are required. I am a wealthy man and I want you. My stepmother was a Spanish princess. I have often envied my father his pleasure with beautiful women. I think we should suit each other well," he added.

For a fleeting instant she heard a voice say, *I love you.* Then it was gone, and she faced the bearded Englishman whose blue eyes were unclouded by romance. "I think we should indeed."

Geoffrey did not return to Brittany with the knights. He too had reached an agreement with Henry Bolingbroke. Declaring himself a man free to choose whom he would follow, he offered his sword and service to Henry in exchange for passage back to England. "I tire of the life I have led," he admitted candidly. "I have served in France for most of my life, yet I am English as my name proclaims."

"I thought you a sworn vassal of Jean of Brittany." Bolingbroke watched him closely.

The two were of an age, but Geoffrey was half a head taller, his frame although well muscled seemed slender and rangy compared with the earl's chunky solidity. Likewise, his clean-shaven face appeared more youthful than the earl's.

"I am not his slave," Geoffrey replied stubbornly. "If he needs me, I can return to his side immediately. My skills grow rusty, and I . . . I grow restless under the sameness."

Henry could well appreciate that. His own life as son and heir of John of Gaunt had not been without its problems.

"Very well," he shrugged. "I can always use a good man. Your reputation has preceded you, d'Anglais. I heard a tale of your saving the duchess. You are no mean fighter."

Geoffrey looked uncomfortable. "I was once thought proficient, my lord."

"Very well. We will return the duchess to her home where you may collect your movables. Then we shall make swift journey for England."

Geoffrey straightened and stared coldly ahead of him. "I would prefer to return with the main body of your men to England, my lord. I . . . I have my gear with me. There is nothing to return for."

Henry Bolingbroke threw back his head and laughed. "A debt or a woman? Or both, d'Anglais?"

Geoffrey's face remained impassive. "A woman, my lord."

Jean de Montfort's face appeared to crumple at the news that Geoffrey had not returned to Brittany with the entourage. He shortly excused himself, gesturing wearily to the lackey who now wheeled his chair. Shortly after, Henry of Lancaster returned to England, and Montfort took to his bed, complaining to Joanna that the winter was the worst in his memory.

During the next year he improved only slightly in the summer and sank even lower in winter. Jean Charles, his twelve-year-old son, was brought home to learn the business of governing the duchy under the tutelage of several of the duke's most trusted advisors.

Joanna spent long hours daily with him. Although she never visited his bedchamber again at night, her abstinence seemed normal in the face of his painful deterioration.

Montfort rubbed his hands perpetually now and slept little. His swollen joints were so stiff that he could not lie flat in bed, but only on his side, his knees drawn up in the position one took when sitting. Like a statue he had to be lifted and moved. Ever the pale, pain-filled eyes searched the room.

"Why did he leave?" he asked Joanna abruptly one day.

She did not pretend not to know to whom he referred since no one was about. She had been reading aloud to him from a petition of one of the local lords. She did not look at her husband.

"I called him bastard," she said, her voice was so low, Montfort had to strain to hear it.

The silence deepened.

Growing increasingly uncomfortable, she screwed up her courage enough to cast a look from behind her lashes at her husband. His face was still, the pain lines deeper than she had ever seen them. His hands, suddenly still, hung limply over the arms of his chair. After a long moment he sighed. "So he is."

When he made no other comment, she resumed reading.

Joanna fled to her husband's side with the alarming message that Bolingbroke had been exiled to France. The news came to Brittany along with other dispatches of general concern. The Earl of Hereford had been exiled for ten years by order of his cousin Richard II. Distressed in a way Montfort could not know, she sat beside him, listening to his opinion.

Montfort emitted a dry mirthless chuckle at the news. "Richard is a fool. Exile, a fool's trick. Never exile a man unless he be too old to return from it. The son of Lancaster may very well bring down the English throne."

"But suppose he is killed as his uncle Gloucester was last year?" Joanna could not keep the anxiety from her voice.

Catching it, Montfort looked at her appraisingly. "Henry Bolingbroke will be watching for that. Gloucester was old, almost as old as Gaunt and I." He exhibited his hands. "Imagine me if I were sent into exile with an assassin on my trail. I would not last the night. But Henry . . . Ha! Let Richard beware."

"We could offer him a place here," she suggested hopefully.

"A place here? In this backwater it takes weeks for messages to reach us." Montfort's color was high, his back straighter. His eyes flashed their old pale fire as his agile mind examined the possibilities for the Earl of Hereford in Europe.

Suddenly, Joanna was reminded that her husband had usurped his own position. What schemes he must have concocted! What plottings and manipulations! What deeds in the dark!

Montfort's eyes focused on the distant past as he stared into the fire. "My first wife was Gaunt's younger sister, you know," he reminded her. "A cruel family. They have little love for one another. Richard is of the same cloth. He has killed his uncle and he will kill again if he can. The Plantagenet is always the Plantagenet's worst enemy. It will be a duel to the death now between Hereford and Bordeaux. I fear Bordeaux will lose. He had his chance."

Joanna sat silent, remembering the events of her early years.

"Have you an agreement with Hereford?" her husband asked abruptly.

She paled, her hand going immediately to her throat. "How can you think such a thing?"

"I would not be surprised, nor opposed," he told her huskily. His excitement seemed to drain out of him as if he remembered his age. "You will not return to Navarre. It has nothing for you. You are too proud and too young to stay here as dowager duchess, accepting sufferance and finally neglect on the part of Jean Charles. You must have discussed something with Henry while you traveled with him."

She studied the pale, pain-lined face of the man who had been called "the most quarrelsome prince in Europe."

"I am your wife, Jean," she said at last.

"And you still do not trust me." He nodded. "'Tis probably just as well. Trust no one and none will betray you."

The fire crackled and leaped, and in the air between them hung stories that would remain forever untold.

"Ring for that cursed lackey," Montfort wheezed, his voice returning to a creaky whine. "His hands bruise me every time he moves me. No one can do for me like Geoffrey."

As she reached for the bellpull, his voice rose again. "You will have to get permission from the His Holiness to marry again since you have no father. I would suggest you begin the petition immediately. I will sign whatever is necessary to obtain a special permission for you to marry whomever you wish. That way if Bolingbroke is successful, you will be ready to go to him as soon as he should send for you."

Nonplused by his behavior, she came to his side and knelt before him, staring up into his face. "Why are you doing this for me?"

He left off rubbing his hands long enough to touch her cheek. "You have never knelt to me before, Joanna," he observed.

Embarrassed, she bit her lip over the words she would have uttered and struggled to gather her skirts around her to rise.

He put his hand on her shoulder. "No. I know you are proud as your father was proud. Sometimes I wonder how your brother can be Charles the Noble. He must take after his mother. You do not kneel for favor."

With his hand on her shoulder, she remained at his knee. Her face was flushed with shame at her lapse.

He lifted her chin, his swollen reddened knuckles hot and feverish to the touch. "Let me guess. Commands, you can understand. Coercion, you can understand. Demands, threats, even torture—all these you can understand. But you

259

cannot understand someone doing you a kindness. Am I right?"

She stared evenly at him even while prickles of remembered pain and terror rippled across her skin. He had reminded her of many things she had buried deep in the back of her mind because to look at them would drive her mad. He must be manipulating her in some way. Perhaps by getting her to sign certain papers, he could renounce her now and send her on her way since he no longer needed heirs and since Geoffrey was no longer here to impregnate her. Her eyes took on a wary expression.

"I can see that you will say nothing," he continued, dropping his hand back to her shoulder. "You are probably cursing yourself for the unconsidered action of dropping down here beside me."

She stirred restively. "Perhaps I should ring for the valet, Your Grace?"

He sighed. "Ah, Joanna, how we have all used you over the years. Were you ever a child, I wonder?"

"I was my father's daughter," she answered noncommittally.

"And he was notorious for his schemes as was I," Jean nodded. "Ah, well, I see I shall get no fervent declarations from you tonight. But I shall always remember that once you actually asked to know my mind. We might have been very close tonight. I would have liked that. I have not been close to anyone in a long, long time." He stared into her impassive face, his eyes unable to read her thoughts. Then he bent to her. "Gently, my dear. Just once more, humor an old man's fancy." His thin lips brushed against hers, lightly, briefly. Then he drew away. "Ring for the valet. I am unalterably weary."

In July less than a year after he had been banished to France, Henry Bolingbroke landed at Humber in the north of England accompanied by Archbishop Arundel and welcomed by Sir Thomas Percy, Earl of Northumberland, and his son called Hotspur.

Coldly and calculatingly he had come while his cousin Richard was in Ireland putting down an uprising. Richard had outfitted his army by confiscating the lands of John of Gaunt, who had died in the late winter of that same year. Henry, Earl of Hereford, had come to claim more than the lands and title, Duke of Lancaster. With his blue English eyes fixed on the main chance he had come to claim the throne.

Plantagenet fought Plantagenet as Montfort had predicted. The Duke of Brittany sat in his chair throughout the long hot summer chuckling over every message that came from England. As he read of Bolingbroke's successes, he would pat Joanna's hand.

"You see, my dear. I told you he should not come to Brittany. Richard missed his chance. In this life almost no one gets a second chance."

Fearful that he might turn on her at any moment, Joanna held her peace, never revealing her excitement at Henry's victories. Would he remember what they had discussed if he should really come to power? The Earl of Hereford was not too high for her to reach. She could even be the Duchess of Lancaster without stretching—but Queen of England? He would want someone else, someone younger, who would bear him sons.

At the thought she winced. Fervently, she prayed that she would never again endure the pangs of childbirth. Surely, eight pregnancies were enough, and Henry had six children by his first wife, four strong sons and two daughters.

She smiled ruefully. She was undoubtedly racing ahead of the game. He had not won. The next dispatch might bring word of his capture and execution for high treason. Even if he won, she had no guarantees. Men forgot or ignored what they had said to women.

261

Still the Papal Dispensation had been solicited, then duly signed by herself and her husband, Jean de Montfort, who listed himself as aged and infirm. If Henry should survive and should remember, she was prepared.

The word came in the middle of October on a bright gold and russet day. Less than two weeks before, Richard had resigned his crown; he had been deposed for misgovernment by the Lords and Commons who had, in the same declaration, named Henry of Lancaster, direct lineal descendant of Henry III, King of England.

Montfort burst out laughing. "He did it. By God! Pulled off the greatest coup of all. Ah! my friends." He raised his cup in salute. "Drink a toast with me to the continuation of the line of raider princes. Drink to Henry Bolingbroke."

The men at his table drank as did his son Jean Charles, the young Marquis of Brest and of Roche-Bernard. Joanna also drank with him, for his eyes met hers significantly. Her smile was hesitant, but then flashed happily for one minute. Surely, one should be allowed one bright smile for one's husband.

Much later, Montfort drank alone, his eyes fixed on a spot in the far distant past where the shades of his old friends and enemies—John of Gaunt and Charles the Bad, Charles of Valois and Charles of Blois—waited for him. His smile was a as twisted as his body, for it carried a hint of longing too.

With the onset of winter, pain and inactivity had finally taken their toll on the savage heart of Jean de Montfort. He lay on his side in his bed, his wife facing him, her hand clasping his, and his breath rattled in his lungs as the fluid slowly filled them. He could no longer rise. His limbs were virtually locked together. He had a fever which nothing could seem to bring down. The doctor had come to bleed him, but he had been driven away.

"Joanna," he whispered.

"Yes, Your Grace."

Around the bed at his back sat men who had long be
instructed in what to do when this time should arrive. I
sons and daughters had been summoned and dismissed,
except the heir, who sat in a high-backed chair draped wi
forest green and gold velvet. Jean Charles sniffled occasio
ally, but otherwise he maintained a creditable calm for o
not quite thirteen and a half years old.

"So stiff, Joanna, all these years, and you have yet to c;
me by my Christian name unless I require it."

"Jean," she corrected herself.

"Thank you," he replied, a hint of his old irony slippin
back into his voice.

"What are the latest dispatches from England?"

"It is as you predicted, Jean. Richard has died
Pontefract."

"Plantagenet against Plantagenet," he breathed. "Hen
will have trouble keeping his throne, but not from Richard

"Poor man."

"You . . . do not sound like . . . daughter of Navarr
Never pity . . . loser."

"The dispatches say he died of a fever, but the messeng
related how horrible things were done to him. He was
young, strong man, who would not die easily." She shivere
despite the inordinate heat in the room. Not only were bo
fireplaces blazing brightly, but a charcoal brazier stood ne;
her right shoulder, only a few feet from Brittany's head.

"Fools . . . die . . . young."

"Jean, you are wiping out all the good confessions th;
you have made to the priest," she scolded.

His attempt to chuckle ended in a hacking gurgling coug
The cough seemed to clear his lungs for a bit, for his voi
became stronger. "My dear, I shall burn in hell. Th
miserable little confession was not worth the time I took
give it. My sins are too deep upon my soul"—he smiled at h
gently—"and upon your body—yours and Geoffrey's."

She tightened her grip. "Do not think of that, Jean. I forgive you. You did what you had to do. Jean Charles is strong and intelligent. He will be a fine Duke of Brittany." She exchanged glances with her son who smiled weakly at his mother.

"I would do it again, but I wish you had not paid quite so dear a price. Go to England. Marry your king. But in your travels do not forget Geoffrey. If you find him, go to him and tell him . . . Ah!"

His pale eyes widened suddenly as pain struck him. He gasped for breath through blue lips.

"Jean!" Gripping his hand as tightly as she might, she motioned frantically for Jean Charles to come to her side. The boy was around the bed in an instant.

"Father!"

He recognized them. His mouth gaped, and his swollen hands clutched at their hands as if by some miracle they might hold him in this life. Then the breath hissed from his throat as his pain-wracked joints relaxed for the final time and the light forever faded from his strange pale eyes.

Part II

The Queen Of England

Chapter 16

"*San Diego y Santa Rita,* preserve us," Doña Isabella moaned hysterically as the ship emblazoned with the lions and the lilies of Lancaster rolled and pitched crazily in the gray-black waves. The slashing rain and frenzied winds had twisted the English standard round the masthead until only one corner flapped dismally. The storm had caught them in midchannel on their way from St. Malo to Southampton.

The Dowager Duchess of Brittany raised her disordered head to glare disgustedly at her old duenna who had done nothing but pray and moan for five days. Both of the duchess' young daughters had been ill most of the time. In the way of children, they seemed to take turns sleeping between attacks of violent nausea and weeping, so their young mother had had no rest at all. Now she shot Doña Isabella the most withering glare she could summon before returning to the business of wiping the face of her youngest, Thérèse.

The little one moaned fretfully as she turned her head from side to side on the damp pillow.

"Poor baby," Joanna whispered. "Go to sleep now. When you wake up, the boat will sit still." Privately, she doubted her own words. In all probability they had been blown past England and into the great ocean beyond. She would not have been surprised to find them teetering over the edge of the world at any time.

Closing her eyes briefly, she swallowed hard against the motion of her own uneasy stomach. In these times of weakness, horrible moments of doubt rose again to plague her, doubts she had often experienced over the past seven years since she had last seen Henry Bolingbroke. These she dispelled firmly by conjuring a vision of his strong face lighted by clear determined blue eyes.

Furthermore, her sense of her own worth was reassuring. She was the sister of the King of Navarre. Albeit she was forced to admit that connection to be nominal, she was indisputably the Dowager Duchess of Brittany and mother of the present duke. No aspersions could be cast on her connections to the powerful houses of Europe. Henry needed her as much as she needed and desired him.

And she did desire him. With a sense of helpless frustration, she acknowledged that the time had grown long since she had known a man's caress. Sometimes at night she reached out in half-sleep searching for the strength and tenderness that had been hers with Geoffrey. Since his departure, no man had touched her. She had slept alone and walked alone. Her women had chattered around her. Her four sons had grown tall and then had been sent one by one, as was the custom, to serve as pages in ducal and princely houses throughout France. The fact that they acted as hostages to the good behavior of "the most quarrelsome prince in Europe" bothered her not at all. She had done her duty by them.

Jean had required her company during the day, but his crippled appendages had precluded caresses of any kind. Instead his hands had inflicted painful bruises on her shoulders when he had leaned his weight on her to move from one chair to another. Otherwise, she had had physical contact with no man. For the most part, her warmly sensual nature lay submerged within her, but sometimes at night she touched her body with dry, hot palms and thought of Geoffrey.

Geoffrey! She looked around her at the dim cabin. Doña Isabella had ceased her monotonous praying and had turned her face to the wall to rest. Thérèse had lapsed into a restless sleep. Marguerite, the elder daughter by four years, had been asleep for several hours.

Rising unsteadily, Joanna stretched in an effort to ease her cramped muscles. Her breasts lifted, making her conscious that the slight coarseness of the raw silk of her chemise irritated her tender nipples. With a shiver she plucked at the material. Then drawing in her breath sharply, she clasped her breasts in both her hands squeezing in an effort to ease the torment of unassuaged desire.

Geoffrey!

She missed him. Painfully conscious of her body's throbbing, she stood alone in the swaying cabin while her blood heated and her mind conjured up pictures of his hard-muscled body and his gentle hands. She moaned softly at the memory of his mouth working its magic on her nipples, her navel, and the sensitive skin of her inner thighs. Dear God! Geoffrey!

Angrily she tore her hands away from her aching breasts and covered her face. Henry! Please God, let him fill her mind.

He was only a year older than Geoffrey. She knew herself to be strong and lusty. Henry would be too. Together they would ... Despite the pain of childbearing, she would willingly pay the price to be made whole again in the arms of a husband who would be her *husband*. She smiled grimly as she reassured herself with that thought.

A knock at the cabin door interrupted her painful reverie. Hastening to answer, she received the captain's compliments. They were within hailing distance of the coast of Cornwall. Landfall would be at noon.

Closing the door behind the seaman, she braced her

shoulders. The coast of England was in sight. She would be its queen. A new beginning lay before her. The old restricted life of Brittany was behind forever.

After an arduous journey through the snow from Penzance, Joanna met King Henry at Winchester where they were to be married in the great cathedral of his ancestors, Ethelwulf and his son Alfred the Great. Gloomy clouds hung over the city, and Joanna's throat was like a raw wound from the cold she had contracted on the day of disembarkation in Cornwall.

Remembering vaguely her other wedding day and Jean's displeasure with her illness, she carefully concealed her pain behind a bright smile that faltered slightly at the sight of Henry of England.

He was much different from the man she remembered. The blond hair of his beard had darkened, thereby noticeably revealing its streaks of gray. "Madam." His gruff voice as he bent over her hand made her wonder if he suffered also from a sore throat.

"My lord." She curtseyed low. Her black eyes met his with timid eagerness. She had worn her most flattering dress today, a gown of deep red velvet, in honor of the red rose of Lancaster. It was embroidered richly with gold threads worked into a pattern of exotic flowers. The floral design was repeated in the gold filigree cowls on each side of her head. A sheer veil of muted golden silk was suspended between the cowls. As she knelt, it floated softly around her.

For a moment he searched her face. She was as he remembered, a little older perhaps, but only a little. Her delicate face was as yet unlined. Her lips were full and red, her cheeks flushed from the harsh bite of the English air. He allowed his tense face to relax into a welcoming smile.

Joanna thought she had never seen a man so changed in so short a space of time. He looked at least ten years older than his thirty-seven years. A quiver of disappointment ran through her body. Was she again marrying an old irascible man? Clear-eyed, she surveyed his body, stocky as she remembered and of medium height. Was she imagining that the joints of his fingers were slightly swollen when he took her hand in his to lead her into the cathedral?

Several times during the protracted ceremony, she glanced sideways at him. Eyes screwed tightly shut, he prayed long, his lips moving soundlessly behind his steepled fingers. His fervency surprised her somewhat. She had not remembered him as a particularly religious man.

"We will have a proper ceremony at Westminster," he assured her at the hastily prepared banquet that night. "This hugger-mugger pleases me not at all. Damn all captains!"

"He could not help the storms," Joanna inserted softly.

"He shall be punished. I entrusted my affianced bride to his care. I expect superior seamanship." Henry's face glowed red with anger as his fist clenched around the knife beside his plate.

"But he brought us safely to land," Joanna insisted. "Surely the man should be rewarded for his *excellent* seamanship. The ships lost at sea and never heard from again are numberless."

Henry turned angrily to her. "Do you have some special interest in this man?"

Suddenly, she was a fifteen-year-old girl again facing an old angry man at a wedding banquet. One word more would jeopardize her position. Yet she must speak. She was no longer fifteen, but thirty-three. As she meant to go on, so she must begin.

Smiling her most brilliant smile, she placed her hand over Henry's clenched fist. "How silly you are, my lord!" she whispered, leaning in his direction so that the floating silk of her veil brushed his shoulder. "Of course, I have no interest in this man. I doubt I should recognize his face were you to bring him into the banquet tonight. 'Tis not that I am

271

unobservant. 'Tis instead that I have no interest in anything behind me. I want to live from this day forward . . . with you. This is the first day of our life together. I want nothing more to do with what has gone before."

His face relaxed almost imperceptibly.

With a winning smile, she hastened on. "Look around you, my lord King. Are we not fortune's favorite children? Do we not wear her stars in our crowns? Through strength and brilliance, you have taken your rightful place as King of England. By your love and honor, I am to be your queen. We shall be happy as most of our rank never have a chance to be, for we have carved our fates for ourselves."

His hand turned beneath hers to clasp her fingers and raise them to his lips. His blue English eyes sparkled for the first time with something very like gaiety. "You are right." He chuckled. "Now I remember why I wanted you above all others, why I have never been able to get you out of my mind."

His lips against the back of her hand sent a thrill through her. Surprising herself with her own temerity, she drew his hand to her lips in turn. Beneath the shadow of her veil, she kissed his fingertips one by one and then his palm. His harsh indrawn breath told her he was as eager for her as she for him.

What they might have said next was interrupted when a noisy Englishman farther down the table rose to propose a toast to the long health and happiness of the king and his beautiful queen.

Thereafter, while the rounds of toasts lasted far into the night, Henry kept his hand entwined with Joanna's, saying no more about the captain, but smiling and drinking without a sign of care. Finally, in consideration for her exhaustion and his own desire for the formal ceremony of union, he excused himself from her bed that night with a beautiful smile that warmed her heart.

*　　　*　　　*

There was a smile on Henry's face when, three weeks later, they rode together through the streets of London to Westminster Abbey. As Henry had informed her, her coronation was a cause for celebration and also an opportunity for him to distribute largesse.

"Is there trouble that you seek to avoid?" she asked pointedly.

"Rumblings," he replied offhandedly. "Mere rumblings. A man does not take the throne from a living king, usurper or not, without creating a host of enemies among those disgruntled supporters who have lost their positions with their man's downfall."

The knowledge cast a shadow on her delight in the elaborate celebration. Again political expediency, not a woman's pleasure, was the reason for this pageantry and beauty. Dressed again in her red velvet gown, she smiled at the sight of the unusual number of men and women wearing red hoods to display loyalty and support for the red rose of Lancaster. The square in front of the Abbey where she was to be crowned was thronged with them.

In answer to her inquiring look, Henry smiled. "'Tis part of my plan to keep the populace content. I caused the garments to be distributed some days ago to add a festive air to the whole city. People will know themselves to be living prosperously and happily if such celebrations occur."

They rode together on horses white as milk at the head of a long procession. In deference to her fear of riding, Henry had placed a lead rein on her mount. Immediately following them came the king's four sons. Prince Henry, the eldest, rode slightly before his brothers—Thomas, John, and Humphrey. All around her the people jostled each other and made comments in voices loud enough for her to understand although her English was limited.

"Smile to the people," Henry commanded softly in French. Withdrawing a purse from his belt, he shook out some pennies into her hand. "Toss these into the crowd." Hesitating, she looked nervously into the sea of upturned

273

faces pressed so close about her horse.

"Throw some this way, pretty lady," yelled an eager voice.

"Jesu bless her," shrilled a woman. "She be goin' to throw some at me."

At these words the crowd pressed eagerly forward, jostling the men-at-arms assigned to hold them back. Joanna's horse sidled and rose slightly to the length of the rein. In panic, she dropped the coins beneath its hooves and clutched at the pommel.

With a concerted cry several men pushed the guards aside and flung themselves onto the cobbles, careless of the hooves. Helplessly, Joanna felt the horse stumble as one iron shoe drove into flesh. A woman screamed in terror.

Cursing viciously, Henry spurred his horse forward dragging her mount after him. Sick to her stomach, Joanna twisted round in the saddle to see a still form crumpled on the cobbles. Around it a melee ensued between guards and those struggling for the few pitiful coppers.

"Poins be dead!" the woman shrieked again. "Oh, me poor boy. She rode him down and killed him."

"Hush your mouth!" a companion commanded, leading her away. "He dived for the coins. He took his chances."

Thoroughly shaken, Joanna reeled in the saddle as Henry pulled their mounts to a halt before the door of the magnificent cathedral. His hands closed round her waist as he brought her down to stand beside him. "Clumsy fool," he snarled. "I wanted the populace appeased, not murdered."

Sick with guilt and shaking with the nervous tension horseback riding always generated in her, Joanna could not be sure she was not the clumsy fool he had declared her. Humbly she clasped her hands. "I could not help it. I beg you, pardon me."

He shot her a black look before turning to face the waiting officials, including the mayor, the aldermen, and the sheriffs, all in their robes of office. "It does not bode well," he muttered in French for her ears only.

Outside the cathedral after the coronation, Henry threw money again to the waiting crowd, as did his four sons, but Joanna kept her hands firmly clasped on the pommel of her saddle and stared straight ahead. If her behavior seemed cold to the people, their opinion was the least of her concerns. Her head ached from the weight of the headdress that towered over her a full two feet. A long heavy scarf of red silk floated from its wire frame. The day had been cold and clear at its outset, but now the clouds gathered and a drizzle began to fall, dampening the cobblestones and making riding treacherous. Several times her horse's hooves slipped, throwing her to one side or the other and disturbing her precarious seat.

The king had caused to be hired a band of musicians from Suffolk to play before them, but the troop made little music, being more inclined to loud bursts of horns and only occasional snatches of tunes on pipes and hand drums. Their stringed instruments had been stowed away from the wet.

At one particularly loud blast, Joanna's horse snorted and threw up its head. It stumbled once, then twice, almost going to its knees. Teeth clenched, she gave up all pretense of holding the reins and clung terrorized to the pommel, her knuckles gone white.

A strong brown hand reached across her and caught the rein, jerking the beast's head up and assisting it to regain its balance. Joanna stared into the face of her stepson, reading there amusement and not a little contempt. "You seem to have trouble controlling your mount," he observed silkily. "Allow me to help you."

Ignoring his attitude, she accepted the gesture as if he had offered it out of consideration. "I thank you humbly, sir." She flashed him a brilliant smile of relief as if his rescue were the most wonderful thing in the world. "I must admit I do not ride well, and the cobblestones are treacherous."

The king pulled his mount even with her on the other side and leaned across them. "I had planned to introduce you two formally tonight, but I find you already conversing together. Joanna, this is my oldest son and heir, named Henry after me, but called Hal."

Joanna smiled again at them both. Their horses were walking three abreast while around them the people cheered and applauded. "He has assisted me, my lord, even as you. I apologize sincerely for the bother." She bowed her head humbly. "I learned to ride too late and must confess a dread of it."

"We are nearing the field," Henry consoled her. "Only a little further to go, and your ordeal will be ended."

Looking ahead, she saw the brilliant gonfalons suspended from the poles marking the lane to the field. The sun, so long behind the clouds, broke through at that moment picking out the blocks of color which formed their intricate designs.

As they rode onto the field, it was obvious that many had come before them; the colorful tents of the participating knights were already erected at either end. They dismounted before a grandstand covered with muted blue cloth on which was emblazoned the red rose of Lancaster.

"Again I shall make formal introductions later," Henry spoke half apologetically. He extended his hand to an elderly woman whose soft, lined face bespoke her years. "This is my aunt, Lady Margaret, the Countess of Pembroke. She is the sister of my father."

Involuntarily, Joanna sank in a deep curtsey. Impossible to forget were the hours spent with Brittany in reminiscences of the fabled family of Edward III, victor of Crécy. As one in awe before a deity she raised her eyes to accept the white hand of the sister of the Black Prince, Edmund of Langley, Thomas of Woodstock, and John of Gaunt. These raider princes of Europe, who had taken the land and the daughters of Spain and France, were the stuff of fairy tales.

"Your Majesty," the old lady chided softly, although her

face reflected her pleasure at the obeisance, "I am the one who should kneel to you."

Henry, too, smiled at this charming show of respect. With unusual solicitude he bent to raise Joanna to her feet. "The pleasures of our new day as king and queen await." He spoke low in her ear.

When they were seated, the marshal gave the signal. At a blast of trumpets, the pageant began. From the far end of the field rode a file of knights clad in every style of armor, all polished to a high sheen for the occasion. Over the glittering metal they wore surcoats of green, black, red, blue, and purple, all charged with a fantastic variety of arms. Their destriers likewise were draped in the huge horse cloths of the same design as the rider's surcoat. From the tips of the lances flew their standards.

Clutching the arms of her chair with excitement, Joanna tried to see everything at once. Around her, servants were serving refreshments. The Suffolk musicians had taken out their other instruments and were playing some recognizable French tunes in her honor.

In front of the stand, the knights formed a line facing the king. While squires held the mettlesome horses, each man removed his helm and dipped his lance in turn. Some ladies leaned forward to attach fine scarves, gloves, or ribbons to the tips as favors for their champions.

The king's champion, a huge figure in German armor polished to a blue sheen, dipped his lance to receive her scarf. As she rose to attach it, her eyes skimmed the line of combatants. Next to last on the left side, a familiar face caught and held her gaze.

Geoffrey, her own Geoffrey, was a combatant in this tournament. As his eyes momentarily met hers across the line of horses, her hands faltered, nearly dropping the rose red scarf. Then a warhorse moved fretfully between them.

Hastily, she tied the favor; the champion inclined his head and, with a tug at his reins, wheeled his horse to thunder

277

away down the field. His movement was the signal for the others to follow his lead. With another blast of trumpets, the joust began.

The old bloody brutal tournaments of the round tables had long been forbidden by the Church. Furthermore, from the economic standpoint, maintaining large numbers of knights to do war against other feudal princes was a thing of the past. They were too expensive to outfit and their vulnerability to archers had been soundly demonstrated by their stunning defeat at Crécy at the hands of the Black Prince. Therefore, the jousts in celebration of the coronation were strictly for show, held between friendly local combatants and knights who moved on a tourney circuit throughout England for the purpose of staging fights. Even so, the shock of horse and lance against a man's shield resulted in many terrible accidents.

Joanna clasped her hands together nervously as the first of many trials was announced. Suppose Geoffrey were the challenger. A man might be disemboweled by a lance slipping off the curve of the shield. Frantically, she realized she could not recognize his armor. Though she listened carefully, she could not understand the names of the combatants. The herald's pronouncements were too distorted by his efforts to be heard.

Then a rumble of excitement went up around her, as did a cheer from the commons lining the field. With a flash of spurs and a thunder of hooves, the king's champion charged down the line, striking the shield of his opponent dead center and splintering his lance. The pounding of the mighty horses, the clang of metal on metal drew a concerted gasp from the crowd as the stands trembled slightly. The challenger was thrown backward against the cantle of his saddle but managed to maintain his balance as the horses swept on past each other. Accepting another lance from his waiting squire, the champion came at his opponent again, this time unseating the man easily.

Wordlessly, Joanna watched as several squires loosened the downed man's helm and raised him to his feet. Dark hair plastered to a sweating forehead, assured her that he was a stranger. As each pair was announced, she listened carefully but vainly for the sound of Geoffrey's name.

At last a name sounding somewhat like his was announced. A knight in a forest green surcoat with a white *barre sinistre* across a black shield reined a heavy gray destrier into the line. The emblem confirmed his identity. "Geoffrey." Her lips formed his name as he set spurs to his mount's flanks and leaned forward to yell in its ear.

Two passes the knights made without either doing more than rocking his opponent. Joanna drew a deep breath. But her relief came too soon. On the last charge the lance of the knight in green snapped. The challenger leaned forward with redoubled effort and thrust him from the saddle.

A general round of applause accompanied the action while the commons cheered lustily. Forgetting herself in her anxiety, Joanna half rose from her chair.

"What is it, my dear?"

From far away Henry's voice penetrated the roaring in her ears. What if Geoffrey were killed? Her heart beating like thunder in her chest, she stared at the still form face down in the churned muck.

The squires ran forward to turn the downed man over, but before they could do more, he began to struggle upright himself.

"Sir Geoffrey is a stout man," Henry remarked. "Unusual to see him unhorsed. Bad luck with the lance. Not his own fault."

"The luck is about all that makes jousting interesting," languidly interposed an older man to whom Joanna had not been introduced. "Everyone knows who will win. There are only a few superior knights. The rest are incredibly mediocre and all are cowards. I beg you, Your Majesty, to declare your champion the winner and get on with the melee. Everyone is getting bored and drunk."

Turning to Joanna, Henry raised an eyebrow at her white face. "Has something alarmed you, my lady?"

Without thinking, she spoke her mind. "I believe I recognized Sir Geoffrey d'Anglais from Brittany, my lord. I was fearful in his behalf."

Henry scowled at her. "You did, my dear. I had forgotten you knew him."

The squires had pulled Geoffrey to his feet and relieved him of his helm. With an impatient hand, he pushed them away. Slipping his mailed hood back, he revealed the distinctive silver blond hair she had caressed.

A piercing pain shot through her as he faced the stands, his stance proud. Again their glances met, longer this time, hers naked with love and pity, his all smoldering defiance. Hurt by the feelings his face revealed, she felt her color recede.

"He is unhurt," Henry remarked as he raised his goblet and laughingly toasted the standing man. "'Tis all in mockery. They do but jest."

Reaching for the goblet of wine on the small table at her side, Joanna took a slow sip, hiding her white face. In her delight at seeing Geoffrey, she had forgotten the circumstances under which they had parted. Evidently, his jealous anger had not cooled. The *barre* on his shield further proclaimed his dissatisfaction with fate. At that moment she understood his shame and his anger at her.

Watching him through her eyelashes, she noted that Geoffrey limped badly as he strode away. The fall today had probably not caused such damage. Had he been wounded in service to the king and not healed properly? Setting her cup down, she drew a deep breath, remembering as she did so the meticulous care with which he had been treated when he had saved her life. How she regretted this more recent damage to his lean strong body.

Shaking her head after his disappearing figure, she turned her attention to her new husband. In Henry she had everything she could ever want. All around her the occupants of the stands were raising their cups in response to a toast to the king and his beautiful new queen.

She had achieved more than her father had ever dreamed for her. A warm wave of satisfaction swept through her as she placed her hand in Henry's and rose beside him to acknowledge the tributes.

Chapter 17

Prince Henry, heir apparent to the throne, had been born at Monmouth to Mary of Bohun, daughter of the Earl of Hereford and one of the richest young ladies in England. Unfortunately, she had been dead nine years, so long that the prince could barely remember her. Only sixteen, he nevertheless considered himself very much a man. His father, he considered incredibly old at thirty-six.

He regarded his new stepmother with angry, resentful eyes. Her undeniably beautiful presence seemed to extend the time before he reached his own majority. Seeing his father as a lusty virile man gave the lie to the idea that the king would soon die and leave the kingdom to his eager son, while the idea of these two "old" people locked in the pleasures of the bedchamber repelled Prince Henry. Furthermore, if the beautiful queen should conceive, he would have more heirs to contend with in a climate that would become more explosive as his three younger brothers attained their majority. Therefore, he scowled menacingly at his stepmother from under his dark Bohun brows.

Smiling at him now, Joanna recognized the signs of jealousy and uncertainty that racked all the royal princes and princesses of Europe, herself included. Like animals defending their territories, they snarled at all intruders whether threatening or not. "May I call you Hal?" she asked him sweetly. He had sat silently on her left at the elaborate banquet following the tournament; on her right her new husband quaffed fine wine as if it were water and called for more.

"If it pleases you to do so," the boy replied after a moment, "but I shall always address you as Your Majesty."

Joanna put a gentle white hand on his arm. "Why such formality among family members?" she asked, smiling her most engaging smile.

"We can never be anything but enemies." His serious face was grave beyond his years, just as hers had been. Vaguely, she remembered her brothers' sufferings under French torture. But why was this prince suffering? He was the undisputed first-born of his father.

"I am not your enemy, Prince Henry," she informed him gently. "Your father's marriage to me is one of convenience. My connections in Europe are useful to him."

His hand clenched around the stem of his goblet. In stubborn silence he raised it to his lips, refusing to look at her again.

Shrugging, she turned her attention back to her husband. His blond mustache glistened with drops of wine. Even as she sought to get his attention, he held his goblet over his shoulder for the hovering servant to refill. Taking her courage in her hands, she smiled tremulously at him. "Perhaps I should signal some of my ladies that I wish to retire?" she suggested.

In the act of bringing the wine to his lips, Henry stiffened. Setting his goblet down carefully, he avoided her inquiring look. "I cannot come to you tonight, my dear," he announced after a short pause.

At his cool rebuff, she drew back in confusion. Shame at her boldness flooded her features with a dull red wash. Hastily, she reached for her own scarcely touched wine. "I beg pardon, my lord," she whispered in some agitation. "I did not think . . . that is, I thought . . ."

He interrupted her, shaking his leonine head irritably. "I go to the wars. For that reason I married you in such unseemly haste in Winchester. For that reason I have packed all the coronation festivities into one day. My enemies gather around an illegal claimant to the throne, an upstart boy whose uncles by marriage, the earls of Worcester and Northumberland, seek to take the throne from me."

"I see," she whispered through stiff lips.

"Ah, but I think you do not see. The boy is my cousin. He is Edmund, Earl of March. His father was the heir presumptive to the late usurper Richard who died without issue. But his father's claim was as false as Richard's, for it was through the female line." His voice began to rise and thicken.

Talk around the table ceased as Henry's anger built. Joanna stared at him in growing dismay and not a little fear. What had she married into? Revolt and threats of revolt did not disturb her. Montfort's suzerainty had never been quiet. But Montfort had maintained an icy sardonicism throughout his lifetime. With nerves like steel, he had faced the devil with aplomb, and he had never drunk to excess nor given vent to useless fits of temper.

Beside her, Henry of England began to rave. "These Percys!" He spat the name from foam-flecked lips. "Thomas and Henry and now Henry's son. Hotspur! I have offered them all, but they want more. Bah!" He threw a furious accusing look at his own son sitting quiet and still beyond Joanna. "And I get little or no help from my own son while this Hotspur fights for his father."

Feeling herself in the line of fire, Joanna pressed back against her chair, as the prince met his king's accusation with an angry scowl. Father and son faced each other across her body.

"*You will* ride with me. By God! I won this kingdom for you. You will help me to defend it." Henry slammed his goblet down on the table so hard that the golden stem crumpled and ruby wine splashed across the white cloth. Rising so quickly that the table was nearly pushed from its trestles, he threw the heavy oaken chair backward before addressing the assembled men. "Prepare yourselves tonight. I bid you all go pray. I had planned with my new wife to go on Crusade, but this must be set aside, as must she, when trouble threatens our kingdom."

Without a backward glance at his bride, he stormed from the room. At once there was a rising rumble of voices: commenting, questioning, bidding one another farewell and good luck. Hastily, the men of Henry's cadre quit the table, leaving the ladies sitting aghast amid the remains of the banquet. Last to leave was the prince.

White to the lips, he rose, setting his chair back with silent care. A slight stiff smile curved his mouth as he bowed formally to Joanna. "I felicitate you on your marriage, Your Majesty," he murmured ironically.

Lying in the royal bedchamber where she had hoped to become a bride, Joanna stared dismally at the canopy overhead. Henry was too beset with revolution to make her his wife in truth. And if he were killed, what then? His son would become king immediately. Then where would she go? Her marriage contract gave her a substantial allowance and the beautiful palace called Havering-atte-Bower, which she had never seen.

Would she ever see it? If Henry did not return, would she be paid the allowance and allowed to live in peace? Remembering her own father and his failure to pay her marriage portion, she knew she could not trust the word of king or prince, especially a prince who so obviously hated her.

Sadly, she smoothed the thin silk of what was to have been her nuptial gown. So much for her naïvely romantic dreams of a golden king who would make her his wife. Good-bye to her private fantasies of happy hours spent in the marriage bed while he led her in a man's way to heights of ecstasy. Good-bye also to her dreams that he would come to love her with true affection and welcome her own expressions of sensuality with excitement and delight. Disappointment stabbed at her with a pang so fierce that her entire body tensed in reaction.

Sternly, she forced herself to relax. Her thoughts turned to Geoffrey. She wondered if he had ridden with the king and his men. Undoubtedly, he had done so. Although she had not seen him at the banquet tonight, he was well spoken of by the king. What if he died before she had a chance to renew their friendship? Breathlessly, she remembered his kiss in the corridor the night she had met Bolingbroke. Did she long for that fierce burning passion again?

Angrily, she sat up in bed. First Henry and now Geoffrey. Her body must be in dire need. Since there seemed little likelihood of her finding relief anytime in the near future, she sought to calm herself. These thoughts would drive her mad if she persisted with them. She must compose her mind and give herself some respite. Always women must wait and pray. The knowledge of her role made her clench her fists in frustration.

In his own bed, Geoffrey smiled slightly at the thought that Henry would march westward tomorrow. His own sources had informed him of the king's angry retreat from the banquet. Acknowledging his jealousy, his hatred, his embarrassment at being unhorsed in front of his former mistress, he reveled in the knowledge that she would be denied the consummation of her marriage.

Dog in the manger, he named himself with a heartfelt curse. But she had been so beautiful, so incredibly beautiful in her red velvet dress with her flawless white skin and her magnificent black eyes. How many times had he drowned in their dark pools? Had he lost his soul in them as well as his heart and mind?

Seven years had passed since he had seen her. She should have grown old and twisted. As God knew, he had. Ruefully, he ran his hand down the outside of his left thigh at the same time he gingerly flexed his knee. The grinding, snapping sound of improperly meshed joints made him wince. The only blessing in this whole unfortunate accident was the fact that the limb did not hurt. Recently he had been exercising it with some results. Perhaps eventually it would regain some ease of movement. Nevertheless, he was resigned to walking with a limp for the rest of his life and never regaining the facility of movement he had always enjoyed.

He had not worn greaves that day. Most knights left them off in the hope that they would be able to move more easily if unhorsed, for the shield protected the left leg down to the boot and the horse's body protected the right. No one could have foreseen the freak accident that had driven the edge of his own shield into the side of his unprotected knee. The force of it had smashed bones and torn ligaments while the skin had hardly been broken. Not even a scar was left to show the extent of the damage to that most sensitive and valuable of all joints in the body.

He cursed softly as the leg crackled and ground when he straightened it beneath the covers. To the epithet *bastard,* she would now be able to add *cripple.*

Proud bitch! The memory of her incredible beauty made him writhe inwardly. How he wanted to hate and despise her! He had searched diligently but futilely for a living woman to replace her. Most of the females he'd approached were so stupid that he'd felt himself to be talking with children. If he met an occasional one with intelligence, he found her unresponsive at worst, at best only passive. Yet he knew himself to be unfair. They were only pallid by comparison to her because he loved her to the point where no one else could even interest him. Groaning through his teeth, he remembered Joanna's fierce passion, her wild sweet kisses, her strong white thighs clasping him and forcing him close.

He threw an arm across his eyes, writhing as he felt his manhood harden despite himself. God! Would he never be free? The scar she had caused to be placed on his body—the brand on his belly—white now, but clearly outlined, was nothing to the brand in his heart.

For half a year Joanna maintained an uneasy presence in the English court. Not quite queen yet certainly not a visitor, she presided at table and in Council, taking the chair of state and receiving deference of a tentative sort. The ladies puzzled over her as did the lords who did not fight in the west. The Percys had been joined by the Scot, Douglas, and the Welshman, Owen Glendower. Reports from Henry were varied. Sometimes he seemed to be winning. Sometimes the news was not good. When it was bad, she knew by their lack of deference that her authority was presumptive, but who could gainsay her? She was the legal wife and the crowned queen? Her stepsons were all too young. Still many murmured about the Earl of March.

Those who came to support her were unquestionably loyal to the king, and they clearly saw that she was accustomed to the business of ruling. And so she was, Jean de Montfort's declining health having required her presence almost continuously during his last years. Yet her calm demeanor and wise adjudicating in Council created no resentment on that score. If Henry were angered at her behavior, he would be the one to throw her down. On the other hand, if another tried to do so, the king's ire might fall on that unfortunate soul.

The first of August, the king returned victorious from Shrewsbury. Worcester was executed for treason, Douglas of Scotland was captured but released and Hotspur was slain by an arrow through the forehead. The Welshman Glendower had retreated into his impregnable mountains to lick his wounds once more. All was serene in the west.

In his victory, however, Henry looked like a man who had lain in hell through all the hot summer. Though Joanna had arranged to welcome his returning army, again furnishing the citizens of London with red hoods, the procession to the Abbey pleased him not at all. His blue eyes, red-rimmed and bloodshot, stared around him angrily. His fair face was blistered where the sun had burned him.

Within the Abbey, Henry was conducted to the tomb of Edward the Confessor where he knelt and prayed fervently. Kneeling by his side, Joanna stared at his steepled fingers. They were definitely swollen. God forbid that he should develop the terrible crippling arthritis that had made Jean's life such a hell on earth.

Beside her, Henry suddenly slumped back on his heels. Dropping his hands to his side palms up, he threw back his head, so he appeared to be staring into the vault of the ceiling.

"My lord?" Joanna whispered uncertainly, glancing upward into the gloomy arches.

"I have killed my friends," he whispered. "God forgive me. I have murdered . . . *murdered* . . . my friends." The tears started from his eyes and poured unchecked down his cheeks.

Catching up his limp hand, Joanna chafed it between her own. "They were your enemies, Henry."

He shook his head as more tears trickled into his beard. "No. They were my friends. When I landed at Hull, Percy met me. They gave me support, and I have murdered them." His hand trembled in Joanna's grasp. "We were like brothers. A man who murders his brother is damned." His voice sank to a dry whisper. "Damned for a fratricide . . ." He began to sob in great wrenching gulps of sound.

"Damned for a fratricide," he repeated. "I did not do it for this. Dear God! I did not do it for this."

"Henry!" Joanna edged closer to him, throwing an arm around his now-heaving shoulders. She kept her voice low as she resorted to sibilant whispers, her lips against his ear. "You are exhausted, my lord. No king likes to kill his subjects, but they were traitors. Do you think they would be kneeling and weeping if they had killed you? Brace up. Give thanks to God who has given you the victory. He must mean for you to rule wisely and long."

"Joanna," Henry closed his eyes and rested his head on her shoulder. "Ah, Joanna. If you only knew . . ."

"I do know, Henry, my king," she soothed him. "I do know." As if he were a child and she a mother, she patted his wet cheek.

Helping him to rise, she motioned to his aides-de-camp to help him from the Abbey by a side door. Her instructions to her stepson were concise and brooked no argument. "Say the king is exhausted and heartsick over the deaths of so many of his loyal friends. Say that while he rests to regain his strength, he bids his men continue the celebration."

Then with her silk veil floating behind her, she hurried after the aides who supported the faltering king to apartments in the White Tower. When they had stripped him of his armor and laid him on a bed, she sent them away. Dragging a chair close to his side, she took his hand.

For many minutes they remained silent. His face was careworn, and his bright red-gold beard was dulled by numberless strands of gray. As she stared, she found she could detect few traces of the handsome adventurer who had offered her hope of happiness. With a sinking feeling, she watched his chest rise and fall as his lips moved ceaselessly and tears flowed from the corners of his eyes.

At last he seemed to sleep; then his eyes opened. "I must take the Cross," he announced. "I must go on Crusade. 'Tis my only hope of Heaven. I must go to Jerusalem." He looked at her as if seeing her for the first time. "You will go with me, will you not, Joanna? It will be an adventure such as I promised you." His eyes beseeched her as his words told her he remembered the plans they had made so long ago.

The stories she had heard of crusades made her certain she did not want to go. Filth, heat, flies, and death were the major subjects discussed by the crusaders who returned from Outremer. After the jongleurs had sung their lies, stories came forth of men who fell dead from their horses, their brains cooked within their helms; of a barren land whose people hated the very sight of a fair European; of a long arduous way to a tomb that when all was said and done was nothing but an empty hole.

Madness! she thought. Then she looked at his pleading expression. Now was not the time to argue with him. Smiling gently, she patted his hand. "I am yours to command, Henry. The fact that you ask me to go, when you could order, makes me all the more bound to your will."

Sighing as if relieved of a great burden, he closed his eyes. "The kingdom is riddled with traitors and heresies, Joanna. I caused to be passed a statute against heresy shortly after I became king, but it has not helped the Church. I cannot bear to see a man burned for what he believes, yet if his pain be brief and he escape the fires of hell . . ."

He rambled on, mulling his problems over, talking them through as she listened. So had she done with Montfort. Automatically, she inserted a word here and there, but her heart ached within her. If a victory plummeted her husband into depression, what would a defeat do?

After what seemed like hours, a knock sounded at the door. Joanna admitted Henry's personal physician, a small Italian with sharp black eyes that missed nothing. He was accompanied by the king's gentleman of the chamber. With a niggardly bow, she stepped out into the hallway, feeling as if she had wrestled with the problems of the world.

In the great hall below, the nobles and knights had

assembled to await word of the king's condition. The seat of honor, far from being left empty, was occupied by the prince, who rose anxiously as she approached. "How does my father?"

"Well," she replied immediately, summoning a neutral smile. "I beg you, my lords, to partake of the feast I have prepared in celebration. He is merely tired. As the prince has told you, he feels strongly the deaths of his friends."

The sober mood of the assemblage was dispelled as servants passed among them with cups of wine, ale, and beer. Long tables had been set up with every type of meat and various breads and cheeses. Knowing the tastes of hungry men, she had ordered the servants to set out exotic candied fruits from faraway lands and nuts coated in honey to tempt their palates. After months of field rations, the men fell to with a will.

The celebration begun, Joanna soon seized the opportunity to slip away. No other women had been invited to this strictly male activity. Soon the talk would become ribald, the curses and oaths vile. With a sigh of relief, she closed the door and hurried down the long hall toward the apartments prepared for her.

Behind her the door opened and limping footsteps proceeded in her direction. Recognition sent prickles up her spine and she purposely slowed her steps. Geoffrey had followed her. Thrilled by his advance, she turned, smiling, to face him as he caught up to her.

"My lady." Bowing slightly, he offered her his arm as he had done so often. As if they had never been separated, she rested her hand in its accustomed place.

"Sir Geoffrey."

They were walking now. But her hand trembled, and her normal breathing seemed shallow as if she could not take enough air into her lungs to supply her racing heart.

"How does the king?" His voice sounded deeper than she remembered.

"He is troubled. He hates the deaths of his loyal subjects."

Geoffrey coughed drily. "He hates the deaths of all his subjects, loyal or no." He nodded grimly. "His guilt rides him hard. The Percys helped him to the throne. He gave them much, but they expected more from him. When he failed to show what they believed to be proper gratitude, they rose up. Great fools they. A bit of patience would have served them better. Hotspur, the son, who was his great favorite, had already been greatly elevated. Young Percy had been much at court as a mentor for the prince who . . . ah . . . lacks something of true filial devotion. In doing battle Northumberland cost the son everything including his life."

"You speak of patience." Joanna smiled. "Obviously, you have profited from it. You have been much rewarded and have grown in his service." Joanna could not gauge his attitude. Where did his sympathies lie? Surely with Henry who had made a place for him in England.

"Oh, indeed." His tone was carefully level. "I have a couple of fine horses, armor, a squire, a small townhouse; and my sword arm is still as strong as ever."

She thought she detected a note of bitterness. "How did you . . . that is . . . Did you hurt yourself at Shrewsbury?" She knew he had not. The minute the words were out, she realized her mistake. She bit her lip.

His face darkened at what he correctly interpreted to be pity. Proud as ever, he forced himself not to limp although a twinge of pain made him regret his strained movement. "An accident on the tourney circuit last year. It heals slowly."

They had arrived at the door of the royal apartments. Guards stood at attention on either side. "Oh, but that is not so long," she consoled him. "I am sure it will heal with no trace. I should be glad to provide an accomplished physician. . . ."

He drew back instantly, inclining his head in a stiff bow. "You need not trouble yourself, Your Majesty."

To her dismay she realized he was leaving her with so much unsaid. "'Tis no trouble. I would be happy. Only say the word."

"Good night, Your Majesty." He turned to leave her.

When he would have turned away, she put out a hand to detain him. "Geoffrey." She switched to the language that had been her second tongue. "I would speak with you at a later time. I would know of your adventures and I have many things to tell you that you will want to hear."

He raised a pale eyebrow but followed her lead by replying in French. "Such as?"

She hesitated as she dredged her thoughts. "Jean missed you," she blurted.

"Indeed. I would have thought he would have been glad to see me gone. My purpose, after all, had been accomplished."

Her eyes shifted warily to the impassive guards. "I missed you too," she told him softly. She could not forebear to lay her hand on his arm.

He looked at it quizzically and then up at her. "I remember how you begged me to stay," he replied meaningfully. He dropped his arm to his side, so that her hand fell away.

"I did not know you were leaving," she called. But he was already hurrying down the hall, trying proudly but vainly not to limp.

Within the privacy of her own room, she covered her face with her hands. So much she had wanted to say to him remained unsaid. Deliberately, he had followed her from the hall but to what purpose when he abandoned her after a brief meaningless exchange. Her heart hurt her badly.

Shivering, she wrapped her arms around her body as her blood heated. The feel of his arm beneath her hand had stirred her almost unbearably. If the corridor had been deserted, she doubted that she could have controlled herself. She was the queen, yet she lusted not for the king but for a baseborn knight. She set her teeth to keep from sobbing.

Banked fires of desire had burst into bright flame within her, yet the realization that her long-suppressed passion was overcoming her reason frightened her.

She could not afford to play such a dangerous game. Queens had died for less—and their lovers with them. Wearily, she climbed into the deep bed. The room was warm from the heat of the day and the unnecessary fire which some overzealous servitor had laid. Throwing back the blankets, she covered herself with the sheet and stared upward at the writhing shadows the flames cast on the canopy above her.

"Geoffrey," she whispered through lips that barely moved. How she longed for his body. In the grip of a powerful fantasy, she pressed her hands to her breasts. Swollen and aching, they begged for a relief that she could not give them. Only a lover's lips could do that. She would not want him to be gentle either, she acknowledged. Her body hungered for savagery that would drive away the years of abstinence and allow her to revel in her womanhood.

Geoffrey would be such a lover. His own desire for her would be increased by anger. They would come together in a crash of blinding pleasure that would leave them both exhausted. How she longed for his touch.

Moaning softly, she squeezed her breast as her other hand traced the warm V at the top of her thighs. Dear God! Would no one ever cool her desperate fires again?

She gave no thought to her position, to the highness or lowness of birth. She desired him for himself, as Geoffrey, the only man who had ever possessed her body, the man who had taught her to desire him and who had saved her again and again both in reality and in dreams.

With a sob of despair, she rolled over onto her stomach, gripping the sheets on either side of her head in an agony of frustration. No one could hear her. The room was empty and silent, and the fire had gone out completely on the hearth. But a fire raged, unquenched, within her.

Wearily, she shivered. At last, like one who has been

punished severely and seeks only to hide away and lick her wounds, she dragged the covers over her, careless of their rumpled twisted state. She was alone and fearfully lonely. The silence of the tower loaded her heart with grief.

Gradually, her breathing steadied as sense returned and emotion faded. Nevertheless, she acknowledged a bond she had not recognized before. She must come to terms with Geoffrey. She must seek him out and speak to him of the past which bedeviled her. Together they could come to some sort of understanding.

Fondly, she remembered the easy companionship of the days in the garden at Rennes. He had been the only real friend in her life. She longed for a resumption of their friendship. Remembering the condition of Henry and the antipathy of her stepson, she found herself desperately in need of a friend.

Chapter 18

Because Joanna had never been prone to headaches, the throbbing pain that woke her drained her of her usual energy. Weakly, she pushed herself up on one elbow as Doña Isabella herded the maids into the room. With hands poised to peel back the covers, the older woman stared at her mistress' white face.

"You are ill?"

Joanna nodded once, then moaned softly, placing her fingertips gingerly against her throbbing temple.

"You are not made of steel, my lady," the older woman remarked unsympathetically. "You have set yourself to do the task of two these past six months. What did you get for your efforts? No thanks and a headache."

"The king is tired," Joanna said in defense of herself. "When he recovers, he will be pleased to find his Council has maintained good order."

Doña Isabella shook her head knowingly. Ordering one of the maids to fetch a small quantity of warmed brandy to ease the pain, she returned to Joanna's bedside. Bending over her mistress, she confided in a husky whisper. "He is sick, but he will never recover. He has the sickness of the soul that comes from the curses of those he has wronged." Her knowing black eyes glittered as she lowered her face to within inches of Joanna's.

For the second time someone had ascribed Henry's depression to guilt. Turning her cheek toward the pillow, Joanna closed her eyes against a painful reality and sank back to wait for the brandy to deaden her pain.

"If he wanted you to sit with him last night, he will want you again," Doña Isabella told her sagely. "You will be expected to listen to his troubles. Your burden will grow heavier and heavier. You need someone to talk to. It is time you took a confessor like all good women."

Joanna raised one eyelid and regarded her duenna balefully. "Go away, old woman."

Fussing with the bedclothes, Doña Isabella remained imperturbable. "You will see I am right. Here is the brandy. Sip it very slowly and lie still. Bring a cool damp cloth," she called over her shoulder. When she had covered Joanna's forehead and eyes with the cooling relief of the cloth, she stood back. "You should choose a confessor, my lady. You have carried the burdens of old sick men on your shoulders long enough. Your flesh may be willing, but your soul will hear things that it cannot carry with it to heaven." Her voice droned on and on until Joanna thought her head would burst.

Why do I keep this creature near me? she thought. Aloud she whispered wearily, "I will consider your words, Doña Isabella. Now go away and leave me to rest."

An hour in the dark left her quietly relaxed. She had just sent for a maid to help her dress when the messenger arrived.

"His Majesty requests your presence to break the fast."

Hopeful of finding him refreshed and in better spirits, she donned a gown of pale tawny linen with an overdress of fine embroidered gold silk. Her hair, having been swiftly braided, was coiled over her ears in shining black rosettes threaded with gold ribbons. The very informality of her dress and hair, unadorned with jewelry, she hoped he would take as a sign of her wish to be friendly and familiar. When

300

she glanced hopefully at herself in the mirror, she found she was pleased with her appearance. Perhaps Henry would be too. Perhaps he might even decide to be loving. Many a man found peace in the embraces of a woman.

Ushered into the king's presence, her hopes were lifted by the sight of his pleasant though weary smile. "I fear I said more than I should have yesterday," he remarked when they were alone.

"Your spirit was overburdened, my lord. Things seemed very black to you when probably they should have seemed bright."

"Bright," he muttered. "Yes, I suppose they should have seemed bright. I look forward to unburdening my soul in the Holy Sepulchre. I should start at Canterbury, I think. Yes, I shall go there first and do penance. A retreat . . . I need to make a retreat from the world."

Joanna groaned inwardly. "Your people need you, my lord. They need your guidance and direction in peace as you have given it in war."

With thumb and third finger, he squeezed the bridge of his nose and rubbed the corners of his eyes. Despite his good night's sleep, a network of tiny red lines streaked the white around their pupils.

They sat in silence for a minute. Then he roused, taking his hand away. "You are right. They need my attention. Tomorrow . . . I will convene them tomorrow."

The servant brought ale, boiled eggs, and fine white bread still warm from the ovens. At the sight Henry's face lighted. "'Tis long since I partook of luxury such as this. The rations in the field were poor. No crops grew this year in Wales where we campaigned over the land." He paused; then his face hardened. "Hotspur died in a bean field."

Joanna tried to head off this reverie. "The ale is delicious, my lord. So cool and fresh." She pushed his tankard toward him.

"The beanpoles were high, but the plants had withered in

the sweltering heat." He lifted the mug, staring ruminatively into its depths, his eyes slitted as if hurt by the light reflected off the shimmering surface of the liquid. "He took an arrow between the eyes. The fool had pulled his visor up. Good God!" He slammed the tankard down and pushed his chair away. "The first thing a knight learns when facing archers is to duck his head and cover his face. He was ever a gallant fire-eating fool."

Henry had begun to stride back and forth, rubbing the palms of his hands down the sides of his robes. Helplessly, Joanna watched him. "Richard did not starve at Ponte-fract," he informed her suddenly. He stared wildly at the door, then strode across the room and lifted the tapestry that covered the stone wall.

"My lord," Joanna rose in alarm at the mention of the former king whose throne Henry now occupied. "Sit you down and eat. You must get hold of yourself."

At the sound of her voice, he glared murderously in her direction. "We will depart for Canterbury tomorrow," he decided, ignoring her yet speaking to her all the same. "I will pray and do penance. Henry of Anjou did penance for the death of Thomas à Becket."

Seizing upon that thought before it left his mind, Joanna seated herself and tapped a hard-boiled egg with the handle of her knife. "And then he was rid of his sin," she agreed, pretending to eat with enjoyment. Tearing off a piece of white bread, she smiled up at him invitingly. "Your prayer and penance will rid you of your guilt. Come, eat and gain strength for the journey."

He stared at her suspiciously. "You think I can rid myself of this burden?"

"I know it."

"Then I will eat." Like a child, his tantrum abated, he reseated himself and took a long cool drink of ale.

The journey from London to Canterbury was completed in less than a day. Henry rode in the royal coach with Joanna beside him. People came out of their houses to stare at him, holding up their children to see him and occasionally cheering.

Henry's spirits were calmed and reassured by the time they arrived at the cathedral where the archbishop's own rooms had been reserved for the royal penitent. Since the archbishop was Thomas Arundel, the king's great-uncle, who had placed the crown on Henry's head, the welcome was a warm one.

Immediately, Henry quitted the luxurious apartments, dashing Joanna's hopes of consummating their marriage. With only the briefest of apologies, he vanished into the monks' dorter upon their arrival. In a sackcloth robe and sandals Henry joined the Benedictine monks in their daily activities. Thereafter, he rose at half-past two in the morning to begin psalms and prayers that went on at intervals for almost six hours. After a scant breakfast he worked and prayed for another six hours. Then, after eating a crude meal in the frater, he worked another four hours until time for vespers and sleep.

The retainers accompanying the royal couple took lodging in the comfortable guests' lodgings. Nevertheless they were bored and complained constantly of the poor food and lack of activity. Geoffrey was among the men who had returned from the wars hoping for diversion. Now a round dozen of them, himself included, cooled their heels in a monastery a good day's ride from London's pleasures and entertainments.

While recognizing their displeasure, Joanna could do nothing. Her own worries were divided. In London the King's Council had been left nominally leaderless. Factions who thought the Percys ill used and supporters of the Mortimers might already be practicing a subtle sedition. Here in Canterbury Henry showed little sign of recovering his spirits.

Dispatches arrived daily from London. He either ignored

them entirely or read them and fell to his knees to pray over their contents. Joanna's fingers itched to reach for them, both for his sake and for her own. Should he decide to remain here, who would rule in his place? What would her status be?

"Can you not influence him, my lady?" the Earl of Buckingham, Henry's cousin, entreated as they sat stiffly in the public parlor.

"What can I do?" She raised her shoulders in a Gallic shrug. "I see him less than you and his men do. At least you may eat with him in the frater if you choose. I am forbidden to enter."

"But a woman's . . . er . . . charm . . ." Buckingham halted diffidently.

Seated across a table from one of the younger men but facing in her direction, Geoffrey d'Anglais raised his blond-white head from the study of a chess move. One of his eyebrows rose cynically as he surveyed her body. His gaze stripped away the gray wool gown embroidered with rose silk thread and his insolent look seemed to mock the failure of her sexuality to seduce Henry out of his religious fervor.

"I have not seen His Majesty except at a distance since we arrived here," Joanna told Buckingham sadly. "Surely, you should be able to influence him more than I, milord. You take him the dispatches every day."

"He counsels me to pray," the earl groaned disgustedly.

Joanna nodded as she took up her embroidery again. "Under the circumstances, prayers will help as much as anything."

When Buckingham flung himself out of the parlor to ride out his frustration, Geoffrey excused himself from the chess game. Aware of him as he came toward her, Joanna pricked her finger. To keep the drop of blood from irrevocably staining the heavy linen she was stitching, she flung her hand away from her lap, only to have it caught by Geoffrey.

Holding its softness between his hard palms, he bent his

head to examine the wound. A crimson drop welled from the tip of her thumb. Before she could speak or wrest it away from him, he raised her hand, took her thumb in his mouth, and sucked it.

A thrill shot through her; sweet pain pierced her vitals as his tongue caressed her sensitive skin. The wetness, the heat, the smooth sharpness of his teeth, the rough titillation of his tongue combined to torment her. She felt torn apart by the tidal storm of sexual desire that thundered through her veins. Dear Lord! How she wanted him! Her very soul craved his touch. Oh, that his lips and tongue were working their exquisite torture on her breasts and her thighs. Because she had been so long without a man's touch, her longing was intensified. She began to tremble. Tears started in her eyes.

Then he raised his head and grinned cruelly, transforming his beautiful face into the face of a demon. "Regretting your marriage, Joanna," he murmured. "Such capital crimes as usurpation and murder must occupy his mind and spirit. I doubt he thinks of adultery, especially with such a willing partner as you."

"Adultery?"

"The betrayal of his host with the wife."

She shook her head. "I do not—"

"I am surprised that you live. I would have thought Jean of Brittany a perceptive man."

Her face flamed as she sought to tug her hand from his grasp. "I never committed adultery. I entered no man's bed except that which he thrust me into."

He sneered as his grip tightened painfully. "This king has no need of more heirs. He would not hesitate to dispose of a queen who betrayed him. I merely warn you. He has killed so many, one more would not matter, be she ever so well born."

Dropping her hand, he strode away, leaving her in the chill parlor. As she watched him go, she touched her thumb to her lips. It was still moist where he had taken it into his mouth. It no longer pained her, but in her heart was a throbbing ache.

She loved Geoffrey d'Anglais. The knowledge made her humble. Rising in response to her deepest desire, she made her way to the Lady Chapel where she fell to her knees. Bowing her head above her clasped hands, she began to whisper her confession to the Virgin. Because she no longer felt shame for her feelings, she begged pardon for the betrayal of her royal blood, but she could not sacrifice the living for the dead. She was a princess, a duchess, and a queen; but in her love for Geoffrey, she was only a woman.

Alone, she faced squarely the acute disappointment she felt at the dissolution of her dreams of a happy marriage. Clearly her husband suffered from wounds that would take many years, perhaps forever, to heal. The dreams she had entertained of nights of passion in the arms of a great king, an aristocrat of her rank as well as a handsome man of her own age, were clearly only dreams. As dreams they swiftly evaporated in the exhausting heat of the English summer.

The walls of the chapel seemed to close round her as unreasoning claustrophobia gripped her throat. Far from her marriage freeing her, it had entrapped her further. The man who should have been her protector and companion knelt in monk's robes, seeking to cleanse his soul of damnable sins, while his son prowled like a young wolf around the outskirts of the pack, awaiting his opportunity to challenge the leader. The man she loved hated her for acts she had never committed. Furthermore, she was practically a stranger in a land whose language she spoke with difficulty.

Tears of disappointment mixed with fear began to trickle between her fingers. Once begun, they would not stop. She, who never wept, wept now in the empty chapel dedicated to Mary the Mother of God, but she felt no comfort. She felt no heavenly spirit beneath its vaulted ceiling, no help for her soul-crushing problems.

She could not guess how long they would have remained

at Canterbury had a message not arrived that shocked Henry into action. Selfish of his gains, he cast off the monkish garments at the news that Henry Percy, the old Earl of Northumberland, was stirring again.

"We march north," he declared to his assembled men, his voice ringing like a clarion in the vaulted room. Geoffrey blinked. The king had not spoken above a dull whisper in all the time they had been at Canterbury.

Standing to one side, Joanna smiled to see Henry now garbed in the robes of his rank. On his head he wore a hood of red velvet trimmed with gold and pinned with a gleaming ruby. His fine blond beard and mustache bristled as he talked. He looked every inch the king.

"Norfolk has sided with Percy, and Richard Scrope, the Archbishop of York, has turned traitor," Henry continued.

A growl went up among the assembled men.

"Hearing of their action, that most infamous of outlaws Owen Glendower has chosen to name himself ruler of all Wales. He thinks we cannot fight on two fronts and hopes to bleed our people of illegal tribute." The blue Plantagenet eyes flashed fire. "But we are more than a match for them."

"Give us your commands, Your Majesty." Buckingham's hand darted across his body to close on the hilt of his sword.

"Even now, Prince Henry leads an army to meet Glendower in Wales. I deem this only fitting since he is its lawful prince. Who should better defend its people than their true hereditary leader?"

He paused while several men spoke loudly in praise of the young prince. Then a scowl darkened his face and he clenched his fist. "We showed great pity for the white hairs of Henry Percy when we spared him and restored to him his lands after the death of his son. He has repaid us by gathering forces against us. This time we shall smite him low and drive him and all his kind from the face of England. Go you now and prepare the horses. I will join you after one word more."

When they had left, he held out his hand to Joanna, smiling as enthusiastically as a boy. "My lady, I must go to fight. Forces threaten the kingdom that I have built for us. When there is peace again, I promise to take up the reins of government and be a husband to you. Until then I beg you to pray for me and be patient."

Sadly, she searched his face for some sign of true regret, but she could find only excitement barely restrained behind a façade of calm acceptance of duty. He is at his best in crisis, she thought. Perhaps he should never have been king at all, but a maker and defender of kings, a general of the armies. Like his father and uncle before him, he seemed best as a raider prince who cared little for the day-to-day business of being ruler of a country.

Even as she entertained these thoughts, her husband bestowed a chaste kiss on her forehead, then spun on his heel and strode rapidly out into the bright sunlight.

Reports came to the Council that the prince had triumphed in Wales and the king in York.

"He has captured Archbishop Richard Scrope and Thomas Mowbray, Duke of Norfolk," the messenger announced.

"His Majesty is successful," Joanna smiled.

"Their execution is to be within the fortnight," the man continued.

A general muttering rose. Joanna slammed her palm down against the Council table. "You are mistaken in your report!" she scolded the messenger. "His Majesty plans to execute the traitor duke. The archbishop must be turned over to the Church for punishment."

His face white, the messenger nevertheless shook his head. "No, so please Your Majesty. He will execute them both. The king says they are both traitors who deserve no mercy. Since he has them in captivity, he will take no chance that they will escape to rise again."

Joanna stared, horror-stricken, at the faces of the council

308

members. "He must be better advised," she said at last through stiff lips. "I shall send a message with greatest speed."

Arundel nodded angrily. He had sat in Council beside her while Henry had been in the field. Generally he approved of the actions of the king, seeing his battles as terrible but necessary. However, the execution of an archbishop, a lord of the Roman Catholic Church was heresy and a grievous offense. "He must be stopped."

Unfortunately, though a fresh messenger was dispatched immediately, the advice of queen and Council was ignored. Henry beheaded the traitors and buried them without ceremony.

"He is doomed!"

Joanna found Doña Isabella crouched in a shivering heap before the altar in the chapel adjoining the royal apartments. When the older woman had not appeared to dress her, she had been informed that the maids and other ladies had no knowledge of her. When Isabella's room had proved to be empty, her bed still smooth, Joanna had felt a stab of concern.

Her own feelings for the duenna were mixed. Although the woman no longer wielded any power, she remained the single link with her misty memories of Navarre. Furthermore, Doña Isabella was the only one in the entire court with whom Joanna could occasionally converse in Spanish.

In the way of servants who have grown old with their masters, Isabella scolded her mistress and voiced her disapproval with a temerity that set Joanna's teeth on edge, but she managed to ignore the woman's increasing bitterness.

Joanna bent over the heap of rumpled black and gray cloth. "Doña Isabella, are you ill?"

Black eyes opened to stare out of dark sunken pits in La

Alcudia's sallow face. "I have prayed, Infanta," she whispered. "I have prayed and prayed, but God will not answer the prayers of my will. His Will, not my will, be done." Two more tears squeezed out to slip unheeded over her wrinkled cheeks.

"How long have you been here, *amiga mía?*" Kneeling, Joanna put her hand on the other's shoulder, a bit startled by the skeletal thinness beneath the gown.

"Since the word came, Infanta." Her use of the Spanish address for princess puzzled Joanna. What was Isabella thinking of?

"What word? What are you talking about, Doña Isabella? You are exhausted from praying so long, I warrant. How long have you been here?"

"The good archbishop . . . he is killed."

Then Joanna knew what word had reached Isabella's ears. She bowed her head a moment. If Isabella felt this way, so must many of the people of England. La Alcudia did not care about Englishmen. The deaths of the Percys, of the Duke of Norfolk, of the hundreds of men killed on either side had not garnered so much as a sniff from her at the telling. But the beheading of an archbishop, a prince of God's church, terrified her.

Her hand trembling, Joanna shook the older woman's thin shoulder. "You must get off this cold floor, Isabella. You will make yourself ill."

Clawlike hands grasped Joanna's wrist. "I have prayed for your husband, Infanta. I have prayed all the night long, but it is God's Will, not my will. You know it was ever thus. God's Will, not my will."

"I know, *amiga.* Come."

Isabella sat up although her knees remained doubled under her. "He is doomed." Her voice rasped from her throat. Her face was contorted into a mask of horror. *"Infanta, escucha me. . . ."* Bowing her head, she began to recite the ritual for the casting out of demons. At least

Joanna guessed she was reciting it. The words were wildly distorted by the old woman's fear and were spoken in a puzzling mixture of Spanish-accented Latin.

"Doña Isabella," Joanna scolded sternly. "You must give this up and come with me."

"The king is doomed," came the reply.

"Stop that!"

"Doomed!" Isabella's voice rose to a hoarse shout.

Angrily, Joanna shook the hysterical woman. "He is not doomed. He is victorious."

"Doomed . . ." It was a whisper.

Unable to get the woman's attention any other way, Joanna struck her across the cheek. "Get up, or I shall fetch a guard to carry you to your chamber."

The blow was only a light tap, but it returned the proud fire to Isabella's glazed eyes. They flashed angrily at Joanna, reminding the queen that she had once thought of this woman as a *hechicera*. Then the fire subsided, but a sly smile remained. "Help me to my feet. Never again will I sacrifice myself for the ungrateful."

Placing her hands under the old woman's arms, Joanna lifted her, then supported her while she moaned and tottered as feeling returned to her numb limbs. "You shall spend the day in your bed," Joanna promised, placing an arm around the duenna's waist to lead her from the chapel. "I shall send the maids with warm brandy and breakfast and warming pans for your legs. You are appreciated, Doña Isabella. I do appreciate why you were praying. You have pleased me with your concern and loyalty for my husband."

"Him!" Isabella cackled drily. "I care nothing . . . nothing . . . *nada* about him. You. You are the one I care about."

"His doings can have little affect on me."

Isabella shook her head. "Look at his face when he returns. You must never let him touch you. Never. Never. *Jamás*. Do you understand?"

Joanna sighed. "You will feel better after a rest, Doña Isabella."

"Promise me, Infanta."

"Old woman. I cannot promise you such a thing. The king is my husband. I am his wife. He will do with me as he wills and I will submit. Besides, you of all people have always told me that my duty is to submit to the will of my husband." She smiled a bit sadly.

They had arrived at the door of Doña Isabella's room. When Joanna would have left her, the older woman caught her hand and pulled her in through the door. Bolting it behind them, she tugged the queen into the middle of the room. "Best not stand too near the door. Someone might be listening."

"Doña Isabella, you are not yourself."

"You will see?" The older woman began to wring her clawlike hands. "No one will fail to see it in his face? When he returns you will see it, and you will not let him touch you ever again."

Her distress alarmed Joanna. "See what? What is there to see?"

"The curse of God. He has killed the archbishop. He has killed a prince of God's church. He cannot escape. Him. Pfah! I care nothing about. He deserves what will come to him, but you . . . Not you . . . My lord, Charles of Navarre, long years ago bade me protect you and guide you. I have always done so, though you did not thank me for it. But this time you will. You will. For you are not a fool."

"What are you talking about?"

"You will see it in his face. The fires of hell. They will burn his skin. They will roast his body. It will swell with the dreadful heat. Eruptions will burst forth. If you look in his eyes, you will see the fires burning behind them. As he writhes in agony, parts of his body will begin to die, but he will live and suffer. He is God's message to heretics. God will avenge His own."

Joanna put her hands to her ears to escape the old woman's chatter. "I beg you. Be quiet."

The duenna's hands grappled at the queen's wrists. "Only one word more, then I am finished. You will see it for yourself, when he returns. But you are young. You might not recognize it until it is too late to save yourself."

"What? Recognize what?"

"Leprosy!"

Chapter 19

A black tide of horror rose around Joanna threatening to engulf her where she stood. More feared than the plague, leprosy's hideously disfigured victims lived on and on, despised and ostracized, the outcasts of the earth. Terrible sores covered their bodies while their extremities rotted and fell away. Swathed in dirty bandages, they roamed in pitiful bands or lived alone in wretched hovels.

Shuddering violently, she shook her head as she struggled for reason. Henry showed no such signs. His fair skin had been burned by the sun of summer during the Shrewsbury campaign. When he returned to his normal round of activities, his skin would heal. Reassuring herself, she angrily pulled herself from Isabella's grasp.

"You know nothing, old woman."

"He has slain an archbishop of God's Church," Isabella insisted without inflection. "He has no hope. He has lost all."

"The king has won final victory over his enemies," Joanna argued. "He will return in triumph. His reign will continue in peace."

Isabella shook her head sadly. "I know what I know. You will best be warned. You have no one but me to help you now."

Joanna caught the other woman's arm and shook her

hard. "You do not *know* something so horrible. You claim to know the will of God. That in itself is heresy. To speak such an evil thing is wicked. To speak it of the king could lead to your death."

"Why do you think I pulled you into the center of the room?" Doña Isabella slid her glittering eyes over to the door. "The necessity for caution is stronger now than ever."

Joanna took a step backward as the woman's baleful eyes finally fastened on hers. "I have no necessity for caution."

Doña Isabella shrugged her shoulders wearily. "Even as you speak those words, you do not believe them. I know you better than you know yourself. I am exhausted. I will go to bed now."

As if all strength had left her frail body, she tottered to the bed and lowered herself upon it. Joanna followed her to pull a coverlet across her and tuck it around her. "I will send a maid to undress you and put you to bed. Shall I send something to break your fast as well?"

Doña Isabella turned on her side and put her hands together under her cheek like a child. "I require nothing except sleep. I can wait until the afternoon meal to eat. Leave me."

The king did not return to London immediately. Exhausted from the campaign in the north, he rested at Arundel, the home he had gained when he had married his first wife.

Joanna felt a chill when she heard that he was not on his way. Her marriage was still unconsummated. He could renounce her at any time should he so desire. Perhaps even now Prince Henry spoke against her. Although many in the Council regarded her with favor, fully as many did not. The Archbishop of Canterbury had returned to his diocese, thereby condemning Henry's act by withdrawing his support.

With the armies disbanded, the knights were returning to their duties and estates.

In vain Joanna waited for Geoffrey to show himself at court. Although she could not discover his exact position, she knew he was an important figure in the royal retinue.

Finally, when even Buckingham had returned to resume his place on the Council, she sent a messenger to inquire at Geoffrey's lodgings. The man returned with the news that Sir Geoffrey d'Anglais had returned some time earlier, but the press of personal business had kept him from the court.

When Joanna heard this reply, she felt a surge of unreasonable resentment. When Geoffrey returned, he should first have made a report to the Council. Each of the members of the king's cadre had done so, except him. Summoning the messenger again, she penned a missive commanding Geoffrey to appear before the Council to make his official report.

As she signed it, Joanna the Queen, she felt a twinge of conscience. If Geoffrey had been wounded . . . but the reply had pleaded personal business. No mention of a wound had been made. True enough, the Council was not particularly interested in hearing any more old news, but she felt sure his report would be valuable.

Perhaps she should call the messenger back and temper the message. Perhaps she should merely request Geoffrey's presence for a personal report to the queen. But no, Geoffrey would make his report to the Council; then, afterward, she would invite him into her apartments to talk over his personal observations on the condition of the king.

At that time she would beg his pardon for whatever wrongs she might have dealt him in her youth and she would reveal her sincere affection for him and her desire to be his friend. She smiled to herself as memories came flooding back. Those warm young days in the gardens in Brittany were almost tangible, as was the passion they had shared.

The very thought of that passion made her feel choked and

hot. She had not known how to value it. Furthermore, she had known nothing else. No other man had done more than touch her. She might have been Geoffrey's chaste wife all these years. What would her life have been like had she been in fact?

A shiver rippled through her body as regret tore at her heart. Geoffrey had loved her. He had called her his own; he had been jealous of Henry. But would she have made a different choice? She stiffened her proud back. She was the daughter of a king, and now she had achieved her true destiny. She was a crowned queen. In honest appraisal, she would have done nothing else.

Seated at her desk, writing a letter to Henry on the following day, she was interrupted by Doña Isabella. "He begs to see you privately, milady," she hissed dramatically.

Joanna looked up in surprise. "Who?"

"Geoffrey, the former servant of Brittany."

The pen squibbed from her fingers and blotted the paper. "Geoffrey is here to see me."

"He waits without. I told him you might have a few minutes for him."

Joanna touched her hair, left loose today to hand down her back in a rose mesh snood. "I do. I shall be pleased to speak with him."

Isabella nodded. "Remember we need friends, milady. He was ever loyal to Brittany. Perhaps he can be used to good advantage."

Joanna grimaced. "Ever plotting, Doña Isabella. Your plots will be your death one day."

"We need friends," the duenna replied sagely. "I will remain in attendance. . . ."

"No." Joanna cut her speech short. "You will not remain in attendance. I need no attendant with Geoffrey. We have spent long hours together. He is more like a brother to me

318

than any man alive."

"You are a married woman and the queen."

"As a married woman and the queen, surely I may speak with one of my husband's most loyal subjects?"

The duenna's lips thinned. "I will admit him, milady." she curtsied stiffly, disapproval in every line of her body.

That he looked older was her first impression. The silver blond hair was still the same, although perhaps a shade lighter, as if white hairs had besprinkled it. The features were thinner and lines crinkled around his pale gray eyes.

But his frame was as it had always been, not an inch of spare flesh about it. Indeed, his belt was dragged low on his hips by the weight of his sword. As he entered, she noted with satisfaction that his walk seemed easier, the limp not nearly so noticeable or binding as it had been.

He was so like her remembrances of him from the days of their youth in Brittany that her eyes misted at the sight. With her love in her eyes, she held out both hands to him. "Geoffrey."

He took one hand in exaggerated politeness and made an elegant leg to her.

When she would have drawn him close to her, he drew back. "You sent for me, Your Majesty?"

Sensitive to the tone of his voice, she set about putting him at his ease. "We have not heard your report in Council. Since you are here to see me privately, perhaps you have some news of Henry? I shall be glad of anything you have to tell me."

He interrupted her with a mirthless chuckle. "I have nothing to tell you about your husband, madam. I am no more privy to what moves him than are you."

At his tone, her stomach knotted apprehensively. Clearly, the reunion she hoped for would be harder to initiate than she had anticipated. Smiling bravely, she ignored his tone and asked another question. "Did you complete your business then that kept you from court?"

His gray eyes were stormy, his voice heavy with irony. "I cannot think that the Queen of England has summoned one so lowly as I to inquire about mere personal business."

Rising, she walked toward him, extending her hand. "Geoffrey—"

"Say what you will and be done, madam." Coldly he cut into her speech.

Whipping back her hand as if from a fire, she clasped it around her upper arm and hugged herself protectively. "I would have personal speech with you," she protested. A slow flush dyed her cheeks at the contemptuous expression on his face.

"Is the queen unhappy with the absence of the king?" His voice was like a dart of venom in her heart.

"No . . . no," she protested. "That is, of course, I miss His Majesty very muich, but that is not my reason for summoning you."

"Oh, yes." He sneered. "I forget you summoned me for my report on the battle, a battle that took place many weeks ago—a battle that no one cares about anymore."

She shook her head. "I did not summon you to report on the battle," she admitted. Her voice was low. She clasped both arms around her body and hugged herself tightly. His antipathy was tearing into her, ripping her poise to shreds. Shivers of anxiety vibrated along her slender frame.

"What then?" he prodded, his voice a sharp sword.

"I . . . Geoffrey, I beg you. Look not so angry at me. I am trying to tell you. I want to tell you." She held out her hands to him, palms upward, fingers trembling. "Geoffrey . . . can you not be my friend?"

He stared at her, his eyes burning, his face set in grim lines. Then he threw back his handsome head and laughed like a mirthless demon from deepest hell whose soul was damned long ago. His laugh sounded the note of tragedy . . . and of revenge, the most bittersweet of all sounds.

As she recognized his hostility, the passionate entreaties

she had just made to him embarrassed her. Angry at revealing any weakness, she spun away.

Instantly, he was upon her, grasping her shoulders in hurtful hands and dragging her back against him. One arm slammed across her chest under her chin, holding her firmly against his hard body. "So you would be friends," he hissed in her ear.

For a moment she was shocked into silence. Then her sense of worth and dignity reasserted itself. "Release me," she demanded in her iciest tone of command.

"Not until you tell me what you want from me." His breath was hot against her neck.

She shrugged her shoulders hard and twisted her body. "I wanted to be friends. However, I see that friendship is impossible with such as you."

"Oh, very . . . yes. Very much indeed. I am so low, so common. What then does Her Majesty require from me?" One hand fastened in the rose mesh to pull it loose and let fall the long heavy mass of black waves. "What can she require?" He sneered again.

"Let me go, sir. You are behaving like an animal."

"Why so I am? But then we bastards are little more than animals." His hand stole round her waist as his teeth fastened in her earlobe. "Little more than animals . . ." His teeth nipped her hard.

"Geoffrey . . ." Her voice did not sound like her own. The pain made her blink, and the roughness of his hands was frightening her. She began to struggle.

"What can Her Majesty want?" he crooned. "What can she want with an animal like me?" One of his hands slipped round her waist, hugging her back against him before sliding upward to the buttons of her surcoat.

"Geoffrey, you forget yourself." She caught his wrist and sought to pull his hand away, but his arm was like a band of steel.

"No!" he roared in her ear.

The violence of the sound made her cringe. Frantically, she clawed at his wrist, kicking backward at the same time with her heels, trying to hurt him or at least startle him into releasing her.

"Gently," he chuckled. Her ineffectual struggles pleased him. A wave of excitement made him shudder. The heat of her body released the perfume she always wore, the same floral scent he remembered. Against his will, he recalled the passionate tenderness of their best times together. Then his resolve stiffened. She had rejected him when he would have treated her with all honor. Now she would offer him dishonor. He would not accept that. With a growl, he pulled the surcoat open, ripping the cloth when the buttons did not immediately yield to his fingers.

"Geoffrey!" she cried aghast, her fear *of* him combined with her fear *for* him, should they be discovered.

"What could Her Royal Majesty want?" he snarled. He spun her around, his eyes stormy with anger. "Does she want another heir?"

Horrified that he had so misread her intention in summoning him, she could only shake her head speechlessly, her eyes filling with tears.

"'Tis as I thought," he grated. "The young prince resents you and your ambitions. So now you wish to supplant him in his father's affections. Do you wish to solidify your position by producing a young Plantagenet for the king? When the king dies, who would be more powerful than the mother of the young king?"

"No," she gasped. "Never. I have never sought to take anything that belongs to the prince."

"No?" Dark color flooded his face. His gaze slid insolently down to her breasts covered only by the fine white wool of her gown.

She followed his gaze. To her disgust, she saw that the struggle against him and her horror at his words had hardened her nipples, revealing their clear outlines beneath the wool.

"Ah, I see. The queen feels no obligation for an heir, but the woman wants more than her husband can provide for her." With a cruelty so contemptuous that her heart began to throb unsteadily within her, he grasped one nipple between his thumb and third finger with the pressure required to make a snapping sound.

A cry tore from her, but the pain of her breast was nothing to the pain in her soul. He had totally misinterpreted her summons. As if she were naked, she bowed her head in embarrassment and crossed her hands over her chest.

He laughed at her gesture. "Never fear, Your Majesty. You have nothing more to fear from these animal hands. I would not touch you if you paid me to do you service. I am no whore. No gigolo. I did what I did for Brittany under pain of torture, you recall. Life was sweet for a man so young as I was then. Now . . ." He roughly thrust a hand beneath her chin and snapped her head up to look him in the eye. "Now . . . I do not set my life on a pin's fee if to preserve it my hard-won honor would be stained."

Tears wet her cheeks now. She could not control them. She stared at him as through a streaming leaden pane that distorted his beloved features, making them unlike themselves. That was the problem she told herself. She could not see clearly.

Like a hail of stones, his words continued, crushing her emotions, bludgeoning her spirit. "Do you miss a man's touch, Your Majesty? A queen can have so many things—rank, position, jewels, rich clothing—but she can only have one man . . . the king. And if the king be away, busy, neglectful, disinterested, then what? What can a queen do? Especially one whose body delights so in the pleasures of the bedchamber." His voice insinuated evil things.

"Geoffrey," she whispered. I beg you—"

He caught her roughly against him, one calloused palm covering her mouth, forcing the words back into her throat.

"Oh, I pray you, Your Majesty. Do not beg. You are the queen. Do you forget that? You bargained for it. Even while your first husband lived, you were bargaining for this. Navarre's daughter. The true get of Charles the Bad."

She stared upward into his face only inches above her own, her eyes terrified, her breath coming fast against the side of his hand. Locked against him, crushed by his hard grip, she stared at him hopelessly. As suddenly as he had gripped her, he flung her away. She staggered backward against the desk and toppled sideways to the floor. This time a wail of despair tore from between her lips.

Once his emotions were unleashed, his control could not be recovered so easily. Swooping down beside her, he slammed her over onto her back, roughly grasping her shoulders to press her down to the hard floor. "Do you miss it, Joanna?" he grated.

A whimper of pain escaped from her tight-pressed lips in answer. She closed her eyes to shut out the sight of him.

His hot breath fanned her cheek. "Ah, you may close your eyes and your mouth, but your body will tell all."

Then she did cry out as his hands slid down her body, squeezing her breasts before dragging up the hem of her gown and chemise. "No."

"Do you miss the caress of warm skin on skin?" One of his hands moved over the curve of her hip, his fingers tracing the bone then moving onward until the index finger found the scar. *"B,"* he whispered. "We were branded on the same day at the same hour. Have you missed the delights that followed?"

She could not answer. The touch of his hands no matter how rough—how humiliating—was driving her mad. So long deprived, her heart pounding, her nerves taut, she bit her lip and clenched her fists to try to restrain the flood of passion that threatened to drown her. Her efforts were to no avail. Beneath his hands, her belly convulsed and shuddered.

His bitter chuckle pierced her heart. With calculated

cruelty, his knowing fingers slid into her warm curls and found them moist and welcoming. "So eager," he jeered. "So hungry. You have been alone a long time, Your Majesty. Poor lady. A queen should have her every wish granted. Is that not the way of the world?" His hands parted her thighs and began to stroke their soft inner surfaces in small circles.

Where his fingers stroked, her skin tingled. Whimpering again at the terrible pain created by the tension building within her, she dug her heels into the floor and arched up to meet him.

With a laugh he placed his palm flat on her belly and pushed her back down. At the same time, he bent to bring his lips close to her ear. "Do you ache, Joanna? Does your hungry body ache for the food of love? Is it starving? Tell me."

Stubbornly, she shook her head.

As if he accepted her answer, he pulled his hand away instantly. "Well, then . . ."

"No," she whispered, involuntarily raising her hips to follow his touch.

"No?"

Her eyes flew open. He had told her not to beg, but the ache within her was fast becoming a torment she could not bear. He had been her first lover, her only lover. He had trained her well to respond to his body. Now her body remembered the training. "No," she cried. "Oh, please, no. That is, do not . . . I mean, do . . ."

"Is this what you want?" he asked softly, his tone a seduction in itself. If she had not already surrendered, she would have fallen beneath its gentle onslaught. His hands closed over her breasts still beneath the white wool, squeezing them gently before he concentrated on the sensitive nipples that throbbed agonizingly beneath the soft fabric.

She moaned at the delicate fondling.

"Answer me," he demanded. "Is that what you want?"

"Yes."

"And what else do you want?" his voice continued inexorably.

Embarrassed despite her throbbing desire, she hesitated. To expose herself so completely before anyone was foreign to her nature. No one had ever demanded such complete surrender of her soul.

As punishment for her reticence, he pinched her nipple more sharply. "Tell me."

"Oh, please." She begged for mercy, but he was adamant. In the barest of whispers, she capitulated. "Please touch me between my legs. Please . . . I ache so."

With agonizing slowness, his hand slid along her silken thigh to its joining. After much delay, during which time she writhed and whimpered helplessly, he found the throbbing center of her pleasure. "Is this the spot you want me to touch?" he asked, stroking it with the tip of his index finger.

She began to sob. "Oh, yes."

He rested his palm on her thigh, while his finger circled enticingly without actually touching her as she craved. "When was the last time you were touched here?" he asked gently. "When was the last time a man made love to you?"

Mindless now with desire and pain, she would have opened her heart for him had he asked her. "You were the last," she cried. "You, Geoffrey . . . only you."

Her answer surprised him, although he could not doubt it. "Me?"

"You are my only love," she sobbed. "Please . . ." She ground out the word, desperate.

"What about Brittany?"

"He never touched me . . . ever. He was too crippled."

"And Henry. Surely you do not tell me the king has not made you happy? He was accounted a lusty lover. His sons and daughters are proof."

"No, he . . . I . . . Dear God, Geoffrey. *I cannot bear . . . please.*"

He asked her one more question. One more admission from her would fill his cup to the brim with bitterest revenge. "And why did you summon me today? Why am I here with you?"

Her teeth sank into her lower lip, so that a drop of blood welled from its center. "Because . . . oh, Geoffrey . . ."

"Tell me, Joanna."

"Because I love you."

He let out his breath in a long sigh. One hand whipped from beneath her skirts even as the other left her breast to lever him from the floor.

"Geoffrey."

Her cry of agony was music to his ears.

Her eyes flew open, to stare up at his tall frame, his face, the face of a demon who laughed at her very real physical pain as well as her despair.

"Suffer, Your Majesty," he snarled. "Suffer as I did. I was the despised one. I loved you, protected you, fought for you, gave you pleasure to make your life fulfilled. Brittany used me, but at least he gave me an honest wage for honest labor. You took my labor and gave nothing in return. You owe me the pain."

From his full height, like a conqueror, he surveyed her plight, emitting a snarl of satisfaction.

Her mouth gaped in her white face. Her forehead was beaded with perspiration. Clenching her fists at her sides to still the tremors that ran through her body, she stared up at him. "You say you love me," she whispered hoarsely, lifting her drowned gaze to his. "Yet you treat me like this when I have only sought you out to declare my friendship and love. How could you treat me so?" Bitterly defeated by him and by her own body, she turned her face away from his triumphant one.

Her prostrate body seemed to wilt before his eyes. The bright flush of passion faded from her cheeks, leaving her like a corpse. Joanna proud, Joanna imperious, Joanna begging—all these he could resist, but Joanna conquered and despairing, he could not. The sight of her wrenched his gut, dropping him to his knees beside her. Her hair spread on the floor around her shoulders in a disordered mass of black waves. Against his will, he touched it, noting that his fingers trembled. Her deep rose surcoat, so rudely pushed aside, now bound her arms to her sides, exposing her breasts, their mounds upthrust through the white wool. He had left her skirt pushed up around her thighs.

His face contorted in anguish as all thoughts of vengeance left him. She was his love, and he could not leave her sprawled in shame. Others had treated her badly and would continue to do so, but he could not bring himself to join their ranks.

Gently, he gathered her into his arms, pressing her face against his tunic, hiding her eyes from the light while he clumsily returned her clothing to some semblance of order. At first she lay like one dead in his arms. Then gradually her tears started, the bitterest she had ever known. She did not weep for what she had done to their love when she had contracted the marriage to Henry. Though that was a sad thing, she knew she could have done nothing else.

Instead, she wept because he had so misunderstood her desire for this meeting. Yet how could he have thought anything else of her? She had wanted above all things to be Queen of England, and she had not valued her gentle companion and lover. "Geoffrey," she whispered at last, "I am sorry."

She felt his lips against her hot forehead. "Joanna, I am too, but I cannot be what you want me to be. I cannot go back to that shame and degradation."

She sighed. Useless to deny his accusations. He would never believe her. Undoubtedly, he was safest believing the worst of her. He should not suffer again from a hopeless love. "You are wise."

Recognizing the selfishness inherent in her arranging

328

this meeting, she said good-bye at last to her childhood. Selfishness and vanity she had had in plenty. Now she suffered for them. But Geoffrey must not be made to suffer more.

As though her body had been doused with ice water all her hot emotions disappeared. Stiffly, she climbed to her feet, not looking at him. Her hands fumbled as she did up the buttons of the rose plastron. One eyelet was torn, but by twisting it and tucking it inside the facing, she decided it would escape notice until that evening.

Finished, she bent to pick up the rose mesh snood and stuffed her hair back into it. That, too, would have to do until evening.

At last she faced him extending her hand. "I thank you, Sir Geoffrey, for your informative report. I shall take heart from all you have said and shall study to see how your information can be turned to good."

With a sad smile, he bowed slightly. "Ever Your Majesty's faithful servant." Turning on his heel, he strode from the apartment. His footsteps echoed down the corridor, their fading sounds tearing at her heart and mind.

At last, when all was silent, she drew a quick shuddering breath, and stared round her. The room was exactly as it had been. Somehow she had expected to see it changed, so violent had been the emotions that had filled its space. However, she must continue to carry out her duties. A queen has many duties, she reminded herself, especially when the king is away.

Chapter 20

David Nigarelli of Lucca, the king's physician, met
Joanna at the door to the audience chamber on the day the
king returned from Arundel. His words delivered with
unctuous gentleness accompanied by solemn looks, prepared her for the worst. "It may be that he has been infected
with St. Anthony's fire, Your Majesty. There was much that
was unfit to eat in York. The bread was moldy. Many
refused to eat it for fear of ergot."

They were of a height, her headdress making her appear
taller by several inches. Through clear eyes, their black
depths swimming with iridescent flecks, she measured the
slight Italian. "And if he does not have St. Anthony's fire,
Doctor?"

The Italian shrugged evasively. "I would not want to
disturb your mind with injudicious diagnoses."

"May I enter?"

"Be prepared to see him changed," the man warned. "But
be assured he is recovering now. He remained at Arundel
until the worst was past."

When the doors opened, at first Joanna could not see
Henry. The cadre had gathered in a semicircle before him,
their broad backs obstructing her view. From behind this
human wall, she heard his voice giving orders. Hesitant to

break into the doings of men, she waited quietly.

A man on the edge of the group happened to glance in her direction. Hastily, he nudged his fellow who looked also. Almost reluctantly, the circle parted. Men glanced hurriedly in her direction, then back at the king, who continued his speech, oblivious of her entrance. Their faces reflected disturbing emotions as their eyes darted from her to her husband.

She had dressed for the reunion in a gown of deep rose, the color of Lancaster. Her hair was caught up into horned cauls made of filigreed gold. From their tips was suspended a veil of sheerest rose sendal that floated behind her as she moved forward. Every man in the cadre responded to the freshness of her beauty and winced inwardly at the prospect of her meeting with the king.

The man who had returned at last from Arundel was as one unknown to Joanna. Muffled from head to foot in black wool and silk, not an inch of his skin visible except his face, he stared at her with burning wary eyes. The Italian physician had told her to be prepared, but his warning had not been accompanied by graphic description. The sight of her husband's face caused bile to rise in her throat. Frantically, she swallowed, one small fist clenching at her bosom. Only her quick presence of mind kept her from pressing it against her mouth and thereby revealing her horror at the king's condition.

Scabs marred his forehead, his cheeks, his eyelids, his swollen lips, even the patchy beard on his chin. Most hideous were his nostrils, grotesquely swollen by large pustulant boils. Defiantly, he stared at her, daring her to scream, to cry, to vomit, to faint. With a faint rustle of fabric and a shuffle of shoes, she heard the men close the circle behind her. She felt menaced by them also as if they, too, dared her to despise the king.

Calling on reserves of strength she did not know she possessed, she willed her frozen lips to smile. Her trembling hands plucked at the sides of her skirt. "Your Majesty." She sank to one knee, bowing low in a deep curtsey.

When she raised her head, her eyes met Henry's. The bright Plantagenet blue at least had not been dimmed. As she smiled gently, his defiant wariness abated somewhat. Suddenly his eyes seemed to glisten, as if with tears; then he blinked, and the impression was gone. With a gesture of his black-gloved hand he bade her rise.

As she moved to take her place to the left of his chair, she came face to face with Geoffrey. As his mouth twisted sardonically, each knew the other's thoughts. In his eyes she read cruel pleasure in relishing what he believed to be her torment. Now her marriage would certainly not be a true one so long as the king suffered such a grievous disease.

She shivered, recalling Isabella's prophecy. Could her old witch of a duenna have spoken the truth? No, she reassured herself. The doctor had diagnosed St. Anthony's fire, a fairly common disease in the late spring and fall in England. The rye grasses produced the black mold ergot, beloved, so the legends said, of witches who used it to cause miscarriages among the cattle of someone who had earned their ire. Worse yet were the stories of unfortunate women who had taken the poisonous substance to rid themselves of unwanted pregnancies.

Equally to be avoided was rye bread not baked fresh but kept overlong until tendrils of black mold threaded through it. Many a starving peasant who had eaten it had found himself disfigured by the disease that now ravaged the king.

"Buckingham tells me that you have won great admiration among the members of the Council," Henry began, his querulous tone tinged with jealousy.

Joanna smiled faintly. "If I have won admiration, I am pleased, Your Majesty, for my behavior reflects on you. In most cases I acted merely as a mediator among the knowledgeable men you gather round you."

Henry nodded slowly. Her answer was well chosen to

abate his displeasure. "That is the real duty of a king. First, of course, he must surround himself with good men. Then he must mediate their strong opinions."

His eyes studied the faces of the men assembled before him. Some few had been with him almost from the beginning when he had returned to England from exile, ostensibly to claim the Duchy of Lancaster confiscated by his cousin, Richard. Most of his followers had joined him in the intervening six years. All their loyalties were suspect. He knew them to be opportunists and adventurers even as he himself had been. In that sense, he supposed they were as loyal as could be. Self-interest was the most powerful force in the world.

Even his queen, whom he acknowledged with a cynical smile in her direction, had taken her place beside him for the position he offered. No, perhaps not quite. She had made her choice when he was yet Earl of Derby and of Hereford with naught but the Duchy of Lancaster as a prospect. He had not offered her a kingdom, and she had accepted him before he had won it.

He shook himself irritably, remembering where he was. His reverie had caused some impatient shufflings among the assembly. "I shall resume my place in Council," he announced officiously. "My queen has labored too long at my office. She will be glad to be able to return to her duties." With these words, he offered his gloved hand to his wife.

Steeling herself to appear unmoved, she placed the tips of her fingers on the top of his. His thumb closed over them forcing them down into his palm. The black suede was soft and elegant, but the thought of what might lie beneath it made her stomach heave.

Moving like an old, old man he levered himself off the chair, grimacing as his clothing shifted on his body. With Joanna on his right, he led a progress among the men, speaking to each of them in turn, reminding one man of a time when he had fought beside his king, inquiring after an absent friend of another.

When they came to Geoffrey, the king smiled pleasantly. "Ah, d'Anglais, your knee does not trouble you so much?"

"No, Your Majesty." Geoffrey inclined his head. "It can do whatever I will it to, and your will is my will."

The king clapped him on the shoulder with his other hand, purposefully bringing the three of them close together in an intimate circle. "Well, said. You remember him, do you not, Joanna? He came to me many years ago from the service of your former lord, the Duke of Brittany. He has been ever faithful—a strong and gallant man. We know well how to value such men, do we not, my lady?"

The three standing so close together reminded Joanna forcibly of the arrangement among Brittany, Geoffrey, and herself. For a terrible moment she misread his meaning. Her eyes darted from one man to the other betraying her agony before she recognized the remark as being merely a general compliment.

Geoffrey's smile hinted at irony as he read her thought. Again he bowed low, this time reaching for her other hand and carrying it to his lips. "The service that I owe to you, sire, would be as willingly performed for the queen."

His breath warmed her hand sending a little thrill through her. Not surprisingly, a feeling of disorientation swept over her. Holding her hands were two men, one whose flesh made her skin crawl, one whose touch aroused her emotions to fever pitch. Her sensations must be closely akin to madness she thought. How could such overwhelming desire and revulsion exist side by side in one body?

Then Geoffrey released her hand and stepped back with a bow as Henry led her on to the next man.

The following day Henry returned to his rightful place at the head of the Council, and Joanna returned to the bower to resume her duties in the idle world of women. It was a world she had come to despise, for she had tasted the excitement of politics. Her life at Montfort's side had only been a prelude to the position she had assumed on the Council. She knew she had performed the ruler's part well. Now it was abruptly taken away from her.

Bored with idle chatter in the women's quarters, she purposefully sought out Henry, encouraging him to talk about the business of the day. Sometimes she was pleased with his decisions; at other times, she bit her tongue at the effort to keep from voicing her objections.

Acknowledging herself nearly helpless to influence the many divergent forces in England, Joanna nevertheless began to offer timid suggestions. At first, Henry resentfully ordered her to mind her place as the lady who ordered his household, not his kingdom. Yet he was no fool. Joanna possessed a clever brain along with a well-honed gift of persuasive speech developed during her long years in thrall to her father and her first husband. Obviously, she sought only to persuade him to look at an issue from another angle. If, in doing so, she was able to influence him to make wise or just decisions, he came to accept her help as an offer for the common good.

"You make powerful enemies, Your Majesty."

She turned, surprised to find that the voice at her elbow belonged to the prince. As if he delivered a casual remark, his eyes remained fixed on the mummers capering before them for the evening's entertainment.

The intensity of his tone made her tremble. "In what way?"

"Leave off your questioning and harassing of the king. The Council's decisions are not to be gainsaid by a woman exerting her physical influence over a sick man."

Not only were the words an insult, so was his tone. Yet she strove to placate her stepson. "I swear I use no 'physical' influence, as you call it."

"Do you deny that the king comes to discuss private and secret meetings with you?"

"He does not discuss 'secret' meetings. Since when are the meetings of the Council kept secret?"

The prince grunted softly. "If you wish to argue the point, perhaps we should have some speech together tomorrow," he suggested.

"I am ever at your service," she whispered sarcastically, but he had left her side as quickly as he had come.

After breakfast Isabella admitted the prince to Joanna's study. In the manner of the arrogant young, he made no effort to conceal his distaste for the cronelike figure dressed in dusty black garments more suited to a Spanish nunnery than the English court.

When Isabella had scuttled out, he made an exaggerated leg to the woman his father had married. "Your Majesty."

"Prince Henry."

He ran his gaze over her garments, taking in especially the gold rings on her fingers and the intricate gold design of her necklace. "You have enjoyed my father's generosity," he observed drily.

She touched her fingertips to the dark gold topaz suspended at her throat. "If you are referring to this, it was a gift from my late husband on the birth of his second son."

"Ah." Hal shuffled his feet uncertainly. Face to face with her in private, he found he did not know how to proceed. Although he told himself he did not fear her, he found himself in awe of her beauty and dignity.

"Please be seated." She indicated a chair across from her own.

Hesitantly, he lowered himself to its edge, feeling more and more uneasy. After a moment's silence, he drew a deep breath and thinned his lips. "Madam, you are making dangerous enemies."

Joanna regarded him soberly. Everyone at the court had hosts of dangerous enemies. She told him so, adding, "And just as quickly, they become friends. The wind blows north then south. My father knew better than most how to judge its vagaries."

"Your father, madam?"

She stared at him in amazement, suddenly very much aware of the difference in their ages. This callow young man had been born two years after Charles of Navarre had met his hideous death. He was not yet twenty, while she was thirty-seven. Her reverie was interrupted by the realization that he was staring at her, probably attributing her silence to her advanced age.

She smiled brightly. "My father was Charles of Navarre. He was thought very . . . clever among the European monarchs."

Clearly the name meant nothing to him. He shrugged slightly. "Men deal with men," he informed her loftily. "They do not tolerate women who do not know their places." His words were cold and vaguely threatening.

Concealing her irritation, she took a firm grip on the arms of her chair. "The king needed to know how matters stood after his long absence."

"Such information should have come from others," the prince objected sullenly. "There are many more qualified than you—many who have the best interests of this kingdom at heart."

"Such as you?" she asked gently.

"England will be mine someday—and France too," he replied arrogantly. "I should be the one to rule when my father is incapable."

"He is not incapable. He has been physically ill, but he is recovering."

Shrugging his broad shoulders, the prince purposefully let his eyes wander around the room. It was singularly unfeminine. Not a sign of an embroidery frame, not a lute, not even a flower relieved its austerity. He might have been in a man's room. Not that he was used to feminine trappings. He had spent no time with females since his mother's death. One corner of the small study contained a desk with two stacks of papers. Possibly, he had interrupted her reading. At last he looked back at her, his irritation evident. "There are those who say he is cursed."

"Only the superstitious and unlearned."

"He has many sins on his soul which God may have chosen to punish in a way exemplary to all." Even as he spoke, he shrugged slightly. Watching him closely, Joanna recognized that he did not believe what he said.

"He has brought peace to England," she replied serenely. "He has sacrificed his health in the effort."

"He is foul." The words were uttered like a curse.

Joanna drew a deep breath. "For shame. He is your father. Moreover, he is the king. Why do you despise him? He cannot be condemned because he has caught a disease while campaigning to protect the throne. Remember that throne will be yours someday."

The prince scowled. "Inheriting it from him will not make it mine."

She misread his meaning. "Of course, it is yours. You are your father's first-born son. No son to come after you shall take it. Even if I had twenty sons, they would not be the first-born."

With piercing intensity, his answer hissed across the intervening space. "I mean it is not his to give."

Her eyes flew to the door, ascertaining that it was firmly closed. "You speak treason," she whispered.

"He stole the throne and murdered the rightful heir at Pontefract."

Her black eyes studied him carefully. What did this impassioned young man mean by making this dangerous statement to her? Such reckless unthoughtful speech could lead to his downfall.

Yet his eyes were angry, his color high. Undoubtedly, he lived with the burden of guilt as well as resentment. All the court knew the tales of his scandalous roistering around the streets of London, drinking and fighting in the lowest taverns in Cheapside. He was rebellious by nature, and his rebellion was directed against his father.

At last she spoke, measuring her words carefully. "Powerful men make many enemies as you have seen fit to remind me. Richard was a powerful man at one time. He had a chance to kill your father, but he was foolish. He did not seize the chance when it came. Brittany laughed at the time. He would never have freed a man under those circumstances. In so doing, Richard let his most powerful enemy go free."

The prince groaned. "Do kindness and mercy count for nothing?"

The daughter of Charles of Navarre looked at him cynically. "Perhaps Richard was not really kind? Perhaps he was cowardly and weak. Perhaps he feared to destroy the only son of John of Gaunt? To show kindness and mercy would have been to allow your father to return, forgiven, before his father died and to inherit the lands which were his by birth."

The prince sprang to his feet. "How do you know so much?" he cried angrily. "Who are you? A French duchess? What do you know of England?"

"My first husband was much interested in England. Brittany and England have always been close. Montfort's claim to the suzerainty was supported by the English who gave him refuge when he was exiled," she reminded him.

Frustration released his hot temper. He had come to threaten his stepmother, instead he found himself being given very reasonable arguments against the beliefs he cherished. Furthermore, he found himself understanding why his father respected and listened to her. Still, he wanted to believe that his father was a monster as many believed him to be. Otherwise, his own bad behavior was nothing but silly youthful rebellion, not the proud defiant act of showing his independence from a bad king.

"You flatter him to gain power for yourself," he accused loudly.

"How can I flatter him by advising him?" she countered.

Grinding his teeth with rage, he stood over her while she remained seated, small and calm, in her chair. "I warn you, madam."

"I thank you, but I shall serve the king even if there is danger to myself, even as you would. Calm yourself, young prince."

When she called him 'young,' she broke the last hold he had on his temper. With a foul oath he strode across the room and flung himself out of the door, slamming it behind him.

Joanna remained in the chair for a long time, staring sadly at the floor. His anger had made her weak, for though he was immature and spoiled, she recognized his power. He was hard and determined. He would not hesitate to rid himself of her should his father die. Furthermore, his anger at his father seemed real enough. Jean's words came back to her. *"The Plantagenet is always the Plantagenet's worst enemy."*

The next day when she walked in the garden, Geoffrey stepped into her path. "Dismiss your women," he commanded darkly.

His presumption made her angry. Defiantly, she thrust her chin out at him. "You do not give orders here, Sir Geoffrey."

His gray eyes glinted like armor plate. "Pray, forgive me, Your Majesty," he hissed with elaborate sarcasm. "I beg you dismiss your women, unless you wish them to hear of your shameful behavior."

Instantly defensive, she nodded to Doña Isabella and the two English dames who served as her ladies-in-waiting. "You may withdraw to a distance. Sir Geoffrey would have private speech with me. We are old friends from many years ago," she explained. "Doña Isabella, you may return to the

341

apartments where I will join you later."

When Joanna's attendants had walked away, casting curious looks over their shoulders at the pair, she seated herself on a bench in the garden, folded her hands neatly on her knees, and waited. "Now, Geoffrey."

"I had forgotten you had a taste for young men," he began angrily.

She stared at him, puzzled. Having no idea what was stirring his anger, she did not know what his remark implied.

"Of course, I was very young," he continued, "but I should have thought your tastes would have matured. Here I find you still seeking to ensnare callow youths."

"What do you mean?" A slow flush of anger stained her cheeks. It struck her that she was getting very tired of Geoffrey d'Anglais presuming to dictate her moral behavior. His condemnation was particularly irritating since the sins of which he accused her were solely and completely in his own mind.

"I mean the prince!" he snapped.

"The prince?"

"I saw him come from your apartments. He was fiercely angry." Geoffrey's own anger could scarcely be contained. He clenched and unclenched his fists as if he struggled to keep from hitting her. "Your tastes have changed for the worst, my lady," he accused her.

"On the basis of a young man's angry face, you accuse me of trying to ensnare him," she exclaimed, aghast. She made as if to rise, but he dropped a hand on her shoulder, holding her firmly. At a distance his act appeared to be the act of one friend talking earnestly to another. "No, you shall sit here and listen, while I hold a mirror to your soul."

"You have no right," she fumed. "You are not my judge. Furthermore, you do not have the truth of the story. I wager you have not even inquired."

"Ah, I do not need to make inquiries when I know you so well." He sneered. "You planned this meeting with the prince. It must be easy to betray an old sick husband now since you have done it before."

"You are wrong," she insisted. "So wrong. He sought me out. He insisted on meeting with me to warn and threaten, even as you."

Gazing into her earnest face upturned to his, he could almost believe her. Her hands, the palms uplifted, reached out to him in supplication. He had felt those hands caress his body. Those lips had parted just as they did now in tenderness and sweet passion beneath his own.

Suddenly he pictured her in the arms of the diseased king, and the young troubled face of Prince Henry rose before him. Instantly, his imaginings turned him into a savage.

"Your beauty would corrupt a stone," he swore breathlessly.

"I swear I did not seek to corrupt him. He is ambitious—"

"He is the prince. He declares you cast a spell on him."

She could not restrain a chuckle even in the face of his rage. "He is a young boy reared in the company of men. He knows little about women." Her voice became serious. "You may have observed that there are few enough in this court."

"I have noticed that you never cease scrambling to maintain a position of power. You are planning again as you have always done. Before Brittany died, you had already found a soft bed to receive you. Now, with England seriously ill, you look to his son."

"No!" It was a wail of protest. His words cut her to the quick. Would he always consider her to have the very basest of motives?

"You are beneath contempt," he gritted, ignoring the pain in her voice. "To seek to lie with both father and son is an abomination. I am ashamed that I ever . . . that I ever cared for you."

His insulting accusation was the last straw. White as chalk, she pushed herself upright despite his heavy hand. "Leave me," she spat. Her face was inches away from his, her

343

eyes flashing volcanic fire.

"With pleasure," he snarled back, his face contorted with rage. "Only heed my warning. Leave the prince alone."

Toe to toe they stood. His hands were doubled into fists at his sides; hers, likewise, were clenched at her hips.

"I do not seek the prince. He is but a youth. I am old enough to be his mother. In point of fact, his own mother and I were the same age exactly."

"That would mean nothing to such as you."

"Such as me!" She almost shouted the words. "You know what I am. I am a political pawn. I was the bride of Brittany to insure diplomatic amity. I was bedded to you to insure the continuation of the line. Henry Bolingbroke wanted me to insure his strength and support on the continent against the Valois kings. I can do nothing. I can only be used. If I can manage to better myself, I do so only because I am valuable to men."

"You manipulate them," he contradicted her. "You use your beauty and your guile to lure men, to bewitch them." He was spluttering now, the cogency of her words carrying home her argument despite his desire to believe the worst of her.

"I have never manipulated anyone."

He pounced upon that denial. "Even now, you use your influence over the king to carry your will in the Council."

Dropping her eyes, she shook her head. "I am bringing him up to date on what has happened while he was in the field and recuperating at Arundel. I can be counted on to give an unbiased view since I have naught in England but his interests."

Geoffrey stared at her demure posture. He could not deny she spoke the truth. She was defusing his anger. Then he remembered the prince. "Witch!" he spat out. "You twist and turn, making crooked seem straight, but I will not forget my purpose. I warn you. Leave the prince alone. He will make a great king someday. He does not need his emotions entangled with such a lustful piece as you."

Turning on his heel, he left her reeling from shock at his horrible words. Her tender approach to him had only erected a barrier impossibly high and thick between them. Desolate, she sank back down on the bench. She had never felt so bitterly alone or so besieged in her life.

Chapter 21

"Jerusalem! Jerusalem!"

Henry had fallen asleep again on his couch; now his recurring dream of a Crusade disturbed him. Joanna shook her head sadly as she studied the papers before her on the desk. Their afternoons invariably were spent in the same way.

The king reclined on a couch specially moved for him to his wife's study, while she read to him the reports of the day. Then they discussed the deliberations of the Council. More often than not, he dozed lightly, sometimes waking abruptly, sometimes drifting in and out of sleep like a child. Many times, unfortunately, his sleep was troubled, usually when his body pained him most severely.

The hideous taint of leprosy could no longer be denied. Besides Joanna and his sons, only the Council and the cadre saw him now. His skin had thickened over most of his body, particularly on his face which now remained perpetually reddened and swollen, and the lines on his face had deepened, making him appear much older than his forty-six years. Nerve damage to the muscles of his legs and feet had crippled him, so he moved only with a cane now. On bad days he could not walk at all.

As she glanced up from her reading, he jerked spasmodically, groaned, and reared halfway up. Looking around him dazedly, he raised his gloved hands to rub his eyes. The whites were a network of broken veins that extended into the blue irises. His sight had been steadily going as the inflammation and pain had increased.

Delivering himself of a bitter oath, he settled back on the couch and lay blinking at the ceiling. "What were you reading, Joanna?" His voice was hoarse and raspy as if his throat were in the same condition as his eyes.

"I had finished, Henry." She put down the paper. "It was not very important anyway. It is a Council report on the spread of Lollardy in the universities. Your uncle, Arundel, wants to revoke the charter of Oxford."

"I care not." Henry sighed.

Joanna sat in silence, weighing her chances. "Oxford is a great university," she said at last.

"The chancellor is not my friend," Henry replied irritably, twisting from side to side on the couch in a futile effort to find freedom from his terrible disease. "He swore an oath to Richard II."

"England needs great universities. Spain has them. France has them . . . Italy." Softly she enumerated the countries.

"You speak truth," Henry agreed at last. "We will do nothing. Therefore, Arundel will be only slightly discomfited, and the university may go on as it pleases."

Joanna laid the paper aside and picked up another. Before she could begin reading it aloud, Henry spoke fretfully. "I care not. I shall leave the country soon. We shall go on Crusade, you and I. I shall leave Exeter in charge. He is my brother after all. My father sired us all, and Richard legitimized them just before my father died. A brother would not take a brother's throne." He looked in her direction hopefully.

Still Joanna did not respond. Her eyes remained directed to the papers before her. To argue with him was useless, but she did not take him seriously. Henry of Lancaster might dream of Jerusalem, but his love for the throne of England was too deep and abiding to risk leaving the country in the hands of any but himself.

"Richard," he whispered, swinging his legs gingerly over the side of the couch and staring into space. "Richard . . . Thomas Swynford, my stepbrother, was his gaoler at Pontefract. He was to keep him safe." He drew a shuddering breath. "Piers Exton was a lie. There was no such man. I had Richard's body displayed to the people, so they could not dispute his death. Oh, God. God . . ." Slumping back onto his couch, he lay on his side and drew his knees up toward his chest.

Joanna closed her eyes as a nauseating odor rose from the king's body. He had been less able to control his bodily functions this winter and suffered occasional accidents. St. Anthony's fire still left him disfigured with hideous pustules that swelled and burst, leaving behind scabs that eventually formed deep scars. She had not seen his body in years, and she now wondered at the faithfulness of his valets. The men must have the patience of Job.

When his mutterings had died away, she rang for the servant whose duty it was to care for the king that day. When the man appeared, she dispatched the king to his care. Shivering as if the room had suddenly turned cold, Joanna made her way as silently as she could to the small private chapel adjoining her apartments. Succumbing at last to Isabella's importunings, she had taken a confessor to whom she unburdened her soul on occasions. Privy to her husband's feverish monologues, she had been forced as her duenna had predicted to listen to secrets she should not know. The hidden torments of a king's conscience revealed the fates of many men.

The chapel was little more than a closet with a simple prie-dieu and a crucifix hanging on the wall over a small altar table. Two candles on either side of a missal were the only source of light. Dreary as a cell, it suited her needs, for her confessions were better done in the dark.

Even as she knelt alone, awaiting the appointed time when her confessor should appear, she regretted the burden thrust upon her. For years she had resisted telling her thoughts to anyone who might reveal them. First she had feared the knowledge might be used against her by her father and then by her husband. The situation was no different now, for plots were fomented everywhere. She still feared for herself, but the strain on her coupled with the absence of any person in whom she could confide made her desperate.

Hands clasped tightly together on the shelf of the kneeling bench, she thought of Geoffrey. How she had trusted him in Brittany! Ironically, she had not known how to value him in those halcyon days when she had strewn her careless thoughts before him, certain that they were safe with him. Not even torture could have caused Geoffrey's tongue to condemn her. He had been tortured for her sake and had yet remained her friend. A tear squeezed from between her tight-shut lids.

The faint creak of a floorboard behind her signaled the entrance of her priest. Raising one hand surreptitiously, she wiped away the self-pitying tear to raise to him a face cleared of all violent emotion. With a cynical twist to her lips, she reasoned that she confessed all to no man.

"Your Majesty?" came his gentle, inquiring voice. Friar Randolph was a small dark man, a Celt from Cornwall, the descendant of a conquered race that had held the British Isles before the Roman invasions.

She raised her eyes as he knelt before the altar table and took up the missal. Opening it, he began to recite the mass. His darkness reminded her vaguely of Brother Francisco, the tutor of her girlhood and practically the only friend of her youth. Such a resemblance must be superifical, she reasoned, and superficialities are a foolish base for trust.

The better part of an hour spent with Friar Randolph left

her feeling stronger for the rest of the day. At least she would not have to struggle to keep from bursting into tears at the least trouble. Of late, Henry's irascible behavior had driven Council members wild. The cold of winter and the fasts of Lent had shortened his temper until Joanna occasionally doubted his sanity.

Relieved of the searing words Henry had poured into her ears and with the taste of the Eucharist still on her tongue, she walked back toward the study. At these times, she had formed the habit of thinking of nothing, of driving all recriminations and plots from her mind. Such moments of serenity were more necessary than food and drink to her these days. God grant that she could maintain her steadiness as Henry grew worse and worse.

"Practicing to be a widow?" a familiar voice asked nastily.

Coming at her so unexpectedly, the words made her flinch. Caught with her mind unprotected, the ramifications of the question pierced her to the heart. She tottered to the wall and leaned against it, one hand clenched tightly at her waist, the other shielding her face from his all-seeing eyes. Tears, which she had controlled until now, slipped down her cheeks.

She heard a muttered exclamation behind her before a hand touched her shoulder. "Joanna."

Once she had loosed her hold on her feelings in his familiar presence, she could not stop. Like an icicle melting, her substance turned to water and she slid down the wall, crying helplessly as her heart leaped and pounded within her.

Shocked at her emotional outburst, Geoffrey went down on both knees beside her, grasping her shoulders to turn her into his arms. Unsurprisingly, she resisted these efforts. Rather than distress her more, he contented himself with rubbing his hand soothingly up and down her spine and across her shoulders.

For several minutes Joanna found herself incapable of practical thought. Geoffrey's words—their prediction of what must surely be the very near future for her—drove her into a great gulf of despair.

"Joanna." His voice, softly importunate, echoed in her ear. "Joanna, let me help you to rise. Forgive me, lady. I did not mean to cause you so much pain. I beg you—damn my soul for being an unfeeling swine!—please let me assist you to rise. Let me guide you wherever you wish to go."

Her tears had stained the front of her garments, for she had no handkerchief about her. Instead she had crumpled into a tight ball hiding her face from him by pressing it against her knees.

His words only elicited from her another storm of weeping. "Why do you not go?" she gasped. "Oh, why do you not leave me alone? Why do you linger to mock my pain?"

His voice was gentle in her ear. "I do not mock your sincere pain, Joanna. Forgive me for speaking so cruelly. Let me take you to a place where you may calm yourself, and then I swear I will leave you, Joanna."

"Oh, God," she begged. "Just leave. You have said a terrible thing to me. I want no more from you. What was once between us is no more. I was thinking of that when you spoke to me of the future. Now leave me."

"Joanna . . . Your Majesty . . ." Despite her stated wishes, he slipped one hand underneath her knees and lifted her body into his arms. "Let me take you to your women."

Her sobbing continued as he hurried along the hall with her. His knock at the door of her apartments brought a very wide-eyed young lady-in-waiting.

"Her Majesty is ill," was his excuse. Behind the young girl's shoulder, he caught sight of Isabella, her eyes glittering amidst the sallow wrinkles. His hands tightened protectively around Joanna. Even as they did so, he knew his gesture to be futile. She was the queen.

As the women hastened forward commenting and questioning, he carried his burden to a chair before the fire. "I have brought her to you, Doña Isabella." He addressed the woman purposefully. "She collapsed in the hall on her way from chapel. I think she may be overtired."

Joanna buried her face in her hands, her breath coming in shuddering gasps. She had no more tears to shed but was drained of all emotion. She longed to look at Geoffrey, but his question, which had triggered her outburst, had been intended to be cruel. She took the cold wet cloth that one woman pressed into her hand and held it to her eyes. Better not to see his leering, mocking face.

"We will take care of her," Doña Isabella promised. "No doubt you are right. She has been nursing the king for hours at a time. Her Majesty has had more than her share of nursing in her life as I am sure you remember, Sir Geoffrey. You may leave her in our charge now."

Wishing to remain but having no reason to do so, Geoffrey reluctantly allowed himself to be herded toward the door. Over the duenna's head he saw Joanna's slender bent figure shudder violently. A shaft of pain lanced through him along with the desire to take her in his arms and beg her forgiveness.

She had told him she had been thinking of him. Despite his disgust with her for greedily seizing every opportunity to gain rank and power, feelings stirred within him that he thought he had buried long ago. Sternly he forced his eyes away from her only to meet Doña Isabella's accusing glance.

A shamed flush stained his cheek. The old woman's eyes narrowed to mere slits as if she measured him and found him small. Her lip curled. "Go," she commanded gruffly. "She has need of friends, not enemies."

An instant later, he found himself standing outside the door of the apartments and wishing with all his heart he were within.

Despite the heat of the fire, Joanna could not control her

chills. She had cried until her eyes were swollen almost shut, their lids red and puffy. In an effort to relieve her throbbing temples, she thrust her fingers into her hair and pulled at it.

"My lady," one of the young women begged, catching her mistress' wrists, "please let go. You will injure yourself. That will not help."

The duenna was beside her immediately, thrusting her wrinkled face into the face of the queen. "Stop!" she commanded in Spanish. "Princess, stop!"

But even the Spanish words did not penetrate Joanna's distraught brain. Her mind was filled with chaos. To her disordered consciousness Isabella's hands felt like hooks tearing at her body. "Leave me alone!" With a scream she tore herself free so violently that she staggered across the room.

"Joanna!"

"My lady!"

"Your Majesty!"

"Leave me alone!" she shrilled. "I must . . ." She swayed where she stood. Closing her eyes to try to clear her blurred distorted vision, she drew a deep breath and released it in a shuddering sigh. "I must see the king," she finished.

"Princesa." Doña Isabella moved slowly toward her, arms outstretched, her voice low and soothing.

Joanna darted toward the door. *"Hechicera!* Keep away from me! I will tell the king."

The other ladies made no move to stop her, and Isabella was too slow. With a flutter of skirts, she was gone, dashing through the antechamber and out into the hall.

"Your Majesty!"

"Princesa!"

Joanna slowed to a walk only as she approached the guards outside Henry's apartment. Summoning an air of dignity that belied the condition of her dress and the wild light in her eyes, she strode arrogantly past them. If they noticed her beleaguered condition, they made no attempt to detain her.

Henry was not in the study. The valet had taken him to his rooms and had summoned the physician, Nigarelli. The Italian greeted her at the door to the bedchamber. "My lady, he is resting easily. You should not have upset yourself so."

His quiet words steadied her as they gave her an excuse for looking as she did. Yet her body still shivered and quaked from the effects of the hysterical outburst.

"Doctor, I must see the king."

"Madam, he is asleep. I have given him a draught. I fear he has a fever. This February has been unusually cold and he has not eaten well of late. His body is thin, for he has lost some flesh. Generally, however . . ." The physician droned on and on, oblivious to the growing agitation of the woman before him.

"When may I see him, Doctor?" she interrupted at last.

He paused, cocking his head to one side as he directed his gentle scrutiny for the first time to her condition. "Madam, he will doubtless sleep the rest of the day and into the night. Once the drug I have given wears off, he should slip naturally into a healthful sleep. I think you will find him much rested and refreshed tomorrow."

Her shoulders slumped. A wave of disappointment crushed her. How she needed to reassure herself. Only a word from Henry would help her at this time. "Doctor, may I only see him? I . . . I have been distressed by his condition."

"Madam, you have my assurance. He is well."

At that moment Doña Isabella entered the antechamber. "Your Majesty," she called nervously, ". . . and Dr. Nigarelli." She dropped a perfunctory curtsey. Looking from one to the other, she faltered, then bravely spoke to the man. "I have come to remind Her Majesty that she must eat and rest."

"I quite agree." Dr. Nigarelli smiled unctuously at the

duenna's announcement. *"Madonna,* return with your lady and rest yourself. The king can see no one else tonight."

The king and queen attended devotions at Westminster Abbey during Lent. Praying at the tomb of Edward the Confessor with Joanna beside him, Henry suddenly gasped for breath. As he had done once before, he sank back on his heels, palms turned upward toward the vaulted ceiling.

Thinking he would weep, Joanna turned to face him, reaching automatically, for his hand to offer comfort. Horrified, she stared as his mouth fell open and his body slid backward to lie in a tangled heap, his legs doubled under him.

Even as she called for help, his half brother, Dorset, sprang to his side.

The king's face was blue and for a minute he did not seem to breathe.

"Summon the physician," Dorset shouted over his shoulder.

"Ho! Guards! Bear the king to the abbot's chamber."

"Be careful," Joanna cried, as the heavy-handed men seized Henry's limbs and twisted them roughly. "Be careful, dolts. His body is hurt. Oh, do not pull at him so." She pushed herself between Henry's leg and the hands that gripped his ankle and calf to straighten him out.

The man pulled back, alarmed at her vehemence.

"Your Majesty," Dorset chided her. "He did what was necessary. Henry's limbs must be straightened in order for him to be lifted off these cold stones."

Reluctantly, she gave way though she winced at the treatment. They could not know how painful the scabs were when they were abraded. "Be careful," she whispered between clenched teeth as she followed them to the abbot's chamber.

For what seemed an eternity, Henry lay on his back, his mouth slackly open. After each stentorian breath the watchers shivered in agonized suspense until he drew the next. Joanna clung to his hand and willed him to continue. "Please, Henry," she whispered once when the time seemed longer than the last.

"My lady." Dr. Nigarelli came panting to the bedside as if he had run a long distance, which indeed he had. "I must ask you to leave while I examine His Majesty."

She raised her eyes to his. "Examine him from the other side of the bed."

"But his heart is on this side," the physician objected.

"Yes, but do it anyway." As she had waited, she had become obsessed by the belief that if she let go of his hand, he would slip away.

Nigarelli first removed the crown from Henry's head so that he might rest more easily. Then he called for bolsters to be placed behind the king's frail shoulders to lift them up and ease his breathing. "I must loosen his clothing, Your Majesty," he said pointedly.

Dorset was at her elbow. "You must leave, my lady."

"No," she protested.

"You will hinder the physician's work."

"Yes," Nigarelli insisted. "I must work undisturbed. He is very ill, but with immediate care, he may recover."

"No," she insisted stubbornly. "He must have someone to hold fast to." She tightened her grip on Henry's left hand.

Both men shrugged in frustration. The abbot came forward and offered his assistance, putting every facility of the Abbey at the disposal of the doctor.

As the king's chest was bared, Joanna swallowed thickly and turned her face away. A putrid odor rose from his sweating body at the opening of the thick garments. Dark red, lumpy skin stretched over a rib cage so covered with sores that Henry seemed to be rotting already. Her stomach

357

heaved, and she gagged, emitting a stricken sound.

Nigarelli's lips thinned. "I warned you, my lady," he said tautly.

Ignoring him, Joanna concentrated on the magnificent tapestries covering the walls of the chamber. They portrayed scenes of the Holy City picked out in gold and silk threads. "What chamber is this, milord Abbot?" Joanna asked curiously.

"It is called the Jerusalem Chamber, so please Your Majesty, because of the tapestries."

"Oh, God, do not tell him so," she whispered.

Too late.

The red-rimmed eyes flicked open. Hearing still acute when all other senses were fading, Henry Plantagenet responded to his dream. "W-where?"

The hands of Nigarelli were stilled in surprise.

Joanna twisted her body frantically, trying to catch the abbot's eye, but the good man had stepped forward eagerly at this sign of his sovereign's revival. "The Jerusalem Chamber," he repeated clearly.

"No," the queen moaned.

Henry stared for a moment at the abbot; then his eyes searched for Dorset who stood aghast as did Joanna. Both knew the prophecy made at Henry's birth stated that he would die in Jerusalem.

The sons of John of Gaunt stared at each other. Never had Dorset felt such love and pity for his magnificent elder brother. Henry's blue gaze flickered weakly, then passed on to his wife. He closed his eyes momentarily, opened them again. His wife's stricken face hovered above him.

"Jerusalem, Joanna," he whispered through cracked lips. "Jerusalem . . . but not as I dreamed."

"Henry," she begged. "Hold fast. You will yet see it."

The hint of a smile flickered across his slack mouth. "Not as I dreamed," he repeated. His eyes closed, and he seemed to sink into himself before their very eyes. The hand to which she had clung so fervently seemed heavier than before.

Her eyes flew to the physician who leaned forward with a mirror to see if the king's breath clouded the glass. "He lives. However, someone should summon the prince."

As the abbot hurried out, Nigarelli withdrew from the bedside, folding his hands helplessly. Life was escaping from the stinking, pustulant body. He had no remedy for a spirit that no longer wanted to live. The word *Jerusalem* had somehow discouraged his patient. When he had bent over him the first time, he had felt life surging strongly through him, driven by the will of the king. Now that will was gone. He shook his head.

Dorset took his place on Henry's right, first removing the royal crown to a stool beside the head of the bed. Together they watched the silent monarch, unconsciously holding their breaths each time until he breathed again. The room grew dim as the shadows of day's end lengthened.

A noise in the corridor presaged the arrival of Prince Henry. His young face was white and still as stone as he thrust the door open and beheld the tableau.

Dorset rose and came to his side. "He has spoken but a few words since he collapsed. Perhaps you can get him to speak."

"Yes." Hastily, he took his uncle's place beside the bed. "Father! Your Majesty!"

The ghastly face on the pillow remained immobile, its scaly reddened skin stretched tight over the bones. The long aquiline nose of the Plantagenets jutted forward grotesquely like a gargoyle from a gothic cathedral, but gargoyles were carved from dark gray stone, smooth and damp. The skin on the king's face was hideously pitted and dry as if it had been baked in the fires of hell.

"Father!" the prince called again.

At the same time Joanna tightened her grip on the flaccid fingers. Was it her imagination? No, the grip was answered.

"He can hear you, Hal," she gasped. "I felt him grip my fingers at your words."

"Yes." The prince nodded grimly. "He can hear my words." His eyes never leaving the face on the bed, he ordered them all to quit the chamber. "It is our wish!" he snarled, when Dorset protested in the name of Joanna.

"I cannot let him go," she begged piteously. "I cannot. Oh, do not bid me leave."

Implacable, Hal shook his head, grasping his father's right hand in both his own. "I will hold him even as you, Your Majesty."

"No, you will let him go," she hissed.

His bleak eyes met hers across the body. His were filled with tears much to her surprise. Suddenly, they were united. "I will not let him go, madam," he repeated, "but I must have private speech with him."

"Then speak in front of me," she begged. "Believe me, Hal, I have heard the secrets of my husband's soul. And if you seek to unburden your own before him, do not, I beg you. 'Tis too late."

"I will have private speech," the prince reiterated firmly. "Uncle Dorset, I beg you, escort the queen from the chamber and you, Doctor, and Abbot, go too."

With a sigh Dorset capitulated. The prince could do no harm. Of a certainty, Henry was dying. His next breath would probably be his last. Moving forward slowly, he placed his hands gently on Joanna's shoulders. "Come, my lady, you have done all you could. Leave them together."

Sobs burst from her throat then, deeply wrenched from the core of her being. She shook her head again and again as she held fast to the king's hand with a death grip.

Dorset was compelled to reach over her shoulder and pry her slender fingers loose. "Come, Your Majesty."

As Henry's hand fell limply to the bed, she turned into the marquess' arms and allowed him to lead her away. At the door she looked back over her shoulder. She would never see him again. Her last sight was of the son, placing his hand on his father's shoulder.

"Oh, my lord Father," he said clearly and firmly, "hear me, I beg you. I must know one thing. . . ."

Henry's eyelids might have flickered—Joanna would never be sure—then Dorset led her through the door which closed behind them with a final thud. What Henry told Henry would remain forever behind the door.

Chapter 22

Her heart heavy, her face white, her eyes veiled by lids so gray they looked bruised, Joanna led the procession of ladies into Westminster Abbey. Preceded by trumpeters, her train borne by pages, she took her place as first lady of the realm. Until Henry V married, she would be the queen. A step behind her at her right shoulder came Lady Hereford, the king's grandmother, and at her left shoulder Lady Margaret, Duchess of Clarence, the second lady in the kingdom, wife of Thomas, Henry's brother.

Also attending the coronation was Lady Margaret, Countess of Pembroke. Had ten years passed since she had met this singular lady? How sadly she must go to the coronation for her grandnephew.

The new king had not set eyes upon his stepmother in the three weeks since his father's death. Her invitation to attend the coronation had been couched in terms which offered her little choice so she had obeyed. Her grief at Henry's sad death had been tempered by gratitude to God that his suffering at last was ended. His soul full of woe and his body a living hell, these two burdens had killed him at age forty-six.

She had not been required to attend to the disposition of the body. Dr. Nigarelli had pronounced it so badly rotted that it was immediately lashed to a barge and floated with all speed to Canterbury Cathedral. Henry of Lancaster had already prepared a tomb graced by his effigy in alabaster. Its site was close to the tomb of his cousin the Black Prince and only a few feet farther on from St. Thomas à Becket's resting place. Because of the Lenten season, he was interred with little ceremony by his uncle, Archbishop Arundel.

Now, with the cynicism that had almost become part of her nature, Joanna regarded the splendor before her. The night before Passion Sunday, an unseasonal snow had covered the ground outside Westminster and had blanketed the whole countryside as well. Nevertheless, the press of people and the blaze of candles rendered the Abbey stifling. The light gleamed off cloth of gold and silver thread, off satin and silk, off oil and water. The faces of the men glistened with sweat as their garments weighted them down.

Even after Archbishop Arundel finally placed the Crown of St. Edward on the king's head, the ceremony was not over. The king was then brought to the throne and, in turn, each of his nobles swore fealty to him. Watching his face grow whiter as the strain upon his body and his emotions began to take its toll, she wondered why a man would be king.

What consuming passion had driven her husband to the throne of England when he had not been born to it? While her black eyes stared, unseeing, at the glittering spectacle before her, she slipped into a reverie. She had never really known Henry Bolingbroke. He had swept into her life, promising her adventure and excitement when she had begun to feel her whole existence to be hedged in by Jean de Montfort and his endless quest for heirs. They had made a pact as practical and loveless as that of infants whose fathers had planned their marriages.

She had come to England hopeful to experience a true marriage with the handsome man she remembered, only to find him beleaguered on all sides by enemies so that he had no time for her. By the time the enemies had been dispatched, he had been a sick man. He had not approached her, knowing his disease would revolt her as it did himself. For ten years she had lived with a man who had hardly touched her hand. For the last seven years of their married life she had not touched his ravaged skin or placed a ceremonial kiss upon his cheek.

Her sexuality had slept within her so long that she wondered what she would feel if a man were to seek to arouse her. She was older now. Over forty. Perhaps the fires that had blazed long ago had died, leaving nothing but a residue of memory.

Her eyes focused suddenly as Sir Geoffrey Fitzjean d'Anglais stepped forward to make his obeisance. He had been a member of the late king's cadre, and he had moved smoothly into the same position with the new monarch. His fair white blond hair caught the light as his lean height brought his head above those of the smaller men.

Dressed in dark gray with muted silver threads decorating his tunic, he looked somehow alien in the midst of the bright heraldic colors and the metals that flashed and clashed in the flickering light.

An emotion akin to pride stirred within her. Despite his treatment of her, she loved him. Here in this Abbey of William the Conqueror, Bastard of Normandy, Geoffrey's presence was a reaffirmation to the world that a man must be measured by his acts, not by the circumstance of his birth. Her heart stirred within her, and her breathing quickened as he went down on his knees with folded hands between the king's palms.

As a tear welled from her eye, she turned her head aside to surreptitiously lift it away with her finger. To her surprise, the Countess of Pembroke also dabbed at her cheeks with a scrap of linen. When the eyes of the two women met, the older woman smiled slightly before returning her gaze to the spectacle.

The feast at Westminster Hall was the most elaborate that Joanna had ever seen. Throughout the full seventeen courses, some brought in by servants mounted on white horses, the king disdained food but sipped wine occasionally. His face pale as an angel's wearing the Crown of St. Edward, he sat in state on the marble chair draped in cloth of gold, a golden canopy above his head. At his right hand was a small table on which food and wine were set by a servant who mounted a ladder to reach it, for Henry was elevated several feet above the company on a dais especially constructed for the coronation banquet.

Seated only a few chairs from her stepson, Joanna felt his eyes on her on more than one occasion. His scrutiny made her stir uncomfortably and look away. To her amazement, Geoffrey approached her and made a leg, which she acknowledged by extending her hand.

At her request, he bade a servant bring a chair so he might sit behind her. The reason for his approach puzzled her, but she waited patiently for him to speak. "The old king is dead and with him the old memories of his usurpation. Henry of Monmouth seeks to establish himself once and for all as England's rightful monarch."

"He does well to do so," she replied evenly. "Else the crown will sit as painfully on his brow as it did on his poor father's."

Even as she spoke she could have bitten her tongue. Geoffrey's face hardened. "And, of course, sons must ever bear the burden of their father's wrongs," he remarked sarcastically.

Her face reflected her sadness. "Such is the way of the world, Sir Geoffrey. 'Even unto the third and fourth generation.' I did not make the rules. I do not even live by them."

"Ah, but I think you do."

"No." She shook her head. "But you choose to believe that I do."

He clasped his hand tighter on the hilt of the dress sword that rested at his side. "What will you do now?"

She folded her hands in her lap and stared at her fingers. Her hands were still as white as ever, but their skin had begun to crinkle slightly as a sign of her age. "I suppose I shall do as the king requests . . . or commands. I strongly suspect I will retire to the country."

"Your lot will not be particularly comfortable in a strange land with very little to smooth your way," he pointed out gently.

She shrugged. "Not in a strange land, no; but Henry left me his castles and estates and the revenue from them so long as I lived. I shall not be poor or in want."

At her words Geoffrey's expression changed. He seemed to swallow what he had been about to say; then he coughed and cleared his throat. "So you have emerged triumphant again." His voice held a thread of tightly controlled anger.

"I seem to have done so. Does my comfort and ease offend you?"

"It seems undeserved. So much for so little." The cold words were like a knife to her heart. Nevertheless, she had not made the mistake of hoping that he had come to wish her well.

"You are cruel, my lord."

"I have had cruel teachers."

"At least one of your teachers was also mine," she reminded him. "His lessons did not make me cruel."

He scowled at her, an angry flush rising in his cheeks. "Did they not? I beg to differ, madam. I bear the mark on my body to this day."

"As I do on mine, Sir Geoffrey," she flared. "Even as I do on mine."

His mouth snapped to, and the silence grew between them.

He pushed back his chair and rose to leave. As the servant removed the chair, he stepped forward, bending his head to her. His voice was flat and expressionless. "Take your houses and your revenues and leave. You have seized that which you wanted to keep you safe. A very enterprising and ruthless woman. When you leave the court, I doubt that we shall meet again. Therefore, *adieu.*" Stepping back, he made an obeisance, almost insulting in its formality and grace.

Her face frozen as his, she acknowledged his gesture with a stiff nod. When he had walked away, she lifted her eyes to heaven for strength only to meet the eyes of her stepson who was elevated on his golden dais. His piercing eyes had taken in the whole encounter, undoubtedly recognizing the antipathy between the two. His eyes held a speculative look. In an effort to recover her poise, she reached for her goblet and raised it high to him, smiling a glad smile of congratulation.

In June the funeral feast honoring Henry IV was finally held at Canterbury with the whole Council attending as well as many of the cadre. The ceremony had been planned as the culmination of a progress the young king had made through the southern towns of his kingdom. Joanna and her ladies were summoned to the feast and provided with gowns of black and white to wear. Again the spectacle was brilliant and beautiful demonstrating to all the world that Henry V declared himself to be the unquestioned King of England.

Joanna found herself again close beside the tomb of the Black Prince. In the coolness of the cathedral, the alabaster effigy of Henry IV had no meaning. The Henry she had known had never looked like this portrait. Perhaps before guilt and suspicion, rebellion and disease had marked him, he had looked so bluff and hearty, his beard and mustache curling splendidly. Perhaps he had looked that way at the beginning of the century when he had triumphantly wrested the throne from Richard of Bordeaux. She closed her eyes and earnestly prayed for the peace of his soul.

Joanna met with King Henry V the next morning in the president's chambers of the cathedral. With a stern face, he motioned her to be seated before he picked up a paper before him. "I have here a list of lands belonging to the Crown of England and the House of Lancaster, madam."

Regarding him steadily, Joanna braced herself. Nothing stood between herself and this man's resentment. She must face him and assert her rights or lose all. "Then I believe some of them must be mine for the space of my lifetime, Henry," she told him evenly.

He scowled at her. "That shall be as I decide, madam."

"My late husband provided for me in his will," she asserted calmly. "You are most generous to offer more, but I am quite content with the estates and revenues that he provided in our marriage settlement."

"My father was not in his right mind at the end of his life."

Frowning, Joanna shook her head. "I beg to differ with you, Henry. Your father was sure of himself until the end. For that reason he did not make any effort to provide for my care. He had already provided for me handsomely at the time of our marriage."

"So long ago . . ."

"But nonetheless, the contract is binding. I am entitled to take residence as I see fit at Windsor, Wallingford, Berkhamsted, Hertford, or Langley."

He blinked at her memory as she recited the terms in a clear voice. "Those are the property of the Crown."

"I am the queen."

"I suppose there is no harm in merely taking residence," he began sternly, "but—"

"Furthermore, I am to have my own private residences at Hereford and at Havering-atte-Bower as well as the revenues from those estates to provide for my maintenance and the maintenance of my household." She did not finish the sentence before he leaped to his feet, his voice thundering over hers.

"Hereford was my mother's home. You shall not have it. He had no right to give it to you."

Anger made his handsome face ugly. Used to dealing with the rages of powerful men, Joanna feared him nevertheless. This man hated her. He had always done so. Gripping the arms of her chair until her fingers ached, she faced him sturdily. "I brought him a Spanish as well as a French alliance. He knew my true worth, and we bargained accordingly."

Seeking to intimidate her, he stood over her, glaring down into her face. "My mother brought him land and bore him sons as well."

"I do not denigrate what she did for him, Henry. I only—"

"Do not call me that!"

"Why not? It is your name."

"You have not the right."

"Few do," she remonstrated, raising her voice to answer him. "And they will grow fewer until someday no one will call you Henry or Harry or Hal. You will be sorry then and will long for the sound of your own name." Here she lowered her voice to speak in a gentle tone. "'Your Majesty' grows tedious and cold. Many times it carries a dagger in its smooth folds. Treasure your name for so long as it is left to you. No one called your father Henry but me; his brother, Dorset; and his uncle, Arundel. He missed it sorely."

The king slammed his fist into the palm of his hand, threatening her with his violent desire to smash her in the same way. "You will not have Hereford."

She shrugged. "To deny your father's right to dispense his possessions as he saw fit is to deny his kingship. If you deny his kingship, then you deny your right to it."

"May God damn you to hell!" He swung away from her, too angry to show in his face the knowledge that she was right.

She rose, her face as white as the ermine round the collar of her black dress. "I have lived with your father in hell for the last seven years. As I watched him suffer, I suffered in my woman's heart for his pain. Few can appreciate the agony of seeing someone die by inches and being helpless to aid him even a jot. Already I have been told that I did little to receive so much. He who said it is wrong as are you. But what I did for Henry Bolingbroke, you will have to find out when your need is as desperate as his was. Pray God you have someone who will be your friend since you will not let me fill that office."

"I need no whores as friends."

"I am not a whore. I was born a princess of Navarre where today my brother reigns as king. I am by marriage the Duchess of Brittany where today my son rules as duke. I am the Queen of England, the first lady of this kingdom until you marry. I will withdraw until you have control of yourself, my lord."

He spun round. "I am as controlled as I will ever be with you, madam. Hear me!" He stabbed a finger in her direction. "You shall depart immediately for whatever residence pleases you, so long as it is not where I am residing and so long as it is *not* Hereford. I will allow you to keep the other houses and revenues so long as you do not appear in this court again except at my express command."

She drew herself up tall but kept her voice mild. "I had expected little else from you. I shall not go to Hereford, nor do I want anything that was your mother's if my use of her things offends you. I have long loved the palace of Havering-atte-Bower. It shall be my home where I can abide content. I shall do as you command, leaving you with good opinion from all by saying that it is my wish to leave the life of the court and mourn for the king. By this you will see that I wish you no harm and bear you no ill will." She crossed to the door but paused with her hand on its facing. The sight of his angry face made her think of her sons when they were young boys. She hesitated. "You are very young yet," she suggested gently. "I spent long hours with your father discussing the politics of the Council. You could learn much from me that would save you grief."

His face did not change. Indeed it grew redder.

She shrugged. "God bless you, Your Majesty."

As she climbed into the carriage the next day, Arundel kissed her hand. Pleading his advancing years, he had resigned his post as archbishop after the coronation, allowing his nephew to appoint Bishop Chicele, a good man and much younger and stronger. "The king will have need of you, my lord," Joanna chided him.

"No, Your Majesty. By the time he learns to regret what he has cast aside, I will be long dead. The young cannot appreciate us until they have become like us."

"Are we really old?" she asked wistfully.

"Not you, my Queen." He surveyed her face and figure with the look of a connoisseur.

"For shame." She smiled. "And you an archbishop."

"No longer, my lady. And even a common priest may look at the beauty of a madonna." He smiled in his turn.

"Do not go too far away from him," she begged. "He does not know the Council. Henry would have warned him, but he would not listen. Now he will not listen to me. At least half of them believe the Earl of March should be king. He is ignorant of—"

"Let him find it out for himself," Arundel interrupted with a wave of his hand. "I return to Arundel to spend my days in peace. I know you say you go to mourn, but I think you go because he has ordered your retirement. More fool he. No more loyal woman ever existed. In ten years you have never given less than full measure to the throne of England."

With those words, he helped her into the carriage and again kissed her hand.

"Farewell, my lord Arundel."

"Farewell, Your Majesty. Perhaps we shall meet again."

Joanna's eyes filled with tears as she sat back in the carriage. Across from her wrapped in her black garments sat Isabella, muttering over her rosary beads. Only the duenna's eyes, glittering through slitted lids, revealed that she watched all the queen did.

"I shall not care, Isabella," Joanna said at last. "I shall be glad to be gone from the intrigue of the court and the suffering of the king."

The woman in black snorted indelicately. "You were ever the child of Charles of Navarre. Had you been a son you would have gained back the Norman lands that he died so cruelly for. Your brother is a weak fool. What has he done but stay in his own little corner of the world and renounce his rights to what belonged to him. They call him Charles the Noble. Bah! You have guided the accursed king and ruled for him, just as you did for Brittany in his last days."

"I helped when I could," Joanna admitted.

"You were born to rule," the old woman crooned, "but Almighty God saw fit to make you a woman. His ways are inscrutable. Perhaps he does not want his earthly kingdoms to exist for long."

Joanna smiled at her twisted reasoning. Isabella's mutterings were treasonous if spoken to anyone but herself. Sometimes she feared for the old woman's sanity. At others when she was angry with her, she half believed her to be what she had called her so long in her own mind, a *hechicera*. With a weary sigh she settled back against the cushions. The ride to Havering-atte-Bower was a long and tiresome one.

As he had watched from the shadow of an archway, Geoffrey had striven to keep his face impassive. Joanna's departure should have been a triumph for him, but instead he felt old and sad.

Despite the knowledge that Henry had been sick for many years, Geoffrey felt diminished by his death. Henry Bolingbroke had helped him to return to England from Brittany. He had elevated him to a position of power and importance. He had counted him a loyal supporter and had not demeaned him as Brittany had done.

Henry had been the same age as Geoffrey, and so the king's death had shocked Geoffrey into sensing his own mortality. In three years he would have seen half a century. Half a century was very old in the life of a man when few saw their sons grow to manhood and many were dead at thirty-five.

Henry had married the woman Geoffrey loved, not that the king had known of his love. Geoffrey had been at great pains to keep anyone from ever knowing, for he had considered Joanna to be proud and scheming, utterly corrupted by her own power, and as oblivious to the feelings of others, as uncaring, as all of the nobility were. He had torn his love from his breast long ago.

Now as he watched Joanna's carriage rapidly becoming a dot in the distance, he told himself he gloried in her downfall. Undoubtedly her sudden departure meant that she had not been able to seduce King Henry V.

He clenched his fists at his sides. The night of the coronation feast he had almost offered her his protection—almost but not quite. He had thought about doing so every day since the king's death.

Indeed, the morning he had heard of the king's death his first thought had been that Joanna was free. Gladness had pierced him so that he had shaken like a terrified boy. Seated

374

in his chair, he had spread his hands before him in amazement to stare at their trembling. As if he were a youth mooning for the love of his life, he had dreamed of her for days. He had rehearsed his speech to her, planned how he would woo her with soft words.

He had sought her out at the coronation, thinking to find her downcast, her wealth and protection wiped away, her future uncertain. He would have enjoyed her humiliation but a few minutes—she deserved to suffer he had told himself—then he would have lifted her spirits with his offer. She would have been tearful and humble with gratitude. Eventually, after she spent a suitable length of time demonstrating her perfect obedience to her new lord and master, he would have treated her passionately again and they would once more enjoy that which he knew she craved.

But his speculations had all been fantasies. She had landed on her feet like a cat. Freed from the leprous king, she had come away with lands and revenues that could not be compared to his humble lodgings and pitiful estate.

How she would have laughed at him had he offered her his protection. He flushed angrily at the thought of her laughter. A bastard endured much, but it never became easier to take. He knew when he had bowed out of her life that he had been right to do so. She needed no one, now or ever. He could not help admiring her for that—and for other things as well.

In his mind he recalled her beauty, the shimmering cream of her skin, the midnight blackness of her hair, the soft curve of her lips, the aristocratic breeding evident in every line of her graceful body as she moved. She was a star that he could only worship from afar. Head down, he turned away from the arch and trudged back into the cell assigned to him.

He loved her. He would always love and worship her. She was gone from him forever, but he would never forget. Nor could he take another woman, for she had spoiled him for all others.

He flung himself face down on the narrow cot in the monk's cell. The mattress, less than two inches thick, was slung over a lattice of ropes that creaked and protested at his weight. The sheet was coarse brown stuff, rough and prickly to his skin. This was undoubtedly one of the poorest cells in the guest house. Such had ever been his lot—the poorest, the most meager.

And now the only woman he wanted had passed out of his life. He was a fool. All the plans he had made to humiliate her were but fantasies—as far from reality as he was from her. If she had been within his reach, he would have fallen at her feet to worship her. He would have taken her in his arms and loved her until she forgot all the unhappiness she had ever known.

He would wait . . . a few months, perhaps a year. He would strive to win the king's favor as never before. Probably within that time, the king himself would marry and beget heirs. Joanna's position would then no longer be unassailable. She would cease to be the first lady of the realm. At a propitious time, he would request the right to protect her.

Amazed at his own daring, he twisted himself over onto his back. Lacing his hands behind his head, he stared at a cobweb festooning the ceiling beams. Somehow—eventually—she would be his. He smiled.

"You may think we have seen the last of each other, Joanna d'Albret et Montfort and Lancaster, Princess of Navarre, Duchess of Brittany, and Queen of England, but you are wrong. I, Geoffrey Fitzjean d'Anglais, swear to pursue you to the ends of the earth if necessary."

His words sounded strong in the empty room. Then he grinned foolishly at himself. If anyone walked by at that moment and heard him talking to himself, he would be surely thought insane. Perhaps he was insane, but he had his dream.

He closed his eyes, conjuring up a picture of her as his

376

lover when they were scarcely more than children: her fair white skin, her ebony hair, her passion-swollen breasts, each crested with a throbbing nipple of sensitive flesh. Yes, she was the only woman for him. He had never found pleasure with any other. She would open her arms and her sweet thighs to him.

"Joanna," he whispered. "Joanna."

Chapter 23

"You are summoned, Your Majesty."

Joanna raised her eyes from her embroidery frame to regard the messenger as if he spoke some language other than English, French, or Spanish. "I beg you, sir, repeat yourself."

"His Majesty, King Henry V, has summoned you to court to join in the celebration of his victory over the French at Agincourt." The youth's voice carried a thrill of excitement tinged with hero worship.

"All England knows of his victory and has joined in the celebration of it for months now," Joanna replied. "Why am I suddenly summoned at this time? If I remember correctly, the battle was fought on St. Crispin's Day in the spring." She glanced significantly at the windows of the bower. Fine sleet mixed with snow splattered against them, and the wind soughed mournfully.

"So please Your Majesty," the messenger stammered, "there is to be a memorial service on All Hallows. All of England will be there to pay honor."

She accepted a missive from his hand and tore it open. Even as she studied its contents, she chided herself for keeping this simple man waiting. She wanted to return to London. Havering-atte-Bower was pleasant, but she felt stultified by its sameness. For a year and a half she had resided in its pleasant, comfortable halls. How she missed the excitement and the challenge of government.

Lowering the paper to her lap, she smiled at the nervous man. "I shall make all haste," she replied. "If you and your troop will wait for the space of a day, I and my lady will accompany you on your return."

"I was so ordered to do, Your Majesty. I mean"—he turned bright red as her black brows rose angrily—"I was to make myself available as your escort."

An alarm bell rang in her mind. She doubted very seriously whether she would have had the option to refuse him. Her mind cast around for some excuse she might use to break off the trip; then she shrugged that idea away. She wanted to go to London. Whatever awaited her there, she was still the queen, unless Henry had decided to take a wife. Would this man know? She looked at his young embarrassed face.

No. He would not be privy to any news of that nature before she was. She corresponded with the Duchess of Clarence, who would have written her immediately had such exciting news been known.

Her mind was still considering the problem the next day when she sat bundled in her furs across from Isabella. The duenna had objected strenuously to her going. "No good will come of this," the old woman maintained again, clicking the rosary beads, long worn smooth by her endless counting of them when she was distraught. "He wants you for a purpose other than to celebrate his victory. Bah! He should have called you to meet him at Canterbury Cathedral when he first landed in England. You would have added luster to his pageant at the tombs of his father and uncle. He did not want you then. He does not want you now. He wants something *from* you."

"Quiet, Isabella. Your black predictions will drive me to distraction."

The old woman nodded her head sagely and closed her eyes. Her tightly compressed lips and set face radiated disapproval.

Nevertheless, excitement sang in Joanna's veins as the carriage rocked gently along the road, its horses' hooves slightly muffled by the snow. She was going back to London. There she would renew old acquaintances and perhaps make new friends. She might even do something useful again. Henry's attitude must have changed since he had been brought face to face with some of the problems of kingship.

With a wistful smile she thought of Geoffrey. She never failed to inquire about him in her letters to Margaret. Through their correspondence, she had learned that he and many others had returned sick and much weakened from the long campaign in France. She had sent money to Margaret to provide for his care, stipulating that it should be paid to him in the form of a reward from the Crown and that its source should not be traced back to her. Would he look the same?

Ruefully she raised one gloved hand to touch the heavy braid of hair neatly coiled under her hood. Among its thick black strands threads of white were appearing with alarming frequency. Not only were the lines around her mouth deeper, but she had creased her forehead in the past year by working over her embroidery. With a sigh she rubbed her index finger against the offending line that marked the creamy skin between her eyebrows.

Geoffrey would doubtless think her old. But she did not feel old. At this moment she felt young and eager. A little smile curved her lips. She was returning to London, and whatever lay ahead, she would meet it optimistically.

Henry of Monmouth, he who had been crowned Henry V, was more greedy than his father before him. Not content with the throne of England, he wanted also the throne of France. Determined to claim it through the rights of his great-grandfather Edward III, he had landed at Harfleur in

1415 and had marched across the northern part of France claiming each town by making its leaders swear allegiance to him.

Charles of Valois was terrified. His only surviving uncle was an old man. The Duke of Barry was the last brother among the men who had effectively ruled through their ineffectual nephew during the many years of his insanity. Suddenly forced to make decisions for himself, Charles had thrown the flower of the French aristocracy against the rabble of English yeomen. Their numbers should have inspired confidence, but Barry reminded the king of the battle of Crécy when the Black Prince's archers had so devastatingly routed the army of French knights. Barry had cause to remember well. He had been captured and held hostage for a crippling ransom.

Others remembered too, if not the battle then the lesson of Crécy. With trepidation Marshal Boucicault deployed the armies of France. They converged upon the invading king and sought to cut his escape route to Calais and the sea. They thought they had succeeded. His men were so few in numbers; theirs, so numberless. Like a great wall they arranged themselves before him in the green field of fresh spring wheat. So certain were they that they would overrun him with one mighty charge that they did not bother to arrange a signal for retreat.

But their thunder was muffled by the mud. Their field was too narrow to maneuver. Ponderously, they charged toward the line of English longbowmen whose thin-tipped arrows unerringly sought the chinks in their armor. When the first knights fell, others crashed into the barricades of their wounded bodies and piled upon them, smothering the fallen and effectively dissipating their own power. And ever the arrows fell like hail until the dead were too many to climb over.

Henry's victory had been expensive, not in terms of lives lost but in terms of money outlaid. Instead of conquering and sacking towns, he had gained their peaceful surrender. The tribute he had demanded had been minimal. Now in order to pursue his claims, he needed money.

"Your Majesty." Joanna sank into a deep curtsey before her stepson.

His answering smile was stiff, but affable. "Rise, my lady." He offered her his hand.

"All England hails your victory, Your Majesty. You have covered yourself with glory."

"And regained the territorial rights of the Plantagenets," he added smugly. "From the time of William of Normandy, we have slowly been adding to our lands. For a time we were displaced, but I have restored much that was ours."

Extending his arm, he escorted her through the ranks of his court. Familiar faces smiled at her and men bowed, offering her homage as the Queen of England. She felt a thrill of love at their smiling acceptance. These were, after all, her adopted people. Only a dozen short years ago, she had come—an alien—into their midst.

Henry paused before a young man whose different dress proclaimed him to be a foreigner. His hair was light silvery blond; his eyes, in striking contrast, were black.

When Joanna nodded uncertainly, he dropped to one knee before her. "Lady mother."

She stared at his smiling upturned face. Aghast, she realized that she stared down into the face of one of her sons, but to her embarrassment she could not recall his name. Her eyes flew to Henry's face and found there a cynical amusement at her expense.

"Madam," he supplied drily. "May I present François Paul, Count of Richemont."

Thus supplied, she flashed her son a bright smile and bent to bestow a kiss on both of his cheeks. "How good to see you," she exclaimed softly, taking both his hands in hers to draw him to his feet.

"Ah, we meet under the worst circumstances, Lady

Mother." He shook his head sadly.

Puzzled, she stared at him. Why should the circumstances be bad? Had one of his brothers died and she not been informed? Anticipation sent a chill of alarm along her spine. "What mean you, my son?"

His look clearly conveyed his incredulity. Stiffly, he drew himself up, "I am a captive. A prisoner of England."

She stared at him, appalled. "For what reason?"

Clearly he thought her feeble-minded. He looked around him in exasperation. The other members of the court were studiously pretending to ignore the conversation between the two. Only Henry Plantagenet looked on with an amused grin.

"I was captured at the battle of Agincourt."

Now it was her turn to gasp incredulously. "But Brittany and England have an alliance."

"I am a Frenchman," he insisted hotly.

"You would fight for Valois!" A hectic flush stained her cheeks. Her heat matched his own. Her father would have risen from his grave in anger could he but know that a grandson of his had taken up sword in support of the mad king.

"He is *my* king."

All around her the court listened open-mouthed, no longer making any pretense of carrying on conversations. "He was the enemy of your father and your grandfather. You would not be Count of Richemont had Valois had his way. You would not be anything at all."

Both the king and count drew back in amazement at her vehemence. The pleased smile faded from Henry's mouth. The queen's response had not been as he had anticipated. He had expected a mother's horror at her son's captivity to be followed by tearful pleas for his release. Instead she berated the man for fighting for the Valois, for betraying the ideals of his father and grandfather.

"France was threatened by the English," Richemont

argued. He squirmed with embarrassment. He bore no love for his mother, but he had expected her to make a great cry over him as silly women were wont to do. To his horror, she was making him feel guilty. His own brother, Brittany, had written strongly worded letters to him ordering him not to fight. He had ignored them to his sorrow. The expedition that had begun as such a sure victory had ended in disaster. He had almost gotten himself killed.

Now his mother, the one person from whom he should expect unequivocal loyalty, was practically raging at him about his grandfather and father. The whole affair was too much.

"The people of France were in no danger from His Majesty," Joanna informed her son. "He has ancestral rights to the throne of France that are as strong as Valois' ever hoped to be."

Turning her shoulder to the red-faced young man, she deliberately replaced her hand on Henry's arm. "Your Majesty."

Her stepson, somewhat nonplused, had no choice but to bow slightly in acknowledgment of her support and lead her away.

Standing too far away to hear the conversation was Geoffrey Fitzjean d'Anglais. He, too, had been summoned to court for this celebration. The wounds he'd received during the skirmishes across northern France had been superficial, but he had contracted lung fever as a result of prolonged exposure to the elements during the long march.

His body had recovered slowly. Angrily, he had acknowledged himself to be forty-eight years of age. Many would consider him an old man. Henry IV, who had been the same age as he, had been dead two years.

Watching from across the room, he felt himself trembling slightly from the overpowering emotion he felt at seeing the Count of Richemont, the son of his body, together with Joanna, the mother of his children. Their antipathy was

385

obvious. Her behavior provoked in him a surge of anger. Still cold and heartless as ever, she could not even show affection for her own captive son. Doubtless, she feared he would jeopardize her position.

His mouth tightened in distaste. Unobtrusively, he moved through the crowd to speak to the young count. At last face to face with him, Geoffrey was startled by their resemblance. Although the boy's eyes were Joanna's, his hair, skin coloring, high cheekbones, broad forehead, and the shape of his nose all seemed fashioned after his very own. He found himself believing that he would have recognized his son anywhere.

"My lord," he spoke in the accented French of Brittany.

Richemont turned, raising one eyebrow haughtily at the sight of this man dressed very plainly in gray relieved only by the ornamental hilt of a dress sword swinging from his hip on a black leather belt.

"I knew you as a little boy."

The count stared hard at the man before him. "I do not seem to recall . . ."

"I was your father's valet for many years."

"Geoffrey!" The youth eagerly grasped his hand, his relief evident at the sight of a friendly face. "Of course, I remember you. You were always the friendliest of all my father's retainers. My brothers and I often spoke of how you cared for us. We came to depend on you, you know. But what are you doing here?"

"I left your father's service soon after you were sent away as a page."

"How could he let you do such a thing? You did everything for him, absolutely everything."

Stunned by the fervently uttered words, Geoffrey felt himself color slightly. Could it be? But no.

Richemont hurried on. "I never saw anyone else lift him or serve him. He could hardly move without you. The three of you were inseparable." He nodded ruefully toward his mother who was engaged in animated conversation across the room.

Geoffrey remained silent. He could not believe that the youth knew the true nature of the relationship. Yet how close his words were to the truth when even the barest of hints might subject them all to scandalous speculation.

". . . the queen, my mother." Richemont continued unhappily.

Startled, Geoffrey blinked. He had not been listening. "She is very beautiful," he responded vaguely.

The young man nodded. He sensed a friend with whom to share his troubles, to air his side of the adventure and to discuss his subsequent captivity. In retrospect, the whole affair seemed doomed from the outset, and he appeared the worst of fools for participating in it when doing so meant defying the wishes of his family. "She lives in the past." He hurried on with an air of one much abused. "She does not see the new alliances. She reminded me of grievances of people long dead. I cannot be expected to carry on their petty wars and hatreds."

"She but seeks to preserve her place here," Geoffrey remonstrated softly. "She is twice an alien to these people. A Navarrese princess who married a Breton duke."

"Oh, she reminded me. Her words about my own father and grandfather are seared into my memory. I doubt that she will pay the ransom for one whom she feels betrayed his family, but she is wrong. France is my nation. Brittany will eventually join with them just as Richemont has." He spoke with boyish confidence.

"She would not pay your ransom?" Geoffrey asked, incredulous.

Richemont regarded his mother's figure. To tell the truth, he had not asked her, but he did not intend to now. He had his proper pride. "No," he lied by implication. "She would not pay my ransom."

Geoffrey flinched. He remembered his son as a little boy.

How he yearned to tell the boy of his parentage. If he had the means, he would have paid it instantly, would have beggared himself to do so. But he had very little, certainly not enough to ransom a count of France. Glumly, he stared at the queen. Her selfishness was hellish. What natural mother would deny her own son? She was a true daughter of Charles the Bad.

At that moment she turned to catch them both staring at her. The sight of Geoffrey's face, pitifully gaunt due to his recent illness, made her gasp in sympathy.

"Madam?" The king had overheard her.

"I see Sir Geoffrey d'Anglais across the room, Henry. He . . . he looks somewhat changed," she faltered. "Did he sustain some horrible wound in France?" Some horrible wound that she had not heard of, she finished mentally.

Henry looked at her speculatively. Occasionally, he wondered about the current relationship between d'Anglais and his stepmother. The man seemed to despise her, while she frequently expressed interest in him. Of course, they had spent many hours together in Brittany, she as wife and he as valet to the same duke. "He caught the lung fever, I believe. It debilitated his strength severely. He grows old." The king shrugged. "He can expect to take longer to recover."

Her black eyes flashed, betraying her anger as she leaped to Geoffrey's defense. "All men take a long time to recover from lung fever. Many never do. Do not dismiss such a good and loyal man, Your Majesty, for a temporary condition."

The hero of Agincourt nodded agreeably. "Rest assured I do not intend to, madam."

His later confrontation with Joanna did not end so amiably.

"Madam. The Count of Richemont requires ransom."

She braced herself. She had been right to be suspicious when she had learned that the messenger had been sent to bring her from Havering-atte-Bower without allowing her to refuse. "I am sure his family . . ." she began delicately.

"You are his family, madam," Henry interrupted.

"His brother—"

"I repeat, madam. You are his family. We are presently engaged in the ransom of many of the prisoners to their families. Some are understandably difficult to contact. Fortunately for young Richemont, his family is simplicity itself." His words had taken on a mocking tone.

"But I am the Queen of England."

"He has no one else. It would be regrettable if so young a man should languish away in an English gaol. Since he is in excellent health, his captivity would undoubtedly be prolonged."

Silently, she surveyed him. How she longed to rage at him, to wipe the smirk from his face. He had done this deliberately. He had made no effort to contact any other members of her son's family. Richemont had a wife who presently was chatelaine of rich estates provided for her husband by Montfort. A message would begin negotiations immediately.

But Henry did not want a reasonable tribute paid from the coffers of Richemont. He wanted the wealth of Henry Bolingbroke, only legitimate son of John of Gaunt. He wanted the dower lands that Lancaster had settled on his wife in the marriage contract.

Her face set and pale, she rose slowly from her chair. She had dressed for the interview in an undergown of heavy gray wool with a sideless surcoat of rose red velvet. Her black hair was completely hidden beneath a steeple headdress from which was suspended a sheer silk scarf of the same rose hue. With the headdress added to her height, she towered above him.

Hastily scraping back his chair, he rose from behind the table. Her air disconcerted him. Why did she not plead? Why did she not rage? He had expected emotional reactions. All women were ruled by their emotions.

"I shall return to Havering-atte-Bower," she told him icily. "Clearly my presence here is hindering negotiations necessary for the release of the Count of Richemont."

"Madam—"

"I am the Queen of England. Before that I was the Duchess of Brittany. My husbands were enemies of Valois even as you, Henry. To ask me to ransom a disloyal son is infamous." She turned to leave.

He interposed himself before her. Now he could look down into her face and intimidate her with his height. "He is a captive," he reminded her sternly. "If we cannot get money from him, then we must dispose of him. Those are the rules of war. We cannot afford to keep him at court living on our largesse." He stared hard at her, expecting her capitulation.

But she had faced greater men than Henry V. The issues at stake here were minor in comparison to those she had negotiated with Montfort and Bolingbroke. "Send to Richemont," she replied practically. "His estates are wealthy. If you receive no answer to your letter, send to Valois. He should be eager to ransom every knight still living if only to provide himself with an escort."

"Valois has many to ransom." Henry's face turned red with anger. The interview was not going as he had planned. He began to realize what his father had seen in this woman. Her grasp of the situation was astute. Without hesitation she had offered him not one but two alternatives to provide himself with much-needed funds.

He had already thought of them himself. Indeed, he had intended to use both of them to fill the public coffers in addition to securing the Lancastrian estates for his own private use. What angered him was the fact that she had thought of them—and rapidly too.

"Valois will find a way to ransom Richemont," Joanna replied shrewdly. "He cannot afford to have more of Brittany's ill will than he already has."

"Valois will not even ransom Boucicault."

Her smile was a trifle condescending. "The marshal failed him. He was supposed to win resoundingly and bring you in chains to Paris. You were to be exhibited to the populace as the greatest triumph of his infamous reign. Instead, he is the laughingstock of Europe. There will never be a place in France for its marshal."

Henry clenched his fists at his sides.

"Have I your leave to withdraw, Your Majesty?" She turned to go without waiting for his answer.

His temper broke. His hand closed around her upper arm. "No!" he growled. "Do not presume to leave my presence, madam."

Her black eyes flashed to his face, then down to the hard brown hand closed tightly around her flesh. Her breath hissed angrily through her set teeth. "How dare you!"

The hand that had gripped round a sword hilt with tireless strength tightened savagely. "I dare anything with you," he snarled.

She tipped her head back to stare defiantly into his angry face. It was very close now to her own. She could feel the heat of his breath. Stubbornly, she kept her expression impassive although his strength was bruising her flesh. "I am your father's widow and the anointed Queen of England."

"My mother should have been queen. You are a diplomatic whore. A thing bartered back and forth among power-hungry kings. A beautiful bitch who sells herself to the most powerful in return for position and wealth. Wealth that does not belong to you."

The odor of his body rose into her nostrils. He had worked himself into a rage. She was in danger, yet she knew not what to do. To show fear at this time would be disastrous. He might well imprison her and take her property even if she submitted. "My wealth does belong to me," she insisted evenly. "Someday you will find it politically expedient for the good of your country to find yourself a 'diplomatic whore.' If you are wise, you will select one with wealth and powerful trustworthy relations. I wonder what your expedition in France would have been like had Brittany, as well as Richemont, allied himself with Valois. The outcome might have been different."

For a full minute the only sound in the room was their labored breathing. The very air was charged with currents reminiscent of heat lightening before a summer storm. She had defeated him, horse and foot. His anger threatened to choke him, yet he feared to confiscate her lands. Many on the Council had smiled with pleasure at her appearance in court. It would be unwise to turn the favorable winds that blew around him as a result of his victory into angry storms over the queen. Many did not think him to be the rightful king. The Earl of March was very much alive. He could not afford the name of tyrant at this time. He did not dare to take the lands of a helpless widow, especially one who had been his father's wife.

With a guttural exclamation he pushed her away from him, sending her stumbling toward the door. "Be gone! Be out of this palace before nightfall and on your way back to Havering-atte-Bower, bawd."

She thudded against the heavy oak paneling bruising her shoulder and twisting her ankle. Far from cowing her, the pain made her fiercely angry. Always the same treatment for a woman. Had she been a man, he would not have dared.

She pressed her forehead against the cold wood, drawing several steadying breaths. Think, she cautioned herself. He could take your lands by force, yet he wants you to give them to him. Clearly, he dares not take them. But why? Even as the question formed itself, she knew the answer. Better than he, she understood the Council. With a ghost of a smile on her white face, she turned, forcing herself to move smoothly and imperturbably despite the stabbing pain from her ankle.

Gathering the sides of her skirt in trembling fingers, she sank into a deep curtsey, lowering her head in mock obeisance. "Yes, Your Majesty." Her voice was low and melodious, not revealing a hint of the turmoil which raged within her. "I have been pleased to see you are in good health. May you continue to enjoy it."

Rising she slipped through the door, leaving him to his impotent rage.

Chapter 24

The wind, howling like a wolf, flung the iron casement back against the stone with a horrifying clang. The leaden panes shattered, spraying shards of glass across the room.

Uttering a piercing scream of terror, Joanna sat up in bed, staring wild-eyed at the window as an icy gust swirled round her. The blast of cold air set the tapestries on the wall to snapping and whipped her long black hair about her face. Thunder crashed and lightning sheeted across the entire sky. Borne on the gale, pellets of sleet struck the rich hangings of the bed. The lightning flashed again. Joanna covered her ears in anticipation of the elemental noise and shouted with all her strength.

Then she waited a minute, shivering in her bed and drawing the covers up tightly around her shoulders. Lightning flashed again as the storm released its full fury directly above Havering-atte-Bower, and within seconds, thunder exploded like the crack of a thousand cannons.

Cursing fervently, Joanna sprang from her bed. One bare foot slipped on the wet floor, but she managed to recover herself and fling open the chamber door. The inner chamber where Isabella slept was empty and dark.

Alarmed, Joanna pressed back against the heavy carved panels and strained her eyes into the darkness. Where was

Isabella? Because the old woman no longer slept well, she kept a light with her always. Sometimes, Joanna wondered if she slept at all, for at any time of night, the duenna could be found awake. Often she sat in a chair ceaselessly clicking her rosary beads and murmuring prayers in her peculiarly accented Latin. Sometimes her lips moved soundlessly as she read from old books written in Spanish. Many times, she lay on her back in bed, staring upward at the ceiling, her black eyes fixed on the distant past.

"Isabella!" Joanna hissed.

The impenetrable darkness gave no clue as to whether the usual occupant of the room was there or not. Overhead the thunder rumbled again, though not so loudly.

"Isabella?"

Pushing herself away from the door, Joanna made her way, hands outstretched, across the room to the table where Isabella kept flint and tapers. In a moment a feeble glow dispelled the darkness around where she stood.

By the time she could lift her candle aloft and peer into the dark shadows, she was shivering violently. Her teeth were chattering from the cold and from an emotion closely akin to panic. In a nightmarish flash of memory, she returned to France as a child, and the rumble of thunder became the thud of soldiers' boots.

Fearfully, she stared around her, trying to perceive the room in the wavering light. Not only was the room empty, but the covers of the bed were violently disarranged. The bolster had burst open showering gray goose down across the floor. It stirred gently in the icy currents swirling around her feet. Otherwise, nothing moved in the empty room.

"Isabella!"

Shielding her candle, Joanna moved as quickly as she dared into the hallway. There, as before, only darkness and silence greeted her. Where were the servants? Thoroughly terrified, she shouted for her butler. The wind howled eerily in answer.

At the top of the staircase, she paused. Only her nails, digging like claws into the bannister, prevented her from sinking to her knees. The childhood terrors haunting the darkness around her almost drove her scurrying back into her bedroom to cower beneath the covers.

Except the bedroom offered no sanctuary, she reminded herself sternly. The place must be an ice cave by now: the bed, dank and cold; the air, frigid. She was the queen. Her people had disappeared, and she was responsible for them. It was her duty to investigate, to rescue them if necessary. Doubtless, she would discover some reasonable explanation.

Perhaps she was dreaming!

Had the storm really torn the window open? Was Isabella still asleep in her own bed? The icy drafts penetrating Joanna's very bones assured her that she was awake. Yet somehow the idea of a nightmare from which she would eventually awaken seemed very attractive to her teeming mind.

The black hole of darkness below her forbade her descent. Staring into its bottomless depths, she began to tremble. Again she called the butler's name.

Her voice fell away into the silence as if it had never been.

Stubbornly, she forced herself to her feet. How dare they desert her? She paid their wages; she fed, clothed, and housed them. They owed her a debt of loyalty. Whipping her emotions into anger, she straightened her shoulders and descended, the pool of light shimmering around her body.

Her anger sustained her almost to the bottom where panic rose to meet her. Suddenly she realized that she did not know how many steps were left. Even as she cursed herself, she arrived on the landing. She stumbled and her lurch dislodged the candle from its socket. Despite her desperate efforts, the taper fell to the floor where it feebly flared on the damp tiles.

Dropping to her knees, she scrabbled for it, but too late. In a breath she was plunged into darkness.

Clutching the warm stub in both hands, she cursed once before panicky tears began to fall. Something was terrifyingly wrong. Fearfully wrong. "Isabella," she whispered, her voice quavering around her sobs.

She listened intently, staring into the darkness around her, turning her head from side to side to catch the slightest sound. Only the noise of the wind and of the sleet pelting faintly against the windows and doors reached her ears. Inside, the house was eerily silent. The servants of Havering-atte-Bower—her servants—had disappeared in a single night.

Isabella had clearly been taken away by force. Those who had taken her had also taken pains to do their deed in silence and under cover of night. Why? If they sought to frighten her to death, they were succeeding.

Pushing her terror far to the back of her mind, she staggered to her feet. The front door lay somewhere down the hall and to the right. Her most important consideration was to negotiate the distance without falling over furniture or crashing into a wall.

The way seemed interminable. Her overstrained nerves set her body to shivering violently as murderous drafts swirled across her bare feet and around her legs beneath her skirts.

"Cursed house! Foul English weather! Rain, rain, rain! Sleet and snow mixed with rain! Why so? God in Heaven!" This litany she recited between tightly clenched teeth strengthened her. She found the corner of the hall and rounded it to face the great door. A diminution of darkness too faint to be called a sliver of light revealed its bottom edge. Thankfully, she flung herself at it.

Her hands fumbled across it, found its bands, its bolts, its bar. Eagerly she slid it back. Both hands closed around the big iron handle. Bracing herself for the blast, she tugged.

The door did not open.

Unaccustomed to opening it herself, she drew a deep breath and hauled back with all her strength.

It did not stir. Immovable as a boulder, it resisted her frail strength.

Thunder rumbled in the distance, signaling the passage of the worst of the storm. The rain had slowed to a gentle patter. Both hands locked around the iron handle, her forehead pressed against the cold wood, Joanna allowed the tears to fall. Tears of fear, of exhaustion, of loneliness and despair.

"Isabella," she whispered. "Oh, Isabella." Then, "Geoffrey."

She was a prisoner, alone in a palace—her own palace. Suddenly, she began to laugh. Peal upon peal of hysterical laughter burst from her throat to echo in the silent halls. A prisoner in a palace . . . when had she ever been anything else?

". . . confess that she has compassed and imagined the death of the king." The voice repeated the command over and over. At times, another voice repeated the command in Spanish.

"No. She is a good girl. She has wished nothing but good for the king." Isabella de la Alcudia shook her head emphatically. She was so tired she could barely keep her eyes open. When her body would have slumped, a hard hand struck her twice sharply across the face. The insult, more than the pain, roused her. Licking the blood from her lip, she spat it on the floor at the burly man's feet.

"You have been insulted, Barster," a man's voice observed. "You may strike the witch again."

With a grin of satisfaction, the burly man pulled a heavy

leather and metal gauntlet from his belt and raised it above his head. Exercising more force, he brought it down cruelly across the frail shoulders.

The old woman screamed shrilly as her body catapulted sideways to sprawl on the cold floor.

"Not so hard, Barster. You will kill her before she speaks."

"Sorry, my lord." Stooping, Barster hauled the sobbing, moaning Isabella back onto the stool and steadied her.

"Now." The questioner lowered his body until his face was even with hers. "You will tell us about the sorcery and witchcraft practiced by your mistress."

Isabella's black eyes glittered through her tears. Hatred and fear were evident, but stubborn defiance shone in them also. "She practices no witchcraft. She is good." Her rough deep voice had faded to a quavery rasp.

The man straightened with a disgusted, disappointed look. "She is a witch even as you are a witch," he maintained smoothly. "If you speak not, you must be put to the question."

Terror made Isabella blanche. "I am not a witch," she protested. With gnarled hands, she caught at the questioner's velvet sleeve.

Coldly, he shook her off. "Barster. Attach the ropes."

"No-o-o-o." Numb with terror, the old woman made no move to resist as Barster looped a rope tightly across her chest and bound her to the stool on which she sat.

"Now, witch, you have one chance to tell us what we want to know, or we will test your truth by water."

"No. No . . . *Por Favor . . . por Dios . . .*"

The burly man seized the stool by its legs and upended it into a huge barrel half-full of murky water. Isabella's screams of pain and fear ended in a wretched gurgle as her mouth and nose were flooded.

The two men grinned at each other across her struggling form. Her black gown dropped away from her legs, revealing her skinny, hairy calves and knobby knees.

Within thirty seconds, the frantic thrashing of the exposed limbs stopped. "Enough, Barster. Pull her up."

Obligingly, the lackey dragged his victim out, returning the stool to its upright position. Water streamed off the body. Immediately, Isabella began to cough and retch.

"Here now!" Barster jumped back as the old woman vomited the contents of her stomach onto the floor. Angry at the spatter on his boots, he doubled up his fist and punched her viciously in the ribs.

The scream that issued from her throat was like the scream of a rabbit as its throat is being closed off by the snare.

The other man watched impassively, folding his arms across his chest and shifting his weight a bit in impatience. Satisfied with his retribution, Barster stepped back and the questioning began again.

By that time, Isabella could no longer think. Her answers were automatic. Over and over, she reiterated the truth. "Her Majesty is not a witch. She is a good girl. She has been my charge for thirty years. She is a good girl."

At length the questions stopped. While Barster relieved himself on the floor in the corner, Isabella's questioner regarded her angrily. He was wasting time.

"Old woman!" He bent to her again. "I will give you one last chance to tell me what I want to know."

". . . told you . . ." she muttered.

"Not the truth."

". . . truth . . ."

"I know it is not. We have the confessions of all in her household, including her priest."

"Then he lies . . . English dog . . . no loyalty to the king."

"You mean the queen. He is loyal to his king."

". . . my king . . . always loyal . . . my king."

"Barster . . ." The man gestured toward the water.

Isabella did not protest. Her head lolled forward as if to

drink as the hamlike forearms flexed to lift the stool by its legs. With a splash, the waters closed over her head.

When Barster drew her out after barely a minute, she was dead. The questioner cursed his assistant roundly and foully.

When ordered by the prior to confirm the necromancy of the queen, Friar Randolph shook his head in horror. Bowing his head over his folded hands, he begged for forgiveness, but he could not testify to that of which he had no knowledge.

"But she has dreamed of the death of the king and confessed such a dream to you," the prior insisted impatiently.

"Well, yes," Friar Randolph began, "but . . ."

The prior smiled. "Enough. You will sit here and write all you can remember of her dream."

"But her dream is not a spell, Reverend Prior."

"You do not know it was but a dream, Friar Randolph. Her powers are foreign and therefore their methods may be unknown to us." With this pronouncement, he turned to leave the other man.

The weight of habitual obedience to authority bore down hard on the Celt's thin shoulders. The prior might be right. Yet how could he be? The queen was a kind, gentle lady. Her acts of charity in the neighborhood, her regal bearing, and her true sense of responsibility to all in her household had made deep impressions on him. Had he been a man of the world, he would have found himself madly in love with her.

A vision of her face, intent as she knelt with eyes closed and palms pressed together to receive the Eucharist, filled his mind. "Reverend Prior, I beg you. The queen did not have an evil dream. Her dream was merely one of concern for the king."

His already florid cheeks stained brighter red, the prior

turned back. "Father Randolph!" His voice was no longer unctuous, but threatening. "You will write as I bid. Am I not your arbiter in spiritual matters?"

"Oh, yes."

"Then, hear me and believe me." The prior's voice rang like a bell. "I have questioned other members of the household. The old woman was undoubtedly a witch."

"Was?" Randolph's hair prickled along the back of his neck. "Was, Reverend Prior?"

The man crossed himself. "She took her own life rather than admit to her association with the Evil One. Those who questioned her declared that she thrust her own head under the water; and when they tried to lift her out, her body weighed like lead."

"Doña Isabella?"

"The old Navarrese woman, yes. Clearly, pagan customs have clung to her and to her mistress. Their practices are much polluted, I have heard tell. They crown their king under a certain tree whose red leaves and branches are the color of blood and do flourish even in the fire."

"But she was always reciting her rosary, Reverend Prior." Randolph began to feel more and more uncertain. "Doña Isabella was naught but a weary old woman, forgetful and a little strange as all men and women come to be if they love so long as she."

Of a sudden the prior's face changed. The rheumy blue eyes set in pink folds of flesh became hard. "Friar Randolph, do I understand that you are disobeying me?"

The younger man hesitated. His instincts hinted at danger. Mentally, he berated himself for getting involved with royalty. Not only were their own lives fraught with danger, but those who served them were frequently threatened as well. A slight tremor shook him. "I merely seek assurance that all the facts be known," he replied humbly.

"More facts are known than you are privy to," the prior

advised him dryly. "Now set you down and write as I have commanded you."

The only sound in the quiet room was the scratching of the goose-quill pen across the parchment. Not knowing what was really called for, the friar took care to present the true picture of Joanna as he saw her and of the doings of her household.

That done, he left the inner parlor and made his way along the narrow hallway behind the transept. The door opened at the end of the passage. "Brother Randolph." The man's voice was unknown to him.

The friar halted, staring into the silhouette. Its sudden appearance had startled him. Somehow it seemed faintly menacing, for although dressed in robe and sandals, it was unusual for its breadth of shoulder. Most religious men added girth rather than muscle. "I am he," he replied softly.

"Come with me," was the command. "The Reverend Prior has commanded me to accompany you to the Isle of Guernsey."

"Guernsey? But—"

"We leave at once, Brother. Do not tarry. The way is long."

From the broken window of her bedchamber, Joanna watched the small troop approach. They came riding from the west into the bright glare of the midmorning sun. They carried no standards announcing their names. Likewise, their livery was devoid of plastrons displaying coats of arms. As they drew closer, she recognized no one. They were merely a guard.

Determined to present a picture of infuriated royalty, she dressed herself in her most regal gown. Lacking the ministrations of her maids for three days, she had contented herself with merely brushing her hair. Now her hands flew to braid it tightly and coil the thick skeins into a heavy knot at the back of her head. A quick glance at her glass assured her that she looked regal, although the fastenings felt a trifle insecure.

Below she could hear the men knocking and wrenching at the door. With a shrill screech, the nails came free of the wood. The guard would be inside in a minute. Pinching the color into her white cheeks, she hurried forth to meet them. At the head of the stairs, she posed regally. Let them find her thus. Height was a distinct advantage.

Drawing a deep breath, she laid one hand, in a semblance of calmness, on the bannister. The other she held relaxed at her waist. Projecting an air of outraged confidence, she straightened her spine and raised her chin.

Heavy boots thudded in the hall in a nightmare reenactment of the terrors of her youth, but she closed her eyes and took a deep breath.

When she opened them, the men were stalking down the hall toward the foot of the stairs. With one foot on the first riser, the leader saw her. Again her bravado served her in good stead. "I have been waiting for you," she announced haughtily before he could speak. "I demand that you take me to London immediately. The Council will have much to say to whomever is responsible for this outrage."

The soldiers gathered at the bottom of the stairs in some awe. Expecting to find a weeping rag of a woman perhaps cowering in her bed, instead they faced the Queen of England, her black eyes spitting fire. The royal wrath conveyed by her tone cowed the better part of valor in most of them for they were trained to obey orders.

A young man of about twenty, his garb slightly finer than that of the others stepped forward. His figure was spare, his face thin. A fine blond mustache drooped over the corners of his mouth. Joanna could not tell when or if he smiled.

"I assume you are the leader," Joanna continued

405

imperiously when no one else moved or spoke. "Act, man. I require a carriage and horses immediately. Half of you will form my escort while the other half will remain here under the orders of your second-in-command to ascertain the whereabouts of my servants and to put my house to rights."

He whom she had addressed suddenly shrugged himself from his trance. He mounted a couple of steps; at the same time he pulled a paper from his tunic and held it up toward her.

Her eyebrows rose at his rudeness.

A flush appeared on his cheeks, and he bowed quickly.

Acknowledging his courtesy, she extended her hand regally to receive the paper. "At last," she announced, as if she had expected this message all along.

Breaking the seal, she unfolded it and scanned its contents. The words made her blood run cold. Her only chance would be to get to the Council in London. Surely, among its numbers there would be a few friends who would intercede in her behalf against this monstrous order.

Folding it again, she stared at the leader. "I suggest we depart for London immediately, Captain."

He had been watching her closely. His courage had risen as the blood had drained from her face. "My orders are to convey you elsewhere, my lady."

"Then I am countermanding those orders," she told him levelly. "We shall depart this very afternoon for London where I shall be the guest of Lady Margaret, Duchess of Clarence." Let him know the names of her allies, she told herself.

"No, madam," he insisted with surprising firmness. "I was instructed under no circumstances to obey your orders. You are my prisoner. Charges have been brought against you, and you must be conveyed to a place where you can be watched until your trial."

"Trial? I am guilty of nothing," she sneered. "This is all a mistake. One I fear, Captain, of the most dangerous kind for you."

He did not hesitate. "That is as may be, madam, but I have my orders."

She advanced one step down the stairs, two, a third. "Who has more authority than I, sirrah? I command you. Speak. Who has more authority than I, myself?"

"My orders come directly from the king."

"You lie! The king is in France."

"His Grace, the Duke of Bedford speaks for him."

She made an exasperated sound. "Captain, we are wasting good daylight hours. Think, man. You are making a mistake that will cost you your career, perhaps even your life."

His sun-lined face was set; his mouth, a thin white-lipped line. "If I do not obey orders, Your Majesty, I know I will have no career."

She threw the message on the steps in a gesture of royal contempt. "On your head be it." She turned back up the stairs. "I will not leave until I have sent a message to the Duchess of Clarence."

"No, madam. You are my prisoner. You will send no messages."

White with anger, she rounded on him, but he forestalled her. "Madam, hear me. I have my orders. I shall obey them. You have no choice but to accompany me when and where I say. We leave after sunset. May I suggest that you lie down and rest for the day. My men will be deployed about the house. I myself will sit in your room."

"How dare you? You—a man—in my bedchamber."

He grinned pityingly at her. "You have nothing to fear, my lady. I do not slake my thirsts on women older than my mother."

She flushed bright red at the deliberate insult. He saw and smiled. "I can play intimidation too, my lady." He smiled thinly. "Proceed to your chamber. I will follow you."

Once inside he locked her door carefully. Surveying the broken window, he looked questioningly in her direction.

"The panes were smashed in last week's storm."

He nodded at the memory. "'Twas a bad one. It blew roofs off in London."

Still not convinced that this stranger was actually going to remain with her throughout the day, she remained standing in the center of the room. Nervously, she laced her fingers together. "Captain . . ." she began tentatively.

He swung round. "Lie down, madam."

Angry at his tone of command, she strode to the bed and positioned herself stiffly upon it. Folding her hands across her waist like a brass figure on a tomb, she stared straight at the ceiling.

He settled himself in a chair out of the cold breeze from the open window.

For better than half an hour she maintained her hostile silence. At last she spoke. "Captain, were you responsible for removing my servants in the middle of the night?"

He did not answer immediately. She looked in his direction to catch his forehead creased in a frown. "Yes, my lady," he replied at last.

"Where did you take them?"

"To be questioned as to your movements."

"My duenna, Doña Isabella de la Alcudia . . . is she safe?"

He drew a deep breath. "No, madam. When we questioned her she would not cooperate. She was very stubborn."

Joanna clapped a hand to her mouth. "Oh, you did not hurt her. She is but a poor old woman. She has been with me for thirty years."

"She was very loyal."

Tears started in her eyes and trickled down her temples into her heavy hair. *"Was?"*

"She committed suicide. She was a witch who would not reveal her dealings with the Evil One."

A fierce rage boiled in Joanna's bosom. "You lie!" she whispered. "And before God you will pay for that lie and the act that precipitated it."

The hair rose on the back of his neck. A hardened soldier used to idle threats, he was surprised to find her words carried more weight than if she had screamed them at him.

Part III

The Prisoner Of Pevensey

Chapter 25

Not the sight of the mounted men but the sight of the huge horse she was expected to ride almost broke her courage. The captain, following close behind her, stumbled against her when she halted abruptly at the sight of the rearing beast. Stamping impatiently, it nodded its huge head, setting its bridle to jingling.

White-faced, she rounded on the captain, who stepped back murmuring apologies under his breath. "I insist on a carriage."

His expression changed to one of exasperation. "We do not have time for a carriage, my lady. Please mount quickly."

"No."

The last faint purplish strands of day were fading from the western sky, and the wind had died to a gentle breeze. The captain was angry at the prospect of the night ride; he was angry about this entire business. In the first place, the captain did not really believe in witches. In the second place, instead of an old hag muttering unintelligible incantations as she cackled over her gnarled hands, he had found a beautiful, regal woman in full possession of her senses.

The entire command had soured. The servants he had rounded up were peaceful, dutiful men and women. The man the captain had questioned had not the least idea of what the questioning was about. Only the old Spanish lady had fought fiercely, glaring her hatred over the gag thrust ruthlessly between her jaws. When he heard she had died, his predominant feeling had been one of disgust followed by a faint twinge of guilt. Terrorizing old women was not a man's activity.

He wanted this business ended as soon as possible, but now this woman was resisting just as the old woman had.

He struck a belligerent stance. "Have done, madam. We must be on our way. Mount your horse."

"No! I—"

Swift as thought, his temper erupted. He grabbed her shoulder, dragging her in against him. One hand fumbled and found a strip of cloth inside his tunic. This he twisted round her head, gagging her before she could utter another sound. Withdrawing a second strip in the same fashion, he gathered her wrists together and wrapped the binding tightly around them.

Sliding one arm under her knees and another around her shoulders, he slung her onto the horse's broad back, guiding her legs astride in a posture no lady would ever adopt. The man on the other side of her horse leered appreciatively at the length of limb thus exposed.

"You will do as I say, madam," the captain announced, as much for the benefit of his men as for her, for her cries of protest were effectively muffled by the gag.

The savage grin he flashed up at her faded a little as he beheld her starting eyes staring not at him but at the ground beneath his feet. Why she was terrified of the height! More gently he guided her hands to the saddlebow. Then lest he regret his actions, he swung onto his own mount and gathered her reins with his. At a gesture from his hand the mounted troop clattered away, swiftly gaining speed until they were at full gallop by the time they reached the road.

Joanna was almost paralyzed by fear. To the already long

list of horrors she had experienced in her life was added that ride through the darkness of the Essex countryside. The rhythmic pounding of the slashing hooves was torture. The vibration terrified her. In the moonlight she could see the ground far beneath her. Her fingers went numb from clutching the saddlebow so tightly.

Her body rocked from side to side with the motion of the horse. Tears spouted from her eyes to be dried by the wind blowing in her face. At length when she could cry no more, when the miles had lulled her terror to mindless apprehension, her captors halted at a ferry.

The Thames. They had come to the Thames. She heard the boatman grumble briefly at the idea of making the trip at night, heard the clink of coin; then the horses moved uneasily onto the deck.

"Please to dismount," the boatman ordered. "The currents be treacherous enough during the day. At night it might be a bit rough. Mayhap someone might fall."

The men swung down from their horses, but she was not allowed even that respite. The captain kept her in the saddle, commanding his men to form a cordon around her.

Supporting herself on her hands, she sat with bent head, trying to ease some of the pain in her abused thighs. How did men stand such? Her flesh was surely scalded clear to the bone.

Before the ferry grated firmly against the landing, the captain had already mounted his horse. Even as the bow touched, he urged his horse forward and off, leading her mount behind him. The others clattered along as fast as they might, and the nightmare journey continued.

As the first streaks of dawn lighted the sky, they clattered up to the gate of a monastery. The gates swung open at a barked command, and the horses were led inside. Pulling her from the saddle, the captain supported her by holding her against his side and half-carrying, half-dragging her. Without removing her bonds or gag, he pulled the hood of her traveling cape over her face and swept her up into his arms.

"Lead the way." She heard his terse command.

He carried her to a tiny cell where he deposited her on a rude cot. The gray light of morning revealed her face, pale as death with dark eyes that stared at him accusingly.

Moved by a curious pity, he gently turned her head to the side and untied the gag. Stuffing it into his tunic, he freed her hands as well and rose. Looking around him, he noted a pitcher and a basin on a crude stool. "Do you wish to eat now, my lady? Or would you prefer to rest first and eat later?"

She could not answer him. Her throat was dry. She swallowed, moistening her lips experimentally with her tongue. "Later." The word had no timbre.

He nodded as if he had expected her answer. Turning on his heel, he hurried out. She heard the bar grate across the door. Her last conscious thought was that she was thirsty. She should drink some water and relieve herself, but she was too exhausted. Her outstretched hand dropped limply onto the floor beside the cot, and so she fell asleep as she was.

As darkness fell, they were away again. To the mental agony of riding again through the night at breakneck speed was added the physical agony of stiff muscles and bruised skin. Because she did not protest, he did not bind her; but this consideration was scarcely noticed.

Joanna had gone beyond recognition of it. Every part of her hurt. Stiff as a doll, she clutched the pommel of the saddle before her and concentrated on the whipping forelock between the horse's ears.

The wind freshened in the darkest hour before dawn. Borne on its chilly blast, Joanna could smell salt water. They were approaching the sea. They must have ridden south all night. The channel must lie somewhere before them. She felt a faint hope that they might be taking her to France.

Out of the darkness loomed a huge dark shape. A wall.

The horses surged downward, then up again immediately. They had crossed a dry ditch. Now the troop clattered through a gate with guardrooms on each side.

Once inside, she could see a torch flaring ahead. Her escort trotted the horses toward it. By its leaping flames, she could see a bridge across what must surely be a moat around a castle.

"Halloo!" The leader of the troop raised his voice.

An answering shout bade him enter.

Iron-shod hooves clopped across the bridge and between thick walls. Before the door of the keep, she was lifted from her horse, her pain-wracked body supported on either side by members of her escort. A man stepped from the door to wait at the top of the steps. Torchlight dyed his pale hair and one side of his face red.

The captain stepped forward, drawing another letter from his tunic. Your prisoner, d'Anglais."

"Yes," came the soft reply. "Your Majesty . . ."

She swayed where she stood. Her limbs were numb, her body refused to function. The blood rushed from her head. Her full weight sagged on their arms as she fainted.

She could have been unconscious only a matter of minutes, for when she roused, she was lying on a bench with Geoffrey bending over her. His face hung above hers, impassive, but with a strange light in his eyes.

"Drink this." He slipped one hand beneath her head while the other held a cup to her lips. Sweet wine diluted with water flowed into her dry mouth and eased her parched throat. Her hand closed over his wrist and held it as she drank greedily.

At last she lay back, caressing his beloved features with eyes turning luminous in the firelight. Her hand rose of its own volition toward his cheek. "Geoffrey," she breathed.

Abruptly, he swung away from her side, making a sweeping motion with his hand. "I had a simple meal set for you, my lady. When you feel slightly recovered, rise and eat.

417

Then we will talk." He did not look back but crossed to the door and went out. She heard a bolt grate into place behind him.

His rejection wounded her, but she was too exhausted to think what it might mean. Instead she closed her eyes and allowed her tiredness to take her into a state bordering on unconsciousness. More than an hour passed before hunger and discomfort roused her enough to take an interest in her surroundings.

The room in which she lay was plainly furnished. Besides the padded bench beneath her, it contained a small table with a chair drawn up to it. A small open fire flickered fitfully on a tiny hearth. Turning her head, she could see a single narrow cot along one wall. The smallness and rudeness depressed her. Was this her cell?

For a long time, she lay still, not daring to move as the searing pain in her limbs and back gradually subsided to a dull ache. Finally her stomach made its own dire distress known. Tentatively, she attempted to sit up. Apart from her abused hindquarters, she was fine, she told herself. A bit hungry, a bit faint, certainly tired, but these conditions could be quickly remedied. Gritting her teeth, she pushed herself to her feet and tottered to the table.

"A simple meal indeed," she grunted, lowering herself gingerly onto the chair which fortunately had a thin pad made of the same stuff that graced the bench. She sniffed at it suspiciously. "I do not care for fish stew," she announced mournfully to the fire. "But I am sure I shall find it surprisingly palatable. I cannot remember when I have been so hungry."

The warm stew, scooped up with bread crusts, assuaged her hunger. She wished for more wine but found only water in the jug on the table. Nevertheless, it was cold and sweet. She poured some into her cup, drank it, then poured herself some more.

As she set the jug down, the bolt slid back, and the door

opened. Geoffrey strode into the room. His tall figure was as thin as ever. His garments of fine gray wool fit him loosely, yet elegantly. The thought flitted through her mind that very seldom did the most elegant velvet and brocade garments of other men become them as well as Geoffrey's simple clothing suited him.

The horrors of the last desperate hours fell away as she pushed herself back from the table and stumbled toward him. Her arms went round him, and she hid her head against his chest. Even though his arms did not enfold her, she nevertheless drew strength and reassurance from the scent and feel of him. His heart beat strongly beneath her cheek; his chest heaved as he drew a deep breath against her breasts. "Oh, Geoffrey," she whispered brokenly.

Only for a moment did he allow her that respite before putting her from him with hard stern hands. Without preamble he addressed her, his voice devoid of any emotion. "You are my prisoner within the walls of Pevensey Castle, madam. You are to be kept in close confinement until such time as you shall be brought to trial for sorcery and necromancy threatening the person of His Majesty King Henry V."

Her mouth dropped open as she stared at him incredulously. "Sorcery? Me? I am accused of sorcery!"

He corrected her as if he had memorized the charges. "You are *guilty* of the sorcery and necromancy. You and your spies have plotted against the king. I have seen proof incontrovertible."

Shaking her head in disbelief, she extended her hands helplessly. "Geoffrey, you know I have not plotted against the king. For what reason would I do so?"

His mouth twisted angrily. "As to that, I cannot say, madam. I do not understand someone so ungrateful." Even as she watched, his fists clenched at his sides as though he maintained a tight grip on his temper.

"I am not ungrateful," she protested weakly, sinking down

on the bench. His anger wounded her deeply, but deeper still was the wound that his lack of faith caused. Could he really believe she would harm the king?

"England elevated you," he continued, his outrage building. "You are its queen. You have riches, property, a fine palace to live in."

She raised her head, sarcasm dripping from her voice. "As you say, it seems incomprehensible that I would be so ungrateful. Especially when I have so much to lose by plotting against the king."

"Ah, but you could gain more, much more. And you were ever greedy."

"What could I possibly gain?"

"The throne."

Facing him defiantly, she laughed softly. "Over the dead bodies of Clarence, Bedford, and Gloucester," she remarked sarcastically as she named the brothers of Henry V.

He began to pace angrily back and forth in front of the fire. "You were plotting with Navarre—"

"My brother!" She sneered. "Do not be absurd. I have not seen or heard of him in over thirty years. He has his own problems. He has forgotten he has a sister."

"When you were Duchess of Brittany, messages passed through your servants to Navarre," he insisted coldly. "You were ever one for plots."

She drew a deep breath and rose from the bench to limp, stiffly and painfully, toward him. "You are wrong, Geoffrey. Terribly wrong."

He raised his hand to halt her. "Stay away from me, madam. You have long bewitched me with your black arts."

Her smile was soft and warm. "Geoffrey, I use no arts. I have none to use. Messages passed to Navarre when I was first married to Montfort, but they were from poor Isabella to my father. He was ever one for plotting. Believe me. The reports were mostly about me and my attitude. Isabella found me an unwilling spy. I think, had my father lived and had I ever been returned to him, I would have been severely punished for my lack of enthusiasm for his schemes."

"You are as bad as your father," he insisted doggedly. Being alone with her in this room was beginning to bother him considerably. She was just as beautiful as he remembered, but she now revealed a sweetness and gentleness of spirit that he did not remember. Where was the proud and haughty princess who had despised her mating with bastard blood?

And then he knew.

"Do not seek to deceive me," he warned hoarsely. "Do not think by pretending innocence that you will win your freedom from me. Your treachery shall be closely watched. The king knew well who to assign to be your guard."

Suddenly she laughed. The dry bitter sound echoed strangely in the bleak cell.

"You will not have your way, madam," he insisted.

She shook her head. "Oh, Geoffrey," she gasped. "You are the most loyal and yet the most foolish of men. Do you not see? We are both old, useless people to the new, young king."

"I am not old and useless," he denied savagely.

Her mouth curved in a pitying smile. "You may be right, but I am. Worse yet, for me. I am in his way. I have possessions that he wants—"

"You lie. You have nothing that he wants. He is the king."

"Only so long as the Council agrees to support him. Fully half of them favor the Earl of March." She bit her lip, but the words were out before she could stop them.

He leaped on her words. "The Earl of March. Of course. Fool that I am. I should have realized. What will March do for you?"

She shook her head emphatically. "Nothing. Nothing. I swear."

"The king was right to arrest you. You would subvert the Council against him and make the way smooth for his rival." The silver-gray eyes glittered like steel as he came

421

toward her.

"No," she cried throwing back her head proudly. "But I will tell you why your precious King Harry has imprisoned me and will probably kill me shortly. I refused to give up dowager lands. They were my last hopes. I know I am old. I also know I have no chance for anything more." She was panting now. Physical pain and emotional stress combined to weaken her body so that she swayed. Despite the air she sucked into her lungs, she felt dizzy and light-headed. "He has had me arrested so he may take my castle and my revenues from the Lancastrian estates to pay for his foreign wars against France."

"No!"

"Yes!" she hissed angrily. "Otherwise why this secrecy? Why travel at night with me? Why arrest my servants and question them in secret? Why kill my poor old duenna? Why am I not brought to London and tried before the Council? I am the Queen of England. No one can sentence me except the Council."

"You are to be protected," Geoffrey protested angrily. "The secrecy was necessary to protect you. The people might become fearful and demand that you be burned for your witchcraft."

"Witchcraft? Bah! The people around Havering-atte-Bower know me. If any were asked what he thinks of the queen, they would answer to a man in my behalf. Oh, no. Henry does not dare bring me before the Council. He knows his charges are laughable."

"He seeks to spare you. The Council—"

"The Council would look at him as if he were crazy if he brought that charge before them. They know my honesty, my loyalty to Lancaster. Did I not serve my husband with all the strength of my body and mind?"

"You came to me to betray him behind his back," he sneered.

"You with your evil mind misinterpreted everything I

said." She clasped her hands together in front of her in an attitude of prayer. "I wanted to be friends with you again. I desperately needed friends, even as I do now, but you would never have been my friend. You are too unforgiving."

"I would ever forgive a good person, but so wicked a sorceress—"

The rage that she had kept under control for so long, burst from her. Like Charles the Bad in his worst fits of temper, she clenched her fists and screamed at the angry man standing before her. "It is too much to expect forgiveness and generosity from a lackey such as yourself. You left Montfort when his powers looked to be waning. You sided with the young prince when Henry Bolingbroke was dying of leprosy. Harry of Monmouth had better look to it should he ever become ill or infirm."

"Damn you! Damn you!" His rage was equal to her own. Like tigers they came together. His hands fastened in the neck of her garments and ripped them apart. "I was ever loyal to Montfort," he thundered. He bared her to the waist and dragged her against him, lifting her out of the wreck of her dress. "You bear the scar on your body, even as I on mine. Do you remember the pain? Do you remember what he said that night? He asked you whether you believed that I would suffer such torment to trick you."

"I believe that you had no choice," she snarled, struggling against him, her nails curved to claw at his cheeks. "I had the choice. To submit and spare us both or to die. I have always had the choice. You have always done what one or the other of them told you to do."

He flung her out of his arms, sending her reeling back against the table. Her dress gaped open to her navel, but she did not seek to cover herself.

"I did not choose to be the male whore to the Queen of England."

Drawing herself regally upright in the wreck of her clothing, she spat her defiance at him. "I could have had far,

far better than you, should I have needed a male."

His eyes narrowed to slits of molten silver as he ground his teeth in rage. "Shall we see, Madam Queen?"

His hands went to the buttons on his tunic.

Mesmerized by horror and the thrill of a desire that was frightening in its perversity, she watched him rapidly divest himself of his clothing. When his long spare body was nude, he covered the intervening space between them in one predatory lunge. Violently, he ripped the rest of her clothing from her.

He is raping me, she thought wildly. The idea should have terrorized her, but oddly it did not. A part of her she did not recognize welcomed his violence.

One arm snapped round her waist; a hand that held a broadsword with a grip of steel closed over her hipbone. His other hand grasped the white column of her throat, the long fingers gripping her jaw to turn her head up to his ravaging lips. His kiss was punitive. His tongue plundered her mouth as he lifted her tightly against his manhood.

Fully as angry as he, her jangled senses became overcharged by the torment she had endured. Furiously, she writhed in his arms. One arm was trapped between their bodies, but the other was free. Her hand fastened in his silver-white hair and yanked viciously as she bit down on his tongue.

With a surprised grunt he jerked his head to the side and staggered back a step. The movement did nothing to free him since he still held her feet off the floor and her entire length pressed against his body.

When she continued to tug at his hair, he set her down and released his hold on her throat to grab her wrist. "Leave off," he commanded tightly.

"Oh, forgive me," she mocked. "Am I too much for you? You had better go away and lock the heavy wooden door behind you before I escape."

For answer, he clasped her wrist behind her and buried his

face in the side of her neck below her ear. "You are never too much for me," he panted. "A whore like you needs a strong man to satisfy her."

The hateful word set her wild. She twisted again in his arms sinking her teeth into his shoulder until he cursed and caught at her hair to pull her head away. Her braids came loose from their moorings and the silken skeins began to separate. His mouth came down to kiss her again while he ran his fingers through them. His passion mounting to white heat, he bore her to the floor, taking her slender body beneath his, on the rough planks.

Her own body would have responded in any event to his, but in her anger she sought to punish him as well. Furiously, she raked her nails across his shoulders as he groaned his pain and desire into her mouth. "Devil," she moaned. "Devil. Devil. Devil. Devil."

His weight bore down on her hips as he used the hard muscle of his manhood to grind against the soft mound at the juncture of her thighs. Far from begging for mercy, she cried her anger and defiance into his mouth. His shoulder was slippery with blood where she had bitten him, and he tasted blood against her lips where his mouth had punished her own.

His pulse pounding in his ears, he raised himself above her to survey her. She did not look as he had expected. No conquered quaking rag, she bared her teeth at him. He saw the flash of anger in her eyes just as she brought up her knees and tried to roll away.

"No," he growled. "Oh, no. We shall finish this, now." With both hands he parted her thighs and positioned himself at her entrance even as she twisted angrily in her effort to prevent him. "Now," he gasped.

Joanna could not contain her cry of mingled agony and ecstasy as he filled her. She had been so long without him that she welcomed him with every part of her that was female. Conversely, the cruelty of his revenge coupled with the perversity of her own feelings filled her with revulsion.

Almost mindless with desire now whipped to fever pitch, Geoffrey began his movements immediately, not waiting for her body to stretch to accommodate him. The tightness of her sheath generated wave on wave of voluptuous pleasure through his body, so that each movement wrung a groan from him. Bathed in sweat, he set his teeth as he endured the exquisite agony which, try though he might, he could not prolong.

With a mighty lunge forward, he exploded within her, shouting his pleasure to the rafters.

At the same time, he thrust her body over the edge of ecstasy. Like ripples from a stone dropped into a brook, her own release sent the sensations flooding her body. They emanated from the spot somewhere deep within her that he had touched with his climactic movement. Her breath sighed slowly out of her lungs; her eyes closed as her body melted in the burning heat.

For some minutes they lay joined together, her body sprawled beneath him. Yet he had not collapsed across her. His last conscious thought had been to twist his body sideways and gather her in against his chest, so they lay facing each other, their limbs still tightly entwined.

Gradually, she regained her senses. The floor was hard beneath her. Her body was cruelly bruised and overtaxed by the violence of the encounter. Now that it had ended, she felt tired and faintly nauseated. Her hair, tangled beneath her, kept her from moving her head. Wincing, she tried to raise her upper body.

"Uncomfortable?" Geoffrey whispered in her ear.

"Yes, very." She did not look at him but gazed straight up at the ceiling. Her words were cold as ice.

His hands clutched her tightly as if he meant to repeat his act; then they relaxed. With a moan he rolled away.

They sat up back to back, he staring into the fire, she drawing her knees up in the circle of her arms and laying her cheek on them. For several minutes they remained thus, each alone, alienated from the other.

Joanna felt tears starting to form, but she blinked them back. Under no circumstances must this brute of a gaoler know that he had the power to make her cry. And yet their coming together had been so wonderful. For just a few minutes she had forgotten everything except that he was Geoffrey. She was back in the arms of her love, and his passion filled her. The memory of deprivation of her years as the wife of Henry IV moved her to self-pity. How she longed to confess everything to Geoffrey, to tell him that he had been her only love but that she had been too stupidly young and proud to recognize him. Now he would not believe her. He was determined to believe what he wanted to believe.

At length he gave a slight shudder and rose, reaching for his discarded clothing. Silently he drew it on. Then, without looking at her, he crossed to the door. She raised her head to stare defiantly after him, her black eyes flecked like obsidian in the dying firelight.

From the doorway, he looked back at her huddled figure, feelings of self-disgust and revulsion clearly visible in his face. He had betrayed his position as gaoler before he had her in captivity twenty-four hours. "I no longer have any doubts," he snarled hoarsely. "You really are a witch."

Chapter 26

Once the door had closed behind him and the bolt had grated into place again, Joanna began to shiver. Her teeth started to chatter, and nervous rigors twisted her stomach muscles into knots of pain. She threw an agonized glance over her shoulder, but only warm ashes remained on the hearth. Its fire had died untended while their own fires had raged out of control.

· Moving like an old, old woman, she gathered her knees under her and crawled to the bench. Then by carefully steadying herself, she managed to balance on legs so weak she feared to trust them. But trust them she must. To remain as she was beside the cooling hearth was unthinkable.

So quickly was the reaction setting in that she could hardly close her trembling fingers around the heavy woollen material of her cape. Groaning softly, she slung the garment around her, then shuddered as its cold silk lining slid over her naked back. The bed was impossibly far away.

Staggering drunkenly, she crossed to it and flung back the covers. At least the sheets were clean. Gathering her cloak tightly around her, she sat on the edge to pull off her boots. Beneath her abused thighs, she could feel the bed slats through the thin mattress.

A wave of despair swept over her. Bread and water and

fish stew, one small fire at night, a mattress so thin she could feel the boards beneath it—and a gaoler who raped her. Dry-eyed, she buried her face in her hands. Very likely, this prison cell was her last home on earth. If Henry did not kill her immediately, she would not long survive under these conditions.

As a chill spread through the room she became aware of the sound she had not noticed before. The sea was pounding against the shore not very far away. The sound was soothing. Concentrate on that sound, she told herself. Let it lull you to sleep. She pulled the cloak more tightly around her and thrust her feet beneath the chill covers. Huddling in a tight ball, she cupped her hands together at her lips and began to pray soundlessly.

She forebore to pray for her deliverance, for she had lost all hope of freedom in her life. Instead, she prayed for the courage to make a good end, to live proudly as befit her heritage until she should die of the conditions of her imprisonment. She prayed for the soul of Isabella. She had never been able to bring herself to do more than tolerate the old woman; yet lying in her cold prison bed, she felt hopelessly bereft. Who would be her friend now? Of a sudden, she thought that all whom she had loved in this life were gone from it. No, not quite. Geoffrey still remained, but he was as removed from her as if he stood on the other side of the world.

Her prayers did not last long. Her breath warmed her chill fingers even as she plunged into a dreamless state more near unconsciousness than sleep.

The wind from the sea blew outside her walls, but she could not feel it, nor could she see the water. Her cell had no windows. Bare gray walls such as prisoners have known for hundreds of years filled her eyes with their oppressing sameness.

Yet she did have a skylight. High above her head, set in the slope of the ceiling, was an opening covered by transparent skins. Scraped thin and oiled, they allowed diffused light to enter. At least she would know day from night, she realized with a kind of gladness. Soon even the difference between day and night might become a welcome diversion for her.

Carefully, she straightened her body from its cramped position. Utterly exhausted, she had fallen asleep immediately, and her body had barely stirred from its tight ball. Her very bones ached after the jolting horror of her ride. Tentatively, she ran her fingertips over her inner thighs. As she had expected, they felt raw and stipples of dried blood showed where her thin skin had been abraded by the saddle leather.

Her hand moved higher, touching the soft hairs at the top of her thighs. The slight stickiness she felt there startled her. So many, many years had passed since they had last come together that she had been almost as tight as a virgin. That tightness combined with the rawness created by the ride had caused her to bleed.

She sighed as she squeezed her thighs together in remembrance. In the midst of her fiery anger had been the ecstasy of sexual fulfillment. They had made love, their bodies knowing the way as surely as if their last coupling had been only yesternight. Now she felt like a young girl who has experienced the first exciting fulfillment of her life and looks forward eagerly to the next one. She wondered with a sigh whether he felt as she did. Mentally, she shrugged. He would never admit his feelings to her. The hatred of his last words, the revulsion in his voice were imprinted on her memory. He believed his attraction for her to be the result of witchcraft.

It if were witchcraft, then he was the greatest warlock of them all, for his body was like a magnet drawing her to him whenever she came within his sphere.

The bolt grated across the door. Hastily, she threw back her covers and rose. Dizziness blinded her and a storm of

431

dots whirled before her eyes. She staggered back and sat down hard. As a result, the first thing Geoffrey heard as he entered the room with a tray and a bundle was the sound of the bed slats creaking in protest.

"I have brought your food." He set the tray down on the table and came to loom over her, his hands on his hips, his booted feet astride. Sitting with bowed head, her palms pressed to her temples, she could not see the quick look of concern that flashed across his features. When her dizziness had finally abated, she raised her face to see only rigid control evident in his stern features.

"I thank you," she replied, surprised to find her throat painfully dry.

He paused a moment. "There is a flagon of ale."

She raised an eyebrow. "I thought water was to be my only fare."

Abruptly, he turned away and strode to the bundle that he had set on the bench. "'Tis all you deserve."

Instantly, she regretted her words; they seemed to have closed off the tiny breach in the walls between them. "I . . ." She could find no reply. Anything she might say, no matter how innocent, would be purposefully misconstrued.

He unfastened the bundle. "I have brought your clothing. 'Tis more suitable for your status than the garments you have now."

"Especially since they have been reduced to rags by you."

He shot her an angry look, and a dark flush stained his cheeks.

Proudly she pulled her cloak tightly around her, then reached for her boots.

"Leave them," he commanded. "You will no longer wear fine leathers." A pair of rope sandals such as penitents wear dangled from his fingertips as he came toward her. Before she could move, he had caught up her boots and slung the sandals down in front of her with a defiant air. "Take off those fine hose as well."

Burning with angry humiliation, she stared at the rough, crude things. His calculated cruelty almost made her ill. He must have dreamed of her abasement, perhaps for weeks, perhaps for years. Her eyes flashed upward to read in his stern face a complete lack of mercy. Undoubtedly, he would wreak his revenge for all the insults he had suffered in his life on her person. "You bastard!" The words leaped from her lips like stones from a sling.

She did not know whether they hit their mark, although he grinned whitely. "Exactly, madam."

She sprang to her feet, lifting her chin defiantly in his face. "You have never behaved like a bastard until today. Always you were a gentleman born and bred. Today you behave like the lowest hound. You strike against the weak and helpless."

"'Tis what you and your kind have taught me," he sneered. One hand snaked out to jerk the silk-lined cloak from her shoulders. "Get dressed."

Humiliated beyond tears, she stoically donned the garments he had brought. Besides the rope sandals, she was expected to wear a penitent's robe made of wool so rough it felt like sandpaper against her skin. She picked up the rope belt to gird it loosely around her slender waist, wincing at the rasp of the fabric.

Resentfully, she cast a glance at the ripped remains of her garments before he rolled them into a ball inside her cloak. Beneath this single garment, she was naked. Even a ragged shift would be better than none. She thought of begging but realized he would enjoy denying her even that small request. When she was dressed, she stalked angrily to the table to inspect the food he had brought for her.

He squatted on the hearth relighting her fire and feeding it from a small scuttle of charcoal. At length he rose. "You must tend your fire hereafter yourself," he informed her, dusting his hands ostentatiously before gathering up the bundle.

She did not reply but kept her head bowed over the plate.

She heard his movements, the rustle of cloth. At last he cleared his throat. "I will leave you now," he announced. "I shall return in the afternoon."

Still she did not reply, seemingly intent on using a crust of bread to swipe up a bite of the same fish stew she had been served the night before.

With a muffled curse, he tightened his hold on the bundle of clothing and strode out. The door banged to with unnecessary force after which the bolt grated more harshly than before.

Alone in the room, she let the crust of bread slip from her fingers. Turning her face away from the unappetizing mess, she clapped a hand to her mouth in an effort to retain her food. So this was why prisoners prayed for death: to escape the hatred, the humiliation, the deprivation, the food. Her eyes slid from floor to ceiling over the bleak gray stones.

She had done nothing—nothing. Yet she was being punished as if she were the foulest of creatures by a man who would enjoy every minute of her torment. With one hand she gripped the edge of the table until her knuckles turned white. Self-pity was washed away in a flood of angry frustration.

Suddenly expelling an angry expletive, she pounded her fist on the table. She would not surrender her pride to him. Never would she allow him to add pity to the savage hatred he bore her. Resolutely turning back to the table, she lifted the crust of bread to her lips, holding her breath against the powerful fish odor.

When she had slowly and meticulously eaten every bite, she pushed the chair away from the table and looked around her. The utter sameness of her cell depressed her. How could she exist with nothing to do? She had been used to reading, to writing letters, to supervising the servants, to hunting with the bow in her forests adjacent to Havering-atte-Bower. She had spent several hours of every week with her steward and more among the tenants, listening to their problems and caring for their needs. It had been a full life only occasionally tinged with loneliness. Now it was replaced by nothingness.

Rising, she began a minute examination of her room. The gray stone walls were damp and chill to her touch. The floor was of smooth wood planking, further confirming the hypothesis that her prison had probably been a bower for the women of the keep in happier days. Since the walls contained no arches, she must assume they were inner walls, probably in the very center of the building. The skylights provided sufficient light for the endless sewing required of the ladies of the house. Likewise the room was capacious, which she would not have expected a tower room to be.

A sobering thought struck her. Perhaps the room had been comfortably furnished with fine tables and chairs and decorated with tapestried screens. Perhaps these things, along with the chests of fine cloth and boxes of laces, trims, and silken threads, not to speak of pins and needles, had been hastily gathered up and whisked away by Geoffrey in a desire to make her life in prison as agonizing as possible.

The room seemed suddenly chill. Rubbing her arms, she crossed to the hearth and knelt to blow up the fire and add a few small lumps of charcoal to the fitfully glowing embers. At least she had something to do with her time, if she so chose. She could tend the fire. With the amount of charcoal he had given her, that might turn out to be a full-time job.

When she rocked back on her heels, the rough brown material of her robe pricked the backs of her thighs and calves. Sternly she suppressed the remembrance of the dozens of soft linen and cotton chemises she had owned, of her fine silk hose in all the colors of the rainbow, of the fine wool and silk dresses that Jean had particularly admired on her.

She rose hurriedly in an effort to detour that train of thought and swayed dizzily. She was still weak from the ordeal that had destroyed her old life and had left her bereft of everything in the world.

Perhaps she should try to spend the day in bed and recover

her strength. She returned to the narrow rude cot and stretched out upon it, trying to relax completely. In less than a minute she drifted into a sleep quite different from the semicoma in which she had passed the night.

Albeit her sleep was different, it fell far short of being tranquil. Her body tensed as her mind, overcharged with fears released from the bondage of her conscious will, extended itself into the fantastic realm of nightmare.

Joanna lay in the dark, darker than that of any night she had ever known. No single ray of light managed to enter her wide-staring eyes. Smothering in its intensity, she felt the blackness on her skin as bone-chilling cold. Yet she could not shiver.

She stretched taut unable to move. Able only to feel the chill, she moaned helplessly as it wreathed itself around her limbs, about her hips and waist. As if the rough wool of the penitent's robe were nothing, it laid its bony fingers on the dead white scar marring the skin of her belly. As if fascinated by the brand it traced it until she could bear no more.

Relentlessly moving upward, it closed its dead man's fingers over her breasts, fingering the nipples in a travesty of sensuality that made her cringe with revulsion at the same time that the tips of her breasts shrank and puckered to the touch.

A whimper slipped from her lips, and even as they opened to emit that tiny sound, dust slipped between them. Stifling, tasteless dust it was. So fine it almost seemed not to be, yet there was so much of it that its billowing coated her tongue, gritted between her teeth, clogged her throat, and made her cough.

Whereupon more whooshed in, as if eager to fill a void. Instinctively, she knew it was the dust of the tomb. Her body was bound by a rigid structure that held her feet tightly together while at the same time it pressed her hands against the outsides of her thighs.

She breathed in panic as the same fine dust entered her

nostrils. The shape pressing in around her was a coffin. Her muscles tensed to fight, to kick outward and upward, to thrust with her fists and elbows, but she could not even double her fist. Her legs were so constricted that they could not move the veriest inch.

At the sound of a loud thump a substance fell somewhere just above her heart. She would have screamed in alarm, had not the fine choking dust billowed more determinedly into her open mouth and sifted down into her already filled and aching lungs. Treacherous, overpowering dust that it was, it forestalled all her efforts to escape it.

But one could not escape the grave!

No one, no matter of what rank, could escape the grave. Charles of Navarre, Jean de Montfort, Henry Bolingbroke, all had gone to the dust which now threatened to fill every orifice of her body.

The thud of clods falling on the coffin followed swiftly now. She moaned and writhed. She was not dead. She knew . . . she felt . . . she remembered. She was not dead! They were making a mistake.

Geoffrey! Her mind screamed his name. Where was he? Always he had been the *deus ex machina* of her real world. Why did he not come to her in the realm of nightmare? Geoffrey, her mind screamed, help me. I am being buried alive. Only you can save me.

But would he come in time? Eventually, for everyone, there is a time when the *deus ex machina* does not appear, when the fantasy becomes reality.

Her fighting spirit rebelled at the thought. Wildly, she began to struggle, threshing valiantly and violently. Husbanding her air until her lungs ached and then drawing in a deep breath with a terrified gasp, she managed to stave off the unconsciousness that would surely be the end.

Writhing frantically to one side, she managed to tug one hand up her body to cover her face. Thus barricaded behind her hand she opened her mouth to call his name. "Geoffrey."

Only a dry whisper, wicked like the breath of an incantation, slipped from between her lips.

"Geoffrey," she tried again, this time managing a faint whine through the suffocating dust. Like a talisman from a fanciful Arabic tale, the word tore the lid of the coffin away.

Frantically, she pushed herself upright, struggling against the swathing material that must be her shroud. At last she swayed upright, her feet still entangled so tightly that she was prevented from taking so much as a step. She screamed again, this time her mouth clear of all the horror. "Geoffrey!"

He did not come and the dust began to blow and swirl upward from the coffin, rising about her knees, her thighs, her hips. Rising, rising inexorably. As if it were quicksand, she struggled against it, pushing with her hands and twisting her body, but she could not release herself.

It swirled beneath her breasts and around them, over her shoulders. She turned her face upward. "Oh, Geoffrey . . ."

His face appeared out of the blackness, looking as he had in the dreams of her youth. His skin was smooth and unlined, his gray eyes were softly luminous with love, his hair was a magnificent mane of pale silvery-yellow.

His tall body was swathed in a black cloak, but as he stood before her, he flung his arms outward, billowing the material out like great dark wings. He was nude as she had known he would be. His muscles rippled under the smooth unmarked skin. No scars of war, no brand of agony marred the masculine perfection of him. Despite her dire need, she felt intense desire course through her veins.

"Joanna." His voice was gruff but gentle.

"Geoffrey."

He furled the wings of his great cloak around them and gathered her against his body in a warm secure cocoon.

Her bones melting at his touch, she collapsed against him. Unable to struggle longer, she committed her whole life and

438

care to his strong arms. Her head tipped back against his shoulder; her eyes closed in exhausted sleep.

Feeling her relax, Geoffrey d'Anglais slipped his arm under her knees to catch her and hold her against his chest. Her scream of terror had penetrated to his own room next door. With fast-pounding heart he had burst into the converted bower to behold her standing upright as she swayed crazily beside her bed.

The bedclothes were tightly wrapped round her feet, and her arms flailed wildly as she strove for balance. When he lunged forward to keep her from falling, he had mistakenly thought she saw him. However, a closer inspection revealed her terror-stricken black eyes to be focused on nothing. Their pupils were dilated until the gold flecks that normally ringed them were engulfed.

At that moment he realized she was asleep, in the grip of a nightmare so horrible it had dragged her from her bed to stand upright and sway and scream in terror.

One arm tilted her inner body in against his chest as if he gathered a child to him. His other hand cupped the back of her head to press her face against his neck. "Hush, Joanna," he crooned, rocking his body from side to side. "Hush, my dear."

The whimpers of terror subsided as she clutched handfuls of his tunic and clung for dear life. Her body trembled against his, her chest heaved convulsively as she gasped for breath. Beneath her breast he could feel her heart pounding so hard and fast that he was alarmed.

Was she going to die in his arms?

"You are safe, Joanna," he whispered, his lips brushing her hair. "Be easy. You are safe. Shh-shh. Hush. Hush, Joanna." His vocabulary of soothing, comforting words quickly exhausted itself, causing him to switch to a set of meaningless sounds. No one had ever comforted him in his whole harsh life, so he operated on instinct alone.

He lowered himself to the cot, feeling as she had the thinness of the mattress beneath his shanks. The hardness of the slats was discomfiting in more ways than one. He had slept on much worse, including the hard ground at night, but she was a delicately bred and nurtured lady. How could she be expected to endure such discomfort? Sternly, he turned his thoughts back to her present condition, continuing the soothing meaningless crooning he had begun.

Whether he was saying or doing something correctly, or whether the nightmare had expended itself, he could not tell. But her quivering body began to relax, her heartbeats subsided to a normal rhythm. He felt the small sigh she gave as she relaxed totally. Her hands slipped from their hold on his tunic to lie quiescent upon her breast.

When he held her away from him, he found her eyelids to be closed, the long black fans of her lashes lying darkly upon her white cheeks. How tired she looked even after a night's sleep and another nap this morning, how pale and drawn.

Without thinking, he lowered his mouth to kiss her fair forehead, smooth now with its frown of pain and terror erased. His lips slid to her temple, to her closed eyes, to her cheeks. Involuntarily, his grip tightened around her, tightened as he became aware of the curves of her body pressed in a sensual way against his own.

No!

He shouted the word in his mind. Hastily, he sprang up. As quickly as he could, he must get rid of her body or be guilty of taking her as he had only a few short hours ago.

As he laid her on the bed, he tried manfully to study her face impersonally. She was not young. Tiny wrinkles radiated from the corners of her eyes and a pair of definite creases formed an upside down V between her eyebrows. Her skin had lost the first bloom of youth. Yet staring at it, he admitted that age had bestowed a translucent fragility to it that enchanted him. Somehow she attracted him more now than ever.

Straightening up, he looked angrily around him. When the Duke of Bedford had advised him of the king's command, he had accepted the post of gaoler with shameful eagerness. His reasons, he had acknowledged, were perverse. He wanted power over her. He wanted to make her pay tenfold for the thousand casual insults and indignities she had heaped upon him in the years when he had been her lover on command. Those wounds had never healed but had only closed over to conceal the cankers beneath the surface. He meant to take perverse pleasure in lancing them in her presence and in letting their venom spew forth.

Or so he had supposed. Now he doubted his motives. Had he really assumed the post for revenge? Or had his heart leaped with gladness at the thought of seeing her every day, of accompanying her everywhere?

After bringing her breakfast, he had hurried through his routine as steward of this moldering pile only to find himself in the chamber adjacent to her by the middle of the morning. There he had waited, pretending to study reports, but always with his ears pricked for the tiniest sound from her. When he had heard her scream, his heart had lurched wildly in his chest.

Angrily, he tore himself away from her bedside to stride purposelessly back and forth, his hands clenched into fists. God! Oh, God! Surely, he was bewitched.

He paused to fall on his knees on the hearth and savagely add an unnecessarily large amount of charcoal to the fire, building it up to a fine blaze with the addition of a couple of logs. The chill of this inner room was going to be a problem in winter. How could she keep warm without someone to constantly tend the fire? She would need . . .

In disgust he tossed the coal scuttle down with a noisy clatter. He could not even control his thoughts. His mind ever dwelt on her comfort. Instead of punishing her body, he seemed bent on caring for it. Rising, he pressed the heels of his hands to his throbbing temples.

A small sound reached his ears. He whirled to find her sitting up, staring at him, her eyes wide with alarm.

"What are you doing here?"

"I . . . I came to take you to the chapel for prayer," he improvised. "Finding you asleep, I stirred up the fire before I awakened you."

She did not question him further, nor did she look at him in disbelief. Instead she stretched her head on her slender neck, tilting it from side to side. "I thank you," she murmured. "The chill of the room must have gotten into my spine, for my neck feels stiff and cramped."

"Shall I rub it for you?" The words were out before he thought. Then a slow flush rose in his cheeks as he remembered that gaolers did not touch the bodies of their prisoners, nor did they offer succor. "That is . . ."

She shook her head, not seeming to notice his discomfiture. "No, thank you. It will be all right in just a few minutes. It is already better." She tossed aside the covers and rose, shaking the wrinkled robe out and adjusting its folds around her waist beneath the knotted rope.

Then she raised a hand to her hair. It fell in a tangled black mass, reaching to her waist in back. The sight of her garment, plus the condition of her hair seemed to remind her of her position. Her face carefully devoid of expression, she raised her eyes to him. "I beg a boon, Master Gaoler."

Instantly, he too stiffened. "Speak," he rapped tightly.

"I must have a comb or brush."

"Must, my lady?" He raised a sardonic eyebrow.

Drawing a deep breath, she approached him. Before he realized her intention, she had dropped to one knee before him. Crossing her arms across her breasts, she intoned in a low voice. "I *beg* a comb or brush, Sir Geoffrey. Behold me on my knees a penitent."

He stared at her bowed disordered head. His petty

442

remonstrances generated a hot spurt of shame which he sternly suppressed. She might seem penitent, but he would wager anything he owned that she did not feel so. She was a sorceress after all. They were known to be dissemblers.

"I will see if I can find such," he promised grudgingly. "But for now you will go to your prayers just as you are."

Chapter 27

Only one short month, only thirty-one days had passed, yet Joanna felt herself withering. How could she endure much more of this? She had heard of prisoners who emerged from prison after years and years. What inner strength did they draw on? Shuddering, she contemplated a frightening idea. Were those who emerged not possessed so much of strength of will and character as strength of body? Did their minds escape into madness while their bodies clung doggedly to life? Would she gradually deteriorate into a gibbering, muttering idiot, a mindless old woman who perhaps believed herself to be the witch they had labeled her?

Her fists doubled convulsively. At once she was angry at herself for entertaining such thoughts although she acknowledged that they occupied her waking hours more and more. Disgusted by her lack of mental control, she rolled over on her back and experimentally rubbed her hands over her ribs. She had lost flesh because she no longer even tried to eat the inevitable fish stew. It was not that she minded the taste of it; she had become accustomed to it. She merely felt she was waiting for something that would never happen. In such circumstances, why wait?

Probably her lands and moneys were being utilized as fast as her stepson could collect them. Given that license, he really had no reason to kill her. Her death might create a breath of scandal that would tarnish the shining image of the perfect knight and king. Better to let her live out her life in a dull gray prison. Furthermore, he was a young man. He would long outlive her.

She squeezed the bridge of her nose hard between her thumb and third finger. Adamantly, she refused to give in to tears. She would look at her predicament until it became an ordinary thing that held no terrors for her. As long as she lived, she would be imprisoned in this ancient castle with Geoffrey as her gaoler. There, she had faced it. She turned her face to the wall. Why did she not feel any better?

Briefly, she contemplated Geoffrey's fate as her gaoler. In a sense he was imprisoned too. When she died, however, he would be free to go—if she died before he did.

The thought made her unbearably sad. His manner had not softened to her in this past month, but she had come to love him more than ever. Still she did not want to die. Even under the conditions in which she found herself, life was precious.

Distastefully she plucked at the material of the robe. It had not been removed from her body except when she stripped it off to bathe from the small pan of water he provided. It would probably stink of her body had it not already been heavily permeated with odors all its own. The Council should really pass a law prohibiting the sale of wool of this quality. Inferior stuff like this should be burned. The person who had woven this material was undoubtedly taking monastic moneys under false pretenses. Perhaps collusion was involved. The monk who bought the stuff would have to be a party to the crime, for no one with an eye could fail to discover the quality.

She lifted a foot and contemplated her bare toes emerging

from the end of the crude sandal. For two weeks the rough rope had created great blisters that had broken and scabbed over. Now a set of ugly calluses had replaced them. With a sigh she let her leg drop back to the bed. Instantly, she winced, regretting her action, for her heel landed on a portion of the thin mattress directly above a slat. She would have a big bruise there tomorrow.

If only she could do something, anything. She closed her eyes, remembering. In her imagination she could hear the hunting horn winded by Clothere in the forests of Brittany. The miles she had run. The excitement. The freedom. The thrill of the chase. It was all so real. Her nostrils were full of the scent of pine; her vision encompassed the dark heavy green of the Breton forests.

Her eyes flew open. The walls, gray and cold, closed round her. The light slanting in through the oiled skins far above was filled with motes of dust that drifted lazily downward. They had nowhere to go except to join others on the floor, only to be stirred up again as she scuffled through them.

Suddenly, she felt like a criminal. What a crime to bring dust in on her shoes from out of doors. How sad to think that the dust that she brought in would be a prisoner here too, even as she.

Abruptly, she stood up, shrugging her shoulders and chuckling ruefully. If she did not leave that line of thinking, she would be reduced to a quivering wet rag in a matter of minutes.

The bolt grated. Eagerly she faced the door, involuntarily raising her hands in welcome. As a result of her present emotional state, her fingers trembled with longing for human contact.

Her fears must have shown in her face, for Geoffrey's carefully impassive countenance changed to a frown. What was wrong? One silver eyebrow quirked upward interrogatively.

447

Instantly, she dropped her hands to her sides. Her eyes fell to the tray he carried. She could not suppress a slight shiver of distaste. Pressing her lips tightly together she swallowed heavily. Fish stew. Did he eat the same thing? Did all the men assigned to this moldering pile—her guards—eat the same odious mess? She could imagine such a diet inspiring a mutiny. If it did not, some would begin to sprout scales at any time.

He set the tray on the table and seated himself in the chair he had adopted as his own. "If it please you, madam, eat now, and I will escort you to the chapel for prayer. An unforeseen difficulty takes me elsewhere for the rest of the day and prevents my returning until tomorrow."

His announcement depressed her. The hours would stretch interminably until his return. Her muscles felt limp and useless. On leaden legs she crossed to the table and stared down at the tray. The usual unappetizing mess was accompanied by a lump of black bread so hard that it resisted her best efforts to break it. More wretched than she had been since any time in her imprisonment, she replaced it on her tray with a sigh. "I cannot eat this, Sir Geoffrey." She faced him squarely. "The fish is spoiled, and the bread is too hard for me to break."

Frowning, he came to the table to inspect the tray, but she held up her hand. "Be not concerned. I am not hungry anyway. I beg you let us not delay over this mess."

The chapel of Pevensey Castle stood in the center of the inner bailey. It was a crude structure devoid of any ornament. Instead of an altar, it had a rail with a rough kneeling bench before it. A cross hung on the wall behind.

Hands clasped tightly together, Joanna opened her mind to everything around her, letting her senses respond to different impressions, no matter how poor. She did not concentrate on the meaning of the Latin words. They were of little comfort although she was grateful that they served as an excuse to keep her here in this chapel until she must return to the four gray walls and the swirling dust motes.

Her hair curled riotously down the center of her back. Though tied tightly at the nape of her neck with a bit of ribbon, it refused to lie smooth and straight. Instead it waved and curled and, as a consequence, spread wildly from shoulder blade to shoulder blade. Not only did it not lie smoothly down her back, but wisps of new hair curled round her forehead and over her ears. Her face was haloed by them.

Arms folded across his chest, his weight primarily balanced over his good leg, Geoffrey viewed her from the side as she knelt in the dim chapel in the inner bailey of Pevensey. She had been his prisoner a little over a month now. Each day, he brought her food, saw to her needs, and took her to the chapel in midmorning. Today for the first time when he opened the door to her room, she had seemed different. Her face had worn a look of desperation that annoyed him. She should be accustoming herself to her existence. He had firmly closed his mind to the idea that she would be tried and burned for witchcraft.

Instead he anticipated his visits to her. Until today her eyes had always been bright, her lips curved into a smile as if his comings and goings were the highlight of her day. When she had turned away, no longer looking at him and refusing to eat her food, he had felt mightily disappointed. A tiny twinge of guilt stirred him. When he had told the cook to fix fish stew for the prisoner, he had thought it a nourishing repast but suitably humbling. It suited his idea of taming her and bending her obdurate pride. Perhaps, after all, he should vary the menu? With a frown, he dismissed the idea. Soldiers ate the same rations for months on end and prospered. She was no better than they.

As he studied the lush wealth of her hair, he was pleased to

449

remember that he had brought her a brush and comb the very next day after she had requested them. Periodically, he brought her a small pan of water to wash with. Women were different from men in that respect. Their skins were more delicate. If she but knew such luxuries were unheard of for prisoners, she would thank him for his consideration.

During the day, as now, he lingered beside her while she ate, sometimes allowing her to engage him in conversation, sometimes merely sitting silently and contemplating her. At those times he enjoyed selecting one feature and studying it. One day it might be the extreme translucent fairness of her skin; another it might be the shape of her cheek or the curve of her mouth.

But he was beginning to realize that these pleasurable pursuits were dangerous. His longing for her increased daily. When he brought her the evening meal, he dared not linger. So potent was her attraction becoming for him that he feared his own lust would choke him when he saw her in the evening. Even now the thought of their lovemaking the night of her arrival stirred him mightily. He shifted his weight uncomfortably.

She overheard the movement and hurriedly finished her prayers. Crossing herself, she rose and came to him. "I am sorry that I took so long, Sir Geoffrey. It was not intentional, I assure you." Above all she dared not let him know her real activity during her time in the chapel. He might refuse to take her out again since the purpose of this prayer was the cleansing of her supposedly bedeviled soul.

He nodded courteously. "You did not take too long. In fact, my movement was not meant to disturb you. I . . . er . . . had a cramp." He stamped his foot to demonstrate the necessity for working it out. He dared not let her know the nature of his thoughts.

She regarded him with concern. "Does your leg pain you often?"

"Oh, no," he replied truthfully. "I was in a bad way after I returned from France, but the king provided some money for my care. A physician was sent to me, and I was able to hire a larger staff of servants until I could recover my strength and resume my service to him."

She preceded him out into the sunlight of the inner bailey. "Did the money come directly from the king?"

"Again, no. He is too circumspect to do such a thing. No, I was given to understand from the physician that he had been sent by the Duchess of Clarence, Lady Margaret. I knew well then who my benefactor was, for she knows me not nor does her husband. So the care could only have come from the king." He nodded his head, a smile of satisfaction lighting his face. "Henry V forgets not his loyal men who serve him well."

"I suppose you are right," Joanna strode across the bailey to the well. Leaning her elbows on its rim, she peered down onto its mirrored surface. How ironic that the money she had provided was credited to the man who sought to take everything she owned. She drew a shuddering breath.

Geoffrey's head joined her at its edge. "Would you like a drink?" He moved to draw the bucket from its depths.

"Is this water fresh?" she asked.

"Yes."

"How can that be? I can hear the sea pounding outside the wall."

"The well was once a bubbling spring. This was a Roman fort, probably built here because a fresh spring gushed from the ground at this spot. In the Conqueror's time, he caused the keep to be added. Later the inner bailey and moat were built. But always the most important thing was kept safely enclosed—the well."

As he spoke, he drew up the bucket and held it while she cupped her hands and drank her fill of the cold sweet water. When she had finished, she scooped more into her hands and splashed her face and throat.

As the cool water coursed over her skin, she uttered a soft sound almost like a giggle. The movement turned her face up to his, and she suddenly flushed with embarrassment at the expression she read there. "I . . . that is . . . I felt hot and sticky. I have not bathed . . . ." She stopped in consternation. She feared if he knew of her discomfort, he might find ways to augment it. "That is . . . the day is very sultry." She squinted upward into the sun.

"I did not realize that you wished to bathe."

"Oh, but 'tis not necessary. You bring me water to wash with, and I use it to good advantage." She shrugged as if it were a thing of no importance. At the same time she mentally cursed herself for revealing her desires to him.

He stared at her, trying to study her dispassionately. Was it his imagination or did her face seem thinner? Suddenly, his hand snaked out and turned her face up again to the sun. Its brightness forced her to close her eyes while he stared at the dark smudges beneath them that he had taken for shadows. Likewise, the skin seemed slightly sunken at her temples as well.

At length he dropped his hand from her chin to her wrist. "Come," he commanded, his voice hard. He felt her tremble and pull back slightly, but the slenderness of her wrist in his grasp determined his course.

Their progress to the bower was so rapid that she had to run to keep up with him. Arriving slightly breathless at his heels, she was whirled into the room with unnecessary force.

"Strip off that robe!"

Her eyes widened in fear and anger. Protectively, she crossed her arms across her breasts and curved her fingers over her shoulders.

"Do not hesitate," he commanded, with an imperious wave of his hand. "I would see what I have here. Strip!"

"No. You know what you have here. Do not embarrass me

452

and degrade yourself, I beg you." Her eyes were dark tragic pools in a face altogether too white.

"Must I take your garment off myself? May I remind you that I am perfectly capable of doing so?"

She closed her eyes, drawing in a deep sustaining breath. "No. You need not remind me." Her hands fumbled at the rope belt, pulling its knot loose and letting it slither to the floor. Stooping slightly, she caught her robe around the knees and pulled it up and over her head with a crossing motion of her arms. When her head came free of its folds, she let go with one hand but used the other to sweep it in front of her for concealment.

Although the room was cool, he felt his anger begin to heat within him. Deliberately, he grasped the folds of the robe in his fist and tugged even that crude protection away from her.

With a small sound suggestive of a sob, she bowed her head.

Her body was a fragile painting of light and shade. Yet so thin. She had never been voluptuous, but she had always carried muscle uncommon in a woman. She had hunted avidly, always walking for miles to reach her quarry, frequently running after it if it fled. Now she seemed a dangerously slender shadow of herself.

"You have not been eating," he accused her angrily.

She stared down at her body as if she had never seen it. "I suppose I have not," she agreed sullenly. "What of that? I am a prisoner. Whoever heard of a fat prisoner?"

He ignored the truth of her comment. "I bring you food twice each day. You are not starved."

She raised her head but studied a stone in the wall a couple of feet to the right of his stormy eyes. "I do not care for fish stew," she said at last.

"A prisoner has not the right to complain of the fare."

"But a prisoner has the right not to eat it." She was having trouble keeping herself under control. Her anger seethed beneath the surface. A pulse throbbed in the base of her throat.

"Look at me when I address you," he commanded angrily.

Her angry eyes flicked back to his face where they locked with his own.

Ignoring her defiance, he continued his catechism. "What do you think you are doing? Are you trying to hurt yourself? You will not remain in this condition."

She set her chin stubbornly. "I have no appetite. My body tells me that I do not need to eat in order to sit or lie within these four gray walls day and night. I need no energy to walk down the hall and out across the bailey and back once a day."

Shaking his head, he set his doubled fists on his hips and stared around the room. "This room has light and heat, a bed, a table, a chair. For a prisoner to live—"

"I do not wish to live."

He gaped at her. "You lie. That is childish. Of course, you wish to live."

"Not as I am. Why should I prolong my life? Either I will live long enough to be tried for witchcraft and sentenced to the fire by a Council picked from Henry's cohorts, or I can live here as a prisoner until death releases me. I do not expect anything else from Henry because he has always hated and resented me."

Her fatalism enraged Geoffrey because it rang of truth. "You cannot know that," he objected half-heartedly. "You are liable to be found innocent."

Joanna laughed mirthlessly in his face. "By whom? If I cannot convince you who have known me all my life, how can I convince men who are seeing me perhaps for the first time?"

"The king will probably relent. He frequently grants amnesty to all prisoners." Even to himself, Geoffrey realized

454

his words sounded feeble.

Her face settled into impassive lines. "May I dress?" she requested icily.

He blinked. He could not believe that he had lost all awareness of her nudity. His eyes narrowed. "No. Wait as you are." Spinning on his heel, he practically ran from the room, slamming the door behind him but failing to bolt it.

Shrugging angrily, Joanna started to slip the robe on again but changed her mind. Let him return with what he will, she thought. I shall still not do as he commands. He will have to force the food down my throat.

Only a few swift minutes elapsed before he returned, carrying an armload of clothing. "Here." He tossed the lot on the bench and held out her boots. "Put these on. I am going to work up an appetite for you. You will be so hungry and tired that you will eat everything on your tray and then sleep soundly throughout the night."

"What do you intend?" she asked suspiciously.

"We shall go hunting."

The sparsely wooded fields beyond the Roman wall of Pevensey were not the thick green forests of Brittany, but they afforded small game and birds in plenty. The true nature of her condition was brought forcefully home to him. Before they had walked a mile, perspiration dripped from her forehead and darkened her back and the armpits of the tunic he had loaned her. Likewise, her skin flushed a bright red with the unaccustomed heat of her body.

She could not have jogged a quarter of a mile, let alone run. In the light of her weakness, he cursed himself for his foolishness. Remembering her unusual strength and speed in the hunt, he had attached a lead line to her neck and fastened it at his belt. Now her breathing sounded loud in his ears as she labored to keep up with him. She could not possibly have run away from him despite his limp.

As the sun warmed their faces, the cooling breeze from the Channel dried their perspiration. Each of them had a quiver of arrows strung at his waist, but he carried both their bows.

As they neared a wooded copse, he slowed his pace, allowing her to walk abreast. Stealing a glance at her, he was rewarded by the sight of her face alive with excitement. Her black eyes, sparkling with their old fire, scanned the area for signs of game. Her little feet walked softly, testing each step automatically, ready to withdraw if the surface on which she trod threatened to betray her presence by the slightest sound.

He put his hand on her shoulder to detain her. Silently, he slipped her bow off his back and handed it to her. His smile was reassuring as her eyes widened in amazement.

She had not really expected him to arm her for the hunt. She had hoped that he might allow a little target practice later as a sop to her feelings, but to turn her loose in an open field or forest with a bow and arrows was too much to expect.

While she stood dumfounded, feeling the fine yew grain beneath her fingers, he loosened the noose around her neck and slipped it off. Her lower lip quivered and her eyes shone with a bit more than their normal brightness, but otherwise she gave no sign that he had done anything out of the ordinary. Then, with a motion of his hand, he directed her off to the left.

Separating, they approached the copse some twenty yards apart. Each of them seasoned hunters, they made no sound. The cross breezes blowing from the Channel carried no scent into its shaded interior. They were almost within it when a tiny roebuck sprang to its feet, looking around itself with great startled eyes.

With the fluid motion of long practice that does not allow itself to be soon forgotten, she drew the arrow from the quiver and nocked it into the string. The buck was in her sight but slightly to the right was Geoffrey. He stood motionless, waiting for her to have the first shot. He also had nocked an arrow but held the bow loosely across his body, the head pointed toward the ground.

She could kill him at that moment if she chose. The broadhead would drive with deadly force into his chest, wreaking incredible damage to his lungs. If it happened to nick his heart, it would wound that muscle so that his blood would bubble out of the cavity in all directions. She could take his weapons and his purse and leave him lying there while she followed the seacoast to a town and took ship for France. Once in Brittany, her eldest son would offer her sanctuary.

In that split second as she stared at him with thoughts of murder flashing through her mind, he feared her. She was after all the daughter of a ruthless murderous prince who had never stuck at any vicious act to win victory for himself. Still, Geoffrey did not move, nor did he make an effort to raise his bow and take aim at her.

Then her body pivoted smoothly to the left. The bowstring twanged as the arrow left it. With a thud it brought the roebuck down. Before the creature could know the terror of its own wounding, it was dead, its heart and lungs torn by the cruelly efficient game arrow.

"Well shot!" he called as they moved in toward the fallen animal.

"Thank you."

Kneeling beside the carcass, he slipped his hunting knife from its sheath and prepared to field-dress the kill. "As clean a kill as I have ever seen."

"Yes," she replied. She walked a few steps away and sat down beneath a tall tree, her legs drawn up in front of her. "I could always kill whatever I chose."

The singular choice of words made him pause. Looking up quickly, he saw she sat with her bow lying athwart her knees, an arrow nocked in the string, the point aimed at his heart.

He did not still his busy hands. Long familiar with the task of field-dressing game, they continued their routine. He did not look at her again until he had finished, wiped his bloodied blade on the grass, returned it to its sheath, and wiped his fingers on a rag of cloth that he carried for that purpose.

Those simple activities finished, he rose and regarded her steadily. "Now is the time to take your choice, Joanna."

"So it would seem."

Smiling sadly, he spread his hands out from his sides. "I wait."

"No." She smiled ironically in return. "You do not. You know I will not kill you. I only choose to hear you say it. I desire to hear you say that you know this entire drama to be just that—a drama."

He dropped his hands. Instantly, the smile was wiped from his face as if it had never been. "I am loyal to my king."

"And I am your queen. As before I was your duchess."

He stared at her with eyes that turned dark with pain. "What do you want me to say?"

"I want you to tell me why you are so anxious for me to live—why are you imprisoning me, professing to hate and despise me, punishing me with coldness and with petty deprivations?"

He threw his head back, shaking it nervously in a fashion uncharacteristic to him. He had always been so controlled in his feelings. Now they seemed to be controlling him. "You speak of drama, madam. End this one."

"No. Not yet. Tell me why you became alarmed when you realized that I was allowing my life to slip away rather than continue this nonexistence?" As she spoke, she drew back on the bowstring a bit as if to test the weight of its pull.

He drew a deep shuddering breath. His gray eyes were pools of agony. He dared not give her such control of him. Yet his own desires were screaming to be heard. Suddenly, he wanted even as she did to end the drama they had been playing one against the other for over thirty years. His mouth curved in a gentle sweet smile. "Because I love you, Joanna. I love you desperately."

Her eyes filled with tears. She flung the bow and arrow aside. "Geoffrey," she cried. "Oh, Geoffrey, please come to me."

Chapter 28

Joanna lay with closed eyes while Geoffrey worked his own sorcery on her body. When his arms gathered her against him, she was almost overcome by the exertion of the hunt and the violent emotion she had endured. Her head fell back and her eyes closed as she tried to draw air into her exhausted lungs.

In a daze, she allowed him to undress her gently until she lay nude on the grass, the sun dappling her body with spots of purest gold.

His strong hand covered her breast, cupping the fullness, before titillating the nipple until it swelled with desire. "Did you ask for me?" he whispered against her ear.

Though she moaned her acquiescence, he was not satisfied with her wordless acceptance. "Tell me," he urged. "Beg for me as I have begged for you in my heart for so long."

"Please, Geoffrey, please."

"Oh, yes, Joanna. Yes, my love."

He began to kiss the tender skin beneath her ear, his lips finding her quickening pulse. "Does my kiss excite you, love?"

For answer, she clutched at the sweat-dampened locks of his silver blond hair and arched her breast upward to receive the agonizing pleasure of his mouth.

"Does that mean you want me to kiss you there?" he prodded, his words not allowing her to keep even the sheerest veil of mystery.

"Yes, oh yes . . . O-o-o-oh." Her moan was desperate. With one hand she held his head against her so he might kiss and suckle her nipple. With the other she fumbled against his thigh trying to grasp him and guide him into her.

He chuckled softly as he resisted her efforts by deftly turning his body and trapping her hand between them. "No, love. No, Joanna." He punctuated each kiss with a word. "No, Your Majesty. No."

"But, Geoffrey . . ." Her teeth were clamped tightly together as ripples of desire tore through her body. Digging her heels into the deep grass, she pushed her hips upward.

Ruthlessly, he pressed her down, using his hip and thigh to hold her immobile as he continued to kiss and tongue her throbbing nipples with exquisite precision.

"Oh, please . . ." she begged frantically.

He slipped downward, sliding in between her parted legs and mingling the stiff curly hair on his chest with the soft hair of her mount. While his hands slid under her buttocks, his tongue slipped into her navel, teasing that sensitive spot.

"My God, Geoffrey . . ."

Even as she spoke, her body stiffened. He had taken her to her limits as he had wished to do. As the waves of pleasure began to break, he pushed himself back onto his knees and plunged into her hot moist center. Her scream was high and keening, as another wave of pleasure began before her first could end. She was carried higher than she had thought possible. Her body vibrated like the string of a musical instrument so highly tuned that to play it threatens to break it. She would break. In the back of her mind was the fear that her body might be totally swept away, that she might die of love.

And yet she withstood his onslaught. Once he released

462

himself from the self-imposed bondage of the past month, he lost all control. She was his love, his woman, his wife, the mother of his children, his queen. She was every woman in the world to him. They had burned together in the fire of unrequited passion; they had suffered pain and risked death for each other. They had weathered great hatred and cruel misunderstandings from which their love had emerged whole and tough as tempered steel. His joy was such that it tore him apart. He gave and gave to her, worshiping her with the strength of his loins and the adoration of his tongue which drove into her mouth even as his manhood probed the center of her being.

So bright a flame can only last for a few minutes without consuming those who lit it. As a feral growl erupted from the depths of his being, Geoffrey poured his love into her.

Even as she felt his ecstatic shudders begin, she clasped him closer and allowed herself to surrender to the joy and the sensual pleasure of love with the only man she had ever embraced. Their soaring was a prolonged expending of power followed by a gentle descent, a floating down . . . down . . . into the security of each other's arms.

Geoffrey's last conscious act was to slide to the side, so his body would not press too heavily upon her frail strength. With his arms around her Joanna allowed herself to slip directly into a gentle untroubled peace, devoid of every sense except the sound of Geoffrey's heart beating in her ear.

"Did you die?" she whispered at last.

"Why, yes, now that you mention it," was his soft reply. She felt his lips brush the top of her head. "I believe I did . . . and soared up to heaven with an angel in my arms."

"I never felt anything like that," she confessed. "Not even when we were younger." She hugged him close.

463

He smiled faintly. "You were so determined to hate and despise me, I am surprised that you felt anything at all when we were younger."

She stirred restively against him, uncomfortable in her shame. "I can never make those days up to you," she whispered.

He hugged her close. "Precious idiot! You have nothing to make up. I have no regrets. Those days were wonderful. You were a generous woman even though you felt you were being shamed. You never withheld of yourself. My pleasure was such as many men dream of. I had a magnificently beautiful, sensual partner who matched me in youth and eagerness. That I found myself in love with her adds to my joy. My memories of our lovemaking were the happiest of my life . . . until today." He began to move his body so that it fitted itself to hers.

She raised her head from his chest to look into his face. "Truly? You truly loved me?"

He ran a deliciously probing hand up the back of her thigh, making her squirm. "Truly. How could I not?" His hand left her thigh to pull the ribbon free from her luxuriant mass of black hair. He brought its ends to his lips. "Ah, your hair. I could drown in it."

"It is turning white," she sighed softly.

He studied it in mock criticism. "Indeed. I believe you are right. There is a white hair. I shall have to devise some punishment for every one of them. What shall it be? Spankings?" He popped her behind impudently. "No. So many would hurt my hand. Kisses? Ah, the very thing. I shall kiss you in punishment for every white hair in your head."

She laughed softly and delightedly.

"I shall begin right now and . . ."

She ran her fingers through his own fair locks. "I will never know whether your hair has turned white or not," she mourned. "It is so fair that the yellow has always been silvery. Someday when I am all gone gray, people will say, 'Look at that handsome devil. What does he see in that old woman he escorts about?'"

464

Then it was his turn to laugh. "Ah, well. When that time comes, mayhap I shall look around for someone younger to avoid the shame." He yelped as she bit the tiny nipple on his chest in retribution. "On the other hand I may be so crippled by that time I will require two canes to creep about. When that time comes, people will say, 'Who is that strikingly beautiful woman? What does she see in that pitiful old derelict that she leads about by the hand?'"

Dropping an impertinent kiss on his mouth, Joanna slid down his body, kissing as she went, until she reached the misshapen mass of his knee. She began to kiss it over and over, rubbing her hair over it as if she were a Biblical woman adoring the Christ.

When he was moaning with excitement, she raised herself slowly, kissing and biting his inner thighs until he growled low in his throat and rolled her over on her back to receive his love again.

After dark when they returned to Pevensey, he did not lead her to the bower but to his own room next door. "I had wondered where you slept," she murmured as he tenderly helped her to bathe.

He led her to the bed before he made his own ablutions. "I slept as close to you as I dared. Sometimes I slept too close. I would wake up in the night aching with desire. I was determined not to repeat the shameful act I committed the first night you were in my care."

When he came to her, she welcomed him into the bed with open arms. "Geoffrey, you did not rape me. We came together out of mutual need. I loved you and accepted you."

"But you needed comfort and care."

"Forget the past," she whispered against his mouth. "The past is gone beyond recalling. We have today and tomorrow."

A December storm tossed the waves twenty-five feet up the side of Pevensey's Roman wall. White froth flowed across its twelve-foot thickness and poured down the other side. Though the rain had stopped, the day was a fall of icy turbulence. However, in Geoffrey's rooms, the fire burned brightly, and Joanna hummed a snatch of a tune as she set stitches in the embroidered hem of a pale gray tunic of softest virgin wool. When she had finished, the tunic would be decorated with an intricate design of silver, green, and red silk flowers and fanciful beasts. This motif extended four inches deep around the hem and two inches deep around the neck.

The appearance of a troop of riders galloping in through the west gate brought a guard on the run for his commander. Geoffrey hastily drew his heavy cloak around him and descended to the main hall of the keep. On the steps outside its door, he met the men. His own guards were ranged around him, their flambeaux flaring in the whipping wind.

"Who goes there?"

"Harry of Monmouth," came the terse reply.

Geoffrey gaped, peering into the blustery darkness. "Harry of Monmouth is in France."

"Was," the voice admitted. "Now he returns to prepare his way." The figure dismounted wearily from his horse and mounted the steps, his hand outstretched.

"Your Majesty." Geoffrey made to sink to one knee.

"Rise, man," the king admonished. "I come without colors."

Geoffrey stepped back to admit his monarch to the keep. "Have hot mulled wine prepared for our visitors," he ordered his aide.

While it was being brought, other guards, hastily pressed into service as footmen, scurried round, lighting the fire in the great hearth in the hall and setting a board to serve the king. The obvious rudeness of the place, the lack of a fire, the gloominess, Henry regarded approvingly. Not at all the sort of surroundings the lady was used to.

"You live in exceedingly Spartan conditions, Sir Geoffrey," he observed.

"Yes, Your Majesty. There seems little point to do otherwise. No one uses this hall. The men have taken quarters in the gatehouse. I occupy one room above; she, the other."

"I would meet with her immediately."

Geoffrey held his breath. The observation about the bareness of the hall had not gone unnoticed. What would the king think of the warm comfortable room in the tower? How would he regard Joanna in her fine wool dress with her embroidery frame before her?

"Bring her down after the meal. Sweet Jesu! What a night! I had all but forgotten that the coast of England could be so cold." He turned from the fire to face the candles now blazing on the table. The guards began to bring in platters of bread and dried fruit as well as a tureen of soup, hastily heated by the cook. Geoffrey found himself staring at the man's face. He had not seen Henry V in over three years. Although the king could not be many years over thirty, he looked almost of an age with Geoffrey. His fine dark hair was streaked with white; his smooth fair skin, reddened and chafed by the harsh wind, was deeply lined around the mouth.

D'Anglais felt a stab of pity so deep that he feared it showed in his face. Hastily, he looked away into the depth of his beaker of wine.

When the king had eaten a little, he settled back in his chair and pushed his plate away. "You set a good table, Sir Geoffrey"—he smiled tiredly—"for soldier's fare."

"Thank you, my lord. The cook is talented with soups and stews. We do very well."

"And does she do well?" Henry probed. He glanced meaningfully toward the smoke-blackened rafters.

"As well as can be expected," Geoffrey replied. "Her time

467

was not easy at first."

This time Henry's smile was cruel. "Well, send for her. I would speak with her."

Pushing back his chair, Geoffrey bowed. "With your permission I shall fetch her myself. I tend her exclusively. No one else goes near her."

"Excellent," the king nodded. "The fewer who know the better."

Motioning to the guard to pour the king more wine, Geoffrey hurried up the worn stone steps. Once inside his room, he stared at Joanna for almost a minute. Her smile of welcome gradually faded at his silence and at the sight of his stricken face.

Moving with martial sternness, she rose and came to him, placing her hands on his shoulders. With luminous eyes, she looked inquiringly into his face. "What is it?"

"The king is below. He commands your presence."

"Dear God!" She looked down at the clothing she wore. The gown was simple and fine, as were her boots and hose. Geoffrey had taken pains to buy the best materials. "He will know I am no maltreated prisoner if he sees me in this. Where is the penitent's robe?"

He shrugged as he gathered her hands together and kissed them. "I know not. I would have you go to him as you are. The sin is mine, not yours. If someone is to be punished because you are wearing decent garments to keep you comfortable and warm, then let him punish me."

She shook her head. "Are you mad? Do you wish our idyll to end in death for both? If he would destroy me, then let him. But his wrath need not fall on you too." Putting her arms around him and hugging him hard, she pressed her face against his broad chest. "You are too precious to me. To reveal what you have done for me would be useless folly."

"But—"

"We will play a little game. The king will not stay at

468

Pevensey longer than the night. He has business elsewhere in the world, and we know he does not come for a brief rest and respite from affairs of state. Anywhere else in the kingdom would be preferable to here."

"My love, he—"

"Go." She pushed him away firmly. "Find that cursed robe. Hurry, while I strip off these things and let down my hair."

A pale woman with long disordered hair hanging down her back descended the steps in a penitent's robe of coarse brown wool. Her feet were bare, for search though he might, Geoffrey could not find the rope sandals.

At her coming Henry rose from his chair, sweeping her a mock bow. "My lady."

She stiffened at the sight of him but said nothing.

He took her hand in his, pleased to find it cold and trembling. "I find you much changed," he observed, guiding her to revolve before him. "Your gown will never set the fashion at court circles, and bare feet . . . Too drafty for most. Will you sit and have a beaker of mulled wine?"

Much as she would have loved to tell him to go to the devil, Joanna found her curiosity piqued. Her spine stiff with pride, she allowed him to escort her to a chair and set her in it. "It is kind of you, Henry, to ride all this way to have a beaker of mulled wine with your stepmother in these gracious surroundings. You come in honor of the approaching Christmas season, I assume?"

"Captivity has not filed your sharp tongue, madam."

"Nor my mind. Suppose we stop insulting one another and come to the point."

His mouth tightened, then smoothed into a semblance of a smile. He hefted a beaker and regarded the contents before he spoke. "You must know that I was in France when these charges were brought against you. Tom acted as he thought best. However, on looking into the evidence against you, I

469

find your imprisonment was somewhat premature."

"Indeed? I thought so myself. I was abducted in the dead of night and brought here in secret. Most illegal for a country that boasts to the world of trial by jury."

He took a hasty swallow of wine. "Exactly. The cleric who brought charges against you has proven himself to be a disobedient troublemaker. He told tales once too often and met with an untimely end. In short, since his character is impugned, his testimony is suspect. You can be free of this place by Christmas, Joanna."

She regarded him coldly. "I assume the cleric you speak of was Friar Randolph, my confessor. So he is dead as well as my old duenna, Doña Isabella de la Alcudia."

Henry could not meet her eyes. Instead he took great care in selecting a date from the platter before him. "I believe that was the man's name. I was told the woman of whom you speak killed herself. Most unfortunate."

Joanna sighed. Two good and useful people dead for nothing . . . She tapped one forefinger on the table. "My freedom would be unconditional, with all my properties restored?"

"Unfortunately, some have been disposed of. Others were found, upon careful study, to have been illegally handed to you in the first place. Documents must be signed which will clarify all transactions and absolve all blame. Furthermore, you will have to sign over to me certain revenues which I have spent to find the truth of this matter and to prove your innocence . . . ."

"How terrible for you to have been out any moneys on my account." She made a mock-sympathetic *moue*. "I cannot imagine why the king could not say, 'Do this!' and it be done. Do you mean to tell me that not all England is eating out of the palm of your hand?"

"I tell you nothing of the sort. But I do not want an unpleasant rumor started when a signature and an appearance by you can stop it all." His mouth was hard, his jaw set in a stubborn line.

"Do the nobles of the Council whisper about the Lancastrian kings, both father and son?" She sneered. "You are not the man your father was. Whether or not he killed Richard, he never went to him for aid in his own ruin."

At the comparison to his father, Henry's face darkened with rage. "Damn you, Joanna. I need money."

"Why?"

He drew a deep calming breath. "After Christmas, I shall marry the French princess, Catherine. I sent her a gift of jewels by messenger, but they were stolen. I have not the money to replace them at this time. Her mother expects that they will be forthcoming."

Shaking her head in horror, Joanna sank back in her chair. "Henry. Oh, Henry. You cannot marry a Valois. Indeed, you must not. The blood is tainted. Catherine's father is a maniac."

Angrily, he sprang up. He had heard this argument from his brothers and from his grandmother. Gesticulating with his beaker of wine, he thundered, "Damn you all. She is beautiful and sweet. There is no taint about her. I doubt that she is Charles's daughter anyway. Queen Isabeau makes no secrets of her liaison with Burgundy."

Joanna threw up her hands at this twisted reasoning. "King or duke, they are still Valois. Mad and treacherous, every one of them. If she be Burgundy's, what sort of man would cuckold his own nephew? Until France is rid of them, the nation will be troubled."

Slapping his palm down on the table, he leaned across it toward her, his eyes alight with excitement. "I mean to see that France is rid of them in the next generation. With this marriage comes the treaty that will place me next in succession to the throne of France. I will have finished what my great-grandfather began—a union of England and

471

France under one king." His face took on a feral expression in the flickering light. With sickness in her heart, Joanna realized that ambition ruled him. He was embarking on a course that would lead to disaster for all, but he would proceed in it.

She bowed her head. With her hands clasped as though in prayer, she gave him her answer. "You cannot have my gold for a Valois."

He stared at her bent head for a full minute. His ears could not take in this defiance of his will. "What did you say?"

She raised her head. The candles' gleam reflected in her eyes. "You cannot have my gold for a Valois."

"Sweet Jesus!" His voice rose to the rafters as he smashed the beaker into the fireplace. "Can you not forget your stupid blood feud? The old days are dead. The new order changes. The old men who died hating each other—one and all are gone." He clenched his fists, enraged at her refusal.

"They may be gone," she replied fiercely, rising and stabbing her thumb toward her chest. "But I am not gone, and neither is Charles of Valois. Leave us to our feud and go marry his get if you must. But you will never line his coffers with Navarre gold."

"Navarre gold!" he howled. "Navarre gold! 'Tis English gold. To be specific, it is Lancastrian gold. She will marry a Lancastrian king. She is entitled to Lancastrian gold."

"Never."

He hung menacingly over her smaller form a moment before turning away and smashing one fist into the palm of his hand. She could hear his heavy breathing. At last he turned back to face her. "Need I remind you, madam, that I hold your life in my hands. I can bring you to trial at any moment."

"You may bring me to trial before the Council, Henry, but you have no guarantee that they will find as you want them too. No one will believe the truth of your accusations after so

472

many years. All will wonder why you have waited so long to bring charges against me."

"I have spared you out of pity because you were my father's wife."

"Then let me go free if you pity me."

"I would do so, if you will give me that which I require. My father was insane to make those marriage contracts."

"No," she replied proudly. "He knew for whom he bargained. I am the sister of Navarre and the mother of Brittany and Richemont." As she spoke the words, she knew they were true. Even though her kinsmen might be far away, they would rally round her should she ever need them. They would not do so because they loved her, but because where she stood she held the key against their adversary, Valois. Never had the power of alliance meant so much to her as at that moment. Suddenly, all the schemes and dreams of the raider princes made perfect sense. "You are protected from the full power of France by my kin," she reminded him.

His expression changed minimally, as if he suddenly realized the truth even as she did. "They reject you one and all," he sneered. "Richemont will never forget how you refused to pay his ransom."

"My refusal reminded him where his real loyalties lay," she replied smoothly. "He had already met defeat through Valois' stupid tactics at Agincourt. He felt deeply the shame of his actions."

"He does not feel so much shame that he would ransom you," Henry insisted sullenly. "You are alone. Navarre, Richemont, Brittany. One and all, they reject you. They would not know whether you lived or died."

"You need them. You must keep me alive."

"Only if you give me what I need." He caught her wrists and held them, forcing her to face him. "Think, Joanna, a signature on a paper and you can return to Havering-atte-Bower. You can even come to court again. Give me what I need and I will spare you." When she tried to look away, he shifted his hold to her shoulders, his eyes dark with anger and something more. A flicker of admiration burned there.

Wearily, she shook her head. "I cannot give you the money, Henry. Believe me when I say were it for any other than a Valois I would do it. You need to marry. Your father wanted a Lancastrian dynasty. But Valois is not the way."

With a wild oath, he flung her from him. "Damn you. Who are you to gainsay me? You are in prison in this ancient ruin. Yet you dare to defy me. By God, I shall sign the order for your execution tomorrow."

She stumbled away from him but caught at the side of the table and righted herself. "You dare not. 'Twould mar your wedding plans for sure. The Council must have mixed feelings about this Valois marriage. You need them behind you to a man. You spend too much time in France as it is. An absent monarch is always a temptation. How does the Earl of March fare these days?"

He struck her then, hard across the face with the back of his hand. The traditional queen's ring which he had donned on his little finger to give to Catherine on their wedding day, the ring which Joanna herself had worn until she had surrendered it to him at his coronation, cut her chin. She cried out more from shock and fear than from pain.

"I bid you good night, madam. I shall not see you again in this life. Remain here for so long as you live."

"God keep you, Henry," was all she said.

With a loud shout, he called for Geoffrey. "Take this creature back to her cell and see that she is kept close," he commanded. "I will stay the night here in the hall. Have a bed prepared for me and for my men."

"'Tis only your bed that is lacking, Your Majesty. All the others have retired in the gatehouse with my men." Geoffrey's silver eyes flashed at the sight of the blood on Joanna's chin. Her back to the king, she shook her head slightly in warning. He placed his big warm hand under her arms and began to lead her from the hall.

"Do you not curse me, witch?" Henry's angry voice halted them in their tracks.

She turned back with a sad smile. "I have no need to curse you. My curse would be a waste of breath and time. Your curse will come from Valois, not from Navarre . . . never from Navarre, my poor ambitious princeling."

Chapter 29

"Damn his immortal soul to hell! Damn! Oh, damn him!"

"Shh-shh, Geoffrey! He will hear you!" Joanna laid her fingertips across her lover's lips. She had never seen Geoffrey so angry. His face was literally drained of all color. Deadly white he seethed with a rage so terrible that he could barely articulate the words.

"I carried out his evil orders to punish you. If I had not been so in love with you, I would have continued to do so, making your life miserable, torturing you with rough quarters and bad food. You might be dead now. Oh, my God!" He caught her to him, burying his face in the long loose fall of her hair. "Oh, my God!" he gasped, his words sounding more like a sob than ever.

"Geoffrey, oh my dear." She took his face between both her palms and pressed feverish kisses on his lips. "Oh, I do love you."

"He is a thief. The King of England is naught but a cowardly skulking robber of widows." He was off again, his anger boiling within him. "Worse! He blackened your name with a charge of witchcraft. You could have been burned at the stake after being subjected to hideous torture."

She kissed him again to silence him, holding his face with her hands while she moved her body against his in a long, tender caress. After a moment, she felt him tremble as his rage turned to awareness. Beneath the penitent's robe, her body was bare. She wore no shoes or hose, no undergown or chemise. His heat began to seep through its coarse material.

He caught her wrists in both hands and pushed himself free of her. "Are you trying to seduce me from my purpose?" he whispered huskily.

"Me?" She stepped back and bowed her head. "Surely you see that such a thing would be impossible. I am clad in the rudest of garments. Beneath this simple robe I am as bare as the day of my birth. A fine lady in silks and velvets might seduce you. A lady whose soft white body was perfumed and powdered might seduce you. Unfortunately, I am only a humble and repentant prisoner, heartily sorry for my sins and eager to make restitution in any way I can."

"I know a way," he growled. Grinning wickedly, he stepped forward and whisked up her gown. His hands swept up her thighs and clasped her buttocks. Holding her tightly, he lifted her against him, allowing her to feel his manhood, hard and ready for her.

"My sins are many," she gasped clasping her arms around his neck.

"Then you must pay for them one and all."

She kissed him deeply, caressing the interior of his mouth with her tongue and running her palms over the nape of his neck and around his ears. He gasped with pleasure and hugged her even closer.

"Should you not be seeing to the comfort of the king?" she whispered.

"Let him find his own comfort," he replied, kissing her throat and sliding her body ever so slightly up and down.

"But . . . Geoffrey, please . . . I cannot think . . . did he not expect you to return . . . oo-oo-oh?"

He lifted her higher, until her thighs clasped round his waist. His teeth nipped the ruby tip of her breast. "I do not care whether you think or not. I want you to feel."

Arching her back, she tightened her thighs around him. "Ah, Geoffrey . . ."

One hand fumbled at his clothing unlacing the points of his codpiece. Joanna could not suppress her small cry of excitement as she felt his hard maleness touch her softness. His hands rested on her hips to guide her as she sank onto his throbbing shaft.

Then they were moving in unison, the only sounds in the room their groans of exquisite pleasure. He had never felt so strong and hard before. She had never felt such a depth of pleasure. She wanted to scream and shout. Instead, tears of happiness wet her cheeks as she experienced a sweeping climax that left her entire body limply impaled on his rod.

A second later, he was consumed by his own fiery explosion.

With a final expenditure of strength he was able to move the few feet necessary across the room to the big bed they shared. He tumbled onto it, Joanna still locked in his passionate embrace. "My love." He kissed her ear and the side of her throat. "Did you enjoy that?"

She lay on her back, staring at the ceiling as if hypnotized. "I did not imagine that such pleasure was possible," she responded at last.

"Anger is a powerful stimulus."

"I thought the stimulus was love."

"Of course, you are right. I was only angry because of my love for you. 'Twas your kiss that drove me wild." He kissed her again.

"I am so glad," she whispered as she stroked his nape and back. Her touch sent little erotic shudders of pleasure down his spine, and he set his teeth to suppress a feral growl. "I love driving you wild."

"This is madness!" he exclaimed at last, as he rolled off her to sprawl on his back. "I must attend the king."

"I know," she agreed. "But now you will be calm and dispassionate."

He winced at the word dispassionate, rolling his head from side to side. "How can you make jokes at a time like this?"

"Because I am happy. I am incredibly happy. At last you know the truth. The last terrible doubt is erased from your mind forever." She raised herself on one elbow to stare into his silvery eyes. "Now you belong to me forever."

His hand lazily rose to cup the back of her head and bring her mouth to within an inch of his. "Yes, I do. I really do." With that, he kissed her long and lovingly.

"You must escape this hole, " he told her the next day.

Her entire face lighted at the word.

The king and his troop had ridden out at dawn, bound for London and the brilliance of the Christmas court. From the window in Geoffrey's room, Joanna had watched them ride away. Her tiny sigh of disappointment had not gone unnoticed.

"I will make arrangements for passage to France for both of us."

At his words her face darkened. She shook her head. "I cannot go to France, and neither can you."

He looked at her inquiringly. "Why not, pray tell?"

"That move would offer him a perfect opportunity. He could take everything without a murmur of protest from anyone. Furthermore, where would we go but to Brittany? Our arrival would cause embarrassment for Jean Charles. If Henry were to bring about this French marriage, then Brittany would be in a precarious position. Both France and England would be aligned against her." Her forehead wrinkled in thought.

He folded his arms across his chest. "I am willing to take you anywhere you say, for this much is certain: you cannot stay here for the rest of your life in this one room, nor for that matter can I."

She shrugged unhappily. "I suppose you could leave at any time."

Disgustedly, his eyes slid away to study a spot on the wall some distance beyond her head. "Of course. Why did I not think of that? I will pack up and clear out tomorrow. I can think of nothing to keep *me* here."

His sarcasm brought a smile to her face. "Well, you could," she insisted in a small voice.

"No." He bent over to kiss her on the forehead. "I could not. Not ever."

She caught his hand as he straightened and pressed her cheek against it. "There must be someone who can help us. Someone in England must have some influence on our behalf."

"Henry is king." Geoffrey's voice was eloquent with despair.

"Is there no one on the Council to whom he would listen?"

Geoffrey shrugged. "He trusts no one. He sees them all as possible supporters of the Earl of March. Anyone who opposes his wishes, he regards with suspicion."

"His brothers?"

Geoffrey shrugged. "He trusts them, 'tis certain, but none would be willing to do us a favor."

"Until this happened, I exchanged letters with Margaret."

Geoffrey looked puzzled. "Mean you the Countess of Pembroke?"

Joanna whirled. "The king's great-aunt! I had forgotten about her. No, I did not mean her, I meant Clarence's wife. But, of course, Lady Pembroke is the one to help us . . . if she will. The king can have no cause to doubt his own great-aunt." Joanna clapped her hands excitedly. "She is our best hope. I have talked with her on several different occasions. She can, indeed, help us if she only will."

"She will be hard to reach." Geoffrey shook his head doubtfully. "She is old. She comes very seldom to court. I doubt she will be there for the Christmas festivities."

"She is the one who can intervene," Joanna reasserted positively. "Somehow you must reach her."

"As soon as may be, my love." He kissed her soundly.

Fully half a year elapsed before Geoffrey found his way to the side of the Countess of Pembroke. Before Christmas, Joanna contracted an inflammation of the lungs that kept her in bed for the whole of the season. While the channel gales howled outside the windows and the sea leaped high on the walls of Pevensey Keep, Geoffrey tended the fires all night long to keep the room warm.

Even after the fever had subsided, Joanna could do little. She had lost flesh, and sometimes the look in her eyes frightened Geoffrey.

When she thought he did not watch, Joanna allowed her mind to drift. As she thought back, she could never remember being ill. Even when she had given birth to her children, she had not spent more than a few days in bed, and those more for form's sake than from actual weakness. Now she felt drained of energy as well as desire.

Why fight the smothering rattle in her lungs? Why try to lift her head or bend her back when her spine hurt if she attempted to do so? Why drink the liquids Geoffrey constantly offered her when the warm darkness beckoned?

Only by constant attention did he drag her back from the edge. His efforts left him fearful and exhausted but doubly determined to secure her release. Seeing the dark shadows under her eyes and the hollows beneath her cheekbones, he rained deep curses on his king.

At last, in June, he felt he might leave her. Her strength was much improved. Although her complexion remained pale and colorless, the trembling weakness had left her limbs.

"I leave tomorrow," he told her the night before the solstice. "I dare not wait too long. The countess must communicate with the king, and then he must sign letters of release and restoration."

Joanna shivered in his arms. "I want you to go, my love, yet I am afraid. Perhaps . . . oh, I dare not say it. Who knows what may happen? The countess may be dead; we might not have heard. If she be alive, she is still a very old lady. She may not give you an audience, or she may not be sympathetic when she hears your plea."

He raised himself on one elbow and looked down into her pale, drawn face. "We have decided on this course of action. Do not contemplate failure. If all happens as you say, then I will simply take you away from here. You cannot survive another winter in Pevensey. If she will not free you, you and I will simply disappear. You will come with me while I sell my sword. Perhaps we shall go on Crusade." He kissed her forehead, her nose, and her lips.

She returned his kiss with a tremulous smile. "I would go anywhere, so long as I could be with you."

Later in the dark, he lay beside her, flexing his right arm. He might tell sweet tales to her but never to himself. He was too old to sell his sword. He had not couched a lance in a joust in years. A thin film of liquid formed on his forehead as he realized that their only hope lay in the Countess of Pembroke.

To Geoffrey's surprise, he was ushered immediately into the presence of the sharp-eyed lady. The last surviving child of Edward III, the Countess of Pembroke could no longer stand unassisted. Her face was a mass of wrinkles and the widow's peak in the center of her forehead was white as snow.

"Who did you say you were?" she asked without preamble.

He made a deep reverence to her. "Sir Geoffrey Fitzjean d'Anglais, Your Grace."

"Ah." She drew a little gasping breath and raised one withered hand rubbing it quite vigorously against the center of her forehead. "Who was your father, sirrah?"

His face stiffened at the affrontery of her question but he answered with good grace. "I have none that I know of. I am a bastard taken from a monastery."

"Ah," she nodded. "By whom?"

"I beg your pardon."

"I asked, 'By whom'?" she repeated impatiently. "By whom were you taken from a monastery?"

"I was taken into service by His Grace the Duke of Brittany, Jean de Montfort," Geoffrey replied haughtily.

"Ah," she smiled. "My sister Mary's husband."

He looked startled. He had forgotten the duke's first wife had been a Plantagenet.

"Poor Mary," the countess sighed. "Never able to have children. How we all pitied her. Such a handsome man, the duke."

Geoffrey looked doubtful. In his own memory the duke was not a handsome man. Montfort's twisted, almost demonic figure rose in his mind, and at the same time he could almost feel arthritic hands clutching his flesh.

The countess caught his look. "Oh, I do not doubt you do not remember him so. What do you see before you now? A woman who once laughed and flirted and danced with the best of them? No, you see a crippled, wizened old crone. So it was with Montfort. *He* laughed and danced and flirted with the best of us. You are young yet. You will see."

"Your Grace, I see a beautiful woman whose spirit shines from her eyes." Geoffrey kissed the fragile hand.

"Ah . . ." The countess seemed pleased. She smiled up at him, confirming the charming compliment he had paid her. "Please be seated, Geoffrey. I may call you Geoffrey, may I not? I will have a light refreshment brought to us. Then later this evening when we dine, you may continue to pay me those wonderful compliments." She rang a small bell and then placed it on the table at her side. A servitor appeared with a tray of candied fruits and a very pale ale in a crystal pitcher. "Now." She folded her hands when he had gone. "Tell me why you come to Pembroke."

Geoffrey found he could talk to this kind lady much more easily than he had ever imagined. Her sweet smile relaxed his vigilance. He felt himself to be a youth telling a favorite aunt a story. At least, he thought briefly, this must be how a youth who had such a relationship would feel. He began at the beginning, telling of Joanna's marriage to the duke because of her connections on the continent.

"You need not go quite that far back, young Geoffrey," Lady Margaret interrupted, selecting a candied date to pop into her mouth. "The life of the Duke of Brittany is well known to me."

A slight frown creased Geoffrey's forehead. Was she perhaps toying with him? Did she intend to help him or did she not? Mentally, he shrugged. Whether she did or not, he must fulfill his mission. She was his hope of freedom. He smiled. "Of course, Your Grace." He took a deep breath. "Queen Joanna served Henry of Lancaster long and well. Through the long years while he fought the Percys and the Welsh, she presided over the Council. During his extended illness she was ever faithful."

"Ah, yes, poor Henry." Margaret sighed. "He suffered much. Did he look bad toward the last? I never saw him, you know."

"You would have found him much changed, Your Grace."

"Do not spare me, Sir Geoffrey. Was he hideously disfigured?"

He paused only a second. "Yes, my lady. Most hideously."

The countess bowed her head. "Poor man. He so wanted to be king. What a terrible price to pay. Did he believe he was accursed?"

"I fear he did," was the reply. "The disease was so painful, and yet he did not die. He thought he was being punished by God while he was on earth as a sign to all his subjects. He spoke often of Crusade. He longed to go to Jerusalem. As it was, he died in the chamber of Westminster called Jerusalem."

Fumbling for a handkerchief, she shook her head. "I had

heard that he did, but thought it superstitious rumor. So much of rumor and half-truth is attached to my unfortunate family. The death of my brother Edward was the most terrible loss that England ever suffered. Had he lived, he would have been the unquestioned monarch. He was reared by our father to take the throne, and he would have demanded and received loyalty from his brothers. As it was, they fought among themselves."

Geoffrey waited impatiently. The old lady's memories were precious to her, but he felt his own nerves begin to wear thin. "The queen suffers today for something she had no part in," he prodded gently.

"Doubtless," Lady Margaret agreed. "She has been an extraordinarily valuable pawn. Do I understand you to say that she still is?"

Geoffrey nodded.

"Dear me. How tragic! Usually when a woman passes childbearing age, her usefulness is at an end."

Geoffrey spoke carefully seeking to prove Joanna's worth without damaging the king's reputation. After all, to do so was treason and his listener was the king's great-aunt. "For loyalty and service to him beyond that of a mere wife, King Henry IV rewarded her with many lands and revenues."

"Ah. Then I see. She is very wealthy." The countess looked around her at her modest bower. The tapestries were a little faded. "Sometimes I think I would like to have a bit more than Pembroke left me, but then I hear of something like this." She shook her head. "'Tis not uncommon, unfortunately, the imprisoning of a helpless woman when someone stronger wants her lands."

"The present king is badly in need of money," Geoffrey continued softly.

"He would not be asking if he were not," came the dry response.

"He has recently married the Valois princess Catherine. To impress her and appease her father, he needs money for rich

486

gifts. He also needs money to pay for the war in France."

Margaret sighed. "He has many ambitions. To marry a Valois . . . Tsk! I dislike the combination. Plantagenet blood runs hot enough without pouring in a cup of Valois madness." She looked thoughtful.

"So the queen warned him," Geoffrey hastened to insert.

"Poor Joanna," Margaret mourned. "I would not be in her shoes for anything."

Geoffrey took his courage in his hands. "Lady Margaret, can you help us?"

She looked startled. Her bright blue eyes opened wide, then closed appraisingly. "Me? An old woman like me? Surely you have wasted your ride for nothing, young man. I have no influence. I can help no one."

"But perhaps you can. You are his great-aunt. You take no sides in this thing. No member of the Council can speak against him without his springing to defend himself. He fears they side with the Earl of March."

"He has right to fear. The Marcher lords stir every so often and the Welsh to the north are always restless."

"If you would write him a letter. Intervene in Joanna's . . . that is . . . in Her Majesty's behalf."

"I heard you call her by her name the first time, Sir Geoffrey. So you have fallen in love with a royal widow. How nice for her!" She touched her own cheeks lightly. "There was a time, shortly after Pembroke's death, when I would have eagerly welcomed a knight errant such as yourself."

He smiled wanly. His voice lowered in the depth of his intensity, he said, "Lady Margaret, she has been imprisoned for nine months in Pevensey Castle. She was very ill this winter. The lung fever. I thought she would die. She cannot live another winter in that hulk. The sea comes crashing in during great storms and leaps over the walls. It is no comfortable manor house such as this." He looked around him at the elegant shining furniture, the light and air in this bower room, the fine foods on the silver tray. "The keep is only three rooms. A hall downstairs and two rooms above. One is mine, the other hers. Her captivity does not even allow a woman to care for her needs. I have only a small troop of guards, mostly old men like myself as yet too young to be released from service."

When his voice choked at the end, he rested his forehead in his hand.

Her voice came softly to him. "My dear young man, I feel very deeply for her and yet I envy her. You have traveled halfway across England to seek help for her. Despite her desperate plight, she is fortunate. I would that someone loved me as you love her. How may I help you?"

He threw up his head. His gray eyes were silvery with unshed tears. "By interceding for her with the king. Surely, he will not deny your petition. He has married the French princess Catherine. He will in all probability declare a general amnesty. With your petition, he would release her to return home to the small palace Henry left her outside of London. There a modicum of comfort could be restored to her life."

Margaret looked at him for a full minute. His tall, spare form retained its youthful slimness. The skin of his face, though lined, stretched over good strong bones. Because of the extraordinary lightness of his hair, he would go completely white before the change would be noticeable. She drew a deep breath. "My dear Geoffrey, you should carry more weight than I. After all, you are the illegitimate son of the Duke of Brittany. Jean de Montfort was your father."

Geoffrey's face drained of all color. Abruptly, he rose and strode across the room. With every nerve in his body on fire, he quivered like a highly bred horse. At last, he turned back toward her, his face stripped of all emotion. "I had always thought perhaps I was. He named me Fitzjean and knighted me at the christening of his first son by Joanna. I believed then that he was trying to give me status to make up for being born without any."

"He would have legitimized you if he could." Margaret nodded sadly. "I am glad to hear that he did such. It was a great family scandal. No one knew quite what to do about it."

He shrugged an expressive shoulder. "Why should it be such a family scandal? Bastards are born every day. Either the father claims them, or he tucks them away in monasteries to be raised for the Church. No shame falls on him."

"Oh, the shame was not on him." Margaret held out her hand to him. "Come here, dear boy."

When he came, she took his hand and pulled him down to kneel before her. Taking his face in both hands, she kissed him gently on both cheeks. The sapphire blue eyes shone with tears. "Dear boy, the Plantagenets owe you so much, you should have whatever boon you ask."

He looked up, puzzled, into a face alight with love and pity.

"You are my nephew. You are the son of my sister Joan. She was the younger sister of Mary, who was Jean's first wife. I had two sisters you see. One married him and one loved him."

Geoffrey shuddered. His lean brown hand fumbled to catch the arm of her chair to keep from toppling over. "What are you saying?"

"Joan was a beautiful creature. I like to think that we were all beautiful young girls. There were four of us. I am the last now. All of us gone. Out of nine children, I am the last. I married Pembroke; he was a good kind man not much given to court politics, but loyal. Isabel married Ingelram de Coucy. Poor Isabel, a political marriage that did not serve her well. Her troubles are happily over. Mary married Jean de Montfort, another political marriage. My father wanted the suzerainty of Brittany in the pocket of the English crown—so the marriage. But Jean could not assume his seat immediately. He remained for a long time in England. There we saw Joan. She was beautiful and wild and young—a most dangerous combination. Mary had miscarried. Dear heaven bless her! She never did have any children."

The countess paused for breath. Now that she had begun, she shivered in the grip of intense emotion as memories flooded her mind.

On his part, Geoffrey sank back on his heels mesmerized. The shock was too much. His mind refused to function. He could only gape in astonishment.

Helping herself to a sip of ale, Lady Margaret continued. "Jean saw Joan after he was already betrothed to Mary. She was the youngest of us. Her hair was like spun gold, even as yours must have been when you were a boy, and her eyes were blue as cornflowers. I cannot tell you how blue. And she loved to dance. Mary could not dance after she grew so heavy with child, and since Jean was a fair dancer in his day, they danced together and laughed together. Poor Mary watched in agony. Oh, it was terrible to watch. After the child was born dead, Mary withdrew into herself. I doubt that she would let Jean touch her. She got so thin and pale that we feared for her health. Then Jean had to go to France to claim the suzerainty. He fought a great battle and was terribly wounded there."

"While he was gone, the whole terrible scandal surfaced. Joan could no longer conceal her shame. Our father was furious. He shut her up in a convent. Of course, no blame was attached to Montfort. He was by that time the duke. Joan admitted that she had desired her sister's husband and had deliberately sought his love. After she entered the convent you were born and then she was sent away through the religious houses. No one knows where she went. She was dead to us all."

"Dear God," Geoffrey breathed.

"Ah, yes." Margaret sighed. "After Montfort won the duchy, he came back for Mary, but his gray eyes searched everywhere for Joan. I think Isabel finally told him. She hated him, for she had always taken Mary's part. They were much closer than Mary and I were. I never did hear what his reaction was. Mary went with him to Brittany, but she did not live long. When she died, he came to England for you and took you back with him. I sometimes wonder if he ever found Joan."

Lady Margaret sank back in her chair, exhausted. "Dear heaven"—she looked at the lengthening shadows—"we have talked the afternoon away. That is to say, I have. You have listened until you must feel numb."

Geoffrey blinked like a man coming out of a deep sleep. He rubbed a hand across the lower half of his face. "Are you saying then? . . ."

She smiled sweetly. "You are the grandson of Edward III and my nephew. Henry IV was your first cousin. You are the king's uncle."

He rose, his figure as straight as a lance. "Does His Majesty know?"

She shrugged. "I am sure he does. The Plantagenets know their own."

Chapter 30

The king was at Leicester, the castle of his grandfather, John of Gaunt, when Geoffrey found him. The castle had passed from the hands of Katherine Swynford, old Gaunt's mistress, back to his only legitimate son, Henry Bolingbroke. At his death it was among the dower lands and revenues settled on the queen. Since Mary of Bohun, the king's mother, had died five years before Gaunt's death, she had probably never been in the castle.

Appreciating the irony of the king's using his mother as an excuse to possess it, Geoffrey requested an immediate audience. To his surprise, he was ushered into the royal presence with dispatch. Though he would have denied any alteration of his feelings about himself, anyone who knew him well would have noticed that his bearing had changed perceptibly. He did not hold his head higher or his back straighter, but the look in his eyes was different.

At the sight of his monarch the older man frowned. Henry wore a scarlet tunic elaborately embroidered with the golden lions of England and the silver lilies of France. Above the rich colors his face looked unaccountably pale. Purplish smudges made his dark eyes look more deeply set than normal. Round him stood the strong young men of his cadre, his brothers among them. By contrast, the king seemed almost out of place; his fragility was apparent to even the most casual glance.

When he caught sight of Geoffrey, he frowned. Bending his lips to the ear of his small queen, he excused himself, first to her and then to the small circle surrounding her. His dark eyes grim despite his smiling face, he came forward with arm outstretched. "Perhaps we should walk in the garden, d'Anglais," he suggested.

"If it please Your Majesty to do so," Geoffrey smiled pleasantly.

"I think it would be most appropriate. I fear to hear the news you bear. 'Tis sad, I am sure." The gaunt pale face showed no emotion.

"Sad indeed."

Together they passed out through double doors into the quiet garden. The bees hummed about the riot of colorful blossoms. The king walked carefully as if he feared to take a step that might jar him. When they came to a small bench in a circle formed by a hedge, Henry lowered himself gently to the bench. "Now, d'Anglais, tell me what has happened."

"Shortly after you left, the queen fell very will with lung fever."

"I see." The king studied a white pebble to the right of his shoe.

"I nursed her faithfully, and with careful tending she recovered. She is even now at Pevensey, awaiting my return."

Henry looked up, startled. His dark eyes flashed. "She did not die."

"No, Your Majesty. Although her spirits sank to a frightening depth, they rose again when she began to regain her strength." Geoffrey's eyes locked with the younger man's.

If the king was disappointed, he masked his disappointment well. "She is in health even now?"

"She was when I left her."

Henry released a long breath as if he had been holding it and himself tightly in check. With the toe of his boot he turned the white pebble over, exposing the moist earth beneath it. When he spoke, his voice was low and vibrant. "Then why have you left her?"

Geoffrey's expression did not change, but his pale gray eyes darkened slightly, taking on a more metallic sheen. "I have come to effect her return to her palace at Havering-atte-Bower."

The king's jaw tightened as his eyes narrowed menacingly. "Her return?"

"Yes, Your Majesty. Her health has proved to be precarious in the straitened conditions imposed upon her by her residence in Pevensey Keep. The elements on the Sussex coast are too harsh for a lady of her fine breeding to bear."

The king rose, planting himself toe to toe with his vassal. Their eyes locked in a combat of wills. In his mind Henry could hear Joanna's ironic voice. *"I thought the king could day 'Do this' and it be done."* Apparently, the king could never say anything of the kind. His anger rose. "My last command was that she was to remain as she was."

Geoffrey did not move. His silver-blond leonine crest rose at least four inches above the king's cap of dark brown. "I felt Your Majesty might reconsider since the time has been so long and the charges are nonspecific."

"The charges are witchcraft and necromancy."

"But there has been no proof advanced. No notice his been given to the Council of a forthcoming trial." Geoffrey chose his words carefully. Beneath the gray tunic he could feel the sweat rolling in great drops down his spine. "My understanding at the time of your visit was that efforts were being made to secure her release."

"Witnesses have been questioned, but nothing has been done," Henry acknowledged sarcastically. "I have been busy as you see with affairs important to the nation and the whole of western Europe. What is one person compared to the welfare and safety of thousands?"

"My feelings exactly," Geoffrey replied smoothly. "She is of little importance. Her situation need not merit attention. But until such time as you may turn your attention to her, since she is the Queen Mother and therefore subject to you and only you, I thought to preserve her."

"She is safe enough where she is," Henry insisted mutinously. Why did he feel as if he were being addressed like a recalcitrant child?

"Ah, but she is not. 'Twould be a great tragedy should an innocent woman, particularly one of such stature in the eyes of Europe, die through neglect on your part."

Henry clenched his fists. "She is not neglected! God! Your very presence here demonstrates how carefully she is protected. She was charged with endangering my life. High treason! The Council would make short work of her if she were brought to trial. When I put her in your care, I sought to preserve her until I could devote more time to her case."

"I fear for her life if she must endure another winter at Pevensey." Geoffrey insisted.

"I found the evening I passed there adequate."

"You are a hardened campaign veteran," Geoffrey reminded him. "She is a small woman who, moreover, has been cosseted all her life. Until she was taken into captivity, she still retained a duenna who waited on her hand and foot."

At the mention of the duenna, Henry's dark gaze faltered. He had been angry at the news of the woman's death. Her loss had deprived him of an important witness.

He shook his head. "What you ask, d'Anglais, is too dangerous. For myself, I do not really believe all this talk of witchcraft, but I dare not take any chances. She opposed my marriage to Catherine. Now the queen is with child. I would allow no one loose in the kingdom that might discomfort her."

"I shall be responsible for her both night and day at her

own palace in Essex," Geoffrey promised.

"I cannot take the chance. Who are you after all? You were associated with her in Brittany. Perhaps you might be in league with her?"

"I am sure Your Majesty does not believe that. Although I spent my adolescence in Brittany, I returned here with your father in 1397. 'Tis now a quarter of a century since then. Add to that the fact that I was born English. No one has ever had cause to doubt my loyalty to the Plantagenets." These last words were said with a peculiar significance.

Henry's eyes narrowed. "This situation cannot be decided in a few minutes. I must have time to consider it. Will you take supper with us tonight, Sir Geoffrey?"

Knowing he had achieved all he could at the moment, Geoffrey smiled. "I should like that above all things."

The royal gathering in the great hall of Leicester should have been a scene of great happiness. Later in thinking back on it, Geoffrey could only remember that it had been an uncomfortable evening for almost everyone.

Thomas, Duke of Clarence, the king's next brother sat beside Geoffrey. He barely touched his food but kept a servitor busy filling his wine glass. His fair young face shone bright red and was unpleasantly bloated.

Beyond him sat his wife, Margaret, a grim woman much older than he. Their marriage had not been blessed with children. She did not return Geoffrey's smile, but kept darting sour looks at her husband as he became more and more oblivious to the celebration around him. "I must thank you for your physician, Your Grace," Geoffrey remarked in an effort to distract her after a particularly loud belch from the duke.

She blinked as if his statement had no meaning. "I? I sent you no physician."

"I doubt not that you acted as intermediary for another,"

he acknowledged suavely. "But the man was a *nonpareil*. He was able to restore me to the prime of health."

"I sent you no physician," she insisted crossly. "'Twas Joanna that I acted for. She had heard that you had returned from France sick and weak. In all her letters she ever inquired after your health. When I told her of your condition, she insisted on providing moneys for your care."

Geoffrey felt the blood drain from his face. "You are saying that my care was paid for by the Queen Mother."

"Oh, yes. She has dispensed much largesse through me since she retired from court. We correspond, you know. Although I have not heard from her in several months. I have meant to make inquiries, but . . ." She looked significantly in the direction of her husband who now propped his forehead on his hand between swallows.

Incredulously, Geoffrey felt a bitterness rise in his mouth as he remembered his effusive praising of the king's generosity. Joanna had said nothing but had let the king take the credit for her acts. It was even more incredible that she had sent money for his care. Why had she done so, when they had parted on such an angry note? Silently he vowed to broach the subject to her at the first opportunity.

Oblivious to the talk flowing around him, he continued to think furiously. He dared not fail her now. Henry did not seem averse to the suggestion to return her to her palace, but he did not offer any hope either. Somehow the king must be convinced that she could do him no harm.

Geoffrey glanced down the table at the French princess. Catherine was smiling shyly at the people around her. She did not speak or understand much English yet. Although the king spoke fluent French, he conversed more with his brother John, the Duke of Bedford, than with his queen.

On the other side of the duke sat his new French wife, the lady Anne, daughter of the Duke of Burgundy and cousin to the queen. Like a doll she sat beside her new young husband who paid not a whit of attention to her. As Geoffrey watched, she began to trace a pattern with her fingernail in the table linen. Her lower lip protruded in a pout of dissatisfaction.

Looking around the table, Geoffrey studied the faces of the other women. Many were French, ladies-in-waiting to the princess and duchess, and most spoke no English at all. Paired with English gentlemen at the table, they looked supremely bored and drank their wine steadily, the expression in their eyes becoming more and more glassy. Across their bodies the men carried on conversations not understood by their companions. Here and there an occasional couple engaged in a laughing flirtation.

Geoffrey lifted his wine to his lips to conceal a rather rueful smile. He was the old man at the board; his deeply lined face stood out among the smooth countenances. Doubtless young women the world over looked the same. The tragedy of this particular gathering, indeed of this particular court, lay in the absence of gray heads and lined faces. No older generation had been allowed to pass on its advice to its successors.

He stared hard at the king. At thirty-three, Henry V was the oldest man in the room. He had dismissed all the old councilors of Henry IV; he had sent his uncles, Dorset and Arundel, from court; and he had imprisoned the Queen Mother.

As he watched, the king and Bedford were engaged in urgent conversation. Their faces showed worry and irritation. Bedford shook his head adamantly; the king gesticulated with an open hand.

Once he glanced at Geoffrey and as quickly looked away. What his feelings were, Geoffrey could not tell. Geoffrey took another deep swallow of wine, then set down the goblet with a look of disgust. Only a fool would drink wine when he needed all his wits about him. The king might summon him at any moment, or he might wait until the morning. Nevertheless, a representative who was drunk or ill from the effects of drink would do more harm than good for the queen's case. With a deep breath, he put his goblet by him and devoted himself to meat for the rest of the evening.

The conversation that he sought did not come until just before a tennis game the following afternoon. Dressed in parti-colored chausses and a fine loose cambric shirt, the king stretched at ease on a bench in the garden. He looked for all the world like a weary young boy who has played until he is exhausted. Dots of perspiration stood on his forehead and his shirt was stippled with damp.

"D'Anglais?" he asked, without opening his eyes at the crunch of footsteps in the gravel.

"Your Majesty, I fear I intrude upon your rest."

"You do indeed," the king remarked pettishly, "but I want this problem that you pose to go away as soon as possible."

"I beg Your Majesty's pardon."

Henry sat up, swinging his muscular legs about and gripping the edge of the bench. "It is my command that this person remain under close guard until such a time as she can be brought to trial." His voice cracked like a whip in the quiet garden.

Geoffrey did not flinch. "I shall do as you command, sire."

"Then she will remain at Pevensey."

"She cannot survive there. I shall take her to Havering-atte-Bower, where I will guard her with my life. When you are ready to bring her to trial, she will be there to answer to the charges." Geoffrey's breathing came a bit quicker, and his heart pounded a bit faster at the presumption with which he faced the man who had only a few months previous succeeded in laying claim to the Kingdom of France.

The king's mouth dropped open. Again he felt himself being scolded by an older and wiser head. He shook his head in disbelief. "You can be replaced," he said at last.

"Your Majesty will find none more loyal."

Rising, Henry took several angry steps down the path. Over his shoulder, he called, "You would countermand my express orders. I could have you arrested and executed for treason against the Crown. To let loose a dangerous prisoner is a danger to the Crown and to our person."

Geoffrey drew a deep breath. "No one is more loyal to Plantagenet than Plantagenet."

The statement halted the young king in his tracks. He swung back around. "What mean you?"

"I am sure you know."

The dark flush subsided from the features. His anger drained away. Henry's smile quirked only the left side of his mouth, but it was nevertheless a smile. "Welcome, Uncle."

Geoffrey's face did not change. "I have no right to that appellation, but I swear that my loyalty is unequivocal."

As if he ached, the king pressed a hand against his stomach and moved back toward the bench. He did not actually stumble, but his steps faltered as if he had barely strength enough to make the bench.

"Your Majesty?" Geoffrey was beside him in an instant.

Groaning, the king doubled over, catching his lower lip between his teeth.

"Shall I summon a physician?"

"No," was the gasping reply. "He can do nothing. I have these attacks after almost every meal. The burning lasts for a while then I have the dysentery."

"Is there no diet? . . ."

"Nigarelli says that it will pass as my system regulates itself after the bad food and water of the French wars."

The king leaned back now, his head against Geoffrey's strong right arm. His upturned face, dappled by the sun filtering through the leaves overhead, was ghastly pale. Its skin, shiny with perspiration, fell back from his fine bones and long straight nose.

Geoffrey was reminded forcefully of a death mask. Helplessly, he waited while the young body was racked by ague despite the heat of the afternoon.

At last the spasm seemed to abate. The king opened his eyes and sat forward. His hands drooped between his spread knees. Perspiration drenched the back of his shirt. At intervals he shivered convulsively.

Feeling more inadequate than he had ever felt in his life, Geoffrey patted his nephew's shoulder. "Shall I help you back to your apartments?"

With lips tightly sealed, the king shook his head.

"You should rest, Henry."

The quivering frame straightened. "I must play a tennis match with my brothers for the entertainment of my bride."

"Ye Gods!"

Henry Plantagenet's face was pale as death when he turned it to his uncle. "I shall conquer this, or it will conquer me; but I will not lead the life of an invalid."

Geoffrey threw up his hands. "'Tis foolishness, sire. Your bride does not care whether you play tennis or chess. She will be satisfied with whatever you do that will keep you by her side."

Henry smiled. "Perhaps you are right. She is with child. I have at least the assurance that a babe is on the way. Pray God it is a boy."

"Pray God you live long and rule wisely to guide him into manhood."

"As my father did," Henry remarked bitterly.

Geoffrey frowned. "I watched your court last night, sire. You were sadly lacking in old heads. Forgive me, but you were the oldest person there. It is a fearsome responsibility that you have laid on yourself. Surely there are those who would and could advise you."

"Enough, Sir Geoffrey!" The king held up his hand. "I may be ill but not so ill that I do not see the direction this conversation will take us."

"I swear, Your Majesty—"

"She has said often enough that she was the advisor to my

father and held his place in Council during his last years when he was so ill. In my opinion, she was a dangerous influence for Mortimer."

Geoffrey opened his mouth to protest; then he closed it again. To defend Joanna on that score would be useless. The king was determined not to listen to the woman whom he hated and resented. Another argument must be employed.

"I believe the charge was witchcraft, not treason," he reminded the king smoothly.

Henry pressed his hand against his belly. "Look at me. I could very well be bewitched."

Geoffrey smothered a laugh. "Does Nigarelli believe you are bewitched?"

The king shuffled his feet irritably. "No."

"Furthermore, if you are bewitched, the likelihood that an English witch did it is highly improbable. More likely a whole coven of French witches has woven a spell at the instigation of Valois." The gray eyes gleamed with suppressed humor.

"Valois," Henry scoffed, "would not have sense enough to command a dog, much less enlist the aid of a coven of witches."

Geoffrey nodded. "Do you really believe in witchcraft?"

Henry was silent for a long. At last he seemed to throw up his hands mentally. "No."

Geoffrey sighed. "But the punishments for witchcraft are incredibly harsh. I am surprised that you would risk such treatment for a woman if there were the slightest doubt in your mind."

"I did not risk it," Henry muttered. "I would not wish the ducking stool and the fire on my worst enemies. I do not say she is not a witch; I merely say that I cannot prove that she is one."

"'Tis cruel to imprison a woman for life in a moldering ruin over five hundred years old."

"She has only to give up what is rightfully the Crown's."

"You can take what you need," Geoffrey reminded him. "You are the king."

"I cannot abuse widows. The Council would not allow it."

"She has always had your best interests at heart," Geoffrey murmured.

Henry looked closely at his uncle's body. Despite what seemed to him an advanced age of fifty years, the oldest male Plantagenet looked remarkably fit. His lean figure was decorously displayed in his traditional gray and forest green. His silvery-blond cap of hair rising to almost six feet reminded Henry dimly of Richard II, the unfortunate victim of Pontefract. Geoffrey was indeed a Plantagenet from sole to crown and, from the look of him, vigorous.

"So she has seduced you too," he mused.

Geoffrey shrugged. "Perhaps. But I come seeking justice, not license, sire. She is a royal lady. Her blood is the royal blood of Europe. To do her injury or to demean her is to injure and demean all like her including yourself and your royal brothers."

Henry rose to his feet. His hand rested for support on Geoffrey's strong shoulder. Immediately, d'Anglais rose and offered his arm. Startled by the gesture, the king nevertheless took advantage of it, leaning on the older man for support as they began to walk slowly toward the tennis court.

After a few yards, Geoffrey chuckled. "So I used to help the Duke of Brittany, sire. He was arthritic, his limbs badly crippled. He needed support just to stand. I was his valet for several years. It seems I come full circle."

Henry sighed. "I shall soon need a valet myself, I fear. Would I could count on you, my lord."

"Always, my King."

"You will take her to Havering-atte-Bower?"

"We will leave as soon as I can return."

The king's voice was stronger, more normal. His fine mind, ever competent in administration, leaped ahead to the practical. "I shall send a messenger to open the house and have her old servants make it ready. They were all returned to act as caretakers until the property should be disposed of. I cannot return all her revenues or property. Some is already sold."

"She will be pleased to return to her favorite palace."

They walked on toward the fine-clipped greensward where a net had been strung between two poles. A group of ladies in bright-colored dresses and fluttering veils walked toward the court from the house. On the court itself, Tom and John were already batting a small cloth ball back and forth amidst a good deal of laughter. Humphrey stood at the edge of one line and called the shots.

Henry paused. "They are your family too."

"Do they know?"

"Tom does, although he has probably forgotten . . . and John. If something should happen to me, John should be next. Tom is no administrator."

Geoffrey nodded noncommittally.

"I shall dispatch a letter of release to Havering-atte-Bower, dropping all charges. It should reach you within a few weeks."

"Your Majesty. I am eternally grateful. You do a great deed of kindness and nobility."

Henry stepped away from Geoffrey and faced him. "Do you go now?"

"Immediately. I shall ride far before sunset."

The king extended his hand. Geoffrey, Uncle Geoffrey."

"God bless you, Henry."

"Please call me, Hal. Father often did."

"Then God be with ye, Hal."

Henry of Lancaster turned on his heel and waved an arm toward the group on the court. "You call that a volley, Tom! Your belly gets in the way!" Without a backward glance he spurted across the remaining few yards as Geoffrey turned back toward the stables.

Chapter 31

Kneeling inside the chapel, Joanna heard the muted thunder of horse's hooves in the bailey. Her heart thudded within her as she pushed herself to her feet and hurried to the door. The rider was already mounting the steps of the keep with a flutter of forest green cloak.

"Geoffrey!"

He turned, his face alight. As quickly as his disabled leg would allow him, he hurried across the bailey toward her. They came together in the bright August sunlight. His arms closed round her, dragging her against his chest.

"My love—"

"Kiss me first," she demanded.

With a will he bent his head. His mouth closed over hers as if he would drink in the very life of her.

When they were both breathless, he let her go to bury her face in his chest. His body radiated heat and the scents of horse and hard-worked man. "Have you ridden far?" she asked at last.

"From Leicester," he croaked, his mouth against the top of her head. "I have been on the road three days." The hoarse voice sounded as if it had swallowed great lungfuls of dust.

She raised her face, to accept another kiss. "Come in out of the hot sun, my love. While you drink cool wine, I will draw a bath to ease your tiredness."

He took her face between his gloved hands. "Joanna, you will return to Havering-atte-Bower as soon as we can make ready."

She did not actually faint, but her body sagged against his and her eyes closed. However, she managed to retain her grip on his waist. She felt his lips again on her mouth before he bent to sweep her into his arms.

"No," she muttered, opening her eyes and forestalling him. "No. I am able to walk. You are the one who has ridden for three days. Put your arm around my waist."

Together they walked across the bailey together and mounted the steps of the keep. In the cool dimness of the hall, she raised her mouth to him again and again. His kisses grew in passionate intensity.

Together they climbed the stone steps to the upper chambers. Her tears of happiness had begun to fall, but she did not relax her arms around his waist. Instead she tightened her grip on him as her emotions threatened to overpower her.

In the bower room she poured cool wine, placing it in his hands with great ceremony. When he moved to thank her, she placed her fingers against his lips and would not let him speak. Then, with trembling hands, she began to draw off his clothing, beginning with his cloak and tunic. Beneath the heavy wool, his fine linen shirt was plastered to his skin by sweat.

"You must have a bath, my lord," she reiterated. "Sit here in comfort while I draw it."

"I would not . . ."

"Please," she begged him softly. "I must do this for you."

So he sat, bemused, sipping his wine while she drew water from the cistern and carried it to the tub. While she heated

508

some water so that his bath might not chill him, she brought a plate of biscuits and a small round of cheese. "'Tis far from sumptuous," she apologized unhappily.

"I am not used to such. You spoil me," he insisted.

She knelt to pull off his boots. "'Tis no more than you deserve."

He sighed with relief as they were slipped off; then he stood so she might slip down his hose and braies until he was nude except for his shirt.

"You have worked yourself so hard you are little more than a skeleton," she scolded.

Looking down at himself, he saw she was correct. He was a man reduced to the essence of life. He was nothing but bone, tendon, and muscle, but blood coursed through his veins at each pump of his heart. Uncertainly, he glanced at her face. He had never thought about himself in terms of how a woman would look at him. Did she find his body pleasing?

Joanna felt her blood heat as she stared at him. Suppressing her emotions until the end of the bath was becoming more of a task with each passing moment. The straight bones of his long feet were deceptively fragile in appearance. Likewise, his ankles were slender until the hard-muscled calf swelled out above them. The misshapen joint of his bad knee slightly marred the straight line of one leg making her think of a legend that the gods jealously destroyed the perfection of certain human beings lest they be rivals. The swell of his horseman's thighs made her quake.

Her throat was suddenly dry. She clenched her nails against her palms, hoping the pain would quell the rising tide of her desire. Behind her, the kettles began to boil. Thankfully, she tore her eyes away from him and hastened to lift one of the vessels off the fire.

When his bath was ready, she took his wine from his hand and lifted his shirt over his head. The service brought her face within inches of his chest with its curling golden hair. She knew his body well. Pain lanced through her at the sight of the terrible scar at his waist and the white brand on his belly.

He had suffered those for her. He had received the first by thrusting his body between her and the sword that would have slain her, the second because she had stubbornly clung to a belief she now held in contempt.

Dropping to one knee, she pressed her lips to first one and then the other while he shuddered and his manhood rose to throb against the swell of her breast. "My God," he gasped. "Be careful what you do."

Instantly, she drew back. A teasing smile curved her lips. "I am being careful, my lord." Taking him by the wrist, she led him by the hand to the bath. When he was seated in its warm depths, she poured more of the cool wine into his cup and brought it to him.

He leaned back with a contented sigh. "I could grow used to this."

"I mean for you to do so," she promised. Kneeling beside him, she picked up the sponge and began to lave his shoulders and neck. With gentle circular motions, she washed his body, thoroughly.

Leaning back, his eyes closed, he realized that he had never enjoyed a bath before. Like most men of his class, he had bathed in haste when the opportunity presented itself or when the occasion warranted it. On campaign he eschewed that part of his toilet unless the camp was beside a clear running stream. Never before, had he considered it a luxury.

Now every part of his body received her equal attention. When he moaned and writhed at the exquisite titillation of her hands, she ceased immediately but kissed his mouth and bade him drink his wine.

By this method she brought him to a point where he was swollen to bursting yet his muscles felt not the slightest trace of soreness from their exertions.

When she was satisfied that he was clean and that the stiffness of the long ride had been adequately dispelled, Joanna bade him stand while she toweled him dry and guided him again to his chair. "Now," she whispered. "Now, my dearest lord Geoffrey."

Standing before him, she stripped off her garments one by one. Each movement excited him as her white skin and fair shape emerged. When her last piece of clothing had fallen, she raised her white arms and unfastened her coil of heavy black hair. As it tumbled luxuriantly down of its own weight, she ran her fingers through it and swung it around her shoulders like a silken cape. Finally, she cupped her breasts in both hands and walked toward him as if she held offerings for his delectation.

Hypnotized, he allowed her to straddle his legs and press them tightly between her own. Mounted thus, she gave herself up to the exquisite pleasure he aroused as he kissed and tugged at her nipples. In the meantine, she devoted her hands to pleasantly caressing and tormenting his chest and belly until he was groaning and gasping. When his own excitement had built to fever pitch, she lowered herself onto his rampant staff.

"Joanna," he groaned, prolonging the first syllable as her velvet sheath engulfed him in measureless pleasure.

"My lord."

"Joanna, please . . ." His teeth were set. On the horns of a dilemma, he suffered—wild to prolong the incredible feeling, yet wild to end it in the explosion of ecstatic fire he knew must come.

"I only want your pleasure, my savior," she whispered, her body rising and falling rhythmically on his staff. The words were carried on a breath that caressed his ear and the side of his neck before her mouth nipped his earlobe.

He stiffened even more. His hands clasped her waist,

tightened, raised her to the length of his staff and drove her body downward even as he thrust himself up to meet her.

Her cry of ecstasy mingled with his own as they exploded together into fragments of white light that burned away the gray walls of the bower. Like gods their passion lifted them above the present into another realm of pure sensation and emotion.

Only the framework of his bones supported them as they drifted lazily back to earth. With limbs entwined and bodies locked together in a breathless kiss at all points, they only dimly became aware of the present.

At last, she drew a deep shuddering breath and raised her head from his shoulder. "I love you."

"I love you too."

"I had been planning what I would do," she admitted drowsily, planting a soft kiss on the point of his collarbone beneath his chin. "I wanted your return to be special, whether you secured my release or not."

"I thought your plans admirably made and executed," he told her gruffly.

"Do you think they might stand improvement?" She moved her hips experimentally.

"In God's name, not today," he whispered in mock alarm. "As I hope to live, I can stand no more."

"A pity." She straightened herself on his lap, arching her breasts forward and her hips back. "One or two points I was not certain whether I got just right."

"I cannot see how they could be improved."

"Can you not?"

"Well, perhaps later. You are right of course. Practice does make perfect. If I offer myself as a volunteer, will that help you to improve?" He lay slumped back in the chair, his eyelids slitted, enjoying the movements she made on his lap.

"Shall I bring you more wine?"

He reached for the cup and swallowed the last sip. "'Tis

not necessary yet. Stay awhile longer on my lap."

"Do you not fear we will grow together?"

"It is my fondest hope."

She stirred suggestively. "I can foresee problems in dressing and walking about."

"But if we stayed here together, we would not need to dress."

"We might get hungry."

He stretched his arm toward the small plate of food sitting on the table. "Ah well, you are right. And I am hungry. Suddenly, I am ravenous." He moaned as if in pain.

Instantly, she reacted with concern. "How long since you have eaten?"

He ducked his head. "I broke fast yesterday."

Hastily, she raised herself off him. "Why did you not say? I would have brought you a meal before you bathed. I only wanted . . . that is . . . I thought you would prefer . . ."

He caught her hand, turning it to place a kiss on her wrist before she could reach for her clothing. "I preferred it this way, love. Believe me, I did not suffer a single pang throughout your welcoming."

She smiled down at him. "If I had fed you, you might have taken more pleasure."

He rolled his eyes expressively. "I might have died too."

Dressed, they sat together over the meal she had ordered. The cook served it with his own hands, welcoming Geoffrey back with a friendly nod. "My lady planned this meal special," he grinned. "She had me order the foodstuffs all the way from the Hastings market."

"The meal is excellent," Geoffrey complimented him, eagerly sampling the fine white bread and the roasted pigeon. "I have not tasted better at the king's table."

Grinning happily, the man went away.

"Did you dine at the king's table recently?" Joanna asked him.

513

"Three nights ago." Geoffrey nodded. "His brothers were with him and their wives. Margaret sends her best and wishes to know why you have not written in such a long time. I assured her you would write soon and tell her all the news."

"She did not know of my imprisonment."

"No one did except the king and the Duke of Bedford, who carried out his orders while he was in France. No formal papers were ever filed against you. Your servants could give them no information. They therefore had no case. Truly, sweet, I do not think the king ever really wanted to bring you to trial. He hoped you would relent." Geoffrey did not add that the alternative the king hoped for was her death.

She set her mouth. "Has he married the Valois princess?"

"Yes."

Drawing a deep breath, she clasped her hands together before her face. "Fool," she moaned. "Stupid, stupid man. To risk what his father suffered death to gain."

"Perhaps it will not be so bad. She is pretty and biddable."

"Her blood is tainted." Joanna raised her head. Tears made her eyes glisten like obsidian. "All Europe knows what the Valois are like. None will marry them."

Geoffrey nodded sadly. "He seeks a union with France."

"But at what cost? The whole future of the house of Lancaster."

He rose and came round the small table to kneel at her side and take her in his arms. "You truly care about him," he said in wonder.

"I care about all my sons." She nodded. "Besides he is Henry's son. I must do as his father would have done. Henry did not think much of Richard's marriage to Isabella, and her father was the last Capet." She shook her head with a shudder.

Catching her by the shoulders, he turned her to face him. "You can do nothing," he told her firmly. "The marriage is already made and consummated. She is pregnant."

From deep in her throat came a faint but heartfelt groan. Then she was silent. "You are right," she admitted at last. Raising her head, she looked deep into his eyes. "To the devil with both of them."

He grinned. "Right. Tomorrow we leave this moldering pile. Is there anything you wish to take with you?"

She looked around her. "Nothing except the clothes you have given me."

"Leave them," he advised. "They are not fit for the Queen Mother of the Kingdom and the mistress of Havering-atte-Bower." He kissed her triumphantly, and she went into his arms gladly.

The next morning, two horses were led forward. She stared first at the small gray palfrey and then back at Geoffrey. "I shall do it," she declared.

"If you become too fearful, I shall take you up pillion like the veriest farmer's wife." He chuckled at the thought.

Her face was white but determined. "I think I should like that above all things. If I could ride with my arms clasped around you, I would not fear at all."

He kissed her lightly and laced his fingers to toss her up. "Only a few hours, love," he promised her, "and you will be home."

As they rode slowly up the white road through the green and yellow fields, her confidence grew. The little palfrey was a sweet-natured animal only thirteen hands high. Along the way Geoffrey talked constantly, requiring her response and forcing her to think of answers to his questions. Gradually her hands relaxed on the pommel, and she began to feel at ease with the motion.

At noon he took her up behind him on his destrier. Her fear at its height caused her to grasp him with a death grip, but they managed to make a little better time because he urged the big horse to step out more smartly. At the end of the first day, they spent the night in the monastery at Leeds. The nervous strain and the unaccustomed activity had so exhausted her that she fell asleep almost instantly in his arms and did not wake throughout the long night.

The next day was a repeat of the first except that she remained all day in her saddle. "I shall never grow to like it," she confided.

"You need never ride on horseback again," he promised. "'Tis only that I knew you wanted to get home by the quickest way."

She smiled grimly and nodded. Her eyes were fixed on the white road between her horse's ears.

In the middle of the morning on the third day, they crossed the boundaries of her estate.

"Will I still receive the revenue from Havering?" she asked worriedly. The countryside looked wild as if the absence of the landlord had caused the fields to be neglected.

"Yes, and others as well," he told her. "Some of course have already been disposed of, but most will be returned to you. The king has ordered that all the property shall be restored as well as the contents of your house."

"And my servants?"

"I believe they were released and have returned as caretakers until your return."

She bit her lip and stared straight ahead. "All except Isabella."

"She was an old woman, love." Geoffrey could offer no other consolation.

"She did not deserve to die by torture."

"They said she killed herself."

"They lie," she replied positively. "She believed in the justice of God. She would never take her own life. They killed her by accident and sought to clear themselves of blame."

He could not answer. Undoubtedly, she spoke the truth. To argue their case was foolishness.

"And Friar Randolph?"

"I do not know," he lied.

"Did Lady Margaret intervene for us?" she asked him later.

He had been waiting for that question. "No, she told me to ask for your release myself."

He pulled his horse to a halt on the brow of a high hill. She came abreast of him and looked down. Below her the road swept round the curve of a gently flowing river whose bank bordered on the kitchen garden at Havering. "Before we go farther let us rest here and tell each other the truth," he suggested.

She looked at him inquiringly. "I thought we knew the truth."

"In most things we do, but you have kept some things from me." Dismounting, he came round to lift her off her horse and set her on her feet beneath a spreading tree. Removing his cloak from the back of his saddle, he made a place for them both to sit facing the valley before them.

"First," he said when they were comfortable, "I want to know why you paid for my care when I returned from Agincourt."

She studied her hands with pretended casualness before reaching aside to pluck a clover. "I? I thought you said the king paid for your care."

"I have since learned otherwise."

"From Margaret?"

"She was much distracted. The Duke of Bedford was sunk deeply in his cups."

"Ah." She raised her eyebrows. "Well, you needed care and I . . . I had more than enough to provide it."

"But why did you?" he persisted, closing his hand over the nervous fingers that plucked the leaves from the clover. "My

517

last words to you had been vile and cruel."

"Do you really have to ask?"

"Yes."

"Because I loved you. Even as I said I did that day when I asked you to be my friend. I think I have always loved you, even when we were young and you were thrust into my bed. I often worried about my feelings for you," she confessed, bowing her head as a red flush of embarrassment crept into her magnolia cheeks.

"I want to believe you," he muttered. He laced his hands around his drawn-up knee and gazed down at the sparkling water.

"How can you still doubt me? I was a foolish girl whose every waking moment had been spent with people who continually told me that I was different because of my birth. My teachers, my father, my brothers, my duenna—all preached the doctrine of the blood royal. I could not help but believe it."

"So you said."

"But after I grew up and came to England, I was forced to think for myself. The blood royal is a fiction. Valois blood is royal and look at it. Henry's blood was royal, and yet it did not save him from hideous disfigurement and agonizing death. People who are royal are not better or worse than others. Some people are good, others are bad. I have known many who are bad. But as I matured and thought, I realized I had known only one who was truly good and kind. That person was you. You served Jean faithfully with heart and mind and body. You served me and were my friend as well as my lover. When I realized that, I was able to acknowledge my love for you. But I know now it has been there always."

When she finished her long speech, she sat still, staring at the tiny green leaves that besprinkled his dark green cloak.

He cleared his throat and leaned across to kiss her. His tongue teased her lips and bade them open to him. When he had caressed the sweet interior of her mouth in all love, he ended the exchange and sat up, gazing straight ahead. "Ah, well. You have opened your heart to me. Now I have something to tell you as well. I have learned the secret of my birth."

She plucked another clover. "Did you, my lord?" Her voice was unconcerned.

"Yes. It is a long and pitiful story."

She laid her hand upon his arm. "Then do not tell me unless you want to, for believe me, I care not. King or peasant, it makes no difference to me. You are the man I love. Who your parents were makes no difference."

He looked at her uncertainly. "It might make a difference," he told her reluctantly.

"Never. I do not care. I care only for you. In the midst of all this wreckage of kingdoms and of kings, we have emerged triumphant with our love unstained. We have been in love since we were practically children. You are the only man who has ever so much as touched me, and if God is kind, we will have the rest of our lives together to love as we will."

He kissed her hands, his eyes glowing with unshed tears.

Breaking the intensity of the moment, she climbed to her feet. "If we do not go on our way, we will not get home before nightfall, and I have a yearning to sleep in my own bed tonight."

He laced his fingers and lifted her onto the palfrey's back.

"I shall never grow to like this," she moaned as she shifted her weight in an effort to find an unbruised spot on her anatomy.

He regarded her fondly. "You have done very well. You have shown great courage. Many people do not ride, and yet they manage to live full lives. You need never do so again."

As they walked their horses along beside the river, he chuckled softly. "I have never slept in a queen's bedchamber before."

519

She drew herself up haughtily. "It is a very different experience, I can assure you. A queen is much different from other women."

He halted the horse to let it drink from the cool water. At the same time he eyed her critically. "How different? I see two arms, two legs, two eyes, two breasts. How is she different? Tell me. I charge you." Before she knew what he was about, he dragged her from her saddle and into his eager arms with mock roughness. With her held captive on his lap, he pretended to bite and growl against her neck.

Squealing, twisting, laughing in his arms until she was quite breathless, she begged him in vain to stop.

"How is she different?" he repeated.

"She is just different."

"How?"

"She is . . . she is richer."

"Wealth does not make her a better love. It does not make her clasp her thighs tighter around a man's waist and—"

"Geoffrey!"

"It does not make her breasts more full than these." He leered at her in an exaggeration of lechery as he squeezed her playfully.

"Oh, Geoffrey."

"Her wealth does not make her mouth sweeter or warmer than this."

What she might have answered to that observation he never knew because he kissed her thoroughly and with such firmness that they were both breathing hard when he released her.

He raised his head for a moment to look around him. His expression was that of a man whose happiness is in his hands. She saw his pale silvery eyes glisten with suspicious moisture. "How is she different?" he whispered.

"She is not," she admitted at last, throwing her arms tightly around his neck. "She is after all only a woman."

He nodded his head to hold her against him while he

kissed her long and lovingly. She was right, he acknowledged. Just as he was only a man. Prince or peasant, he was only a man. "Then I shall cherish her always because I want only a woman."

Beneath the dark gray material of his tunic, she could feel his heart beating like a drum. "It is all any woman can ask for," she whispered as she raised her lips for his kiss.

Epilogue

Death cheated Henry V of the union of the kingdoms of France and England. Only two years after his marriage to Princess Catherine he died at age thirty-five of a chronic disease contracted during the Agincourt war. At his death his infant son, although only nine months old, already gave evidence of a certain slowness of development that was his inheritance from the Valois kings.

Joanna of Navarre outlived her stepson by fifteen years. She lived quietly and inconspicuously in her palace of Havering-atte-Bower, ever aware of the Marcher lords' ominous rumblings against the House of Lancaster. When she died, her loyal steward arranged for her body to be brought to Canterbury to be buried beside Henry IV.

She was buried with every rite attendant for those of the blood royal.

Bibliography

Asimov, Isaac, *The Shaping of France,* Houghton Mifflin Co., Boston, 1972.

Gilyard-Beer, R., *Abbeys, An Introduction to the Religious Houses of England and Wales,* Her Majesty's Stationery Office, London, 1958.

Gurney, Gene, *Kingdoms of Europe,* Crown Publishers, Inc., New York, 1982.

Hayward, John, *The First Part of the Life and Raigne of King Henrie the IV,* W.J. Jonson, Inc., Norwood, N.J., 1975.

Kemp, Anthony, *Castles in Color,* Arco Publishing, Inc., New York, 1978.

Lofts, Norah, *Queens of England,* Doubleday & Co., Inc., New York, 1977.

Murray, Jane, *The Kings and Queens of England,* Charles Scribner's Sons, New York, 1974.

Scott, A.F., *Every One a Witness, The Plantagenet Age,* White Lion Publishers, Ltd., New York, 1975.

Shepherd, William R., *Historical Atlas,* 8th Edition, Barnes & Noble, New York, 1956.

Softly, Barbara, *The Queens of England,* Stein & Day, Inc., New York, 1976.

Tilley, Arthur, *Medieval France,* Hafner Publishing Co., New York, 1964.

Toy, Sidney, *The Castles of Great Britain,* William Heinemann Ltd., London, 1953.

Tuchman, Barbara W., *A Distant Mirror,* Alfred A. Knopf, New York, 1978.

Vickers, K.J., *England in the Middle Ages,* Methuen & Co. Ltd., London, 1950.

BESTSELLERS BY SYLVIE F. SOMMERFIELD ARE BACK IN STOCK!

TAZIA'S TORMENT	(1705, $3.95)
REBEL PRIDE	(1706, $3.95)
ERIN'S ECSTASY	(1704, $3.50)
DEANNA'S DESIRE	(1707, $3.95)
TAMARA'S ECSTASY	(1708, $3.95)
SAVAGE RAPTURE	(1709, $3.95)
KRISTEN'S PASSION	(1710, $3.95)
CHERISH ME, EMBRACE ME	(1711, $3.95)
RAPTURE'S ANGEL	(1712, $3.95)
TAME MY WILD HEART	(1351, $3.95)
BETRAY NOT MY PASSION	(1466, $3.95)

Available wherever paperbacks are sold, or order direct from the Publisher. Send cover price plus 50¢ per copy for mailing and handling to Zebra Books, Dept. 1670, 475 Park Avenue South, New York, N.Y. 10016. DO NOT SEND CASH.